"With a narrative voice full ⟨...⟩
from page one, the stor⟨...⟩
while painting a hopeful near-⟨...⟩
The cozy pace ramps to a dazzling finale exploring the
resilience of entangled time and the malleability of morality
when love is on the line and power free at hand.
A wonderful debut perfect for fans of *Arrival* and
The Space Between Worlds."
Essa Hansen, *Nophek Gloss,* Orbit 2020

"A cinematic rollercoaster ride through the multiverse and
an imaginative page-turner told in an engaging and original
narrative voice. The worldbuilding alone would be reason
enough to pick up this book, but there is something else
even better here: the real beating heart of the novel is the
compelling gay love story between its main characters, whom
I will remember for a long time: brilliant, flawed,
multi-layered and beautifully human."
Emmi Itäranta, author of *The Moonday Letters* and *The Memory of Water*

"Both poignant and thrilling, *A Fractured Infinity* takes us on
a wild ride through vividly imagined worlds: it's a multifaceted
jewel, with humanity's flaws at its heart."
Stark Holborn, author of *Ten Low* and *Hel's Eight*

"Gut wrenching at times and with razor sharp prose, this
complex, intelligent novel is ultimately empowering. It's a page-
turner of a love story that you'll power through to see if the
world is saved and if Hayes and Yusuf survive together."
Kaaron Warren, author of *Slights* and more

FRACTURED INFINITY

NATHAN TAVARES

TITAN BOOKS

A Fractured Infinity
Print edition ISBN: 9781803360386
E-book edition ISBN: 9781803360393

Published by Titan Books
A division of Titan Publishing Group Ltd
144 Southwark Street, London SE1 0UP
www.titanbooks.com

First edition: November 2022
10 9 8 7 6 5 4 3 2 1

Printed and bound in Great Britain by
CPI Group (UK) Ltd, Croydon, CR0 4YY.

FRACTURED
INFINITY

1
SNEAK PREVIEW

And here, in the cerebral sci-fi movie—not a blockbuster, not my style—based on the next year or so, the title card will roll. SOMETHING EVOCATIVE IN ALL CAPS. Cue the score, the swelling *bwahhh bwahhhh* chest-rattling synth undercut by tinkling wind chimes as the blackness fades. CUT to HAYES FIGUEIREDO on a beach in the furthest part of the multiverse you can dream up, staring out at a sea strewn with stars.

I've seen a million versions of myself, on a million different worlds, so who knows who'd they'd cast as me. Hopefully some unknown who could say he got all Method and really mined his darkness to tackle the role of troubled filmmaker. Troubled, sure, even though the studio will cut most of the depressive bouts of self-medicating, and the functional alcoholism, and the MDMA-euphoria bonfires with the pack of other lost queers I lived with in my twenties, in that crumbling co-op we all called Saint Homo's Home for Wayward Boys. All to focus on the story of the man I love and the futures I've seen where he has to die, again and again, so the world isn't smashed to bits by an asteroid, or swallowed up by a rogue black hole, or nuked until it's a glowing pile of ash.

```
                  HAYES (VOICE OVER)
          Do you see all the stars out there?
          All the possibilities?

          SLOW PAN out, following HAYES'S eyes out to
          sea, then the camera angle flips upside down
          and vaults into space, where an unassuming
          asteroid floats by the screen.
```

There's nothing quite like the sunrise on the beach in this corner of the multiverse.

The juicy lemon wheel of the sun rises over the ocean and torches the horizon with the colors of fruit punch I used to drink as a kid. I rustle on the leaky air mattress, which sends a rubber balloon fart across the pink sand, towards the copse of beach grasses that thicken into what looks like ferns the size of redwoods. That graceful wakeup call would've gotten a smile out of Yusuf, not long ago. Before he left. He hasn't been smiling lately. Just his dark, downturned eyes, and his short sentences.

I mean, of course I get it. It's tough to tip your head to the sunlight when you know that billions of people have to die because you're alive. And the man you love kept that from you.

I putter around the camp for a while, with our ring-of-rocks fire pit and our improvised refrigerator that's a shallow hole covered with palm fronds. The dunes of pink sand and the tropical forest of ferns with their coconuts that taste like bananas and their bananas that taste like coconuts. I'm alone on this island and the whole planet, as far as I can tell.

I knew the end was coming, so I woke up the past few mornings before Yusuf and tried to memorize every detail of him. The shadows on his cheeks from his beard. The swoops of his sooty eyebrows. His halo of black curls. The moles dotting his body like he's a constellation of some ancient hunter.

SCENE: *A sad man alone with a bunch of junk that seems washed ashore from a shipwreck.*

I wish, sometimes, that I never crossed paths with that fucking machine. But then I never would've met Yusuf. The Envisioner— the huge, dark gray box with all its facets and spindly metal spider legs—sits about a quarter mile down the beach. You know how spiders can feel anything that brushes against their webs because all the strings give off a different vibration? I can feel the other universes like glowing threads when I press my hands against the machine.

I don't know how the thing works exactly. Every sci-fi movie I've ever loved has had some hand-waving here and there. *Let's just take this premise and go with it, deal?* I mean, I don't know how airplanes exactly work either, but they do.

Anyway, the thing is a predictive device. It's a gateway, sorta. It's also a plague. A time-bomb fucking with reality on a multi-universal level. Yusuf talks a lot about knots in the fabric of multidimensional space-time, with each Envisioner a point connecting different paths. When he talks like this, words get all crammed together and I can't make much sense of him or anything else.

The thing crunches a bunch of numbers and spits out predictions. There you go. You're all caught up.

———

Yusuf tutored me in physics when I first arrived at the Compound, and I was still interested in not feeling like an idiot around the global brain-trust of the research staff. I use *tutored* loosely since the sessions were him doodling on his bedroom window with a marker and me wondering at what point in his talk about quarks I could slide his underwear back down and get him to swear in Arabic under his breath again.

"In nature, quarks exist in twos and threes," he said one session. "You can't ever find a solo one flying around."

"Why?"

"Because the force that binds them actually increases the farther you try to pull them apart." He squiggled a wavy line between two circles on his window.

"How in the hell does that even make sense?"

"It's like an invisible umbilical cord connects them. Quarks can't exist on their own."

When he told me he was leaving, I wanted to say something about how we're bound together, too. Except it would've been shitty of me to hold him emotionally hostage.

I know it's small-picture thinking to focus on Yusuf breaking up with me with all we've done—surfing across universes and messing up timelines. And I know it doesn't sound self-determination-y to say, but he is what makes me feel the most myself. He makes me know that *this* me is not a random jumble of molecules or events or whatever. Maybe my life is less my own and more an expression of how I love him. That's why I'm supposed to be here.

He bickers with me a lot on the *means* and the *shoulds* and the *supposed tos*—anything that sounds remotely like a bearded, white director set this whole universe up for us and we are just bit players hitting beats in the script. He's all, *in a multiverse where literally every possible version of every possible event exists simultaneously, nothing is meant to happen, and nothing is important, and...* Which is usually when I have to anchor him with a tug on his hand and a joke. Like, *jesus, lighten up. I just asked if we should get dinner.*

I'm aching, like the thread between us is tied to one of my ribs. And this thread pulls tighter with every breath, now that we're drifting farther apart.

This flash-forward teaser is running a little long, but give me a break because with all my universe road-tripping and Envisioner scrying, my sense of time is fucked. Maybe I'm also stalling because I'm not really looking forward to getting into how all of this was my fault.

I pull Junior, my hand-held camera, from the supply stash by the air mattress and plod over to the shade of the fern forest. I rest Junior on a rock, point her lens at me, and flick her little video screen around so that I can see my face during my seaside confessional. I tap the red "record" button and settle on another rock across from the camera.

I look too thin. Sunburned, with green shadows under my eyes. My therapist ex, Narek, told me once that my docs and films are all vanity because everything I make is about me. But he's wrong— also an asshole—because I already exhaust myself with my constant thoughts so I don't need to make whole films devoted to myself. My filmmaking is more about record-keeping and storytelling, as proof that *these people existed* or *these things mattered.* A middle finger to entropy.

This isn't about me, I guess is what I'm trying to say. It's a warning. Or something.

"Welcome to Hayes's Disaster Drive-In Theater," I say to the camera. "You already missed the coming attractions, but that's okay. Sit back and I hope you enjoy the show."

I suck in a deep breath, close my eyes, and trace the threads back to the start.

2
THE HERMIT

I didn't expect to have an audience when I stumbled out of my cabin late one morning to take a leak.

My feet hit the worn wooden steps in the woods of Connecticut, where, like the other artists here, I was supposed to be head-down and plowing through my Great Work. Mostly, my head was foggy from last night's weed. Unlike when I film and all bets are off, I don't like to get high while I'm editing a doc, which is supposed to be all about discipline. Drinking water and eating vegetables and working all day, and all these other good habits I'd heard so much about. But last night, boxed in by the trees outside my windows, everything I'd lost the last few months bowled into me at once, dragging me into a pity-party of one.

I yawned, murky-mouthed, and blinked away the sleep while I battered the grass with piss.

"Sir?"

I jumped at the voice and turned, hand still down the front of my shorts and the other idly scratching a mosquito bite on my bare chest. Four men stood in front of the cabin. The closest guy was dressed in a light sweater and khakis, even in the scorching

July heat. My first sight of the man I'd love so hard that I'd break through universes for him, and I thought, *is this off-duty English lit professor lost in the woods?*

I don't believe in love-at-first sight lightning bolts and angels whispering *you've just found your soulmate.* And I know it sounds weird, but I love that I met him—probably the most important moment in my life—while grasshoppers bounced away from my piss stream in the grass.

"Yeah?" I asked, cocking my head.

The guy at the front cleared his throat and looked down at the ground. The other three were rooted to the earth, all earpieces, clenched jaws, and lumpy shapes under their black jackets. They looked like black ops personal trainers who could kill me three times before I hit the ground.

"Hayes Figueiredo?" the guy at the front asked, peeking down at a tablet in his hands.

"Who's asking?"

"We need you to come with us."

Behind the group, tall grasses swayed in the breeze.

And here's where I die, I thought. I've been chased out of bars and had my ribs broken in alleyways. I've been tear-gassed in political riots. People who come to you knowing your name are never there to just chat. Worse when they're smiling, when they're *needing. We need you to put down your camera. What use are you—really—in this village, or in this school, or in this bar with these sad and twisted people?*

Mostly, I didn't think I'd die while holding my dick in the woods, hoping the little film festivals where I showed my work would have a nice memorial after they screened one of my docs. *Hayes Figueiredo, thirty-three, was gunned down in the woods while at an artist fellowship. This was his final work.* Roll credits.

I shook off, snapped the waistband of my shorts, and slapped on fake cockiness. "I don't fucking think so," I said.

The guy at the front with the tablet blinked, tipping his head. "I'm sorry—what?"

A too-tight string snapped in my chest, and I bolted into the cabin, slamming the door behind me. For fuck's sake, why didn't I bring my mace here? A knock on the door matched my manic heartbeat.

"Mr. Figueiredo? We're actually here because—because we need your help."

"With what?" I called out.

"I can't really say," the guy said. "We're here to *ask* you to come with us, to someone who can fill you in."

The guy leaned at the window of the cabin's door, the glass mashing his thick black glasses to his face.

"Can I see some ID or something?"

"Uh—all I have is my badge from work. Does that work?"

"Sure."

There was some rustling outside until the guy pressed a white card with his picture on it to the window. I wasn't sure what I was looking for, so I squinted at the badge for what I thought was a good amount of time for me not to seem gullible. His name was Yusuf Hassan. On the little picture I saw the same face as the one peeking through the window—a stubbled face with wide eyebrows. Unsmiling full lips and dark eyes that seemed focused on something just behind me. Slightly wild curly hair. I sucked in air to try to douse the fire in my blood.

"Alright. Hold on."

I opened the door just wide enough to look outside.

Yusuf toed my worn front step, only risking eye contact for a second before glancing at the three hired guns behind him.

"I'm realizing that this looks more forceful than we intended," he said.

"You think?"

"Sorry."

His wavering smile eased some of the stiffness in my shoulders. I opened the door wider and stepped back into the mish-mash of my tiny cabin, strewn with notebooks and underwear, with stills from my latest doc taped to the wood walls.

"What could you possibly need my help with?" I asked. "A film?"

I'd done a few guest lectures at my old college before, when my doc about an underground gay bar in Barbados made the festival rounds. I can't say that I gifted the students with a ton of wisdom. I'd overheard some douche professor had bellyached about the film chair even inviting me there to talk about my "smutty fag art." And, oh man, I almost tattooed that badge of honor on my forearm.

Yusuf hesitated for just a second. "Yeah, you could say that."

"Alright. Where are we going?"

He turned to the group for some hush-hush chattering, and, jesus, if this was how all of our conversations were going to work, this was going to take forever.

"California," he said, finally.

"Oh," I sputtered. "*Oh.*"

I'd seen a few of my other film school dropout friends—the bonkers, perfect weirdos who shoved their uncompromising shit on a world that didn't ask for it—get snatched up by studios in LA that wanted new talent to liven up their bizarrely mainstream movies. Each time, I threw them parties and popped cheap bubbly for their Big Break, wishing for them all the luck in the world. *But maybe next time it'll be me*, was the thought that I held between my teeth because you were never supposed to say it out loud.

"Wait. I don't have my passport here," I said.

The Second American Civil War had lasted just over a year and had ended with the secession of California, then Oregon, to join the Union of Pacific States, three years before I was born. I remembered the maps projected onto the boards at school, showing the shifting borders of America shaped by two generations of wars—warring troops, warring truths—without the resources or leadership to anchor what was left of it together. On the map, the borders of Texas and other states shifted and I'd wondered if I'd just been hallucinating—a little too well-done after my wake-and-bake. Before the war, Hawaii had already been an independent nation for going on ten years. Last election, President Whatshisname ran on some platform of mythical *reunification*, his speeches broadcast to a nearly independent constellation of cities sometimes called the Urban Archipelago of America. With wide patches of unincorporated land and rural, self-governing towns stretching between coasts connected by high-speed mag-trains and shared memory. That *reunification* hadn't happened yet and probably never would. My future was now circling the drain because I'd left my passport in Boston and wouldn't be able to get to California. Wonderful.

"You're fine," he said. "You won't need it where we're going."

"Okay." I tried to iron out the jitters in my voice. "Can you give me a couple of minutes to get my stuff?"

"Just be quick."

In the 1980s movie montage, I tried on a bunch of outfits in the mirror before I finally decided on the shoulder-padded threads

I'll wear when I waltz into my studio Big Break meeting. When really, I rinsed in the cabin's outdoor shower and crammed some stuff in a duffel. I was a week into my five-week editing bender away from my life in Boston, and I'd already gone full hermit. I hadn't showered in days and was living mostly on instant coffee and beef jerky, avoiding the other artists because I was *in the zone.*

I'd also been hiding. I didn't need Narek to pull his horn-rimmed glasses off his nose and tell me that. After I finally left him, I threw myself into documenting my friend Genesis's fight for legal protections for synths. Then I lost her, too, a few months back—just as she became the face of the movement. I was here to work and hide and try to pull myself together again. I'd buzzed my hair when I got here. Something about shedding the outside world.

I don't own anything professional-looking—I mostly look like I pinch my clothes from thrift shops. Which is sometimes true. I yanked on a white T-shirt that smelled clean and a pair of khaki shorts that were splotched with paint from my occasional house-painting gigs when film work dried up. I made sure to stuff Genesis's tarot deck, my laptop, and Scarlett, my lucky hand-held camera with her red electrical tape slashes, into my duffel before meeting Yusuf and the others outside.

They followed me down the dirt paths, through the humid July air that was thick with biting flies, to the main house of the grounds, where a black bulldozer of a car idled in the driveway. I'd spent a lot of my twenties getting into cars with strangers, so what the hell. I hopped inside, into an air-conditioned bubble of awkward silence with me alone in the back row.

"Anyone you need to call to say you'll be out of touch for a few days?" the guy in black at the wheel asked, as he rumbled off the dirt driveway and onto the main road.

I guess I could've called someone, theoretically, then and during the previous night's grief bender. I had some friends, still, though the gap that Genesis left in my chest widened every day. The people I cared about were used to me ghosting on them for six months while I worked on a doc. My mom was in the ground, but if you'd asked me how long it'd been I'd have to stop and close my eyes against all the air leaving my lungs because five years still felt like twenty seconds. I'd lost her to uterine cancer before the cures rolled out, and me and my dad, who'd peaced out of half-drowned Boston to live in Florida, had mercifully agreed to stop talking. Once you realize that every phone call ends in a screaming match it's better to stop pretending blood means anything.

"No, I'm good."

Yusuf sat in the row ahead of me. I got the sense that if anyone was in charge here, it was him, though he wouldn't cough up much when I tried to wheedle some info out of him. He didn't mention a specific studio, but maybe it was a superhero thing? The CGI-fueled skull-rattling action movies were on their way out, making room for a return to more realistic filmmaking. I'd heard, anyway, which could be why they wanted me and my hand-held films that zoomed in on sweaty hairlines and the searching eyes of my doc subjects.

The other guys—security guards?—called me "sir" and "Mr. Figueiredo" and asked if the air conditioning was alright. I cracked some stupid joke like *Mr. Figueiredo is my mother*, but I can't really remember because I get all blabbermouthed when I'm nervous.

Slowly, the giant hand cranking a bike chain around my gut eased up. Everything was a fast-forward blur. We drove a while, then hit the highway, then off again to a tiny airfield where the car rolled to a stop by a plane. A plane—what the actual fuck—a *private* plane with gorgeous flight attendants in red lipstick and little sleeper pod things in two neat rows. They were nice enough not to look embarrassed for me, in my paint-splotched clothes and frayed blue hoodie that was *this* close to disintegrating. Only people with statues of dead relatives in city parks could afford cross-country flights, what with the high-speed mag-trains connecting the coasts, and the first-born cost of fuel.

I tried to settle into the white egg of my sleeper pod. I spilled water all over myself and had to cram my eyes shut during takeoff so that my stomach didn't fly out of my ass. I managed to doze for a while, somehow, though I don't remember dreaming, only a blackout worthy of my best tequila benders. A sea of green beneath the plane greeted me when I woke up, with trees that seemed to stretch out forever. I bounced into one of the open pods to get a different look.

"Great Basin National Forest," Yusuf said, a flash of his white teeth poking out from behind his lips. "Have you seen it from up here before?"

Looking back, it lights me up to think about how much courage it must've taken him to start talking to me out of nowhere, when he was usually happier staring out the window in silence. That was the longest string of words I'd gotten from him, with his eyes that seemed to dodge everything finally settling on me. Some accent I couldn't quite clock flavored the low tune of his voice. His secret-identity glasses cut black lines across his face. His dark hair wasn't short and wasn't long, a messy, curly mop with shorter sides. He was handsome enough that it'd take me two drinks, easy, to screw up the balls to make a pass in a bar—*sorry, professor, my dog ate my homework*.

"Never," I said.

I actually cried, just a few tears and a snotty nose, as I looked down at the forest that from here looked like the green crocheted comforter of my mom's bed. She'd told me stories, when I was a kid, of shriveled-up plains, and ozone holes, and droughts torching the green fields of what used to be the United States. Before the trees spliced with quick-grow genes borrowed from bamboo birthed pop-up forests around the globe to suck up the carbon, before the United Arab Emirates-led desalination of millions of gallons of seawater a year to be used for crop irrigation, before the refreezing of the ice caps. Even though that had come a few years too late to stop the flooding of coastal cities, and the sinking into the sea of the small Portuguese island in the middle of the Atlantic where my mom was from.

One night after she'd spread little kids' history picture books on our splotched blue carpet, I'd dreamed of elephants with rib bones poking out, of tigers konking over from heat, and I'd screamed myself awake.

"*Querido*, that was before we learned to work together to fix things," she'd told me, kissing the sweat on my forehead.

The plane touched down in the desert far beyond the forest, and then we all hopped into another black car. A single inky road led us over the flat earth, past a tall wire fence and a security post to a building that looked like a giant beetle with a white, geodesic dome for a shell. And where the hell in California *were* we? Weren't there supposed to be palm trees and models/actors everywhere? I could only guess that we were on some big-budget set. The car rolled into an underground parking garage where the three guys in black took a hike, leaving Yusuf as my only tether through a maze of white halls, bleached overhead lights, and glass doors marked with white block lettering. Cold storage. Dormitories. To Theater.

My duffel bag bounced against my hip as we passed people in white lab coats who gawked at me like a pair of nuts were dangling from my forehead. One woman actually spun away into a side room blabbing a "sorry" behind her. The bike chain started winding around my stomach again. My tongue was a slab of jerky in my dry, salty mouth.

Just as I started to wonder if Yusuf was lost, he flashed some badge at a heavy white door that led down another hallway.

"Good luck," he said.

"You're not coming?"

His only answer was to leave me in my dirty sneakers in front of a plain white door that looked like a broom closet. What the hell. I came all this way, I might as well walk in.

Inside was a small white room with a single circular conference table and a huge screen stuck to one of the walls. The only person there was a slim, white-coated woman with dark hair who turned from one of the big screens to face me.

The screen must've been a live security feed of the room or something, because on it I stood by a wall of glowing hard-candy-colored buttons. But I was wearing some long green coat instead of my traveled-in clothes. And the room didn't look quite like here. And—*what the actual fuck*—the guy who was maybe me but also definitely *not* leaned over what looked like a giant mechanical spider pounded out of shadows, fiddling with some dials.

"Perhaps you can tell me," the woman said, her asymmetrical bob swaying by her chin as she tipped her head, "why this is you."

The bike chain grinding around my gut hit a snag, and the floor dropped out from under me.

3
STAGE

In the editing room in my head, I have a tough time stringing together these early bits of Dr. Nakamori, through all the flash-forwards, and flashbacks, and flash parallel-universes—storyboarding and re-cutting to figure out just who the hero is in all of this.

Not that I think it's me.

I'll call her Kaori soon enough, after I wheedle past her soft voice and stiff back that she rules her staff with, like a doctor bombing cancer diagnoses onto her patients with all the warmth of a bleach colonic. Back then she was cold and mistrusting, with her bored eyes and undercurrent of *I can't believe you're involved in this.* But I like to think I cracked open her armor with my charm, or something.

In the small white room, she didn't move a muscle while I had to venture a hand to one wall to keep from keeling over. The potato chips I'd eaten on the plane wanted to splatter onto her white sneakers. I swept my dizzy eyes up at the screen behind her, where some version of myself in a long sage-green lab coat leaned over the nightmare machine on its angled silver legs. He twisted a few dials with his tattoo-less hands.

"How?" I managed to sputter.

"You're telling me you have no idea where this footage is from or how this device got here?"

It's a trap, Kaori's cool voice broadcasted to me. She knew everything already, she was just waiting for me to goof. One half of her hair swooped and curved past her chin, the other half a blunt shelf that stopped just past the middle of her cheeks.

"You mean how you have video of some guy with my face? Abso-fucking-lutely not."

The cocktail shaker inside my head was crammed with ice and plot points: long-lost twins, cloning, imaging software—banned by governments across the world—that could spin a scene of anybody doing anything, and only forensic analysts could spot the smoke and mirrors.

"We were pretty thorough with the background checks." She shrugged. "But had to be sure."

"Could you please turn that off. It's fucking with me. I'm gonna be sick."

She fiddled with her tablet and—thank god—the video winked off.

"Hold up," I said. "Did you say background checks? Have you been following me?"

"Researching."

"Spying?"

"Please," she snorted, barely looking up from her tablet. "Spare me the Data Rights crusade. Every government is listening to every phone on this planet and that crumbling warehouse you live in has paper-thin walls." She eyed me like she caught me peeking through a hole drilled into the football team's locker room, one hand pumping down the front of my shorts. "Also, you should consider investing in curtains."

I winced, wracking my brain for what I'd been up to lately in my place—*studio* was too generous a word for the single room in the old wharf building I was squatting in, with its chipped brick walls in the drowned neighborhood of South Boston. My mattress on the floor and the card table with the single chair I rescued from the curb one trash day. The collages of doc stills on my walls, along with torn pages from antique beefcake magazines I'd found at a flood sale across the river at Harvard. At the very least, whenever I got home I freed myself from my pants.

"Find anything good?"

"You're..." she trailed. "Nondescript."

"Ouch."

"Sure, you're a unique and beautiful snowflake," she said, managing to crack a tight smile. "Nondescript is a classification. A good one. If I'm being forthcoming here—"

"I'm begging you."

"We had to be sure that you weren't a..." She struggled, looking a little embarrassed. "An extraterrestrial. Or time traveler. Or whatever else, given what we've found so far."

"And what's that?"

Her lips pressed into a line as sharp as the lapels of her white coat.

"Nothing I tell you leaves this facility."

"Alright."

"The *only* reason you're here is because the machine never gives us a straight answer about you, no matter how we ask."

"Wait. What?"

"Best we can tell, we discovered some tech from another universe. And for some reason—here's the kicker—some version of you was in charge of the project and..."

I didn't hear much of what she said past the words "some

version of you." Everything else just rattled around like noise in my brain.

The layout must've made sense to everyone else there, but as Kaori led me around the Compound, the place was a rat maze of white walls, long hallways, and dead ends. Of frosted glass doors that rolled open when I walked by, or others with chrome handles that I was afraid would shock me if I touched them. I followed Kaori, who sucked in a breath as I badgered her with questions. What does this thing do? And how can you keep it and evidence of alternate realities from the public? Just who do you think you are?

With all the conspiracy theories I'd heard on the doc circuit— of a world-wide phalanx of fourteen-year-old geniuses paid by governments to hack into housekeeping synths to sniff out treason and ransom off nudes, of billionaire CEOs strapping cement shoes on their competition and *disappearing* them down deep wells—I never thought any of them could be real. As I hoofed it through a secret, multinational research center, maybe a little suspicion wouldn't hurt.

Before I'd been born, scientists had found evidence of former life on Mars, from back when it had oceans. My third-grade teacher had told the class about the tiny organisms discovered on Titan, swimming through the planet's ammonia oceans and looking like something I'd sneeze up. Public schools had been big on STEM, then, and the teacher had been dropping words like "organisms" and "multicellular life" and "flagella-like structures" in both English and Mandarin as me and the other kids had poked oversized gooey models of the Titan creatures. The Titan news had sparked riots at first, outside of the UN Headquarters and the

Vatican. No one cared much about dead cells from a million years ago on Mars, but living creatures on another planet messed with them. Like, *you're not so special on your little hunk of dirt.*

"It was like being mad at the sky," my mom had told me of the riots, which had happened when she'd been in college.

Me and my mom were already talking a lot more, then, after my little overdose at the tail end of my sophomore year, and I'd shriveled, and wheezed, and screamed for half of that summer in rehab. Self-healing, *blahblah,* and talk therapy, and a journey that I'm supposedly on to this day, which made Genesis give me shit about my weed use and occasional tip-toeing into tequila territory until her death. Even without the Social Skills forced conversations at school, my mom used to sit me down every day—after making me cut off contact with my friends, after taking my bedroom door off its hinges for weeks—and we'd talk. Even if she was exhausted after another overnight shift as an ER nurse at the clinic in Dorchester, she'd sit me down, still in her scrubs. You can't shut me out, anymore, she'd told me. We have to figure out how to be on each other's sides and move forward together.

I'd heard her praying at night through our cardboard-thin walls, begging Mary. *Avé Maria, cheia de graça, o Senhor é convosco. Please guide me. I know you have a son too.*

"Be mad at it if you want," my mom had told me about the Titan discovery, though obviously it was more about the black hole of rage I was carrying around, "but what's that going to do?"

I'd spent years after that apologizing to her for being an asshole when I was a kid. I still have voicemails saved, just to hear her voice. How she'd tell me everything would be alright, even when it might not. The advice she'd serve up with instant coffee and buttered toast in the morning when I'd visit her years later, hungover from an editing bender. I know I'm a wallower—"You ruminate," Narek had told me, in therapist-speak—but I hate that she never got to see me be someone.

A near-death experience, a mom who would sit with an infuriatingly calm face while I screamed at her about how everything was bullshit and I was going to sneak out and do whatever fuck else I wanted, plus a few doc assignments that had me at the wrong end of a cop's bullhorn taught me how to cram my feelings in a lockbox and keep cool. All of which came in handy as I followed Kaori through the hallways, ignoring the part of me that wanted to run for the exits. Instead, I badgered her until she plucked a two-way radio from her belt and *asked* Yusuf to take me to some tests.

I didn't piece together what "tests" meant at first, because the Storyteller voice in my head was already spinning film reels and telling me to chill. There was a story here, itching my brain. The voice was as cool as the air-conditioning against the back of my neck. *Wait this out. Roll over and play nice and dumb.*

Yusuf met me and Kaori at an intersection of white hallways, where half a dozen painted lines on the floor crisscrossed. He'd slipped on a white lab coat—the stiff collar a snowy cliff ledge against his brown neck—since I'd last seen him. He led us through a main hallway of white glossy tile and glass walls. A few short hallways and small conference rooms for whiteboard-brainstorming branched off from the main drag. Temporary rooms for visiting researchers were down that way, he waved, and a cafeteria just big enough for a couple of tables waited down at the other end.

I still had my phone on me, though when I ducked into a bathroom I saw that I had zero service here in the middle of nowhere. I waved off Yusuf's offer for me to leave my bag in his office since my laptop and Scarlett were still stashed inside.

I figured one of the white coats that fluttered around was going to snatch them and tag the back of my neck with a barcode or something. Kaori's researchers breezed the hallways in pairs, their eyes suddenly interested in the clear glass tablets in their hands when we passed. Sometimes they wagered a "Good morning, Dr. Hassan" to Yusuf, who tossed a low *hmm* back.

"What's your deal here?" I asked him.

"I used to work with Kaori back at the University of Oxford. She brought me here to be her..." He trailed. He spoke out of the corner of his mouth a lot, like using the whole thing was too much effort. "Deputy director. Though titles don't matter here."

"And she has you giving tours to the freshman?"

He fiddled with the edge of his glasses, a nervous tic of his I'd already picked up on. "She has a tough time delegating. She'd rather do everything herself. Which doesn't leave a lot for everyone else."

"I gathered. And how long have you been here?"

"A couple of weeks."

He opened a door to a small white room with a padded table. The room—the whole place—smelled new, like the staff had just peeled off the plastic wrap. He mumbled something about hoping the tests weren't too invasive and then fled the room so I could change out of my clothes and into a paper kaftan. My brown, tattooed arms and legs stuck out from the blue paper doll dress. Someone came in without knocking to press a cold stethoscope to my chest and take my vitals. Someone else drew a vial of blood the color of crushed rose petals.

I let myself be poked and the inside of my ears gawked at while I offered smiles and cracks. My Storyteller voice slips out of my mouth, sometimes, when I'm mid-chat with someone and I'm not sure yet if they're a friend or a lead on a doc. The voice is the soothing low drawl of a yoga teacher and its eyes spark with just a little mischief. It speaks mostly in questions. *What if... And why do you think... Do you mind if I just switch my camera on real quick?* And I'll sip my coffee and whoever's talking keeps their eyes on mine and forgets about Scarlett's blinking red light. After a marathon unloading session, more than one person has stood up on woozy legs, clocked the business end of the camera, and remembered it was there.

I tried the Storyteller voice on a few of the people who rolled in. *How's your day going?* And just before the pinch of a needle in my arm, *it's gotta be going better than mine, right? What's up here, anyway?* I got one to cough up something about looking for abnormalities in my blood before she blinked free of the Storyteller voice, like, *waitaminute.*

Each time one of them left, Yusuf popped back in, so it was pretty clear Kaori told him not to leave me alone for a second.

"Babysitting?" I smirked at him.

One corner of his mouth hooked up into a smile. He shrugged.

An MRI machine. A urine sample. Someone asked me about my background of substance use—*why, what're you offering?*—and my family medical history and mental health. Standard-issue depression and anxiety enjoyed by all humans with a pulse, just a dash of all-purpose gay body dysmorphia. I waited for the finger puppets of Jungian archetypes and the *please tell us about your relationship with your father. Were you loved?* Thankfully, the head-shrinking didn't last long.

I pressed my fingertips to my temples in a useless attempt to massage away my headache. The only thing I'd eaten that day was a bag of chips on the plane. I was crabby enough to threaten the next person who walked in with how I was going to rip off the hospital gown and run naked through these goddamned hallways if someone didn't get me some food. Turns out that was Yusuf.

"Did I pass the tests?" I asked in the hallway after I'd shrugged into my clothes.

"You're human," Yusuf said, not meeting my eyes. "So, who knows."

He buzzed us through locked glass double-doors into another maze, trailing a vein of deep green painted onto the floor while I bobbed along, balloon-brained from the blood draws. A cold sandwich in the cafeteria with its sterile yellow walls didn't bring me back to life. Kaori's words about "some version of you" still bounced around the echo chamber of my head.

Two huge glass doors at the end of another hallway were buck teeth in a giant mouth, with the words "Theater One" stenciled across in white block letters. Beyond, I could see walls of screens and panels, with a giant gray machine an island in the white floor.

"You ready?" Yusuf asked.

His eyes finally hit mine. My throat was suddenly clogged with sand. I don't get speechless. I word-bomb. Even when I'd argued with Narek and realized, two minutes in, that I was the one who was wrong, I dug my heels in and rambled. Pestered with brute force until he'd fling his hands in surrender and hightail it, grumbling.

"Any advice?"

Yusuf's eyebrows crowded together in a small V. "She needs you. Don't let her convince you otherwise."

I stepped closer and the double doors whooshed open on their own.

4
VOICEOVER

Forget about film studies snobs bellyaching. Sometimes you need a voiceover.

I hate the sound of my own voice, as much as Narek would get all psychologist on me about malignant narcissism, no room in your life for anyone else, and *blahblah*. Funny, coming from him, who surprised me with how he'd been dating someone else against our "occasional one-nighter with someone is cool" rule. He called it "spontaneous non-monogamy." See also: cheating. By then, we'd been together two years, living together most of that, and it took me all of an hour to cram my stuff into a few bags. I should've listened to Genesis and left long ago instead of waiting for this latest lie of his, which he wouldn't even own. Instead, he spun it as a chance for me to grow emotionally. Like, *don't see this as an obvious betrayal of your trust, but instead an opportunity to reflect on what you can reasonably expect out of a partner.*

```
SCENE: INT. NAREK'S CONDO (and it's his and not
ours, Narek loves to remind, with just his name
on the deed.) - EVENING
```

<pre>
          NAREK (his forced
          calm hiding rage)
    You're a child and no one will ever
    fill that black hole of need in you.
    And you think your shitty little
    videos are doing something? I'm
    embarrassed for you. Embarrassed.
</pre>

His voice likes to blast into my head when I'm low, even still. So let me drown him out with the voice of someone stronger than me. Maybe after she's had a drink and just a tiny bit of her accent slips in, but before she's goofy enough to laugh at her own jokes.

<pre>
          KAORI (VOICEOVER)
    We were hoping to unlock the secrets
    of the early evolution of our solar
    system. What we found on this tiny
    asteroid was so, so much more.
</pre>

Cue the CGI footage—we'll have to bug the studio for a bigger budget—of the Mugen probe, looking like a mirrored roulette wheel, sailing through the black silk of space. In the control room of the Japan Aerospace Exploration Agency, dozens of staff in white and pale blue jackets wait in silence, because the pictures the probe just beamed back at them of the two-kilometer long Endovelicus asteroid can't be right. No way is there a metallic, clearly unnatural *thing* sticking out of its craggy surface. They were expecting to find ice and organic material, not something extra-terrestrial. Especially not *humanmade* since the asteroid spins ninety-thousand kilometers from Earth.

The JAXA researchers fiddle with instruments to adjust the

course of two stag beetle rovers that hatch from the underside of the probe to fling themselves at whatever device is lodged in the asteroid. When the spindly legs of the rovers touch down, the room gushes out one collective breath. Someone pops a bottle of champagne, and one of the staffers screams at the *thunk* of the cork through the heavy silence.

KAORI (VOICEOVER)

JAXA couldn't bring the device home. Not then. Mugen had to circle back to Earth with the samples and thousands and thousands of pictures of what it had found. They shared their findings with space agencies across the globe. Governments were used to working together - begrudgingly, sure - with carbon emissions capped and HIV/AIDS wiped from the planet. But never held to this level of secrecy. The agencies united to build a craft to return to Endovelicus, dig the probe out, and haul it safely back to Earth for study. After a quick pit-stop at the International Space Agency to make sure that this black box wasn't a bio-weapon or alien-made doomsday device.

"And who made the device?" I asked, in the Mexican restaurant in Indian Springs an hour from the Compound and just outside Southern Paiute Country, which became our favorite haunt a few weeks into our time together.

Here's my *favorite* part, which I whipped out during verbal brawls with Kaori like an uppercut finisher to prove I was right, even about dumb things like "this sci-fi movie was better than that one." *And I should know, because I made the Envisioner.*

I squeezed Yusuf's hand to keep me from pounding the table in margarita-boosted bliss. Yusuf just rolled his eyes like, *easy.*

"There's no actual footage of you making the device," Kaori said.

"She can't even say it!" I cackled. Our waiter, used to us taking over the restaurant on weekend afternoons by then, looked over with a lopsided smile. I nodded for another round. "She literally can't even say that *some* version of me—and I will definitely admit that it was not this idiot nondescript version of me—was smart enough to make the Envisioner."

"Waitwaitwait," Kaori sputtered, laughing. "Show me the evidence. Show me!"

"We're scientists," Yusuf said, lowering his voice to sound serious. The voice he saves for when he's trying to explain wave functions, or when he's got me pinned down against my bed in the Compound, rumbling in my ear, *do you want it?* "We need observable evidence to—"

"Such bullshit. *Such* bullshit. Oh my god," I said.

"I will concede that an alternate version of you led his universe's Envisioner program." Kaori tipped her forehead to me.

"Oh, thank you, Doctor, for your concession." I laughed, licking the salt off my margarita rim. "Us fucking serfs bow to the queen."

Kaori had to lower her cactus-shaped margarita glass before she spilled it, and her honking goose laughs got us all cracking up until we swatted the table like *stop, my stomach can't take this.*

"Okay," I said, wheezing air. "Here's my favorite part."

```
            KAORI (VOICEOVER)
We - with permission from the
Timbasha Shoshone, Western Shoshone,
Southern Paiute, and Owens Valley
Paiute Nations - moved to a
temporary facility at the site of
the former Yucca Mountain Nuclear
Waste Repository in the Commonwealth
of Great Basin Nations, once known
as Nevada. We hoped to repurpose the
concrete tunnels and chambers that
scarred the earth and create a safe
environment to study the device away
from the rest of the world. There,
an international team of researchers
first switched on the device and
learned that it is capable of
calculating unimaginable amounts of
data to predict the most probable
future outcomes.
```

"Hold up," I said. "Rewind. Who'd they pick to lead this black-ops brain trust?"

Flashing a toothy fox smile, I locked my eyes with Yusuf's and started a drumroll on the table that rattled the little dishes of salsa against our glasses.

Who, then, to run the Envisioner Initiative? Not that it was called that in the early days. A cosmologist? Astrophysicist? Theoretical physicist? *Blam-o*—Dr. Kaori Nakamori was that and more. Her parents had crammed her with a steady diet of now-banned evil-genius grade nootropics and Mozart symphonies basically since birth, hoping she'd snag a job when she was older. High-sea piracy had been a more stable career than whatever work you could find in Japan. A global life expectancy crawling past 110—even higher in Japan with their healthcare breakthroughs— plus a booming synth workforce meant people brawled into their nineties for whatever non-automated jobs they could find. Suicide, especially after the yearly workforce placement exams, was the leading cause of death in Japan, which had ignited the world population boom with gene-editing therapies and mandatory cancer inoculations. Thirty years after Kaori had been born, the nation would join most of Europe with universal income for citizens—America had been among the holdouts then and now, cramming her fingers in her ears and lighting candles in a séance for the long-dead ghost of capitalism. Kaori had led her class at Tokyo University when she was fourteen and had left for the University of Oxford at sixteen. She'd led the initial JAXA team, so who would they pick to lead the multinational research coalition?

"Dr. Kaori motherfucking Nakamori, bitches," Kaori said, cheersing the air.

I miss those times with the three of us, which I know is weird to say since not long after that afternoon she'd start chasing us across universes and hunting us down like dogs. But that was the last time the three of us were really happy together.

5
HYPOTHESES

Yusuf hung back a few steps while I walked into the lunar landscape of the Theater, with its white-tiled floors glossy like they were slick with rain, and walls of polished steel dotted with huge screens. A security feed played on one of the screens above and I watched myself creeping into the room like I was walking barefoot over hot coals. Towards the hulking spider of a machine in the center, under a latticed greenhouse-like roof.

A dozen or so techs puttered around with glass tablets by two steel workstations, with Kaori nearby. They all froze when I walked toward the machine. Yusuf joined the flock, so no chance he was offering me backup.

The roof must've been one giant FantiSee screen because a flock of seagulls flew across the panes, even though we were underground. A watercolor sky, the vivid blue of Genesis's eyeshadow. Normally, I'd be itching to call her. We had a habit of rescuing each other, her bailing me out of jail that time a guy at a bar had called her a rug-sucking bitchbot and I'd slugged him. Me bailing her out of jail after another one of her protests had stopped traffic in the middle of the city. As I paid her bail after hocking one of my cameras, an officer yakked something about how she was lucky she lived here or she'd be in the fucking scrapheap.

I'd met her around eight years back, just when I'd started thinking, *you should probably quit giving yourself a pass for being a mess all the time and actually—you know—try.* When she heard about my past, she was basically the first person not to treat me not like some damaged thing made out of glass.

"Excuses are so unbelievably boring," she'd told me. "What really grinds my gears—pardon the pun, babe—is that you people run on excuses."

I could have used some of her no-nonsense while I stared at the Envisioner. The machine was the size of a small electric two-door car, held up on six dull metal legs that were jointed at wide angles. Its matte gunmetal gray surface had hundreds of facets, like some giant semi-precious stone worked at for decades by a manic jeweler. The surface barely reflected the fake sunlight from the FantiSee screen above.

I stepped over a snake of black cable that led from the machine to the workstations. My eyes were locked on the machine, and it yanked me closer—some horizontal free-fall like I was bungee jumping while attached to a piano. Four screens, slightly domed and with a greenish tint, were set into its surface, its panels etched with what looked like cave drawings. Oversized dials and switches glowed the color of hard candies.

My first semester in film school, I'd roamed the neighborhood on trash day and had hauled a bunch of ancient TVs into my truck. Then, I'd duct-taped them together, wedged some cherry bombs in between, and filmed the thing blowing up on super slo-mo. A classmate named Rachel, who I'd really wanted to like if she hadn't been so unbearably pretentious, had said something like, "I love that it's a commentary on the destructive power of technology." Sure, I'd told her. That was completely what I'd meant.

Really, I'd just wanted to blow shit up.

The machine looked like the big brother of my duct-tape craft project, here for revenge.

"Sorry about all the tests," Kaori said. She hovered close enough by me that I could smell some whiff of eucalyptus. But she didn't seem like the perfume type.

"Yeah. What's my deal? Radioactive blood? Am I a superhero?" My Storyteller voice, again. I must've been playing it up for the machine, waiting nearby like a spider crouching to pounce.

"Not unless your superpower is mild hypertension."

"That's pretty boring."

"Yes." She paused. "Would you mind stepping closer? And grabbing those two dials there?" she asked so casually, nodding to nubs on the machine that could've been volume controls of a huge stereo.

Sweat pricked in one of my armpits.

"I am one-hundred percent not touching this thing until you give me a little more to go on."

She pressed her lips together in a hard line. "What do you want to know?"

"What does that... *thing*..."

"The Envisioner."

"Sure. What does the *Envisioner* do?"

"It's a modeling device that determines the most probable expected outcome of a given situation."

Even though I flunked my Stats for Idiots class before I dropped out of college, I could wrap my brain around her annoying vaguery.

"You're kidding me. You're saying this machine tells the future?"

"I'm saying that this is about probability and—"

"How are you keeping this away from the rest of the world? They deserve to know."

"We're testing foreign technology in a secure environment."

"I call bullshit. And I still don't know how you got that footage of the—the *other* me."

"The device has a recording function and we've been able to access some of the existing footage. This is already far more than you have clearance to know. I think I'm being very accommodating here. Now, please touch the dials."

On one of the Envisioner's domed screens, my face was warped, like it was reflected on the surface of a green bubble. For all the cameras pointed at the machine and recording everything happening here, the machine was watching right back with spider eyes of its own.

"I'm not touching shit. *You* touch them."

Behind Kaori by one of the workstations, I saw Yusuf shift his weight and look down, trying to hide a smirk. In one clipped motion, Kaori folded her tablet in half and slipped it into the front pocket of her white lab coat.

"Fine. You want a demonstration?"

"Sure. Gaze into your crystal ball."

She plucked a pen from her coat's breast pocket.

"Hide this pen somewhere in the Compound. Here, take my badge and you can scan into wherever you want. Then I'll ask the machine a question."

She actually smiled. With her high cheekbones, she looked for a second like a hornet just before the sting.

I plucked the pen and her badge and breezed out of the Theater. I figured with the security cameras, there was no place in this whole facility that Kaori couldn't see. I dropped the pen in a tank in one of the toilets in the nearby all-gender restrooms, betting Big Sister at least wouldn't spy on people on the can.

When I circled back to the Theater, her hornet smile hadn't faded at all.

"Ready?" she asked.

"I still call bullshit."

"You want to take a peek at that sheet of paper, over there?" She bobbed her head at one of the machine's panels, where a sheet of paper dangled from a thin slit.

I tore the sheet off at its perforated edge. When I flipped it over, I saw a single printed line, the letters made up of tiny dots.

I still call bullshit.

Someone sucked all the air out of the room. I heard a high whine, that day-after-a-concert ringing of slaughtered ear cells. When I looked up, Kaori actually winked.

"Care to know what I asked?"

Yeah, I touched the dials.

They were slick and cool in my hands. I spun them, holding my breath and waiting for lightning to lance me in the gut. Kaori hovered at my side, guiding with, *could you place your hands there, and there?* I ran my palms over the facets, each tiny cliff a drop in my stomach. Nothing. I watched Kaori's unreadable, brown eyes move from me down to the swirling lines on her glass tablet. At least the facets kind of warmed under my touch. She gave me nothing.

"Thank you for your time, Mr. Figueiredo," she said, stepping back after a few agonizing minutes of silence while I brailled the machine. "It's getting late. You're welcome to stay here the night while we work on your travel arrangements home."

And then she turned on her chunky white sneakers and *whooshed* through the sliding doors of the Theater, with the tails of her coat flapping behind her. The other researchers in the room were still as pillars of salt.

Yusuf was the first to come back to life, popping to my side to show me to a room. He tried to smile a little, which I appreciated as I tried to shake the cold in my gut that had seeped down through my palms when I'd touched the machine.

Redness crept up my neck and burned the tips of my ears. I'm embarrassed to say that what stung the most, while Yusuf led me down more hallways, was how really *embarrassed* I was. For a minute I thought I was special. I know that's whiny and obnoxious, and thankfully I got over it once I was eventually alone in my room like *fuck that.* I'd always avoided the delusions of being an undiscovered auteur or whatever, because I knew I was just Some Guy and was mostly happy with what I'd had. I should've died a long time ago, but I didn't, meaning the rest of my life was a bonus even if it wasn't perfect.

But when I boarded a plane for what I thought was my Hollywood break that then turned into *maybe I have a connection to this machine from another universe,* I let myself believe I was important. And now that was gone.

6
CUT

Looking back, I know that Kaori was putting on a show with her pen gag. In case any of her staff wondered if I was going to roll into the Compound with the smarts of Figueiredo, she had to remind them who took top billing.

After I'd parachuted out of me and Narek's toxic relationship, Genesis invited me to share the stage with her one night. Of course, she'd known how to pull me out of my funk.

Soon after we'd first met, she'd fairy-godmothered me out of a mess of benders and into life, and had pushed me to actually finish my first doc. I'd helped her, too, especially when one of the early lawsuits for nationwide synth personhood failed. When the first synths had rolled out, the Supreme Court had been quick to pass the Defense of Human Sanctity Act that spouted some garbage about "only a human born of flesh in the form of our Creator is afforded legal protections under the Constitution" and *blahblah*. Massachusetts was the only state in the nation to grant synths legal personhood and a challenge to the Sanctity Act had been rising up the courts.

Why did she want to be considered a legal person so much, anyway? We're awful. And of course I'd known it was more about legal protection and human rights, but getting her to laugh about how humans were literally the absolute *worst* had been my secret salve with her. I'd helped her create her drag character to skewer and celebrate everything she'd loved so much about people.

We'd always been each other's lifelines and then she had to go on and die, which I'm still so angry about. And I know you're not really supposed to be angry at dead people but the feelings still pour acid into my gut when I think of her. Because in the weeks of editing all the footage I'd filmed of her, some of the pieces started falling into place about how she maybe hit the evac button on life herself. And I can't forgive her just yet. Not when she was there for me so much when my mom died, and would show up at my place with scallion pancakes from my favorite spot in Chinatown after I'd ignored everyone's calls. Most days we didn't need to talk much. She would just climb into bed with me and run her hands along my scalp. And if she could get me out of bed, we'd just walk the city together in silence.

I guess people don't last that long in my life.

So I don't want to think about her dying. I want to remember her the night we were each other's co-stars, after she'd called me up with, "Hon, wouldn't it be fun if you played some rough clips from your doc about your favorite subject, as in me, at one of my shows?"

She had the grace to frame her "quit your wallowing" advice as a suggestion, like I was one of the kids she nannied.

Before the crowd trickled into the bar, I plastered on a smile as I watched Genesis paint her face backstage. She could read my nerves like the spread of tarot cards on her vanity. She always carried her cards, either lazily shuffling them as we strolled the Floating Quincy Market or keeping them in one of her sequined purses.

I futzed with tarot as a teenager, mostly to piss off my devout mom. Genesis and a lot of other synths used the cards as meditation, with the million possible meanings, stories, and futures hinted by each spread offering an escape from the linear data they were always plugged into. Some made their own decks and traded cards with each other. Genesis carried a classic deck, while her girlfriend and fellow synth queen, Dee Construction, favored one based on human history. The ten of swords was the fall of Tenochtitlan. The queen of pentacles was Nobel laureate and activist Wangari Maathai. Justice, the 350-years-too-late pardoning of Galileo. The highs and lows of the past to tell Dee and the others where the future might lead them.

"Shuffle," Genesis told me, handing over her deck. The backs of her cards were flecked with nail polish.

"What am I asking about?"

"Tonight's show."

As I shuffled, I looked down at my tattoo for strength. I have YOU ARE HERE tattooed down my left thumb, a reminder that I'm always where my feet are, even when my brain bounces me to a million different presents. Even when I build a character around myself to slip into a community for a doc. Words to steady myself, even when the memory of Narek dismissing my work wants to paralyze me.

"Enough!" Genesis chirped. "Cut the deck. Pull a card and hand it over. No peeking."

I did. She didn't tell me the card I'd pulled. She just made a smooch noise and told me, "You're gonna be a star."

YOU ARE HERE.

Back in the Compound, where my feet actually were, I was too tired to crack jokes as Yusuf led me away from my failure in the Theater, down hallways that looked too much like a hospice wing. Into the cafeteria where off-duty white coats poked at wilted salads. If my sour, deflated mood existed as food, it was the sad heat-lamp pizza slices we picked at.

"Why do I feel like I fucked up?" I asked.

Yusuf shrugged. "That's just how she treats everyone."

"What's her deal? Synth?"

I only wanted to know because she was so brisk and disinterested, which Genesis and my other synth friends were accused of being. In their case, most current-model synths flowed around a neural network, linking each individual to the millions of other synths across the planet so they could share data. Plus, they were busy running economies, pulling 72-hour shifts as hospital nurses and janitors, or serving as rent-a-uteruses who had zero say in whether their wetware bio-linked synthetic wombs baked the kids of rich customers, so their patience for human bullshit ran thin sometimes. *I know we're limiting your personal freedoms and all, but do you have to be rude?*

People thought Genesis was radical when she just wanted synths to be treated as more than a robo-vac. As more than a few holes for someone to take out their rape fetishes on, or as playthings for the rich who got their rocks off with some casual amputation play.

"You know, they made us feel pain," Genesis had said on stage, once. "That was their decision."

Genesis had been an early model synth, with her gray polymer flesh making her look like one of the mannequins in shop windows down Newbury Street in Boston. One time I'd been with her on the Red Line to South Station when one of the younger model synths, the types you couldn't clock as non-biological unless you noticed that they weren't breathing, had tried to give up his subway seat for her. *Please, gran, take a seat,* he'd said, thinking he was hilarious.

I hadn't spotted any early-models in the Compound yet, but it wasn't impossible that Kaori could be a human-passing synth.

"No, she's flesh," Yusuf said. And bonus points for him saying *flesh* and not *human*. "Just… no-nonsense."

"And at least synths have senses of humor."

"Also that."

"Why'd she even bring me here?" I asked.

"She thinks Dr. Figueiredo—the *other* you—has a… *physical* connection to the machine, which seems absurd to me. More than likely he has some wearable tech that's hidden by his clothes."

"Creepy."

We finished up and he said he'd show me to the hotel hallway, where visiting researchers could stay in temporary rooms while the permanent staff lived in modular housing outside. I clutched my duffel bag as we walked down another hallway with solid white doors instead of glass. I picked a room at the end by the communal bathroom. Inside the small white room, only a slim bed, sink, and a desk stared back at me. I wanted to buckle on a utility belt with hot pink spray paint cans and tag the Compound's bare walls as a big middle-finger to Kaori for even dragging me here.

I tore my eyes away from this end-of-days bunker to glance back at Yusuf. Just beyond the doorway, he was the only splash of life and color in the whole hallway.

"Am I a prisoner?" I asked. "For real?"

"As much as I am."

"I assume you're getting paid to be here."

"Barely. Dr. Nakamori will let you leave whenever you want. It's just that getting in and out of here can be tough. There's a desert between us and the rest of the world."

"See, you're really not helping the non-prisoner case. And you like being here? Or is there a shock collar on you that I don't see?"

He tipped his head just a bit, his lips tightening. "Why would I wear a shock collar?"

I made a mental note to tweak my humor settings, if he wasn't a fan of sarcasm.

"Right. Well. Sorry you had to babysit me all day."

"It's okay."

One corner of his mouth twitched up as he worked at one of the buttons of his lab coat.

The circuits that connect my eyes and my heart were cranked way, way up. I wondered for a second if Yusuf wanted me to invite him in, like Stockholm Syndrome was already tethering the both of us together, and we might as well have some fun. I wanted to. The same way the pounding music and twirling lights on the dance floor would see me hooking a finger into the belt-loops of a nearby guy to tug him closer. The crush of our bodies together, the clattering of lips. The spark in our eyes that lit me up because we were in love for at least as long as it took to find a dark corner or an open bathroom stall. I wanted to run my thumb over the arch of Yusuf's eyebrows, but all of this seemed too weird even for me.

"Good night," I said.

Eyes back on the floor, he bobbed his head at me in goodbye.

With the door closed, the coffin-sized space looked so much like my room a million years ago in rehab that hives prickled the back of my neck. I was finally alone for the first time since coming here.

I bet you're wondering why I didn't creep back to the machine and ask it for lotto numbers or something. Those jokes will come later and so often that Kaori will look at me, squeeze the bridge of her nose, and wonder out loud, "Do I need to restrict your access from the Envisioner or are you going to take this seriously?"

Mostly, I was just trying to keep moving so the swamp of doubt wouldn't suck my feet down, because Figueiredo's face followed me in every room.

Not long ago I would've reached for a little help from the chemically calming department. I don't fuck with opiates anymore since they almost killed me and all. But I've smoked or eaten enough Kaleidoscope Kush to go nebula-diving through thoughts of alternate universes and the mind-fuck of consciousness. Hours spent staring at a chair—between editing marathons of a doc that no one will watch—realizing that we were both made up of the same junk. Maybe there was another universe where the chair was alive and it just took a big bong rip and was staring at something you sit on called a Hayes.

So what do you do when you feel like your bones are too big for your skin? the Storyteller voice asked me.

I dumped my duffel onto the bed and out tumbled Genesis's tarot deck, Scarlett, and my laptop, hidden among my socks and spare T-shirts. I filmed just about all my work on Scarlett, while everyone else used small armies of multi-angle vid drones. I was lo-fi out of a lack of coin more than anything else, though I loved the weight of the camera in my hands, her lens watching everything like an extension of my own eyes.

I've interviewed a ton of people. Beautiful fucked-up artists and a squad of queer cowfolk for a doc called *I Never Left You for a Banjo* about trying to make it in the rodeo circuit. Women who smuggled birth control into End-Days Saints communes before they escaped with their kids because they wanted their daughters to learn to read and their sons to learn to feel. None of them really wanted to be the face of a movement, except Genesis who'd told me as much as she painted the flat, gray planes of her face with a peachy brown California tan.

I'd always lived behind the camera. I didn't want to be in the spotlight, but something—maybe dangerous, or at the very least *deeply fucking weird*—was going on here. If I was connected to it in some way, I had a responsibility to try to find out as much as I could.

I set my camera on the edge of my desk and turned her lens to face me. Her red eye blinked as she listened while I spilled everything.

7
CIRCLING

Yusuf checked up on me the next morning—sent by Kaori, I figured—and took me for breakfast in the cafeteria. He also admitted she didn't know what to do with me. Chartering another plane to fly me out wasn't on the table because they didn't have the funding. I was getting cold feet after my *you need to stay here and document everything* bravado from the night before, after I'd searched my white closet of a room for bugs and turned up nothing. I was still close with the synth community in Boston and could reach out to them for help if I really needed. Taking a cue from the Storyteller voice's soothing rumble about *something brewing,* I told Yusuf I was fine hanging out here.

I measured time in how many naps I could take on the thin mattress that second day. Yusuf came by twice, each time with a list of things, like one reason to see me wasn't good enough. *We're working on getting you a flight out but we're waiting on fuel. And do you need some air?* Hours later, sometime around dinner, he stood in my doorway and dared to meet my eyes. *I brought you some toothpaste in case you didn't have any and are you hungry?* The more he talked about getting me out of here, the low-brass of his voice speeding up just a tick, the more I suspected he actually wanted me to stick around.

After dinner he brought me to a small outdoor track in the shadow of the squat white Compound, saying how he thought I might want to stretch my legs.

I tipped my head to the cloudless blue sky and let the sun bake my pores. We walked the track, our feet kicking up clouds of red clay. Yusuf had ditched his white lab coat but still looked pretty weird outside in his button-down and black pants. I was wearing the T-shirt and paint-splotched shorts I flew here in, though I had at least managed to wash the pits of the shirt in the sink of my room.

"You should know everything," Yusuf told me, after our first loop around the track. "You're a part of this. Secrets are poison."

I'll remember that "secrets are poison" bit when we're on the run. When Yusuf looks at me, his eyes begging, *please just tell me what's wrong,* and I only smile and kiss the corner of his mouth.

"Alright. Is it safe to talk here?"

Yusuf shrugged. "Seems so. We're beyond the Compound walls."

"Should we at least pretend to run? We look suspicious as hell."

"Alright."

I set a slow pace, both of us looping this track to nowhere over and over, until the sweat dripped down our faces.

They called the machine the Envisioner, he said, speaking in more complete sentences than I'd heard from him so far. They weren't sure what it was called in the other universe—the staff in the video footage used a word that sounded like a noise a blender would make if it had a mouth, which maybe had a connection to the Proto-Indo-Iranian word for "eye." Russia wanted unilateral power on all Envisioner-related decisions if they housed the facility, while China offered to keep the device on their lunar base. No other nation held a candle to their space force—I'd heard rumors from some nut-bags that the global superpower had been testing time-dilation devices on the moon that would crank up the passage of time within a certain field, in hopes of terraforming Mars so they could peace out of Earth within the next decade. When it came down to equal access for all the project's member states, the thing had to stay on Earth. Japan had the tech and the money but not the space, with its ballooning population crammed onto every last bit of the archipelago.

Remember me! screamed scrappy little America. *Remember when I meant something, before the economy imploded and the brain-drain to the Union of Pacific States?* Once they got a green light to host, the American government rented a parcel of land for a few billion dollars from the Commonwealth of Great Basin Nations—*so long as we're clear on the rental part and you guys don't fuck us over, again* was the general feel.

Kaori thought that the machine was a gift sent to us— somehow—by the Envisioner team from the other Earth, who likely had multiple machines helping them avert natural disasters or apocalyptic events. Why not do their alternate selves a solid and help them clean up the dumpster fire of their planet? Sure, JAXA had stumbled on the machine ninety-thousand miles away, but astronomically speaking, that's like a package accidentally sent to your next-door neighbor instead of you.

I already knew that the machine told the future. Well—*a* future, Yusuf corrected me. The most likely one, and sometimes they could get it to cough up hints about the present. Kaori had told him that the machine could also model past events but outright banned everyone from going down that rabbit hole. The past is masturbatory, she'd said, because all you find out is that everyone lied or otherwise tried to kill each other, and that only victors get to tell their stories, which was nothing new. They were there to shape the future and with all the Theater's cameras and shift logs, anyone sleuthing about the past would be canned. Already, Kaori had thrown out one of the researchers who'd been caught trying to ask the Envisioner what had happened during the month that the machine had been on the International Space Station for preliminary study before heading to Earth.

To commune with the machine, you had to hold two dials on one of the panels and speak into a small microphone. The answer popped up on the screens or you could print it out. The answers were often evasive, incomplete, or half in whatever language Figueiredo and his team spoke. Kaori and her researchers were still calibrating the Envisioner to work in English. Here, Yusuf lost me with talk about dice-roll sessions and ambient language and I pictured Kaori reading kids' books to the machine and tucking it in at night.

Annoying, though, was that the machine seemed to have—and here Yusuf looked a little embarrassed—a temperament. The answers got wonky depending on how you asked and maybe who was asking. For starters, Kaori couldn't get the machine to give her a straight answer about how I was involved, because it seemed to be confusing me with Figueiredo. And he'd probably restricted the machine from answering questions about himself to keep anyone from snooping. Sometimes—like when you asked about events too far in the future—the screens spat out lines and lines of equations the researchers couldn't make sense of. Or the answer was a bunch of electron shell diagrams, or star charts of constellations either too distant to see or viewed from some other planet.

The sun and all of Yusuf's words fried my brain. The gross cafeteria dinner churned around on spin-cycle in my stomach.

I was trying not to puke as we were jogging, with each sentence that mentioned something about "this universe" or "the other you" just making me more nauseous.

Kaori and her team had no idea how the Envisioner worked. Nothing—MRI, lasers, infrared cameras—could peer through the machine's gunmetal casing. They stopped just short of bringing in a psychic and having them gaze through their third eye at the spidery box. Kaori was also not someone used to being stumped. Yusuf had never seen a mind like hers, even with all the institutes he studied at, the conferences he attended, the papers he co-authored. She took him under her wing at Oxford, where he'd been her research assistant for years before he rose to full professor once she left for Japan. It was basically the honor of his life that she asked him to help her research here. She, more than anyone else, would figure out the true nature of the machine. Just a matter of time.

Best they could tell, the machine's outer temperature raised a tiny fraction of a degree when it was asked a question, meaning there had to be some sort of energy manipulation inside. Maybe it was a particle collider? Maybe it was a fancy birdcage for a miniature black hole, or a wormhole that led to a web of alternate Earths that the Envisioner peeked at? Proof of at least one alternate dimension had already fucked up their current understanding of the singularity that kick-started this universe, so why not throw most of physics out the window? I had to reel Yusuf back in or he would've rattled off theories for hours.

"And we know the thing is safe?" I asked between wheezes.

"From our best estimates so far."

"You know I'm going to say that's a cue for a huge explosion, or a giant fucking black hole that sucks in the Earth, or something."

"Humanity will probably nuke itself long before the Envisioner does anything close to dangerous."

"That's not reassuring."

"Sorry?"

We had to walk for a bit for me to catch my breath. As crazy as all of this was, I loved that Yusuf wasn't holding anything back, like I was an equal here. As much as Kaori barely tolerated me.

"Alright," I said. "Keep going."

Kaori mentioned that the Envisioner recorded video footage and they were able to access some of it, Yusuf said, but she didn't tell me just how *much* footage. The tech leads on her team had been able to retrofit some twenty-year-old laptops to connect to the machine's storage banks. Which was when they found thousands and thousands of hours of recordings all in scrambled order— north of sixteen years' worth at best guess—that would take forever to sift through.

Here, I floated away from my body, tugged upwards by the Storyteller voice. *Shouldn't you get your hands on that footage?* Yusuf said something about bringing in linguists to help crack the speech from the other universe, which was likely related to some Paleohispanic languages. I watched his lips but all I could hear was *you need to get your hands on that footage.*

"Put me on the video team," I said. "I know jack shit about all else, but film I know."

"That's not my call. It's Kaori's. I can talk to her."

I watched the muscles working at the sides of his jaws, maybe out of doubt or regret that he just spilled all of this out to me.

"Let me. I don't want you to get you in trouble with her."

"She'll know I spoke to you about this, anyway."

"Yeah, but I can be convincing. And obnoxious."

"I can see that."

I snorted a laugh. Yusuf's dark eyebrows just knitted together. "How you're convincing—that is," he said.

We rounded the corner of the clay track again, our feet trampling over our past footprints.

"You built the machine," he continued. "A part of you might understand how it really works."

"The *other* me."

"You're connected to him. *Everything's* connected. Theoretically."

Even with the sun sizzling on the back of my neck, I'd rather have wandered out there for hours with him than lock myself back in my room. We looped once more before heading into the vacuum-sealed air of the Compound, where he was quiet again. Almost shy.

"I'll see you later," I said, at the crossroads between the little hotel hallway with my room and the Theater. "Theoretically."

Yusuf shook his head a little, rolling his eyes. For the second before he smiled, I thought, *ugh*, I was a dick again when I was trying so hard to be funny.

He started down the hall. "And your cardio sucks, by the way," he called without turning back. "Later."

I watched his back until he banged a right down the hall towards the Theater. I could still hear his footsteps, matching the quick time of my heartbeat. The happy little merry-go-round head-spins trailed me back to my room while I tried to think of whatever joke I should've yelled back at him. But he snatched all the words out of me, and already I loved it.

Kaori had to eat at some point, right? I staked out the cafeteria until she floated in from the kitchen with her red plastic tray and sat alone at a table. I let her have a few bites of her food—I'm not a complete dick—before I swooped in across from her.

"Oh, goddamnit," she said.

She thought I was there to give her shit about not getting me back home sooner. I mentioned how Yusuf told me about the footage team and I could already see the arguments building up behind the hard line of her mouth. The longer side of her hair was tucked behind her ear. "Think of all the secrets that are buried in that footage," I told her, playing to her rational side. She needed more hands on deck. I was already here and I knew to keep quiet.

"I'm not a physicist or whatever, but film I know. And…" I trailed, breathing deep and nodding slowly, beaming a quiet aura of deference out to the cheap seats in the back. "I really want to be part of something this important."

With her sigh, I knew I roped her in.

"We'll keep you around for a few weeks," she said. "Probationary. The second you get in the way, you're gone."

"That's all I can ask for."

In my head, the Storyteller voice rumbled *attaboy*.

I guess my biggest mistake in all of this was thinking I pulled one over on Kaori, or that I had her figured out at all.

I'm going to interrupt our regularly scheduled programming again to talk about some plot black holes that you might think are going to suck in this whole narrative.

Most of my life I've heard my teachers tell my mom things like *I really wish he'd apply himself more* when they thought I wasn't listening. Yeah, since applying myself like a thick coat of paint would make me smarter or something. I'd like to think my brain works in ways you can't really measure with grades. It spins me waking dreams I try to capture on film and makes me feel so connected to everything else that a holo-ad on the subway for donations to an animal shelter sends me into a nosedive for the rest of the day. Most days, my brain is a jiggly pudding of conflicting emotions. Which is to say I know I'm not a rocket scientist.

Maybe someone else could've seen some of this coming. Or not, because what you need to know is that if this is Hayes's Disaster Drive-In Theater, Kaori is and has always been in the projection booth calling the shots. She controls what we see. If she doesn't like what's playing, she can splice in some of her own footage, and we won't even notice the change.

Because of course Kaori planned all of this. She brought Yusuf over from Oxford and had him pick me up from my little cabin in the woods. She gave him nothing to do here except babysit me, knowing we'd connect because we were both new and equal parts bored and overwhelmed. She knew he was basically unable to keep secrets or lie to anyone—what I love about him so much—so of course he'd spill everything to me.

She already knew the order of the videos from Figueiredo's universe. She wanted me on the team—I convinced her of jack shit—because that way she could release a little breadcrumb trail of footage to lead me wherever she wanted. The whole Compound, the whole Envisioner project, was probably a ruse when she could've just spirited the machine into a lab in Japan or Oxford and studied it herself. This big multitrillion-dollar shell game to change me into who she needed me to be. Except she counted on me being an experiment that would unfold according to her theories, when I don't know what the hell I'm doing at any given moment.

Honestly, I'd be more pissed if I wasn't so weirdly honored that all this trouble was because of me.

8

ORIENTATION

In the rom-com satire movie trailer of our relationship, a smiling baritone informs the audience, "Yusuf Hassan never thought he had time for love." Cut to Yusuf sighing over a glass of wine with an Unnamed Female Friend.

"I'm the deputy director of a secret multinational research organization. I don't have time to date!" he bemoans. Born in Egypt and raised an army brat who bounced with his family to Prague, then Sydney, then East London, his accent falls somewhere in the "British actor trying to sound American" range. He's quiet, with eyes that prefer to skim the corners of rooms. Thirty-six, though he looks younger, with his slim waist and muscles hidden by too-big cardigans. Cut to a scene of him whipping down a Compound hallway while papers fly off the stack in his hands, his glasses crooked on his nose because he's *just so busy* he doesn't even have time to straighten them.

"And Hayes Fig," the voice continues—notice the nice white bread last name because this movie can't have two ethnic-y leads, not when it's *already* a gay story, I mean really—"was so used to helping others fight for their rights and tell their stories. But what about his own story?"

On a morning run along Boston Harbor, I ask my Unnamed Male Friend, biting back frustration, "What about my story? My *love* story?" Cut to a scene of me filming a street protest—the cause isn't important, just pick one—where the pan-racial crowd holds signs with EQUAL RIGHTS NOW.

"But when a machine that can see the future brings them together..."

Here, Yusuf calls out to me that first day at the artist residency, and I turn in slow motion like I'm flipping a blond mane of hair off my shoulder, leaving Yusuf swoon-struck. "Can they really escape their *own* future?"

Except no dreamy baritones chimed in with helpful exposition while I followed Yusuf from the guts of the Compound and outside to a small field of green pavement where twenty or so four-bedroom modular homes baked in the heat. Yusuf, Kaori, and the other staff all lived in their own houses, and now that I was officially one of them—probationary, Kaori kept reminding me—I needed more permanent digs.

We walked up the folding metal stoop of one house and inside to find a doctor's office waiting room of a shared living space, a kitchenette, and two bathrooms. One of my housemates was a woman named Lana who worked the custodial staff. I picked one of the empty bedrooms and dropped my duffel on the twin bed.

"It's a good thing I dig minimalism," I said, zooming Scarlett across the room, with its single chair and desk. Someone had left me a potted cactus as a house-warming present. At least I had a window that looked out over the red desert and the security fence in the distance.

"You've had a camera this whole time?" Yusuf crossed his arms, frowning.

I shrugged and panned over to him. "Smile!"

After unloading my bag, he left me at a security office where I got a fancy official badge, which let me into the inner ring of the Compound. I followed the painted line—the blue of the electricity that buzzed in my veins—up a couple flights of stairs to the Video Mezzanine. A door waited for me at the top of the stairs, its brushed metal like a dull razor. I pushed through.

The dim room was lit mostly by an enormous slanted window that overlooked the Theater, like the mezzanine of a theater where you'd watch actual plays. The FantiSee screen projection of a forest canopy cast a greenish glow into the room, adding to the light from the workstation screens at three long tables. Twelve people wearing headphones like warring DJs sat hovering over keyboards. I was lucky number thirteen.

A few pairs of eyes flicked up at me. Then more—widening as I toed the ground. Screens flashed with footage of a wide gray room where people in dusty green coats puttered around an Envisioner, which must've been Figueiredo's Theater. In more than one screen, I saw him talking with the green coats, or waving wildly at the machine, mid-argument with someone who was definitely losing.

No wonder the footage team looked scared of me. I might as well have crawled, horror-movie style, out of their screens.

"I should've brought popcorn," I said, trying to clear the air.

With all the pep of a park ranger, someone named Arjun introduced himself and the others, who waved politely enough. Arjun was older than me, with a choppy almost-Mohawk slicked back down the back of his head. There wasn't a white lab coat in sight, with everyone in jeans and T-shirts. At least I didn't look completely out of place. Arjun got me settled into my own workspace and explained the rundown of their days here at the Video Mezzanine, though everyone just called it the Footage Farm.

Arjun and his team had thousands of hours to comb through, between the separate files of twenty-four-hour chunks that the Envisioner recorded of the other universe. With additional footage of each time someone asked the machine a question, like a camera from one of the panels was pointed at the questioner's face. Plus, Arjun thought the tablets that Figueiredo's staff lugged around were synched to the machine, meaning there was likely tons of video footage from those, too. The individual files weren't in chronological order, because, as far as they could tell, the transfer from the Envisioner using the ancient laptops scrambled things up. But they were lucky, still, that Kaori's tech lead had been able to dump all the footage from the Envisioner onto a separate server. From there, Arjun had created a work queue that all the footage techs logged into, watched a few hours at a time, and recorded their observations in a digital report for the whole team.

No one had any idea what the people in the footage were saying, of course, with reports mostly full of educated guesses while they waited for linguists to fly in, hopefully. Sometimes when they needed another opinion one of the footage techs would play a clip on the big screen in front of the panel of windows. *Subject A is clearly angry at the results here. No way, see that smile? He's satisfied. Or gassy?* Subject A was Dr. Figueiredo, a helpful shorthand to help distance myself from the footage, plus the other film techs butchered my last name.

I was dying to get into the work queue myself but I had to be *on-boarded*. Ugh. I hated the business-douche language. I burned the morning reading employee conduct handbooks, signing NDAs, and watching work queue tutorials. I shadowed one of the other Footage Farmers for a while, which meant sitting at their side and watching them watch footage. Thrilling. I wished I'd brought

Genesis's tarot deck from my room me to give me something to do with my hands. After lunch, by the time I was ready to wade out of the kiddie pool, Arjun and the others started packing up their things for the day.

"What gives?" I asked him.

"You didn't hear? We're closing up shop early," he said. "Staff supply run. You coming?"

I jumped from my seat. "Get me outta here." At Arjun's tipped head, I let out a nervous chuckle. "I mean, sure."

"Esteemed colleagues," Kaori started from her position by the doors that led into the facility's underground parking garage. She'd ditched her lab coat and was wearing gray slacks and a short-sleeved black knit top that showed off toned arms. The crowd of two-dozen or so Compound staffers listened from a loose semicircle.

"For those who I have not yet met, it is my distinct honor to welcome you to this facility. And to you all, I welcome you to this special, and might I add, *singular,* group supply run. I apologize if I did not sufficiently express to you, via my individual phone calls, many encrypted emails, and detailed pre-arrival packets, that this is a purposely remote facility. And not a college campus where you can run to the student center for cigarettes and condoms."

"Yikes," Arjun whispered at my side. I bit back a snort at seeing resident-advisor Kaori all worked up.

"Our extremely hard-working and capable facilities staff is here to keep the Compound stocked and its residents fed and comfortable, and, sadly, are unable to assist you with your personal haircare demands," she continued. "Thus, this cell-phone-free supply run to Indian Springs. A place some of you may request to visit again on a limited basis using one of our limited vehicles during your limited off-hours. All of which are, again, limited."

I could practically feel the collective wave of nausea through the crowd. At least I had an excuse for coming here empty-handed. I let Kaori's painfully polite reaming bounce off me.

"As far as the residents of Indian Springs are concerned, we are a tour group stopping on the way back to Las Vegas after a day trip in Treaty City, the diplomatic capital of the Commonwealth of Great Basin Nations, which is two hours north." Here, she tugged on a beige sun visor, which I guessed was her tour-guide getup. "I will be joining you to ensure that no one blows this cover. While in town, you are encouraged to discuss—audibly for townspeople around you—the many marvels of Treaty City. Talking points include the city's vast network of hydroponic farms, the majestic eagle sculptures of Unity Square, and the gorgeous and ornate beadwork found in the Commonwealth Cultural Museum." She hit the group with a toothy smile. "Anyone deviating from said talking points will be left in the desert."

"She's joking, right?" Arjun whispered. "Like, she has to be joking."

I shrugged. "All I know is that the beadwork at the Commonwealth Cultural Museum is really something."

Now that she'd torn us new assholes, Kaori led the way through the parking garage and into a white electric minibus. I tucked into a solo seat by the back, and the minibus whizzed through the tunnels and out into the sunlight. Soon, the Compound disappeared in a cloud of red dust behind us.

Technically I was getting paid to work at the Compound as of that morning, but tell that to my malnourished bank account. I could make do with the free toiletries in my pod-house bathroom. While the others bounced around the shops of the town's main drag, with rolling red hills in the distance, I wandered on my own. I did pop into a kitschy tourist shop, telling myself that my new coworkers would appreciate me wearing something other than a stained T-shirt I washed in my bathroom sink. I dropped a few bucks on a bright blue tee with aliens leaning out of a flying saucer to snap pictures with old-fashioned cameras, with the words "Welcome to Nevada" in neon yellow. I was about to head to the minibus to wait out the afternoon heat, when I passed a Mexican restaurant with wide windows that faced the street. Inside was the most shocking thing I'd seen since coming here.

Yusuf and Kaori sitting at a table together, *laughing*.

The air-conditioning and the smell of sizzling onions smacked me in the face when I stepped inside. Some of the others from the supply run were there, too, though everyone seemed to know to give Yusuf and Kaori a wide berth. Except me. Because if the half-empty cactus-shaped margarita glasses on the table meant anything, it was that I was absolutely interested in meeting buzzed Yusuf.

"You don't look like you're discussing Treaty City's vast network of hydroponic farms," I said. I plopped down on a chair without waiting for an invitation and tossed a tortilla chip from the basket between them into my mouth.

Yusuf looked at me and grinned. "Rules don't apply to Dr. Nakamori."

She clinked his glass with her own. "You've always been acutely observant."

Yusuf had a few more buttons of his collared shirt undone than usual. The worried line of his lips from that morning was gone, with a half-smile in its place. Salt from his drink stuck to the stubble above his upper lip. Even Kaori had tossed off her beige sun visor and her tour-guide cover.

"I ask out of jealousy and very much not judgy-ness," I said. "How many of those have you had?"

"We are working," Kaori quipped. "Dr. Hassan and I have first-hand proof that occasional, careful application of creativity-stimulating and inhibition-relaxing substances can significantly boost our problem-solving skills."

Yusuf nodded, suddenly serious. "We call these, 'enhanced evaluatory sessions.'"

"Uh huh," I deadpanned.

A waiter floated by, and I pointed to the margarita glasses, then pressed my hands together in prayer. *Please.*

"Do you remember," Kaori trailed, hiding a smile behind a bite of chips, "our session after the translation event?"

"You still owe me for that," Yusuf said. "I fielded emails from overbearing parents for days."

"What the hell happened?" I asked. "Something with translating Figueiredo's language?"

Yusuf sighed. "She conducted her first physics seminar at Oxford entirely in Japanese."

"With hand gestures. And equations. And *diagrams*!" Kaori actually giggled. For the sake of her staff, I made a note to lug gallons of margarita back to the Compound. "I was illustrating that physics transcends language. And that physics is the language of science. Clearly."

"I explained this thesis to our division head," Yusuf said, rolling his eyes. "Who then asked me to remind you that you were there to teach in English, as per the syllabus."

"Babying the undergraduates to cave to that man's lack of philosophical rigor remains the low-point of my career." She stabbed the lime on the rim of her glass and it tumbled into the neon drink. Then, she glanced my way. "Well, until we see where letting you stay leads me."

I fanned my hand over my heart in dramatic horror. "You know, usually I'm into some casual negging as foreplay. But, ouch."

"Did you get set up with the video team?" Yusuf with the pivot.

"What my esteemed colleague means to ask is if you've crashed our footage server yet," Kaori said sweetly.

The waiter, my savior, dropped off my drink. I glugged a catch-up mouthful. "What's with the 'esteemed colleague' garbage? Aren't you two friends?"

"Is a carpenter friends with her hammer?" The laugh was gone from Yusuf's voice. He swiped at the salt over his lips.

"Now, now," Kaori protested. "You're far less blunt than a hammer."

"Thank you."

"Besides. You value science. I value science. Therefore, by the transitive property of—"

"This is gonna be good," I interrupted.

"—of… interpersonal relations, that means I value Dr. Hassan, here."

"You should get that printed up on a greeting card," I said. I glanced over at Yusuf and his eyes were lost on the ice cubes of his glass. I wasn't sure he was in on the joke.

"I'm not sure we'll have time on this specific outing," Kaori said. "I'll consider it."

On my tongue, the margarita was sour and sweet.

Sometime after my second drink, the two of them stopped referring to each other with their fancy titles in front of me. I leaned back and watched them fall into their easy shorthand after years working and teaching together. I goaded them here and there with questions about their research, with my eyes as camera lenses picking up how they reacted.

> **NAREK (VOICEOVER)**
> You're good at this because you're
> a liar. You know what people want to
> hear, what they want to be asked.
> You use all that to get a story out
> of them.

I shook away the voice with another pull of my margarita. There *was* a question trying to bubble out of me while I watched them. I leaned back and loaded it up.

"Just how does the machine work?"

Silence settled over our table. Yusuf looked to Kaori and I got the sense that I'd stepped in it. In the restaurant around us, the other Compound staffers were gathering their shopping bags and closing checks. We'd be heading back to real life, soon enough.

"It shouldn't," Yusuf mumbled. "The Envisioner should not work."

Kaori leaned back in her chair and crossed her arms as I listened to Yusuf. The universe is made up of a bunch of particles that interact in predictable ways, he said. From the faraway look in his eyes, I knew to settle in for a long tutoring session. The only way you could theoretically predict the future is if you knew—with *infinite* accuracy—the positions and velocities of every one of these particles. Never mind that you can't know both the position and velocity of a particle at the same time. Never mind that no computer can calculate anything with infinite precision.

Never mind the randomness that seems hard-wired in a universe barreling towards disorder. The *never minds* kept building up and I understood maybe half of what he was saying by the time he got to the Second Law of Thermodynamics. He still wasn't convinced that this wasn't some big hoax. Sure, have a blast getting theoretical about alternate universes, but it's not like you can jump into one and prove it's even there.

I waggled my eyebrow at Kaori. "Thoughts from the director?"

"I've been trying to get Yusuf to relax a bit. Breathe and be more present."

"Yeah, but what do you think about the machine?"

"Everything he says is right," she said, shrugging. "But at the same time, here we are."

That was her catch-all answer to anyone who complained about the mind-fuck impossibility of what they were doing.

"Uncharacteristically imprecise," Yusuf said.

"Oh, come on," Kaori chirped. "Have a little faith."

Yusuf clammed up after that. I think if I was a scientist being told that by another scientist I'd probably flip a table. Kaori paid for us and the rest of the Compound's stragglers in the restaurant before slipping her beige sun visor back over her brow.

Back in the baking heat outside. Yusuf walked ahead of us, eyes on the dusty sidewalk. I'd catch up to him, but first—my eyes twitching, catching the last hints of Kaori's margarita-buoyed smile on her lips—I stuck to her side. We should do this again, I said. I could crash their enhanced *whatever* sessions, or we could make them something more fun. Margarita club. Who doesn't want to be part of a club? I'll even make T-shirts, I joked. Why not, she said. And while she was in a good mood, I poked again. What if I recorded bits here and there around the Compound? A snip of a reply, a hand-wave. *Just don't get in the way.* She didn't even blink about me admitting that I'd smuggled a camera here. She probably already knew since there was no way some nondescript like me could get anything past her.

Back on the minibus, I sat next to Yusuf. He didn't have much to say before he crossed his arms, leaned against the window, and tried to sleep.

9

FOOTAGE FARM

The *f*-word from Kaori. *Have a little faith.* Who knows if she meant to wound him or if she was just brushing him off.

Weeks later, when me and Yusuf were swapping the obligatory coming out stories in his room, propped up on pillows as the night breeze from the open window swept across our skin, I brought up faith again. I'd been scared to tell my mom I was gay because she dragged me to church every Sunday, where I listened to a priest talk about all the things I wasn't supposed to do. She'd whack me on the back of the head if she caught me dropping a *jesus christ* as a swear, though she'd grumble about the goddamn busted dishwasher when she didn't think I could hear her. She'd fast for days, sometimes, talking about sacrifice and devotion. Looking back, some of those devotions must've been because she only had the cash to feed one mouth.

When I came out of my glass-doored closet to her when I was fifteen—"I'm your mom, I always knew in my heart," she told me years later—I expected her to freak. Of course she didn't. And why would I even think that, she asked? Because of god, I told her through the snot and the tears.

"I believe in God," she'd whispered into the top of my head while she hugged me. "I love God. But I love you more."

I never bothered to have a *this is a Very Special Episode of Your Life*-type sit-down with my dad when I came out, to teach him to be a more accepting person. My mom kicked him out when I was eight and my memories of him involved his pickling himself on the couch after he lost his job at the water desalination plant when the whole operation turned to synth workers. He called me on my thirteenth birthday and I worked up the courage to ask him why he never bothered to help me and my mom out. She'd made games, when I was younger, about digging through the couch cushions and treasure-hunting on the sidewalk for change to buy a gallon of milk. I'd laughed over the sidewalks, snatching coins and stashing smooth pieces of glass and cool rocks in a shoe-box treasure chest in my room. Having no idea then how hard-off we were—how much she probably stayed awake at night—and thinking it was only a game.

My dad waited a long time before answering, "Because I hate her more than I love you."

I didn't let him rent a ton of space in my brain after that.

Both of Yusuf's parents were people of faith. His dad needed something to tether himself to while his work as a Peacekeeper for the UN bounced him all over the world and, *inshallah,* he would go wherever God sent him because that was His will. In some new tiny apartment, Yusuf's mom would quote the Quran to him as far back as he could remember, between kisses on his forehead. I trust in Him, and in Him shall all the trusters put their trust, she told Yusuf. He saw her trust challenged and heard her on the phone with her sisters and her mother. Doctors. School counselors. *He won't look at me. He won't let me hug him. He barely talks. Something is different about him and I'm not sure how to help.* Learning—the order he found in math and science—

was the only thing that grabbed his interest. How, *inshallah* or not, one equation could describe how both a ball that he kicked at recess flew through the air and how the universe expands. His parents enrolled him in a school for gifted kids and got him tutors and fought to place their little egghead on the high school math team. His parents, who—back in Egypt where they'd all been born—had heard of this cousin's cousin or that friend's friend caught in a police raid at some suspected gay gathering. Even though he had told them he was gay before he left for university at sixteen, they trusted that it was just another problem they didn't yet know the answer to. As much as he wasn't interested in their verses and *you should speak to this therapist* or *that imam*, a rift widened between them.

He honestly didn't get it. He never argued faith. In the game of telephone that was their family and the Muslim community in East London, he called his younger cousin Salma, who heard from her mom, who heard from her sister, who heard from Yusuf's mom about *the gay thing*.

"They're bothered by how *unbothered* you are," his cousin Salma had told him on the phone, always his human-to-Yusuf translator. "Like, you don't care that they're so torn up about you being gay."

"They're right. I don't care."

"Duh. You shouldn't. They'll stop being weird soon enough." She'd popped her chewing gum. "Besides, you're at uni. You can, like, shag every boy you want. You still buying me vodka, or what?"

While Yusuf talked and picked at his knuckles, I thought about other peoples' faith in capital-G God and Kaori's faith in science in the face of the Envisioner's impossibility. Really, I didn't care about any of that. I was just thankful for whatever brought me to that room with him. *But at the same time, here we are.*

———

I wore my work badge and fancy new Welcome to Nevada T-shirt for my first full day at the Footage Farm. Even after the margaritas, I was fresh-brained because I'd stopped at two. Genesis would've been proud of my self-control.

One summer in high school I thought, hey, I love movies. Why don't I work at a movie theater? Which is like saying you should work at a butcher shop because you love animals. You see the ugly stuff that kind of ruins everything. I figured I'd sell tickets and shoot the shit with other movie buffs and sneak into theaters when things got slow. The only job I'd been able to get at the theater was as a morning janitor, so I cleaned dirty toilets and swept empty theaters with a leaf-blower—pushing old popcorn, and wadded napkins, and the occasional used condom out from between the rows of seats. Nothing ever turns out how you really want it.

I figured I was volunteering to watch sexy science experiments or a mystery unfold like grainy night footage of a rare mountain cat. Really, I was there to feel all the joy and creativity evaporate from my skin doing an office job, watching a security feed that might have been of a dentist's exam room. That at least would've had blood once in a while. I burned through the day with half-assed reports, like *tech asked the Envisioner a series of eight questions and seemed happy with the results.* Instant coffee dissolved at the bottom of a chipped mug in the kitchenette where I escaped to kill time under the buzzing overhead lights. I know it's obnoxious of me, but sitting at a desk all day long and filling out reports felt like slow death. I'd be in the Footage Farm forever, now, sitting in the dark like a calf waiting to be turned into veal. I almost wanted to take my chances with the heat stroke trying to hoof it over to Vegas so I could hop a mag-train home. Until I saw Figueiredo's face.

I loaded up one of the files in my queue and the first frame was a close-up of his eyes. I knew they were his because they were *mine*. I slammed the spacebar key, pausing the playback while my pulse tried to burst out of my ears. I just couldn't deal with seeing my face plastered over someone else, not at least until the others in the Footage Farm around me trickled away for the night and I could hyperventilate in peace. And I heard the voice whisper across the back of my neck like the bleached air coming out of the vents. *This is what you need to see. This is why you're here.*

I waited until I was alone and hit play.

Figueiredo sat at a slick glass desk twirling a silver pen in his fingertips. Behind him, a sliding glass door looked out to a small stone patio clustered with ferns the size of trees. Some tropical penthouse or a private office where he felt comfortable enough to unload onto this video journal, or whatever this was.

I forced myself to study his face when I wanted to look away because of the acid his wolf eyes kicked up in my stomach. Lines radiated from the corners of his eyes—the same brown as mine—probably from so much scowling. His cheeks were a little fuller, with deep laugh lines carved into both sides of his lips like parentheses. His finance douche haircut of cropped sides and a gelled side-part in place of my buzzed head. A curving fingernail-shaped scar in one of his eyebrows in place of the pinprick scars in my ears from closed-up piercings. On his nose rested a pair of thin, gold-rimmed circular glasses—which he probably didn't even need—that screamed *I introduce myself at parties as Dr. Figueiredo.*

What weirded me out the most was the hush of his voice—lower than mine and edged in gravel. His words scraped out a tired tune in the strange music of his language, unlike his clipped drill-sergeant speak I'd heard so far. I watched his lips move, squinting at the words to see if they'd make sense.

Honestly, watching twisted my gut so hard that I sometimes had to look away or I'd puke. I'd accidentally gotten blackout drunk at a birthday party for a guy I'd been dating a while back. He'd recorded me swaying on the tiny stage of the bar in front of the karaoke machine and hamming up some pop song for him. He'd shown it to me the next day because he'd thought it was cute. I very much didn't. I had to yoga-breathe through the panic and shame. How was I that *thing* I was watching? How did I let some poltergeist possess my body and make me do things I had zero memory of? The Ghost of Blackouts Past poured another cocktail into my stomach.

I projected a life onto my alternate self while I watched Figueiredo's lips move. He'd probably stayed in school and listened to all those visiting speakers blabbing about how STEM careers are cool, and *you too can change the world!* He'd snagged trophies while I over-slept through the race. His teeth were straight and wide without my slight front gap. His neat button-down skimmed his body. I only dressed half as nice as him, slipping white-cuffed dress shirts over the tattoos of lines of poetry and interlocking triangles at my forearms, when I filmed weddings here and there to bring in some cash.

On my screen, Figueiredo scrubbed one hand across his tired face and I caught a flash of gold on his left hand. He was probably at the height of his career—crafting world-upending tech—and he still made it home in time for dinner with his partner. Who was an underwear model or whatever.

Something off-screen caught Figueiredo's eye and the hard edge of his mouth melted into a wide smile. A man in a dusty green lab coat circled the desk and crouched to drape his arms around

Figueiredo's neck, and—*holy shit*—I stabbed the spacebar again. A man who looked just like Yusuf nuzzled the side of Figueiredo's face. A thicker beard with a sharp line angled to his lips and hair that was cropped closer, but still Yusuf.

My heart clogged up in my sandpaper throat. Kaori had never coughed up anything about another version of Yusuf.

The other Yusuf stuck out his tongue at whatever camera Figueiredo was recording on. I didn't need to understand their words to know that this Yusuf, with the same gold band as Figueiredo's, was teasing his husband. *Sorry, I didn't mean to interrupt you talking to your little diary.* Figueiredo laughed something back, elbowing, saying some word a few times that sounded like how my mom would say her brother's name. *Tiago.* Which must be alternate Yusuf's name. They swapped some end-of-day debrief while heat crept over my face. Then they both clammed up, Figueiredo tipping his head at someone else who must've just popped into the room, off-screen.

Figueiredo tossed off some clipped sentence, and then everything moved in a blur. He burst out of his chair, grabbed his recorder, and then all I could see were snippets of the hallway and floor in the jostling footage as they walked somewhere. Next came the heavy footsteps behind them, and the shouting. Someone shoved a door open, sending Figueiredo and Tiago and whoever else was with them breaking off into a sprint. A pterodactyl screech of an alarm pierced the air. Another minute of slamming through the hallways and shouting at each other.

Until, finally, stillness. Only the echoes of heaving breath.

All I could see was where Figueiredo's camera was angled. Best I could tell, he held it at his side, camera facing away from his legs and pointed at another pair of legs in dark pants. A gunshot cracked through my ears—nearly knocking me off the seat and onto my ass—and the camera clattered to the ground. Only the eggshell-white of the ceiling, until a boot slammed down and the footage winked out.

I watched again and again until my eyes felt dusted in ground glass, not realizing I'd been biting my cheek until I tasted blood.

I tried to poke through the footage queue for a while, but there were thousands of hours to watch, and there was no way I was going to find out who'd been shot, by just blind luck. I was already splicing together ideas about some mutiny against Figueiredo, some revolt against his barbs and iron rule that ended with a bullet in his chest. I should have filled out a report like a model employee and told Arjun about what I saw, but I just had to get out. The fuzzy numbers at the corner of my workstation told me it was past two in the morning. My head was full of noise. I pushed away from my workstation and scrubbed my eyes, pacing to the window that overlooked the Theater.

I wasn't alone. Down below in the Theater, I spotted Kaori by the machine. She ripped off a page from the Envisioner's printer, frowned, and added it to the thin stack in her hands. Then, she tipped her head up to the Milky Way of the FantiSee screen, which was when she saw me watching her from the video mezzanine.

I don't believe in dumb luck now—especially with her—after all I've seen. The white sheet in her hand probably spelled out to her *look up*.

I almost ducked. She smiled just a little, but it seemed friendly and not spiked with sarcasm or condescension like the hornet smiles she'd hit me with before. She waved at me and then flicked her hands towards her, cuing some invisible blinking gameshow lights and a cheering studio audience. *Come on down.*

10
ORACLE

I waited tables for a while at an arcade brewpub in Boston, in the shadows of the FantiSee-screen-encased skyscrapers, past the locks that kept downtown dry while plebs sloshed through the flooded streets in the rest of the city. The best part of the job had been this fortune-teller mannequin named Mystic Lady Pythia in a glass booth by the front entrance. Someone must've hacked the machine or else she was completely over the whole Mystic Lady thing, with deadpanned prophecies in exchange for a few bucks. *Your lucky number is green. Your next haircut will be stupid.*

While I looked at Kaori through the gleaming glass doors of the Theater, it was like she was circling in her own glass booth. I hadn't been back to the Theater since my first day on the Compound, when she'd coached me into running my hands over the Envisioner like a director in one of those synth-human skin flicks. The glass doors *whooshed* open and I walked to her by the machine.

"I'm usually the only one here by now," she said, husky-voiced, with green shadows beneath her eyes. She wagered a tired smile. I figured some part of her had thawed towards me after yesterday's margarita bonding.

"I just saw some crazy footage," I said. "A riot or something against Figueiredo in the other universe. I couldn't stop watching it."

"This thing gets into you." She nodded toward the machine, the blunt ends of her hair bobbing. "What happened?"

"I'm still not really sure." Jitters twitched in my voice. "Someone got shot, but I couldn't tell who because of the angle of the footage."

"Show me tomorrow. And tell Arjun—everyone will keep a lookout in the footage."

"Yeah. Did you know there's another Yusuf in that universe? And I think he and Figueiredo are together."

"Interesting." She pinched her eyes just slightly.

"What're you doing here this late?"

She sighed, pale as the stack of papers in her hands. She looked human, finally, not some synth who was sculpted out of ice and ran on self-importance. "I'm still trying to calibrate the Envisioner so I can extract some decent information."

"Meaning?"

"I'm testing the machine's accuracy with repeated queries. I start with simple things. Coin flips. Dice throws. If it spits out a wrong prediction, I scale back the complexity of the questions. Say, nine dice to six. When it notches a number of correct predictions, I move to more complex questions with more variables. So I can feel comfortable that it will eventually predict large-scale and worldwide events. Much like training a dog."

"Really? I pictured you more of a cat person."

"Dogs are reliable. Their behavior reflects the work you put in. Humans are the ones that don't deserve them."

"I hear that. What've you been asking?"

She handed me her stack of ripped-off printouts from the machine. I leafed through the first half, each page punctuated with the same sentence. *Embolism, age 68.*

"Jesus," I sputtered. "You're asking it how you're going to die?"

"Don't ask it anything you don't really want to know."

Her tea-colored eyes softened, maybe the late hour let her shrug off some of her armor. She was small, shorter than me, and almost tiny compared to the machine in this huge room with its starred screens on the ceiling.

"How long away is that?" I asked.

"Twenty-six years."

"Do you know the date?"

"I'd rather not."

"Yeah. I get it. You scared?"

She shrugged. "Ask when I'm sixty-seven. I'd hoped to see the next century, but what can you do."

"I don't think I'd want to know. I wouldn't be able to get out of bed. I'd just picture some big hourglass with skulls hovering over my head until it ran out. I mean, I know everyone's already running on a timer, or something..."

"Is there something you *do* want to know?"

A hard knot tightened in my gut. In the beat of silence, the clanking of one of the vents high above us echoed with the gunshot in the other universe.

"Who got shot in that footage I saw."

"You're welcome to try."

I held my breath. I still didn't really *buy* that this thing worked, even after her pen gag. And I didn't really want any part in it yet. But still—I let the lights of the dials lure me in like one of the jellyfish clouding the water that sloshed through the streets around my apartment back home. Kaori stepped back to give me a bubble of silence with the machine, letting me lean to it and whisper, "What happened to Figueiredo and his husband?"

Almost immediately the thin slit of the printer beneath the nearest screen sizzled to life, whirring out a sheet of paper covered in a digital aneurysm of letters and numbers. Narrow it down, Kaori told me. I tried again.

"Did Figueiredo and his husband survive the riot?"

The constellation of tiny dots in the next printout didn't help much. *You are alive.* Thanks, spirits from the beyond, for all your help.

"Any luck?" Kaori asked.

"No." I crammed the last printout into the pocket of my shorts.

"Well—the machine has to calibrate to you, perhaps. I'm here most nights. Come down if you want and we can use it together."

So unbearably breezy and cool. And of course she snared me.

"Really? I figured you'd rather be alone."

"The others…" She flicked her hand around the room as if to say, *everyone in this whole place.* "You know, they're a little scared of me. Which I don't mind. I might even like. But you're not trailing me looking for a gold star. Which is refreshing."

"Thanks?"

"Besides, the calibrations are monotonous. You can entertain me."

"I'll start practicing my shtick."

"Don't make me regret this. I'll just replace you with a stereo."

"Fair." I could be her jester for a while, cartwheeling around the Theater. I had to bite back a yawn. "Well, I should be heading off to one of those boxes you cram your staff in and try to get some sleep. Good night, Dr. Nakamori."

"Call me Kaori. If you absolutely must."

Her face was as blank as if she'd been working her calibrations. I could read beyond her eyes, though, and the tired patience in her voice. This was the closest she would get to letting on that she was lonely, sometimes, even if for a few scattered hours at night. I know it's frustrating because I'm talking about her from my perch here on the beach after all that's happened. It's hard for me not to superimpose the image of Kaori the projectionist onto Kaori my friend. But back then, I didn't know what we were in for. All I saw was this brilliant, interesting, and occasionally unintentionally hilarious woman who was running this whole show basically alone, and for some reason wanted to hang out with me. Call it self-importance, or maybe she had me a little star-struck from the moment we met.

"Goodnight, Kaori."

"Sleep well, Hayes."

I left her by the machine to head back to my little steel dorm. I only remembered in the hallway that I was still holding onto the stack of Envisioner printouts that Kaori had handed to me. I leafed through a dozen premonitions of her death, and at the bottom of the stack found a different answer: *Drowned, trapped by debris from a crumbled building.*

Jesus. I had no idea what she'd asked to get that answer, but what a shitty way to go. I chucked the stack of papers into the kitchenette trash, except the last one, which I stuffed into my pocket with the other printouts. On my bed, I unfolded all the pages, letting the moonlight from the open window fall on the words. *You are alive.*

I've never asked the Envisioner how I'd die. There's some stuff I never wanted to know, and who knows if it would even give me a straight answer.

Even Kaori admitted that the Envisioner's answers got wonky when she asked about me. Too many variables, or too many versions of myself that it confused me with. All I could hope for was something quick. A bus could hit me while I crossed the street, distracted by the music that blasted through my headphones and that would be it. *Blam.* One second an electronica crescendo was rippling goosebumps down my arms, and the next I'm gone.

I wasn't obsessed with how I was going to die like Kaori, even if she'd argue that she was only asking the Envisioner as a calibrating question with a fixed answer. I was more into how I was going to live, especially with Figueiredo staring me in the face, wagging his finger at all my screw-ups.

I can almost see the perfect, alternate version of myself that I'll be, any day now.

He's not a famous documentarian who's sitting on a load of cash. He's anonymous—just some guy—but maybe some of his work is known and appreciated because it shines a light on the beautiful weirdos like the synths who're trying to make this world less awful. He's a megaphone that's trying to signal-boost the work of others, more than anything else. Maybe he teaches sometimes at a college nearby and still has plenty of time to create. His students like him and he encourages them to *think bigger* or *rewrite their narratives,* as eye-rolly as it sounds, and sometimes he'll force them out of the film lab and onto the quad when it's warm, where they'll talk about poetry or something. He's with a guy who makes him laugh and challenges him and infuriates him sometimes, with his big, beautiful brain that has him pacing the house at four in the morning, turning theories about supersymmetry and magical balls of string around in his head, but also leaving his socks everywhere. For the sake of this hypothetical let's call him, I dunno, *Yusuf.* And the two of them lift each other up without caging each other in.

This hyper-me calls and checks in on his friends. He carries an umbrella with him in case it rains. He's steady enough to keep his promises but still restless enough that he'll disappear on a solo road trip for three days to think about his next project, but he remembers to run it by his husband first because he's not a complete selfish dick. He moves his body and makes art. He's kind and fesses up when he's not. He makes his husband smile, and they still spend nights with their lips and bodies crashing into each other like the week they first met.

I don't need a lot. Just enough.

11
DICE

The bars of early sunlight from the blinds invaded my eyes and cut a gold grid into my wrinkled bedsheets. A fine red dust gathered on the sill of my open window. My eyes felt clogged with the same dust, gritty and tired.

I wrestled with whether to tell Yusuf about the footage of Figueiredo and Tiago, ignoring the sugar-rush at picturing me and him together. I didn't want to mix up whatever was happening between us—this limbo between hanging out as friends or something more—by slamming the gas pedal. *Hey, it looks like we're married in the other universe. Should we at least make-out in this one?* We had no phones and I didn't know how to reach him. I didn't even know which one of these tin box houses he lived in. I've never been into game-playing and waiting some random number of days to text someone. I could practically hear Genesis's voice ribbing me. *You're knee-deep in a multinational conspiracy to keep the most significant scientific discovery ever imagined from the public, and here you're worried about getting dick?*

I buried myself in work for the day. I told Arjun about the riot footage and his teeth glinted through his smile in the lab as he wrangled the others for an all-hands snoop for any clue about what happened. I even made a few bags of vending machine popcorn in the kitchenette and lugged them over to the farm. One of the other techs pulled up some footage of Figueiredo on the big screen and I tossed a few faux-buttery kernels at his face, booing.

"You think this asshole ever smiles?" I asked.

I was the circus ringleader running a room again, killing time by trying to make the others laugh. Until—screw it—I found Yusuf in the Theater before the staff cleared out and told him to meet me before he left for the night. We could walk back to our houses together.

The other techs cleared away one by one, leaving me without the armor of my jokes. Hours of watching Figueiredo and the way he bulldozed everyone, with his staff clearing paths for him and clamming up whenever he was near. As much as he was an asshole, I admired how he took no shit from anybody and knew what he wanted.

Then, sometime past ten when I thought Yusuf had forgotten about me for the day, he knocked on the Footage Farm door and sat down by me with a tired sigh, brushing his knees against mine. For a moment, my whole world shrank to just that warm point of contact between us and I forgot about what I'd planned to say to him. To hell with rushing. I pulled up the scene of Figueiredo and Tiago, and hit play, the whole time watching Yusuf's eyes. This close, his eyes glinted an iridescent brown, like the glossy shell of a beetle.

"What do you think?" I asked him after we'd watched twice.

"Who was shot?"

"I don't know. This is the only angle of the footage I've found so far. We're looking for more."

The only sound was the faint rustling of his lab coat when he leaned forward to rest his elbows on his knees. Closer to me so that his breath prickled warm goosebumps on the backs of my arms.

"Did you know an… *alternate* you was a part of Figueiredo's team?" I asked.

"No."

"You don't seem super surprised."

He shrugged. "More than likely, with a million different iterations of us throughout the…"

In the silence after he trailed off, the idea of a million versions of us, each like a cracked kaleidoscope mirror, spun my head.

"And about us?" I asked, bobbing my chin to the screen. "*Them.*"

"They're together?"

"Looks like. Do you think they look happy?"

"I can't tell."

"I think they do. I mean, before the running and the screaming. And the gunshots."

"Oh." His beetle-shell eyes flitted from mine back down to the floor. "Should that… is that supposed to mean something?"

"I don't know. I mean…" I was doing this all wrong, already. I stared at his intertwined hands and the way they squeezed, pumping like a heartbeat. "There's something here, right? I mean, you hanging around with me when you probably have better stuff to do. And finding reasons to come visit. This is not me being weird or looking for something that's not there, right?" Silence again, and I mentally whipped my back for pushing him too hard. "I like spending time with you." I tried to ignore my jerky heartbeat, instead focusing on where our knees touched. The growing warmth there.

I scored a victory when one of the corners of his mouth tugged up a bit, though he still didn't meet my eyes.

"I like it too."

"Great."

He opened his mouth a few times, bobbing for air like a goldfish out of its bowl and waiting for me to dunk it back in. I gave him the space to breathe.

"It's just that I have a hard time explaining myself. Like everything's scrambled. I'm not good at... I mean, I don't know the rules for..." He trailed, squinting, and then flicked his hands between us. "This."

"Fuck rules, Yusuf. I never know what the hell I'm doing, and you don't have to explain yourself to me. Or anyone."

"Alright." The breath he gushed out swept over my skin, making me almost goofy with relief. "I can do that."

"Cool."

"Then what now?"

I shrugged. "Wanna head home?"

"Yeah."

Our footfalls were slow drips through the white lab rat maze, with my skin glowing brighter than the salt-white lights overhead. We didn't need to talk. I was too tongue-tied anyway. Whenever I went up to guys in bars before, I always opened with who I figured they wanted me to be, but with Yusuf I didn't know who that was yet. He walked me back to my house—he lived alone three houses down, he said—and we both toed the painted green pavement by the folding metal stoop.

From here, everything was a fuzzy dopamine hit in my head. Something about *this place could use a bar* and Yusuf was midway through a sentence about how he gets dinner every night around six when I gambled. Leaning in to stop him mid-word with my lips on his, with the dice-toss rattling around, unsure, until I felt the heat of his hand on my arm. The brush of stubble, the slight parting of his lips, the hand that moved from my arm to my lower back, shrinking the space between us. Under the moth-flecked funnel from the floodlights, I wanted to freeze-frame that moment and just live there forever. Hang it in the gallery inside my head in case whatever we were building here crumbled. Like it usually did. When we found out why each of us was still alone.

Days smeared together for the next couple of weeks—weirdly normal given the completely batshit situation we were in. I spent my days in the Footage Farm watching hours of Figueiredo and his staff and scribbling reports. It was the most stable job I ever had. My dad would've been so proud.

As much as I watched Figueiredo, his eyes watched *me*. Like he knew I was there, eavesdropping on his life. He had to have been mugging for whoever he thought would eventually watch all this footage. I never saw him drink anything but water, never saw him goof off with his staff. I watched him scrawling calculations on the whiteboard in his office and he literally didn't look away—not to scratch his nose, not at a bird fluttering at the window—for three hours straight. I have to nail my ass to my chair when I'm supposed to be editing a doc and I don't feel like it, and instead I lie in bed and pick my fingernails for an hour. Because he never gushed to his staff about their work, I watched how some twenty-second room-temperature speech to them sent rapt looks across their faces like the clouds had just split open and angels were singing their names. When once, after some party where I'd been in full jester mode cracking people up with the story of the Miss Malaise pageant I'd organized while in rehab, Narek had plowed into me. Something like, *you give so much of yourself away to strangers that it becomes meaningless.*

After watching Figueiredo, my reflection in the bathroom mirror looked different, with my eyes too blurry, and my edges soft and watery. Like this whole thing was a funhouse mirror, only I was the one that was squat and warped.

I tried to shake the doubt monster during the evenings I hung out with Kaori in the Theater. We'd ask the machine a million questions, calibrating it to me, she said. Which hand is this pen in? Which card will I draw next? I'd ask the machine, with its answers coming quicker, like it was learning from us. We didn't really ask, we *spun*. A roulette wheel, the Wheel of Fortune tarot card that I'd lay flat on the beer-stained bar of Genesis's latest drag show. I had the Wheel of Fortune tattooed on the top of my right foot. Me making up stories with a deck of cards so that I'd have something to talk about when I hit on some guy at the bar, so that I could seem more interesting. I didn't need stories with Yusuf.

Yusuf and me were basically an arm's length away from each other when we weren't working. Most nights, he'd swing by the Theater while me and Kaori were there and then I'd watch their academic buddy comedy where the genius and her sidekick solved secrets of the universe while slinging sarcastic zingers. I tried to wheedle my way into their in-jokes during margarita club, which we left the Compound for on Saturday nights unless Kaori was slammed. I felt special that I could at least leave the Compound if it was with the two of them, unlike the others. Me and Yusuf didn't bother hiding our feelings for each other in front of her or lie about why we both showed up to and left Envisioner sessions at the same time. One night, while the AI nav of one of the electric cars whizzed us home from Indian Springs and Yusuf was asleep against the window, she bobbed her head over at him.

"You might have to tuck him in," she said. A wink. "Again."

Nights through the maze of halls back to our houses from Envisioner sessions, Yusuf didn't talk a whole lot—no big surprise there—leaving me to heft most of the load. I yammered about my life back in Boston, or the doc about Genesis. He filled the quiet with his lips and hands, on his narrow bed when we were alone. And we'd stop and laugh the first few times, some fumbling with *okay, wait— you get over there and I'll do that.* And I'll borrow some clichés from a different kind of movie, here, some breathy erotic thriller and we can cue the dreamy music and the moody camera angles down the landscape of Yusuf's body. The curve of his muscled shoulders and arms. The lines of his tensed neck—head thrown back—that pointed with compass hands down to a silver medallion that glinted from his dark chest hair. A wine-colored birthmark below one nipple, with my mouth trailing lava down his stomach. The director, later, will watch the dailies and growl, *we need more ass shots.*

I told Yusuf, early on when we were both tangled up together so we wouldn't fall off the bed, how I'd bombed my only physics class in high school with my whole slogging through a swamp of downers thing. I was curious about what he was doing here. And he jumped up like a live wire fell across his bare legs. *Okay, okay, okay,* he chattered to himself, poking through his desk drawers, and a backpack, and his lab coat slung over a chair until— *aha!*—he plucked a green marker and waggled it in the air. Still naked, his back to me, he sketched equations on the glass of his window. *Okay. Wow. Where to start? Right. The basics.* He doodled diagrams of an atom and its parts. Nucleus. Proton. And then a little chart where he sketched the names of all the elementary particles, his hands squeaking across the glass, and speaking so fast he could've sucked up all the air in the room.

"Is this too much?" he asked when he turned around and spotted the grin that took over my whole face.

"No, don't stop," I told him—which was something he said a little while ago, only in a *very* different context—loving how on-fire teaching me something made him.

I was laying on his bed, but I was just as much on an inflatable lounger, bobbing around a bath-water-warm pool in the sun. Because when you're slogging through most of your life and a moment of joy like this hits, you know you just have to wade there as long as you can and let it fill you.

```
SCENE: THE BLACKBOX THEATER OF MY HEAD

          NAREK
     I'd like to remind you that you are
     incapable of caring for anyone else.
     You can save yourself the inevitable
     life-ruining disaster that's six
     months or a year away by just bowing
     out now. If you weren't so stubborn,
     you'd see that I'm just here to help.

(The STORYTELLER VOICE pops his head out, stage
right. He shoves a vaudeville-style hook out
and tugs NAREK off stage)

          THE STORYTELLER VOICE
          (VOICEOVER)
     I think we're fucking done with you
     for now.
```

I know that every time you meet someone you compare them to everyone else you've ever met. That we're all stock characters.

Here comes another emotionally unavailable guy with trust issues, but this new model comes with a cowboy hat so maybe that's enough to keep things interesting. And I'm not some saint who gets his heart trampled all the time, either. You don't get to be alone at my age without reading the character treatments and thumbing ahead in the script in your head. *He's going to do this and I'll get mad*, or *here's how I'll disappoint him*, or *I'm too comfortable to compromise for someone else so why bother*.

But now I was locking everyone else out of the room and watching Yusuf—*just* him, for the first time, maybe—scrawl tiny, precise letters on the window. Because he wasn't just *not* Narek. He seemed happy to let me in instead of keeping us as separate islands. Because you don't meet a lot of people who, after you tell them you don't get something, are so pumped about trying to help you understand that they draw diagrams on a window without bothering to slide on some underwear first.

I guess what I'm trying to say is that with all the people I've ever met—all of the friends, the lovers, the doc subjects, everyone self-producing themselves into what they think people want them to be—Yusuf wasn't a stock character. He kept me guessing. And the same way he'd told me about studying his whole life to try to figure out the big unanswered questions in physics, I wanted to keep looking into what made him tick, too. I didn't want to skip to the end of the script. I wanted to go along for the ride.

He kept drawing on the windows until he ran out of glass and then he came back to bed where we fell asleep in each other's arms.

A week or so after I first stumbled on the riot footage, one of the other film techs found some video from the night of the attack, which must've been filmed from the Envisioner, based on the angle. In the footage, Figueiredo and Tiago stormed into the room and huddled by the Envisioner. A couple of seconds of tense silence passed until the door burst open again and Tiago's arm whipped out in such a blur that I almost didn't see the gun in his hand. He shot the black-clad guy at the other end of the room square in the chest. Which only raised more questions. Why the hell did Tiago have a gun and why was he such a crack shot? Wasn't he a scientist or something?

"I'm glad that Subject B isn't dead," Yusuf said. "That would be like watching myself get shot."

Tiago was "Subject B" to Figueiredo's "Subject A" in the reports. How romantic. *Do you take Subject B to be your lawfully wedded husband?*

I devoured more footage, especially of Figueiredo, following his stiff back and hard eyes across the screen. He was a horror-movie shadow, one that followed me everywhere I went, and when I wasn't paying attention or my back was turned, it moved on its own. His eyes scoured the back of my head. I heard him. I hear him still, sometimes. I say *him* when I really mean *me*, the doubt in my head that uses his voice and his face—his narrowed eyes, the sharp edges of his jaw that could nick fingertips. Which is my voice but with a sarcastic laugh, one that made me wish the voice had a face to punch. His voice needled me in the Theater at night, with Kaori and Yusuf. *They are literally trying to save the world and you're watching videos in a dark room. What good are you, exactly?*

The annoying part was that I knew he was right.

Me and Yusuf snagged a couple of blankets, one night, and borrowed one of the electric rentals to drive into the desert, past the Compound's lights. I'd sweet-talked Lana into getting me a bottle of wine on one of her supply runs. We spread the blankets on the short hood of the car—I suggested the ground at first, but Yusuf had to remind me that scorpions were a thing here—and leaned back against the glass. I poured the wine into coffee mugs.

Overhead, every star that had ever lived seemed to hang in the velvet sky, with the Milky Way gauzed over with light. I was quiet, trying to work over what I was feeling, so instead I counted stars. More than I'd ever seen in the permanent mauve twilight of Boston nights. I'm sure I learned a lot of the names of the constellations when I was a kid, but I forgot most of them. I mapped new ones as I sloshed wine over my tongue. The Lovers. The Sacred Machine. The stars twinkling like the spotlights at one of Genesis's shows.

Figueiredo's voice tried to sneak in on the wind, whispering that me and Yusuf were just using each other. But for what? Sex was too easy to finger-point. I'd woken up after enough one-nighters to know that sex isn't proof of some magic union between souls, or whatever. It just feels good to slam your body into someone else's for a while. Even if—or, especially if, sometimes—both slammers know that it doesn't mean much once the sheets are in the hamper. And sometimes when your relationship is imploding, like me and Narek's had been almost from the start, sex is the only thing gluing it together.

Yusuf wasn't just a distraction. Unless I was chasing some ghost of the way Tiago and Figueiredo looked at each other in the footage. Even a quick glance in a room cluttered with green-coated staff, a little smirk. *We belong to each other.* But that wasn't really it, either. I don't think I'm being all *aw shucks I'm such a dumpster fire* with obnoxious fake self-deprecation if I admit that people like Yusuf who have ambition and brains and their shit together don't normally go for people like me. And I don't think I'm some smokeshow who can vaporize underwear with a single glance, but I know that sometimes people see me—the docs, or the tattoos, or me standing at the edge of a crowd by myself—and get this idea that I'm *cerebral* instead of bored. That they're more interested by the outline of a person that they paint-by-numbers into life.

I knew when you'd been with someone for a while, you could look at them and see more of what you projected onto them than who they really were. I just didn't want to go into whatever *this* was with us already thinking that.

Yusuf couldn't look at me and guess what I was feeling. Not that long ago I would've seen the way his head works as a flaw, or something I had to try to fix instead of just trying to understand him. How he doesn't play mind games, and how he's not fumbling through some fog of cynicism like everyone else. How he breaks everything down into particles so he can see and appreciate the smallest parts of the world around him, and only takes the things from his past that he needs. Which made me want to try to do the same. Even if it was weird and hard, I wanted to be honest for him, more than I'd been for anyone else.

I took a pull of wine against the rusty nail I'd dry-swallowed.

"Are we trying too hard to be like Figueiredo and Tiago?" I asked.

"We're not them."

And I was back to floating in that warm pool. I had to make everything hard when it didn't need to be, when it was easy for him to brush aside my worries with facts. We weren't Figueiredo and Tiago. I had to repeat it a couple of times to shut up the doubt that still wanted to fly out of my mouth. A breeze blew past us. I stared down at the small starburst of a scar by his left thumb. The night before, I'd asked him how he'd gotten it and he told me he didn't even remember.

"I don't want to be your mistake," I told him finally.

He squeezed my hand, turning from the starred sky to meet my eyes. He shook his head, his smile a little wolfy and wild.

"The first second I saw you," was all he could say. And all he needed to.

12
THE HIGH PRIESTESS

Margarita club was a hit until it very much wasn't.

Our first official session after the supply run, we mostly talked shop, with me asking a million questions. I wanted to see what info I could wheedle out of Kaori for background on whatever doc-to-be I was filming at the Compound. I got her to gossip a bit about her staff—juicy if not super helpful—until she wised up and said we should leave work at work. Background snooping over. We spent a few of sessions after that mostly talking about our favorite sci-fi movies, with me drawing on my encyclopedic knowledge, and Yusuf and Kaori shredding the scientific accuracy of each plot. Then something shifted between them. We were all set to leave for one trip, when I headed to the Theater and both of them were as rigid as the angles of the Envisioner. Some calibration test had failed, from what I could gather, and she cut off his sentence that started with *perhaps if you would just* as soon as she saw me. Yusuf looked like she'd just thwacked the backs of his hands with a ruler.

I pushed them to reschedule for the next day because it was a month into my time at the Compound—when I theoretically would've been rolling out of my artist residency and back home with my finished doc about Genesis—and I wanted to celebrate. I should've read the grim line of Yusuf's lips and the way that Kaori's bent elbows jutted out from her hips. But all I thought about was myself. Big shocker.

"We should keep our promises," Yusuf said looking from me to Kaori.

I shuffled Genesis's tarot deck in the strained silence of the car on the way. I'd planned on trying to cut the tension by going full jester for them and reading their fortunes. Kaori would often sum up things with one word, out of efficiency. Guns were boring. Money was gross. Tarot was stupid, she told me as the cards rippled in my hands. Yusuf mumbled something about the iconography of tarot actually having valuable psychological significance, which was the first time I'd ever heard him disagreeing with his intellectual hero.

"Ah," was all Kaori said, leaning back.

I should've kicked open the car door and barrel-rolled out into the desert.

In the restaurant, I soft-shoed for my life—yacking about what each card meant and spinning some dumb fortune for us that ended up with me not paying my share of that night's bill. I could see stage-mom Genesis flailing at me from the wings behind Kaori. *Smile! Smile more!* At least Kaori chimed in with a few *ahs* and *I sees* here and there. A round of drinks and a plate of nachos later, Yusuf tapped on the nail-polish-flecked deck.

"What we're doing is like this," he said. "Trying to pull data out of a million possible stories. What you called stupid."

"The entire purpose of this project is to look to the future and not the past." Kaori took a sip of her margarita. No one would mistake the laugh in her voice as playful.

"That's purposely reductive." He broke a stray tortilla chip on the table with one finger. The crack might've been one of my ribs with how his crestfallen face hit me. "You know that's not what I'm suggesting."

"We are not having this discussion again." Kaori thunked her glass onto the table.

I squirmed, my eyes widening at stage-mom Genesis, who grabbed her purse. *Babycakes, you can find your own way home, right?* She kicked open the backstage emergency exit and sprinted off.

"I need air."

Yusuf shoved away from the table, knocking little dishes of salsa together, and plowed out of the front door. I started to follow him but Kaori stopped me with one hand.

"Wait. He's not a child. You chasing will only embarrass him."

I hovered over my chair for a second before I plopped back down. She was right. I'd never seen anything that close to an outburst from him, and he wouldn't want me in his face while he was working through it.

"So," I said dumbly. "I'd offer to ask the cards about what to do here, but this seems out of my wheelhouse."

"We've seen an alternate version of you," Kaori said, pausing for a sip. "I suppose now we're seeing an alternate version of him."

Yusuf's words from our first day here conked me on the head. *Is a carpenter friends with her hammer?* I hadn't known him well enough then to see that he couldn't have been joking.

"And you? What are the other versions of you like?"

"The multiverse doesn't need any other rough drafts of me. I'm already the finished product."

I mean. Answering a question with an equally serious and hilarious middle finger to the questioner was perfectly her.

"Come on." My laugh didn't reach my eyes. To hell with what she said, I was going to chase Yusuf in just another second and apologize for forcing him out tonight. First, I had to know. "I don't buy that you didn't look."

She leaned forward, the gentle curve of her smirk like *let me tell you a secret*.

"Of course I looked. What I'm saying is that even with *all* the footage I've seen."

Stupid. I should've known with the way she leaned into *all* just how much she'd really seen. But I'm fast-forwarding again.

"I've neeeeeever seen a single second of myself," she finished and then stared at me, just waiting for something. When I didn't bite, she added, "What do you think of that?"

"I dunno. Talk to Yusuf about probability. Infinite universes and infinite outcomes, blah blah…"

"I know all that better than he does. Come on. Why does it get to be you?"

"You're the one who said Figueiredo's not me—"

"You know what I mean. I deserve this and not you."

She'd seemed stone cold sober for a second, like she'd knocked back a few of the Antilixir pills that de-drunk someone and they piss out the alcohol they've sucked down. It must drive her crazy, still, that the thread of her isn't somehow important enough—*strong* enough—to tether her to the Envisioner throughout the tapestry of the whole multiverse. Like her ego, her entitlement is so overblown that it's not enough for her to run the Envisioner Initiative in this universe. She should've been the one to invent the machine in the first place.

"Welcome to the nondescript club," I said.

A dark edge crept into her eyes. For a second, I thought she'd dump her drink on my head. Until her cool mask slipped back into place, the moment gone, and I left her at the table. Alone.

I've had plenty of time to snoop for different versions of her on my end-of-the-multiverse beach—using government databases and weird DNA-based social media—and only found a few. So few that I almost thought that she'd jumped to other universes and killed off her alternate selves, leaving her as the only one. Until I found a universe with her as a pottery teacher. Another with her face plastered on bus stops in Miami promising that she puts the *real* in *realtor*.

When I can't sleep at night, sometimes I think about what I'd say to her if I saw her. *You're just a bit player that the multiverse barely bothered revisiting.* Unless she was right about being the final draft.

Silence in the car. Silence in the hallways. Over the green concrete to Yusuf's house, I asked if he wanted to talk. He said he wasn't ready, but that I could stay over if I promised not to ask about it. Or talk too much, since noise was overwhelming him right now. I appreciated the honesty, since other guys I'd been with would've just quietly seethed at my yammering. We tucked into bed and barely said goodnight.

Hours later, I woke to him slipping out of the room. I sucked in a breath and held it until I could see him out of the window, pacing back and forth over the green concrete. The predawn sky threw dishwater light into the room and over pages on the floor, where columns of blocky words filled his notebooks like they were carved stone tablets. *Earth. The Solar System. The Milky Way. The Local Interstellar Cloud.* He'd tried to calm his brain by ordering the universe and our place in it.

———

I wasted time with footage reports the next day, waiting until I could find Yusuf for dinner. He was too busy to eat, he told me, talking of probability waves and Envisioner question parameters, sentencing me to a solo night of reheated pizza slices. He didn't show for our nightly divination session with the Envisioner, either. I found Kaori in her office, where marker equations and notes covered the three glass walls, making it look like her handwriting hovered in the adjoining Theater. Her desk was a slab of glass stacked with Envisioner printouts and abandoned mugs.

"No Yusuf tonight?" I asked.

She didn't bother looking up from her Envisioner readout, her fingers threaded through the handle of a mug that was veined with gold. "You'd know better than I."

"I should go remind him we're here."

"He's a big boy. I'm sure he just got busy."

I frowned. "So we're just going to completely pretend that last night's weirdness never happened."

"Ideally."

"You don't want to… talk this out?"

She finally looked my way. "Hayes, when has the answer to that ever been yes in the history of anything?"

For Yusuf's sake, I bit back a sarcastic crack and sat at the chair across from her. Neither of them asked me to choose a side on whatever they were brawling about, but I felt yanked in the middle anyway. She had to know how much a fight between them tore him up, how he worshipped the ground she walked on, in his own way. Didn't she? She must've seen the war going on behind my eyes and decided to give me a break before I had an aneurysm. She sighed.

"He doesn't like the direction of the research here," Kaori said. "And I almost wish he'd fight. I'd enjoy the challenge. A coup. Rally the researchers and we can duel over who has the strongest vision for our work. Instead of this sulking."

"You have to know he'd never do that to you."

I knew he'd worked under her for seven years at Oxford when he could've left and chaired a university department himself before he was thirty-five—at least that's what he told me. I'm in for the research, not the ladder-climbing bullshit, he'd said of his career.

"He's not that ambitious."

"It's not that. He trusts you."

She scrunched her mouth up to one side. "I have been a bit rigid."

"You? Never."

"You know, he turned down a director position at the Large Hadron-X to come here? I asked him to. I promised he'd be an integral part of this work. I told him that I needed his vision." She took a slow sip of her tea. "I told him I needed his help to change the world. Perhaps I haven't been delivering on that."

"You can change. If you want."

"No one actually changes."

"Look at you! This might be a real conversation we're having about human feelings."

She opened her mouth to say something, but then stopped and narrowed her eyes a bit, like I was seeing her stumped for the first time. Until she laughed.

The rest of the night is the exposition scene the editors will cut for time before the theatrical release because it doesn't test well with audiences, and the studio is pushing for Kaori to get the villain edit. Because nothing about her is delicate—the blunt ends of her asymmetrical haircut, the chewed tips of her fingers, her eyes that always seem to be peering into everyone. And we'll smooth over the fact that I'd momentarily charmed her, and the only way to peek further behind her mask was to *help* her take it off.

I'd found a slip of paper that morning when I'd been straightening up my room. A printout from the first night I'd joined Kaori by the Envisioner, weeks ago. *Drowned, trapped by debris from a crumbled building.* I placed the paper on her desk.

"What's this?" I asked, sliding the paper closer to her.

She eyed the printout with her cool, tea-colored eyes.

"My parents went missing and…" She trailed.

"You asked the machine? I thought the past was a no-no."

A pause, a sip of tea from her gold-laced mug. "Curiosity is a natural human instinct."

I listened as she told me about her family. She'd already been at Oxford when the tsunami hit Japan, twenty-four years ago. I'd been nine at the time and too young to remember or understand the disaster until I'd learned about it later in school. My lungs on fire—drowning was still my worst nightmare.

Kaori had been eighteen. When she'd left for Oxford, her parents had moved out of Tokyo and into Katsuura, by the coast, hoping for more breathing room away from the clogged capital. They'd been the ones who pushed her to leave for graduate school, anyway. Oxford had dangled a full ride, research grants, and the promise of a small army of undergrad research peons for her. Even still, her second year there, she could see that they'd been itching to have her back home. They'd always expected she'd return some day.

Her mom, Kasumi, had taught at a university and made pottery in her spare time. When Kaori had been a child, before the worst of the crowding in Tokyo, her mom had spent long evenings in a tiny bedroom turned art-studio in their apartment, before they'd had to rent it out. Bowls and mugs had bloomed out of piles of wet mud under her hands. She'd fire them, and when they were solid and beautiful, she'd drop them on the floor. From just high enough and with enough heft to splinter off a few shards that she'd lacquer back together with a mixture of epoxy and gold dust. *They're stronger, more beautiful for having been broken*, her mom had told her.

Kaori had helped, sometimes, but she'd throw too hard. She'd pick her mom's favorite pitchers and smash them to bits—bowls went bombs-away on the tile floors, her lips unmoving. *She just wants to help you and doesn't know what she's doing. Give her a break,* her dad, Yoshiki, had told her mom, and Kasumi had grumbled and swept the floors, still finding clay shards in corners of the house for days.

"Did you throw the clay pieces too hard on purpose?" I asked.

Kaori's tiny smile told me all I needed to know. *You bet your ass.*

She'd wanted to punish them for the nightly injections of what they told her was medicine, for the meals delayed until she finished her hours of calculus. For forcing her to practice the shamisen because they didn't want her to lose her heritage when Japan had been becoming more and more Western. She'd sit on her windowsill, plucking her shamisen and singing *sakura, sakura* with her thin voice, watching the kids run in the streets below. In the rare times they'd let her play on the weekends when she got a little older—social development is important, too, her mom had said—she'd dominated her friends in shoot-'em-up survival games with names like *KarmaKiller*. The VR-projections had filled the living room in her friend Makoto's house, the edges of the arena looking sharp enough that they could cut glass. Kaori had always shimmied her avatar up to an arena catwalk and sniped everyone. At first, they'd high-fived her—another blam-o by Killer Kaori—cheering on her quick fingers and cool head. But she'd never eased up on them. Even as a kid, why would she let them win? Soon enough, they'd stopped inviting her.

"But who will take care of you?" her dad asked, one video call shortly before his death. And the silent question there, of course, had been *when will you take care of us?*

They'd talked a lot about family, then, about support and togetherness and *blah,* which Kaori had found both irritating and hilarious. Like, *we lived in the same house when I was a kid, right?* You don't make something out of steel and then complain when it's too hard.

She hadn't given a crap about dating. She still didn't have feelings of attraction or interest in anyone else of any gender. She wasn't big on pets and killed the single plant in her office at Oxford. She had friends and colleagues, yeah, but zero interest in romance. And sex—fluids, and sliding all up on each other, and mewling weepy love poetry mid-climax—*gross.* Nah, she'd pass.

She'd tried to tell her parents this and she could see the guilt welling behind their eyes. The nootropics they gave her as a kid, they'd started to say, must've done something to her. Kaori had dead-ended that before the inevitable *we were just doing what was best, blah.* Her disinterest wasn't a flaw. Side-effect of the drugs or not, she liked herself. She felt like her weak spots had been lacquered in gold, making her already stronger than the ones who'd made her.

That had been the last time they'd spoken, before the waves hit.

"You miss them?" I asked.

Her sigh was long and rustling, and on anyone else it would've been theatrical.

"I'm supposed to say yes."

"Please," I snorted.

I looked down at my mug, where the tea bag had ripped open, spilling murky leaves out into the water.

13
EXPERIMENTAL EVIDENCE

The FantiSee screen in the Theater was a cast-iron sky filled with cathedrals of clouds that blotted out the fake sun. Blunt shapes roiled in the wind. I'd heard the AI in the screens were able to pick up emotional cues from homeowners based on their body temperature and micro-movements and displayed scenes to fit their moods. I don't know if that was bullshit or not and who the screen was tuned to—probably Kaori. I didn't want to be around when a tornado funnel dropped from the ceiling and ripped this place to ribbons.

I could almost taste the energy of the air that morning—the burnt ozone smell between lightning strikes—after my dreams of drowning cities and raining fish. Kaori had called everyone over the PA system and told them to meet in the Theater. The thirty or so members of her research staff must've known what was happening, with their smiles like someone had lit a firecracker fuse and they were waiting for the sparks. The rest of us Footage Farmers were in the dark.

Kaori was a blank-faced statue carved from marble by the

Envisioner. I saw a crack in her mask, though, in the way her white-knuckled fingers jammed the end of a pen so hard that she could've blasted blue ink all over her white coat.

By her side, Yusuf crossed his arms, his furrowed eyebrows carving deep valleys into his forehead. I tried to catch his eye as I jostled towards the front of the crowd.

On one of the huge wall screens, tumbleweeds of crumpled paper rolled past a chipped bus stop bench at a city street corner, with signs in a language I didn't know glowing in the pink evening light. *Universiteit. Trein stasie. Museum van de wateroorlog.*

I tried to ask someone what was up, only for them to shoot a deathglare at me. The Storyteller voice whistled. *Well, this is going to get interesting.*

"Countdown?" someone by the front shouted.

"About thirty seconds," another voice called. "The next bus to roll in."

They seemed to hold their breaths around me. I fought a tiny, mean urge to yell *surprise!* and scare the shit out of the whole room. Someone by the front of the crowd started a New Year's Eve countdown. *Ten. Nine. Eight.*

Instead of a ball all lit up for the New Year hovering above us, a long gray bus with its sides gashed with spray-paint rolled onto the screen. Inside, twenty or so people held onto railings and leaned against windows on their ways home from work. *Four. Three.* The bus puttered at the side of the road, letting a few people off, before it whizzed away, belching a white cloud of water vapor exhaust.

Two. One.

The crowd around me lost their shit.

Someone popped a champagne bottle and the cork sailed across the room. Cheers from the nerd herd, and those little honking noisemakers, and someone by me screamed *speech, speech!* The bottle of champagne made the rounds, even though it was before ten in the morning, and the white coats poured it into paper cups or glugged from the bottle. Lots of back-patting and *we couldn't do this without yous*, with me cheesing for them, contact-high off the energy. Heads tipped to the center of the room to where Kaori and Yusuf waited by the Envisioner, in the invisible spotlight cast by all their eyes.

The way that Yusuf's gaze swept to the floor while he stepped back, I knew he was curling into himself. Someone shushed the crowd, and in the silence, Kaori clicked her pen one last time.

"We're saving lives," she said. "Now, let's get back to work."

"What we first saw here," Kaori will grandstand later in the movie, where she looks out over the crowd of her devotees, "is the evidence of the power of this machine, yes. Even more than that—it's proof of what we can accomplish together." And cue the welling of the string-heavy soundtrack, the close-zoom to her eyes, where you can almost see a reflection of stars.

Our world, our country, wasn't perfect, but I guess it was ours.

What I'm trying to say is that the United Arab Emirates plugging up the runaway tap that was rising ocean levels and funneling millions and millions of desalinated water to new farmland was awesome. So were the trees spliced with genes from deep-earth organisms that munched on carbon and turned it into rock so that Canada blossomed with towering pine forests that filtered the air. These beautiful trees that you'd swear were planted by angels, and you could stand nearby, cram your eyes shut, and almost hear them sing as they breathed out clean air. Scientists in Kyoto had pioneered the tech to regrow a human heart in just under thirty-six hours. A joint, resource-sharing pact by Brazil and Australia replanted the Amazon and the Great Barrier Reef. The Commonwealth of Great Basin Nations, though it was still a new country trying to figure out its way, opened its borders to Greek refugees when almost no one else would take them. And the labs in Mumbai scrubbed childhood lymphoma and other horrors from humanity, while others in Kenya resurrected elephants and tigers from extinction. The Pan-African Union, on the continent that had been robbed of its resources for centuries, closed off an enormous oasis within the Democratic Republic of Congo as a nature reserve—where all the creatures that had no say in what we did to this giant rock could actually roam free without us killing them for their tusks or skin or just to get our jollies.

I repeated all this to myself at night, sometimes, after I'd heard about another bombing. Another shooting. *Thoughts and prayers and now we turn to traffic.*

We had gene-spliced drought-resistant crops but the whole city of Jakarta had to be evacuated before the island of Java sank. I threw out a half-eaten pretzel after coming home from the mall once, and my mom flipped out. Because when she was a little girl on São Miguel before her home island sank, her family would get boxes of clothes and supplies from cousins in America. They'd open the box, she'd said, some mixture of joy and sadness clogging her throat even after decades, and the things inside had *smelled* like America. Like fake lavender detergent and vanilla ice cream. And plenty. So how dare I commit the sin of throwing out good food.

"This is our new American dream," Mr. Gutierrez, my freshman history teacher, had monotoned from a script at the head of the class, while a government-sponsored history video about the New American Investment Act—otherwise known as Gut and Cut—played behind him.

China, Russia, and other nations had sliced up the interior organs of America from across the world, all without having stepped foot on the ground that they were staking claim to first. *You take the Rockies, we'll take the Appalachians.* Vegas was a Chinese vassal state. Oceans of Russian solarfarms across the badlands of South Dakota cranked power all the way up to Canada and past Chicago. Together, Egypt and Ethiopia had leased much of Nebraska to grow the drought-resistant splices of rice and wheat the two nations had pioneered. All of these handshakes had been called a *lease,* as if, seventy years from now, these countries will just hand over the land they'd bloomed to life to a nation that doesn't have the power to take it back.

Mr. Gutierrez had read from the script like he was supposed to, talking about the how the leases and agreements had led to trillions of dollars for America's new investment in the future. I.E., students. I.E., us. Like, *all this is riding on you, now.*

"We tried to fix a lot of stuff. Well, *others*—other countries—did pretty well," he'd said. "*We* did a shit job and you deserve better."

The other kids around me had giggled at the teacher swearing, while I'd just doodled faces on my knuckles because I'd been so high I was blasting out of this galaxy.

"People change, *querido,*" my mom had told me, brushing my hair off my forehead, after she'd kicked my dad out of the house when I was a kid.

My hair had been plastered to my head with sweat. I'd said I'd had a nightmare, when really I'd yanked my sheet over my head even in the full furnace of August heat to try to block out the sound of my parents screaming at each other. My dad had been kind, my mom had told me. But he'd let his anger take over too much, which is why he'd had to leave.

Just like America had been all *sea to shining sea once*—even if that was mostly a myth—before it decided to tell the world, *you know? We're gonna go at this alone.* When the country's leaders had played into fear about what those from the outside could do to the perfect America, which had been a playground for the world for too long, they'd said, a buffet where even the criminals and the leeches from other countries could pile their plates. Then came the home-grown terrorists, and the bombings, and the shootings, all in the name of preserving some fairytale white America that had never existed.

But humanity had cured HIV and had found life on Titan. No more Alzheimer's. Almost no maternal death, anywhere. Here, let me lift the cue cards off-screen.

I guess what I'm saying—and sorry for getting so pissed here— is that I know squat about geopolitics. But I can still hear the bubbly-popping in the Theater after the big countdown when the bus rolled away from the bus stop.

Because the Envisioner filled in the outline of Kaori's story, months later when me and Yusuf were marooned on our beach, about how someone had hired a kid to plant a backpack bomb on a bus outside of Cape Town, where two water cartels were warring for control of the Theewaterskloof Dam and the drinking water supply for six million people. Someone had told the kid his family would be taken care of. Extra gallons of water every day—more than they could ever drink. And I know that he was going to kill dozens of people and that's a fucking nightmare that keeps me up at night. But instead of celebrating how Kaori and the team were able to use the Envisioner to send police to pull the kid out of bed that morning and cart him and the backpack bomb away—and I know I'm probably oversimplifying all of this—they could've done something about the cartels instead.

Unless Kaori chose this exact "solution" to this exact horror to send Yusuf over the edge and over to me for comfort, which—again—has my eyes up to the starry sky of my pink beach at night. As the Wheel of Misfortune spins round and round again.

But what the fuck do I know.

I couldn't find Yusuf in his closet of an office by Kaori's, once the confetti cleared and the champagne bubbles died on my tongue. No one knew where he was. I spotted him circling the outdoor track outside in the afternoon heat, his hands plunged into his pockets and his eyes locked on the ground. He'd ditched his lab coat. Dark storm clouds of sweat pasted his button-down to his armpits and mid-back. He blew past the thin dirt path that led from the track to the Compound without even noticing me there and I had to jog to catch him.

"Hey," I said at his side. "Come back to Earth."

He looked up and jostled his head like I'd launched a spitball at him. I fell into step with him and, since I didn't want to push, we looped once around the track before I screwed up the courage to ask what was wrong.

He filled in the gaps for me about the celebration that morning. I had to tip-toe around glass when I asked, feeling a little dumb about how simple the words sounded, *yeah, but isn't this good?* Something gnawed at my stomach with the idea of people getting hauled in by the cops for crimes they hadn't committed yet. I kept my mouth shut because Yusuf didn't need any more fuel.

"Right," he said, "but how can we be sure he would've blown the bomb to begin with? Just because the machine said so?"

Around the track again, our feet kicking up red dust.

"I've been telling Kaori that this isn't—isn't… We don't live in a periodic and predictable system. We should be studying the machine itself and using it to model and better understand our current frameworks. Just because the machine has predicted thousands of dice rolls or card draws doesn't… I—I mean, we can't even accurately predict weather patterns a week into the future because of all the different factors—humidity and wind speed and temperatures. Then you add people to that, and a million other variables. We're chaos. We're…"

He trailed, squinting at me with his lips pinched into a grim line. I squeezed his hand, knowing that his chattering wasn't really aimed at me. Kaori must not have smoothed things over with him from the other night at margarita club. I spotted his quick blinks and the twitches at the corners of his mouth, the same things that would send me careening into the bathroom as a kid to dig around the medicine cabinet. Or leave scorch marks on the floorboards at night. And I know when I'm spinning out, sometimes the best thing to do is just get away from whatever cage I'm trapped in for a while.

"So what do you want to do?" I asked him with a shrug.

"I don't want to go back inside."

"Then let's get outta here."

"What?"

"Yeah. For the weekend. Why not?"

Not like weekends meant much around here since everyone worked around the clock, but it was Friday and we theoretically had days ahead of us to escape the hamster wheel of the Compound. He squinted again into the sky, and I could see him spinning all sorts of reasons why he couldn't leave. Until he just laughed, and said, *sure*.

14
ELIXIR

Our road-trip montage was a blur of bleached red flatness as the electric car zipped away from the Compound and towards the horizon. Even though the AI-nav of the car was switched on, I gripped the steering wheel so I could live out my James Dean fantasy, tipping my head out of the window and sucking in the dry summer air. Each mile that we drove buoyed me up and up.

I thought about going to Vegas, but I didn't want to be any place where synths were property. I booked us a night at the cheap Gold Rush Hotel in Beatty nearby, a sleepy ghost town except for tourists from Death Valley National Park. When this whole unincorporated corpse of Nevada was still a part of the United States, the nation used it to test nuclear weapons in the middle of nowhere. I guess it's only fair that we were there to lob bombs of our own.

We dumped our backpacks in our small hotel room and explored the tiny town, wandering into an open-air art gallery since you were supposed to do cultural stuff on dates, and soon ending up at a restaurant. We ate burgers and fries and cooled down with bottle after bottle of beer, switching to cocktails for dessert because why not? Not like we were going anywhere. Being in a different place with him made me goofy-brained and giggly, like we were skipping school.

I poured a martini into my stomach to try to drown out the sound of the bus wheels in Cape Town rolling away. I should've seen that Yusuf was on a mission to blast his memories of that same morning to static, too, with how many drinks he knocked back. I'd been there before. I should've known better.

I was the first one to bring up the attack, even though I was the one who'd blabbed about forgetting work for the weekend.

"We crossed a clear line here," he said out of the corner of his mouth. Always the corner when he had to stop and think about what to say, instead of *quark flavors* and *super-positions* that came so naturally during our tutoring sessions.

"Is the whole world gonna start slapping cuffs on people for crimes they haven't committed yet?" I asked, martini sloshing over my hands.

We spilled out of the restaurant and over the dusty sidewalks, all the while flinging accusations meant for Kaori and stabbing the air. Because who does Kaori think she is, playing with people's lives like this? We dumped gasoline on each other's fires, but I took my lead from the Storyteller voice that was prodding me to ask Yusuf, maybe this shouldn't be a secret anymore?

We bought frozen cones from an ice cream truck and laid back in the grass of a public park, watching the clouds warp and blow past us. Chains on a swing set nearby creaked. We were just like the kids running around and playing freeze-tag, right?

Which was maybe why this next part seemed so innocent. Were we tattle-taleing? No, speaking truth to power or something-something. What was the... what was the word? *Conscientious objector,* the Storyteller voice offered. Emphasis on the *conscientious.* Alerting the general public to abuses of power and breaches of *blahblah*. And how long could we really expect to keep the Envisioner under wraps?

I'll admit, looking back now, that some part of me must've wanted to blow the cover of the Compound because I wanted out. Watching videos of the perfect version of myself saving his world every day with his crazy scientific advances wasn't good for me in the long run, when I'd go back to my room feeling like a bag of garbage. I was whipping out the self-sabotage, which I'm good at. I know when you're blitzed and with a mouth covered in chocolate is not exactly the best time to try to white-knight into some situation and save everyone. So I'm going to talk in *hypotheticals* for a bit since this next part is fuzzy.

Hypothetically, I mentioned to Yusuf when we'd managed to find our way back to our hotel—reading the street signs with one eye shut—I knew from my filmmaking about a place where tipsters and informants could anonymously reach out to journalists or watchdog groups or whoever.

I'd read about the Cloud Cold Wars as a kid and my skin had crawled about the idea of handing over all my personal info, clicking past terms of services without reading, because I thought I was just posting pictures of brunch or whatever. Giving faceless companies my current location and DNA. Then had come the mining companies that had scraped the web for all traces of someone—their laugh, their spending habits, their face—and cobbled them together to create an AI template.

An Echo, they'd called it. People with enough coin had been able to get anyone's Echo plugged into a synth body, *for personal therapeutic use,* Galatea Systems had wink-winked. *Think of the closure you can find by interacting with Echoes of lost loved ones or ex-partners.* Sure, just so long as you'd pinky-swear not to use Echoes for good old-fashioned sexual exploitation videos.

As independent AI, had the Echoes been their own legal entities? Or could the person one was based off have it deleted? Who cares, because Echoes had all been Galatea property, anyway, and didn't you read the Terms of Service?

Then had come the terror groups using location services in hookup apps to rain micro-drone strikes, killing gays in Iran and Barbados, or unmarried sexually active women in Pakistan. The white nationalist hate groups had cracked open genetic social networking sites and had stolen user location data, hoping to wipe the Ashkenazi genome from the planet. This politician had been doxxed, these nudes leaked, this kid had been gunned down in the street because she'd trashed a single leaked off some pop star's upcoming album. In school, we'd read about revolutions like the Arab Spring that had started online, which had seemed like the exception instead of the rule. If tech companies wouldn't control themselves—and governments wouldn't or couldn't regulate them—people had slowly decided to log off. Sharing pics of their kids to high school friends they hadn't spoken to in twenty years just wasn't worth all this shit.

But you can't un-ring a bell or turn back progress. Global communication, data, and finance still flowed through the AI-policed web. Personal use was now mostly for education and healthcare—encrypted or otherwise anonymized.

Which—*look over here while I pull a rabbit out of a hat*—maybe was the biggest ruse of all.

Back on the grass of the park, the cotton-ball clouds wafted across a sky so blue that it had to be a FantiSee screen. Nothing that pure could be real. Yusuf wiped the back of his hand across his mouth, smearing away a spot of ice cream. I *hypothetically* showed him an app on my phone that led to a series of hatch doors and bookcase secret passages through the deep web to a message board where we could *very hypothetically* post about the Envisioner.

"You're the one who told me secrets are poison," I said softly.

Honestly, I thought we were doing the right thing because everything wrong in the world started with people in a room with too much power over others. But I know the big gulf between what I hoped to do and what actually happened means about sweet fuck-all right about now.

SCENE: THE BLACKBOX THEATER OF MY HEAD

> FIGUEIREDO
> Oh really? How will it test with
> audiences if you put everyone in
> danger and leak all this because you
> think it's the right thing to do?

(Oh shitballs, the Storyteller Voice must be off on a smoke break. Can someone get his hook? Anyone?)

> FIGUEIREDO (cont.)
> Does it make you more likeable if
> you're not the one hitting send? Less
> at fault?

I know Yusuf wouldn't have done it if I didn't push him. We were playing a game of chicken, and if I really wanted to watch everything burn, I should've lit the match myself.

His eyelashes fluttered down to my phone, at his message board post with pictures of the Envisioner he'd snapped on his phone. He hit send.

―――――

My reflection rippled across the surface of the black coffee in my mug, warping my face. Sleep had sobered us up, enough for us to putter around, kind of shy, in the hotel room the next morning. Unused to our private world of a double-bed and soft sheets, of brushing our teeth together after a shower, with me bumping into him because I suddenly didn't know how to work my body. I deleted Yusuf's post—honestly the thing was up for five hours, tops—after some giggling *can you believe we did that* talk. He agreed that we'd both been wound up and he felt better after venting for a while. We said goodbye to our little honeymoon of a hotel and packed the car. I shifted our seats back so that we could lay down and feel the road glide underneath us.

"I know I don't talk a lot," he said, eyes locked on the gray ceiling of the car. "Or I seem like I'm not... *here* all the time."

"I don't mind. You don't have to explain."

"No." He risked a glance over at me, working at something with his jaw muscles. "I want to."

"Okay, shoot."

He sucked in a breath.

"I've spent most of my life breaking things down into tiny pieces and studying them. And arguing with other people about what the pieces do or don't do. And arguing about whether or not we can objectively even say if the pieces are *there*."

He blurted this all, giving me the idea that he'd practiced this in his office back at the Compound. I could see him frowning at the whiteboard and starting over, *no that's not right.* Then pressing his thumb into the center of his forehead like he always did when he was frustrated. Picturing him like this made my heart flip-flap against my ribs.

"I've told you about the wave-function, right?" he continued. "About how things get strange on the quantum level. Unless you're practically staring at an electron you can't really assume it exists in a specific place. You can think of it as a three-dimensional cloud of probability and only when it's observed does that probability collapse and you can find the electron in a fixed spot."

"Weird."

"I mean, I'm skipping around and simplifying. And physicists disagree about whether the wave function is a mathematical tool or real—for lack of a better term. If probability collapses, or if a separate, alternate universe exists for every possible position of the electron. A universe where the electron ended up over here or over there. An equally valid universe for every possible outcome, branching out into infinity. In Oxford, enough of us would pile into a pub after classes and bicker about epistemology or ontology. And a couple of pints in we'd all start railing about how nothing is real unless it's experimentally useful. And sometimes I get stuck on things, or decisions because it's like I can see every outcome and everything seems equally important. Or unimportant or..." He faltered. "I'm not doing this right."

Another broken-winged bird flap of my heart. I squeezed his hand, my YOU ARE HERE tattoo down my thumb anchoring us in one spot.

"Nah, I got you."

"What I'm trying to say is that when I'm around you, things feel more solid. Fixed."

After he gushed out the rest of his breath, he screwed his mouth up into a smile.

"Me too."

We could've hit a landmine and I wouldn't have noticed, with how I was floating to the car's ceiling. Any words I had flew out the window. Because out of all the infinities out there, I was there in a car with him, following the black thread of the road ahead, and that was all I needed.

I watched Kaori in the days after our trip, hanging with her and the Envisioner at night, snooping for clues from the machine and what she knew. I felt the invisible spotlights and tried to act like myself. *The role of Hayes Figueiredo will temporarily be played by...*

Two days trickled away, with Yusuf his normal, quiet self. I could almost convince myself that the guillotine drop wasn't coming, and I was just overanalyzing like I always did. Until the all-hands-on-deck meeting Kaori called on the third day after our trip, when I jostled out of the Footage Farm with the others, wishing that there was just another breakthrough. Even as my feet hit the steps outside the Footage Farm, I knew what was happening.

Before the crowd in the Theater, Kaori twiddled dials on the machine and asked it questions while three of her white coats floated nearby. Will it rain in Paris tomorrow? When will Hurricane Verona make landfall? Will the levees break? I swear she was hamming it up, with the unmoving gold mask of her face like any other day.

When she turned to us, her chin was level with the ground, her eyes a steady searchlight beam sweeping the room.

"I have one of you to thank for this," she said, so softly—she never yelled—that everyone had to lean in.

She swiped a finger across her tablet. On the overhead screens, a video of a suit at a desk—some news show, obviously—flicked to life. I couldn't hear the guy's voice over the blood in my ears. I could only see the picture of the Envisioner projected by his head.

15
THE MAGICIAN

As the slow-motion bomb-drop rippled through the crowd, I sucked in a breath and tried to use my burning lungs to anchor myself to my body. The sniper beams of everyone's eyes pricked my skin. No—they didn't know. Did they? I tore my eyes from the ground and up at Kaori to try to read the blank screen of her face. Telling myself to act normal. But then wouldn't she *know* I was acting? Ball bearings rattled around in the cement mixer of my stomach. Yusuf's feet were rooted to the ground beside Kaori, with his face so still that he could've been asleep with his eyes open.

I'm still not even sure if the first picture on the news was ours. We'd deleted the post and the pictures from our phones, so I couldn't check. My doubt could've just been my brain looking for a way to shrug off the blame.

"I won't insult your intelligence—you're all smart people—by reminding you what you've done," Kaori continued, her voice still the soft gurgle of a glacier-fed mountain stream. So, *so* cold. "How you've jeopardized the project. Our discoveries. The safety of everyone in this building. On this planet."

She wouldn't meet my gaze, instead scanning the crowd, as

much as I mentally screamed at her to look at me. So I could broadcast with my eyes, *it was me. I pushed him.*

She tapped her tablet again and the volume from the screen above blasted to life. Below the lantern-jawed news anchor, the digital crawl read "Sources describe possible extra-terrestrial origin of unknown, advanced technology."

"Whistle-blowers are calling the device the 'Black Box,'" the anchor rumbled. "We're still unclear about what the device actually *does*. Based on geo-cached information embedded in the image, it appears to be housed somewhere in the Commonwealth of Great Basin Nations, sparking concerns that the country may be developing a nuclear arsenal amid alleged land disputes between..."

The high-pitched whine of my boiling brain drowned out the rest. My first day here, I'd railed at Kaori, how can you keep evidence of alternate universes away from the public? And now my drunk loose lips with Yusuf were going to spark a war. No. I did what I knew I had to do. Just like Kaori—all of them—gave speeches about security and humanity and bullshit. When they were really talking about control.

Still.

I tailed Kaori after she breezed out of the room and into her office, leaving the rest of the staff glued to the screens. Yusuf was still gray-faced, with his lips bobbing for words that wouldn't come. Wait, I told him, trying to shove down my panic.

Inside her office, Kaori perched on the edge of her desk, staring into her gold-threaded mug.

"What happened?" I asked.

"I'm leaving for a bit," she said, not looking up. "Getting out in front of this as much as I can so the Commonwealth doesn't take heat, after they were generous enough to host us."

"You sure this isn't an excuse to get out of margarita club when it's your turn to pay?"

She looked up with distant eyes in her high cheek-boned, hornet face. "You're welcome to stay while I'm gone."

I swallowed. Of course I was staying. She was still on stage, then, dropping a hint for me in the audience that she could get rid of me if she really wanted.

"Where're you going?"

"I have some meetings. I'm going on the funding pole-dance circuit. Maybe this is a blessing in disguise. We need more staff, more security. More *everything*." A beat, then, "I'm leaving Yusuf in charge. He'll love that."

"I'm not so sure."

"I'm changing your security clearance. You can enter the Theater whenever you want."

"Why?"

"Because you should keep working with the Envisioner. I know you want the truth about your connection to Figueiredo and the box, and how it got here. I trust *that*. Not the ambition, the career-making, the peacock dancing of some of the others." She bobbed her head to the Theater.

"Thanks," I said, swallowing a fresh throat-full of guilt. "I'll see you when you're back, I guess?"

"Mmm."

My hand was slick on the cold knob of her office door. I was almost free when I heard an, "Oh." Off-handed and breezy. *Oh, would you mind closing the door behind you?* I turned back and found her sitting at her desk like a piano player ready to hit her first chord. The sniper search beams were back on me, this time centered over my pounding heart.

"Was it you?"

"Was what me?"

She looked up from her computer screen, not buying how I was trying to stall. "The leak." She was smiling, almost, and more bright-voiced than I'd ever seen her. "Was it you? I have to ask."

Gunfire all in my head. *Another blam-o by Killer Kaori.*

I knew Kaori appreciates accuracy—so technically, it was Yusuf who hit the button to post the picture. I mean, *hypothetically* post it, and all of that.

"I wouldn't do that to you," I said, so cool.

Oh, bravo. I could practically hear Narek smarm, clapping. *Classic fucking Hayes. He'll go on about wanting to take the bullet, then when it's time, he hits the deck like a coward.*

I stayed away from Yusuf that day. Even though Kaori was already gone, I could feel her eyes watching us. Only after everyone else in the Theater cleared was I able to track him down in his office. His old office, I guessed, figuring he'd move into Kaori's soon.

"Should I call you Director Hassan?"

Yusuf frowned, standing in the center of the room like he forgot why he was even there. "Interim director," he said. When he caught my eye, I saw a tiny spark. "And only in the sack."

It wasn't the first joke he made to me, but it may as well have been, I loved it so much.

He didn't have time for any *was it us* handwringing, not when he was ready to steer the ship away from what he knew were Kaori's bad calls. We should be looking backwards instead of forwards—literally—using the device to ask about and gaze at the earliest instances of this universe where the laws of physics probably didn't even exist yet. We should be trying to stitch together quantum physics and relativity, not dicking around with predictions. Kaori set some parameters about what kinds of past-facing questions the staff could ask, given the leakers still potentially here—so questions about personnel or other vague non-research topics that might otherwise cause more panic were off limits. He didn't like having his hands tied, but he could deal, and he was on fire already with talk of *what this could mean for everything*. I forgot about Kaori trying to scold us all into feeling guilty because I believed in him.

"This is my chance to do something big, for as long as I'm here," Yusuf said.

I know he meant it like *as long as I'm temporarily filling her captain's seat*, but looking back, his words sound ominous. *As long as I'm alive.*

We were so cut off that watching the world grapple with the news of the Envisioner was just like sitting in a movie theater. None of this was real. The only link I had to the outside world was a TV in one of the breakout rooms that was always switched to the news. During breaks from the Footage Farm, I'd head there for some microwaved food and watch the protests in front of the White House and the Pan-African Parliament in Khartoum, the signs and the shouting so scattered that it didn't seem like the people knew what they were pissed about. *Beam Me Up* scrawled in marker on a sign, next to someone with *Everyone Loses the Arms Race*.

I didn't expect Kaori to be as open about the Envisioner as she was, holding press conferences and calling on reporters with her clipped voice. Answering questions with short sentences and unafraid to dodge and move on, even with all the shouting, especially at first. *It's a modeling device. We have yet to understand the language of its inventors, but they appear to be from an alternate version of Earth.*

There was only one mass suicide I saw on the news, of a cult in the highlands of Scotland who thought they could get to the alternate universe by swallowing a few mouthfuls of barbiturates.

"Fucking idiots," one of the white coats whose name I hadn't bothered to learn grumbled at the screen when the news broke.

My microwaved noodles scalded my insides. I thought of my mom telling me about the Titan riots, and how weird it was that people seemed personally victimized by the existence of alien life and not so much about how they learned about it. I knew there'd be a big reaction to the news that I leaked. But honestly, I didn't feel responsible for anyone else's actions or emotions. They all deserved to know, and it was up to them to hop into their grownup pants and decide what they did with that knowledge.

Kaori seemed to agree. She was the chilly stepmother during her press conferences. Where she really sang were news segments, with her pinned-back hair and the jeweled pins of the flags of Japan and the Commonwealth of Great Basin Nations on the collar of her senator's-wife pantsuit.

I watched her on some late-night news show after I spent hours Envisioner-dipping. Captions on the bottom of the screen called her "Dr. Kaori Nakamori, Director of The Envisioner Initiative." I'd never stopped to ask what our whole operation was called, and "The Envisioner Initiative" sounded culty enough. A makeup artist must've dabbed concealer over the green shadows beneath her eyes, along with painting her a red vampire mouth. She was a publicist fresh off a beach vacation, not the tired woman who'd peered down at her teacup while she talked with me for hours about her drowned homeland.

She could've snapped together some black-ops communications team and sent anyone in her place for this interview—or any one of the other million she did—but that wasn't her style. She wanted the messages to come from her.

"There are just so many questions," one of the anchors said, a former football star with a jutting fist-shaped chin.

"*So* many, Reggie," his co-anchor, Kameelah, chimed in with her massage therapist voice. "I mean another *universe?* That's unreal."

"And what we're looking for," Kaori said smoothly, "are answers to so many of our questions."

She never cracked once during the whole interview, even when the anchors grilled her. Why the secrecy, they asked? All about safety, she said, all about looking out for everyone. She felt confident that she and her team could release this *sensitive* information about the device now after years of multinational cooperation and testing in a secure facility, where each day they learned more about this tremendous gift.

"Well, that and the leak," Kameelah added.

Kaori laughed off the jab. "Sure—the leak. Let's go there. Look, of course, ideally we would've controlled that initial release of information. But the wheels were already in motion. We certainly envisioned—no pun intended—a future where everyone has equal access to the Envisioner and its technology. There were a lot of hard conversations the last several weeks, including before the photos hit the media. We knew we had to balance our need for caution with a sense of transparency with the public."

"And why's that?" Reggie asked.

"Because this is not JAXA's discovery, or mine, or my team's," she said, leaning in slightly. "This is *ours*. This is our shared human heritage—spanning universes. Think about that. This future belongs to all of us."

"Stunning," Kameelah said.

"So stunning," Reggie agreed.

Jesus, some deep part of me sank with how unrecognizable she was, all her hard angles powdered, her lips glossed, her playful voice. Which was the character, the pantsuit or the white lab coat? Her act was all about control. How she even sent us more research staff and a beefed-up security team to patrol the white lab-rat halls, all to prove that she was still pulling the strings even while she was away.

Control, control—the tightening of some vice. Figueiredo's voice followed me from the Theater to my room, late at night. *Isn't this what you wanted?* Sometimes Kaori chimed in. *You don't make something out of steel and then complain when it's too hard.*

I visited the Envisioner alone at night, the first couple of days that Kaori was gone, until a night-shift research team swooped in and kicked me out. Yusuf was swamped with work and I had nothing else to do but press my hands on the gunmetal facets of the machine and try to look for some roadmap. What should I do? I asked the thing. What's going to happen? It answered with charts or equations. Or "Invalid query. Critical variable limit." Which— fair enough—I couldn't even shape my swirling thoughts into real questions, so how could I expect the box to know what I meant?

Soon dozens more staff rolled into the Compound. The latest model of White Coat Researcher now came with a two-way radio and a complete disinterest in us plebs in the Footage Farm. At least we got more kitchen staff and were eating more than heat-lamp pizza slices. More funding, Yusuf told me of the improvements and the staff, admitting it was all because of Kaori and her interviews.

The new staff hooked up more machines to the Envisioner and clogged the Theater all hours of the day and night. No more late-night hangouts with me and the black box. I barely saw Yusuf because he had to lead multiple teams, and they were getting close to significant breakthroughs about the early moments of the universe, meaning his mind was never with me even when we were really together anyway.

I wanted to be a supportive partner, but I'd be lying if I said that waiting for him most nights, alone in his room with nothing to watch but the numbers of the digital clock change, was frustrating. I was his sounding board—not like I offered a ton of wisdom— while he spun his brain out loud. His timing wasn't great, though. One night he kissed up my neck only to whisper a boner-killer in my ear, *tomorrow we start sharing data with the Large Hadron-X*. Moving out of my little dorm and into his would've been easier, but I knew we both needed the space and alone time. He was so spent from *talking* and *coordinating* and *touching-base*—things that practically gave him hives—and I didn't want him to feel like he had to entertain me. He'd come in late, smelling of dried sweat and anxiety. I'd try to fill the silence for a while, running my thumb over the black hairs on the back of his forearm. Or I'd be half-asleep and he'd fold into me, pressing his back against my chest and letting my breath sweep across his neck.

Out of everything that was going on, I never thought about leaving or that I'd made a mistake. I was just bummed more than anything else that our secret club here was gone.

I can't say that the world outside was the only thing changing, or even just life at the Compound with its hallways crowded with more staff.

Figueiredo was creeping into me like a disease.

I didn't see Yusuf a lot, leaving me to dive into work, clocking ten-, eleven-hour days at the Footage Farm. Figueiredo's world and the ant farm of his Envisioner facility became a drama that me and the other footage techs glued ourselves to. The well-oiled machine of his staff seemed to implode around him, with green-coated researchers splintering into bickering groups that clammed up when he marched into a room. We weren't sure if this footage was from before or after the riot. We tried to string the footage into chronological order, sketching out possible storylines and main character relationships on the whiteboard. Placing bets on who was going to flip a table or punch Figueiredo in the face first. Someone started a dead pool. All this sounds grosser than it actually was, because they were characters to us more than people, but saying it out loud now is pretty weird.

I never made bets. I became the person I hated—the one stuck at his desk taking everything too seriously, all *could you guys please keep it down because some of us are here to work.* Irritated at everyone and everything because I was tangled in my own head. Watching the footage of Figueiredo's facility was a dream that I could almost remember if I scoured my brain. In his endless journaling with his portable recording device, I could almost feel through the choppy music of his language and understand what he was saying. He became an itch in my brain that I couldn't scratch that followed me everywhere.

Figueiredo took Tiago to an observatory one night and filmed his husband peering down into a telescope. Tiago waved him over and I could read the annoyance in his eyes like subtitles in a grainy, old-fashioned foreign film. *This was your idea, now put the camera down and come over here.* Figueiredo joined him, bent down, and pointed his camera into the eyepiece of the telescope. In the footage, a planet that looked like Jupiter but with swirling green clouds spun against the blackness.

Figueiredo's eyes seemed to swirl with the same storm clouds in the next bit of footage that I watched—him at his desk again—when I was alone the next night. The fern trees outside his office window were covered in snow, with the gray light through the window highlighting the differences in our faces. The pinkish scar across his nose, the lines around his sharp wolf eyes.

"You must've found the machine by now," he said, his voice a tired whisper. "If you ever will."

16
REWRITES

Static filled my head as I drifted through the Compound and into Yusuf's bedroom, where Figueiredo's shadow crept in under the door. The ball-bearings were back in the cement mixer of my gut, clanging around along with Figueiredo's words. His eyes still kicked up my heartbeat. I felt him gliding along the walls and dipping into the shadows cast by the parking lot floodlights through the window blinds. Yusuf was zonked out in bed—lost to the even, slow inhales of sleep.

Tomorrow I'd tell Arjun everything I had seen, and there'd be lots of scrambling around the Footage Farm and the rest of the Compound. It'd throw everyone's marker-board chronological theories about Figueiredo's research lab mostly out the window. He *knew* about us, and he'd been watching us. Still was, somehow? What if he sent us the Envisioner out of panic because his underlings turned against him?

I didn't care about any of that. All I cared about was that it seemed like he was speaking right to me.

I crept into bed beside Yusuf, who murmured something as he rolled to face me. And then I couldn't sleep—his breath across my face, his elbow jammed in my side—because the bed was too narrow and cuddling always sounds so romantic until your arm falls asleep. My face was somehow on fire and clammy at the same time, my body shivering and sweating the ghost of tequila past out of my pores.

Then leave, came Figueiredo's shadow voice, just a whisper of sandpaper over the low hush of Yusuf's breath.

I shifted in bed, easing his arm off me, and tried to shove out the voice by cramming my eyes shut. My eyelids were just screens for more footage of Figueiredo plucking off his gold-rimmed glasses to squeeze the bridge of his nose in annoyance. *Sure, this is fun for a while, but you know that this won't last. It never does.*

I didn't want to listen. The lamplight through the blinds turned the skin of Yusuf's bent arm into a rolling desert landscape. He needed sleep more than I did, with all the work he was doing. *Sure, sure.* And I was leaving for him, right?

I slid out of bed without a sound and into my clothes that I'd piled on the floor. I had years of practice with these pre-dawn spy-flick extractions. Scootching out of the bed of some guy who had transformed from someone I had to be with, to then get away from, in the space of two hours. Tiptoeing through his place like I was stepping over red security beams of a jewel vault. Bare-assed past his front door where I'd dress in the hallway of his apartment— who cared if one of his neighbors saw because even the jingle of the zipper of my jeans might wake him up. On the stoop of Yusuf's house, the dry desert heat was a furnace to the face.

Sweat trickled from my hairline by the time I reached my door, my skin still smelling of him, and I slept alone.

More changes and shifting sands inside and outside the Compound. I was too busy at the Footage Farm and I couldn't pull Yusuf away.

Genesis would have teased me about hanging up my camera and working for The Man.

I saw Kaori's face whenever I planted myself in front of a TV. Breaking news cut into sitcoms I'd been trying to melt my brain with. Screaming pundits on their weeks-long End-of-Days-watches replayed bits of her conferences and footage of her walking out of buildings to decode if what she wore or how she walked was actually a secret message to the Illuminati or the alien overlords sending her orders from their invisible mothership or something.

She kept up her media pole-dance at press conferences and news shows—shimmying, winking, and only ever showing what she wanted to. Behind the scenes, I figured, she was cashing checks from donors and investors. *Get that coin, Kaori.* I smirked as she bulldozed some suit on an evening news show who clearly thought he was going to invite her on and rake her over the coals about the danger of this tech, especially with what we learned from the Cloud Cold Wars.

For all the shit I gave her early on about keeping the Envisioner and this place secret, I never thought she'd blab *this* much to the media. Looking back, going public and shaping the story had probably always been her plan, and she just had to wait for the right time, art-directing the future into one that she'd always wanted.

> KAORI (VOICEOVER)
> Let's call it "transparency in the
> name of science and social progress."
> Or even "philanthropy" if you're
> feeling generous.

But what I think even she didn't expect or calculate was just what a colossal goof the n-Viz would be. Unless she did, with a spare mini-Envisioner the size of a make-up compact tucked into her slim purses that hung off her elbow when she waltzed into TV studios or angel investor meetings. *Don't look over there,* she burbled playfully, *I've got the goods stashed over here.*

Once she'd swooped back to the Compound after her continent-hopping tour, she told me about one product meeting in San Francisco with some tech bros. She'd planned to offer a subscription service of Envisioner data to the public. Nothing critical, only a limited database of pre-answered questions, mostly boring weather and traffic predictions. Maybe an elite product line for bank-rolling customers to hash out personalized questions with a customer service rep—only harmless non-event stuff, nothing about "when will I die," or "what will this stock price be"—for the research team to consider asking the Envisioner.

She could gouge the public twice over if she linked the service to a device, the tech bros had told Kaori, who steepled her fingers like *I'm listening.*

"The n-Viz is about human connectivity and exerting power over our future and *buzzwords,*" a tech bro grandstanded at her in his slim suit, waving to projected slides of his firm's pitch that detailed the black wrist cuff device. "The *n* is for nexus, or new, or the unknown in an equation."

"I still find money gross," Kaori said in her office after she'd filled me in on her fundraising and her pre-enrollment plan for the n-Viz, where people could lock in a lifetime of savings. "But the n-Viz will pay for the new staff, and plane fuel, and the patron outreach."

Even knowing she meant well, I had to swallow a mouthful of hot tea not to go off on her about how privileged someone had to be to just dismiss money. Sure, rally for the redistribution of wealth and get all post-capitalism. But the only people lucky enough to write-off the whole concept of money never had to hunt the streets for stray change to buy groceries.

>   KAORI (VOICEOVER)
>   Democratization of this information
>   is so critical. But it can't be for
>   free. We need the resources. We need
>   the time. It's too important. After
>   all, this is our future.

"I'd really like to know just who gets to decide who has access to this… this thing," a douche supposed expert in some field, who'd never met or spoken to Kaori, argued on a nightly news panel. "She's turning down United Nations requests for access and information. Then this n-Viz preview is…"

"It's crass, is what it is," the lone woman in the group finished for him. Of the three people on the panel, she went in the hardest on Kaori. Pushing to the front of the crowd to light the stake and burn the witch herself. "Someone has to stop this."

The white walls of my room hugged me close. The hieroglyphics from Yusuf's latest tutoring session still filled the window in my room, so electron shells danced in the red desert when I looked outside. He was tied up for weeks and I was trapped here in this shrinking cell. Normally, I wouldn't care. Even when I was with Narek, I had my own separate life, with my own friends and work. I'd been ready to barricade myself in a cabin in the woods for weeks, after all, before all of this. I'd had my doc about Genesis to work on. At least that I could control, cutting and re-playing the bits of her story. My antsy fingers brushed off the footage on my laptop, trying to find some sense that I could weave with those scenes.

But looking at what I'd filmed slid something sharp and cold between my ribs. I still didn't know how to feel about her now that she was gone, if she really did end her own life and leave me alone. Which pummeled me because just seeing her face used to light me up, because she was my heart walking around on two legs. Her face might've been mostly flat gray planes, but I could read her better than anyone else as we'd trawled vintage shops for her first drag show.

"I don't think I've ever felt more like a person," she'd said, looking in the mirror of the curtained dressing room while I zipped up her sequined cocktail dress. Her voice had trembled just a little. She'd smoothed her hands down the gold glimmers at her waist, straightening out a wrinkle in the fabric, and had tucked a stray honey curl of her wig behind her ear.

I'd tipped my head to survey her in the mirror, knowing I had to brighten the mood or else this shopping trip to distract her from another legal synth loss would go down in flames.

"Yeah, but do we really think you're a blonde?" I'd asked. "I was thinking more, like, recently divorced redheaded vamp having a night on the town with her girls."

"Oh, honey." She'd snapped to attention. "I'm so there. Get me that red human-hair number by the front window. And the highest goddamned rhinestoned heels you can find. Stat."

I didn't hear my bedroom door open the night I'd skipped out of the Footage Farm early to project the footage from my laptop on one of the blank walls. From his hunched shoulders I could see that Yusuf didn't know yet that he needed to vent and needed me to coax it out of him. Before he even said anything to me, his eyes brightened at the sight of my doc on the wall.

"What are you working on?"

I'd already told him about my doc on Genesis and her work with nationwide synth rights. Well—the one-liner pitch version, free from the emotional dump truck of *I think my friend killed herself and I don't know that I can ever forgive her.*

I filled him in on how this scene I was working on was supposed to be the opening of the doc because it was how she'd wanted everyone to see her, on stage in the glimmering lights and in control. I didn't know when to cut the scene because I was too close to it and just wanted to watch her perform over and over again.

It was the night she'd hosted a ball during the week that the Supreme Court had mulled over striking down the Defense of Human Sanctity Act. She'd turned an old vaudeville house in Boston into her inaugural ball—she's elected herself president, her girlfriend Dee had eye-rolled, dressed as a power lesbian Secret Service agent. Genesis had strutted out from the wings of the stage, her hands raised, wearing a prim red pantsuit and a blonde pinned-back wig snatched off some female presidential candidate who bemoaned the loss of American family values. The decaying theater had seemed held up only by filigree and streamers of red, white, and blue, with a banner spray-painted with *United Synths of America* stuck to the red curtain at the back of the stage.

A look of saintly patriotism had crossed her face while she'd lip synched the start of some long-dead pop star's riff of the "Star-Spangled Banner" with overdrawn lips that looked so pumped with filler that they might burst. At "And the rocket's red glare," a sizzling electronic beat had dive-bombed through the song and I'd pulled in tight on the shot of her painted red nails clutching the waist of her suit. Then, she'd ripped off the tear-away fabric—the crowd collectively losing their shit with rapture below her—to reveal a spangled American flag bikini underneath, glittering with each of her burlesque shimmies, the beaded fringe swaying around her long legs.

"How did you know to zoom in?" Yusuf asked. "With everything that was happening, how did you know that was the right moment?"

He scooted close enough to me on the end of the bed that his breath rustled across my shoulder.

"I'm not sure it is."

I was debating on cutting to a wide shot from the stationary camera I'd set up in another corner of the room instead of zooming in on her hands right before the tear-away. Like the whole film hinged on this moment of whether to catch Genesis in her artifice, especially with what me and Dee suspected really happened with her.

She'd gotten death threats before that night—bricks thrown through windows of her apartment, the emails and phone calls with the faux concerned voices telling her things like *I sure hope you don't catch a bug.* Dee's mind had gone right to the rumored synth viruses that terrorists could transmit with just a brush of their hands, sending super-bugs burrowing through polymer casing to shred a synth's silicon neural net. Me and Dee had already noticed Genesis slowing over the past few months, an unfocused look in her eyes here, a stumble there, a slight slur to her speech after a long day. Most of the other synths in her product line had been retired long ago, replaced with newer models that looked more human and could process billions of data clouds per second, the whole race of them networked around the world. Genesis just couldn't keep up, even with a new battery cell and neural upgrades. She was a *lady of a certain age,* she'd joked.

Then, she'd come down with a bug that none of the synth techs could cure the night before the Supreme Court ruling and had live-casted her tearful decommissioning out to the whole world. "Though I'm leaving, I hope the fight will live on," she'd told them. And as soon as the Supreme Court struck down the Defense of Human Sanctity Act and synths in Boston rallied at the State House and held up posters with Genesis's face, I knew that the timing was too perfect. Genesis had sacrificed herself for the cause.

The morning after she'd died, I'd found her deck of nail-polish-splotched tarot cards outside my front door, wrapped in brown paper. She'd left a note with the package. *Make your own future*. After staring at this footage every night that week, I still didn't know how to cut her in my doc. Should I be the storyteller or the friend? Should I zoom in on her hands just before her planned costume reveal, or stay out in the wide and show her like she wanted to be, lighting a fistful of sparklers in the spotlight like some neon Statue of Liberty?

Mostly, I was exhausted and frustrated with her. And everything else. The cardboard filmmaker armor that I tried to duct-tape to myself flopped to the floor. As much as I tried to clamp my mouth shut, the words just came blabbing out. All of them. I know she'd been suffering at the end and everyone should be able to end their pain if they need to. And it's beyond unfair to ask a person to live just for someone else if they're in pain. But also, how fucking *dare* she leave me alone if she really did kill herself? We could've figured out a way to make her better. Didn't she know I really had no one else? That she was the one thing that had glued me back together after my mom died, and how did she expect me to go this alone?

Then came the *beep-beep* of the garbage truck in my head backing up to my mouth to dump another load of hot tears and rage. I didn't know if I could ever get over how she died, and now my anger was reaching back through time with venom-tipped claws to slash up all the memories I had with her. How can you love someone but hate them at the same time?

I hadn't let myself break down since Genesis died because I didn't know if I'd be able to put myself back together again. It was easier to keep my own head at an arm's distance, sometimes, coasting on detached snark. I really tried to slam the door on my tears, at first, for Yusuf's sake. Until I knew I just had to buckle and live here for a while and feel everything. Whatever it was that we were building here, I had to let him in. I had to give him the choice of whether he wanted to be with me—or if he could, honestly—even if I had to explode in a shrapnel bomb of unresolved feelings, sometimes.

Sucking up snot and mumbling *jesus christ* as I wiped at my burning face, I looked at him. Begging with my eyes for him to say something. The muscles worked at the sides of his jaws, his wide eyes like a can of soda just exploded in his face.

And then he started talking about photons.

I don't really remember how he started, just that I was trying hard to breathe and not snap at him with a *I really need you to not be talking about physics right now.* He was speaking in these slow sentences and tracing my palm with his thumb. Looking down at our hands and back up at me, over and over. Yanking my hand away and leaving would make me an asshole. Besides, I was starting to get what he was saying, almost, while he talked about some experiment where scientists shot light beams at a metal plate. Which proved that light was a particle and a wave at the same time, or something. And, yeah, it's strange but also just how the universe works, he said, even if it seems like it shouldn't make sense.

"What I mean is," he said slowly, his eyes on mine, "you can be mad at her and love her at the same time. Even if it seems like it doesn't make sense. That's just how things work."

My whole body felt like it had just finally let out a sneeze it had been holding in for months. My nervous laugh shook off the weight from my shoulders. My kiss told him I wasn't laughing at him, and when I leaned back, a corner of his mouth tugged into a smile.

"I think I get it," I said. I wiped the back of one hand across my nose. "But I might need you to remind me once in a while."

"I can do that." He bobbed his chin over to my laptop. "Can you play that part again?"

I hit play on the scene of my doc. I knew he wasn't big on clubs and drag shows, mostly because the noise overwhelmed him. I didn't need some head-patting from him that I was doing good work or whatever, but watching him watch Genesis's act, a tiny gap appearing between his lips, closed up the rest of the space that I'd convinced myself had widened between us lately.

When the footage on the wall flashed to Genesis's hands, Yusuf reached over and hit pause, freezing the scene at her red nails bunching the shimmery red fabric at her waist.

"It's perfect," he said.

Genesis's voice floated between us. *Tomorrow we strike. Tonight we fucking dance!*

In today's episode of *Home Movies from Hell,* let's watch Figueiredo skip stones across the ocean of the multiverse.

Arjun and the rest of my coworkers had already flagged a ton of footage from Figueiredo's world and organized it into theoretical timelines. Arjun had told me when I'd first started here that all the footage from the Envisioner had been copied to a server, and then chunks of footage were randomly assigned to work queues for the techs to review. I figure, now, that Kaori didn't think I'd be a model employee who scanned the footage queue every day to check out everyone's flagged videos and notes. Because I sure had a knack for stumbling on important-looking footage for the assignments to be random.

Yusuf had a lot of patience for normals like me, which was a lot more than I could say for some of the others at Dr. Nakamori's School for Smarmy Overachievers. But I dropped the word *random* in front of him once and could see the steam erupting from his ears.

"People use the word random when they don't want to look for patterns," he'd said.

My shoulders still felt lighter the day after confessing how I felt about Genesis to Yusuf, when I hit play on the latest batch of footage in my queue.

Figueiredo's face was too close to the camera of whatever device he was recording on, the harsh lighting carving deep lines across his forehead and on either side of his mouth. The flickering overhead lights and the constant filming of his every task didn't help much to quell his serial-killer vibe. Finally, the lights quit their firefly blinks and cast their glow over the airline hangar—or wherever Figueiredo was—with its lead-gray concrete floor, metal walls, and dozens of shadowed shapes that looked like boulders.

He stepped out of frame, talking to himself, and he must've flicked on another panel of lights. White light flooded the gray room, revealing each of the boulders as an Envisioner.

We knew he must've had a whole fleet of them but seeing them all gathered there prickled my skin with cold. I could feel their spider eyes moving on him. He strode to the closest machine, still talking to himself, and the thing's greenish domed screens snapped to life. The one next to it, too—and the next, then the next. The Envisioners whirred and blinked when he strolled by, like puppies reacting to their owner, with answers to questions he probably thought but didn't ask aloud darting across their screens.

One glance back at the camera before he rested one of his palms on a facet of the closest Envisioner. Something sparked under his hand, though for a second I thought it was some trick of light or glitch in the video. Until a wavering, gold-edged circle appeared on the Envisioner beneath his palm with a *sploosh* like waves hitting a rocky shore. A night sky hovered within the circle. I don't know how else to describe what I saw other than that he cut a circle into a glass window like he was some spy breaking into a shop window. Except instead of a storefront, he somehow cut a hole into *reality*, and through the circle was another world.

The circle expanded until it was about fifteen feet across. Just big enough for him to walk around to the opposite site of the Envisioner, plant his feet on the ground, and shove the thing into the hole. The circle fizzled out as soon as the machine passed through.

I had to hit pause on the playback here and just let the facts of what he was doing pound against my brain. I was watching him send his fleet of machines into other universes, and one of those was probably the machine that had crash-landed into ours. I watched with a detached gaze that would've made Kaori proud.

Dark circles of sweat appeared under the dusty green armpits of his lab coat while he worked, pacing to the next Envisioner and the next, opening a portal with the noise of a wave-slosh, and shoving each machine through. He got creative with some of the drops. He'd place his hands on a facet and a circle would bloom between the legs of the machine until it grew wide enough that the Envisioner dropped through. He was showing off—a little jig in his step here, a little flex for the camera there.

I had no idea how important the footage that I watched was. Not just for work—with it being the first evidence we'd seen so far that Figueiredo had sent other Envisioners to other universes besides just ours. Important because it completely changed what happened with me and Yusuf.

He'd told me before about how the machine responded to Figueiredo's touch. But seeing him send the machines away— moving further into the distance so he was little more than a blur against what must've been hundreds of machines—spun my stomach. Like I was in a bomber jet, staring down the open hatch, and dropping bombs onto the cities below.

17
INTERMISSION

There's a question I could've asked Kaori, at the podium for one of her press conferences. I'd be sitting in one of the rows of folding chairs with the other reporters, in my newsman drag of a trench coat and a fedora with *Press* written on a card and tucked into the hatband. I'd raise my hand and she'd nod for me to stand.

"Good morning, Dr. Nakamori. I'm Hayes Figueiredo with *Stating the Fucking Obvious News*. My question is, if I hadn't seen that footage, would I have known just how to rip through the barriers myself? Or that I even *could*?"

"Mmm." Kaori would nod. "Great question, but what we should really talk about is the troops."

Since I couldn't ask Kaori that, I tried asking the Envisioner once, but the *maybes* and *would'ves* fractaled down into forever.

I know I said she'd been the one really calling the shots here. But honestly, me finding footage of Figueiredo showing off how he could cut windows into other universes didn't seem like it was a part of her plan. It was my escape.

Less than a month after she'd left, she was back like it was just another snoozer of a day. From my spying spot at the window of the Footage Farm, I saw her by the Envisioner. I bolted down the stairs and tried to corner her to ask how she was, but she waved me off saying that she had too much catching up to do. Yusuf filled me in that night—actually able to tell me through the side of his tight lips how frustrated he was with her. She was back with zero warning and already she'd given some vague pep talk to the staff, thanking Dr. Hassan for his leadership in her absence and how they were ready to resume predictive work.

I watched him unravel into a breathless annoyance, saying she was undoing all his progress. I was happy to listen, but there was only so many times I could say *that sucks*. I could've screamed that for such rocket-scientists, they could be completely dense if they didn't see that the only way to hash all of this out was to— christ on a cross—*talk* to each other about their feelings.

After a few days of the weird tension between them like an invisible barbed wire, I cribbed a plot-point from some buddy movie and decided to trap them together, forcing them to hash things out. "Let's get out of here for an afternoon like old times," I told each of them. Yusuf met me at the small electric car the next afternoon and I told him to wait in the back. Only when Kaori walked into the garage a few minutes later, opened the car door, and spotted Yusuf already inside did they realize this was a setup.

Yusuf's mouth dropped open. I mouthed *sorry* at him.

"Change of plans?" Kaori asked coolly.

"I thought the three of us could use a getaway," I said behind her. "You know. An hour locked in this car with no escape, with no one else eavesdropping on what's said in this safe space."

After a second of spinning calculations, Kaori sat down inside. Before either of them could change their minds, I scooted to the front of the car. I stayed in the driver's seat even though the AI nav took the wheel, tires squeaking over the pavement of the garage and onto the road outside.

"Thanks, Dad," Kaori deadpanned.

"Don't make me turn this car around."

"Could you?" Yusuf asked.

The awkward silence warped time into an unnaturally long half-hour that had me wondering if sticking myself between them had been a mistake. Until Yusuf spoke up to tell Kaori that he just wanted to be useful. Because why else did she bring him here? Kaori didn't have time for this kid-gloves bullshit, she said, not when Yusuf was acting like an infant because he wanted to be in charge and didn't want to answer to her.

Their sighs rustled through the car as I played marriage therapist with my leading questions. And how does that make you feel? Kaori, what do you think about that? Kaori managed to save the eye-rolling and sarcasm, softening as Yusuf told her that he didn't resent her. He didn't want to be in charge. But with the most complex piece of technology they could ever dream up in their hands, he wanted to think bigger, like she said they would when she convinced him to join her here. Like, grand unifying theory big, instead of gazing at an uncertain future.

Flat red earth stretched out on either side of the road.

"Let's meet in the middle," Kaori said. "We have the resources now. Let's consider this a partnership of two research divisions. You take the past. I take the future."

I dragged them to a bowling alley instead of our usual Mexican restaurant because I'd wanted them to have something to do with their hands in case they were itching to strangle each other. Yusuf was so bad at the game it was almost sweet, with him rocketing balls into the gutter. Kaori's shots knocked single pins off the edges of the frame, until I could see her spinning calculations on angles and force behind her eyes. Halfway through our first pitcher of beer, the ice thawed between them. Kaori scribbled names on the back of a pint-glass ringed napkin, both squabbling over staff like they were drafting some fantasy sports league. *Fine, you take Nazar but I'm getting Vasquez.*

By the time we split cheese-coated nachos at the Mexican restaurant, I didn't have to play therapist. They divided the Compound, with Yusuf and his team taking the day shift, Kaori and her team the night shift after a few hours of calibration and testing between. She always was a night owl, anyway. This whole treaty was so easy that they felt silly about getting so worked up and protective, when their work wasn't about egos—it was about *knowledge.* Now that their kingdom was divided and treaties signed, we all *cheers*ed with our cactus-shaped margarita glasses, and the band was back together.

I missed a lot of warning signs as the gears cranked tighter around us, because—surprise, surprise—I was focused on myself.

Protests erupted across Florida after Kaori alerted the government that they should evacuate the Keys before a monster hurricane knocked the islands into the sea. I watched an old woman crying to a field reporter on the TV in our break room. *Just because some machine tells me to leave, why should I listen? I've lived here for forty years.* Behind her, the winds were already kicking up sea spray. I have no idea what happened to her when the hurricane hit like the machine said it would.

Kaori converted a conference room into a customer service call center for her n-Viz program. The wrist device hadn't officially rolled out yet, though the customers were already calling and screaming about when they could ask the box their questions.

I visited the place once and found four people sitting by phones and computer workstations in tiny pools of light cast by desk lamps, their eyes all flashing me varying looks of *help*. I knew the look from my summers washing dishes at a chain restaurant in Southie, the humid days by the industrial dishwasher that belched clouds of mystery-meat-smelling mist into my face. I'd picked up a couple of lunch shifts here and there, and there was always some asshole wailing to me about a world-ending injustice. A tomato in his burger, and then I'd be in front of a firing squad of *nobody in this goddamn place has ever done a day of hard work in their lives and why don't you cut your hair and get a real job.*

Some patron paid a shit-ton of money—Kaori was cagey about just how much—to come by the Compound and ask the Envisioner a question. I marooned myself in the Footage Farm late the night he came by and peered down at the Theater where he, Kaori, and a few of her aides floated by the Envisioner. He asked the machine whatever he bankrolled Kaori to ask and was soon flapping his arms wildly at the machine, then to Kaori, then to the whole world around him, it looked, until he stormed out.

The *how dare you have something that we don't* hurricane winds whipped around us. An invisible guillotine hung in the air.

I was too busy poring over footage from Figueiredo's universe and trying to find an hour or two at night when the Theater was empty and I could work with the machine alone. Then, creeping to Yusuf's bedside long after he'd been asleep. Trying to work up the courage to tell him I was losing myself and couldn't explain how or why. That this world was starting to feel less real, less *solid,* even after what he told me in the car on the way back from Beatty.

When I'm around you, things feel more solid, he'd said. *Fixed.*

Instead I told him, "We're getting out of here," and I wouldn't tell him to where.

Sometimes you need an intermission. A swelling of the score from the theater speakers and then the red velvet curtain plummets down from the ceiling and covers the screen. The manager flicks on the house lights that dazzle the eyes of the audience and everyone stands up, all *huh?* and fumbles from the movie-fog back to real life. I worked an intermission into one of my early docs as a palette cleanser—an hour into a deep-dive into a gay bar in Ukraine that was raided by the police—a five-minute break when I wanted the audience to get up and dance. Cue the retro-jingle. *Let's all go to the lobby and buy ourselves a Coke.*

Yusuf and me were silhouettes in the observatory, alone except for an employee who lingered on the fringe of the circular room, knowing to give us space. This section of Commonwealth University in Treaty City was closed to visitors, and we were only able to creep in because I'd called and maybe *hinted* that this was Official Envisioner Business. The lie was completely worth it just to see the outline of Yusuf peeking down the telescope in the room lit by dim red bulbs.

I guess I should thank Figueiredo for the inspiration from that date video of him and Tiago. I even brought Scarlett with me. I looked at Yusuf through the viewfinder of my camera because looking with my own eyes sent a dull ache through my chest.

"Would you put that thing down and come over here," he said. "This was your idea, anyway."

It was only fair, somehow, that Yusuf would say the exact same thing that I knew Tiago had in his exact position. All of us were hitting marks in the same play, over and over again.

Maybe Yusuf's talk about parallel universes was all wrong since it made me picture two lines of light streaking through empty black space, never once touching. From what I've seen, it's like the universes intersect at points. The Envisioner. The times me and him spent alone together. The way he kisses like he's resurfacing from a deep dive and I'm giving him air.

I lowered my camera and walked to the telescope. I peeked down, the fingers of one hand interlaced with Yusuf's. Whatever sight offered by the telescope's lens blurred in my eyes.

"Do you see it?" he asked.

"Yeah. It's beautiful. So, so beautiful."

I've heard a million shitty songs about how love is like a drug. Many of those songs while I was swaying on a dancefloor under a disco light, with the music thrumming in me, watching time ripple away in waves that I could reach out and touch. *Oh, your love is making me high.* I got what those hack songwriters who rhymed *love* and *above* meant. Love lights you up and torches your brain. For me, actual drugs were an escape. A way to strap on armor so I didn't feel so much, and the metal might weigh me down enough that I'd fall asleep. Yusuf was sharp and real and raw—something bright that burrowed past my ribs and stayed there.

The car we'd borrowed slipped over the black thread of the road on the way back to the Compound, the only sound the faint hum of the engine.

"I think I love you," he said.

I'd been spacing off, staring into the night sky for what felt like hours. I could barely hear him over the engine, dropping this casual factoid like he was telling me our exit was up ahead. Normally, I'd poke him about the *I think*. What, you're testing some hypothesis? You can't just say "I love you?" But the way his beetle-shell eyes beamed out *please say something*, I knew I could joke later.

The breath caught in my throat. The wires in my head got all twisted up, sending little aftershocks of warmth all down my body. I turned from the windshield and reached for his hand, forcing his eyes up again.

"I love you," I said.

I'd tossed Scarlett in the trunk. I wished I could wriggle back there, grab her, and ask Yusuf to say it again. I could record it and re-watch again and again, especially now that I'm stranded in the sand without him. But the moment was already gone.

18
COLLIDING

On a *how fucked are we* scale from one to ten, I guessed everyone in the Compound currently hovered around a million.

Shoulder-to-shoulder with other staff, I couldn't tear my eyes from the overhead screen in the Theater where four vehicles ripped from a post-apocalyptic survival thriller plowed through the desert. A beat-up black van, two jeeps, and a black pickup rumbled down the same road that me and Yusuf had driven on the way back from the observatory just hours before. One of the jeeps actually had a steer skull mounted to its grill.

Kaori's tight voice had blasted through the PA system in the Compound and over the green-painted pavement of our cookie-cutter houses, ripping us all from sleep before dawn. *Code bravo bravo bravo. All staff to the Theater.*

"We've been warned that some people are coming," Kaori said, even-voiced and straight-backed. "And that they're angry."

What freaked me out the most was the total silence in the Theater. Only the breaths of the people around me as Kaori's words died in the air, in front of security footage and the growing crowd.

The surge of my pulse at the side of my neck was a silent alarm.

Well, we're doomed, the Storyteller voice deadpanned. *I'll just see myself out.*

We could fight about *how* later, once we were safe. Finger-pointing at how Kaori baited the fringe crazies with how open she was to the public, or with the insane price of the n-Viz pre-registration. Or bringing that sponsor here, who'd stormed out because of whatever the Envisioner had told him. Or me and Yusuf's leak to the tipster board.

What mattered now was that the Commonwealth of Great Basin Nations had no standing army and couldn't guarantee the safety of the Compound. And that my skeleton was trying to vibrate out of my body. The security drones were already zipping out to meet the group, who picked them off like clay pigeons, causing the screens around the Theater to dissolve into static. By my side towards the front of the crowd, I watched Yusuf's lips move—*Earth, the Solar System, the Milky Way, the Local Interstellar Cloud*—as he fell back into his ordering.

"We got word from the Nations border that a couple of civilian vehicles blew past," Kaori said. "It's just idiots with torches and pitchforks who don't like when other kids on the playground have toys that they don't."

"How many?" someone at the front of the crowd shouted.

Another white coat leaned towards Yusuf and whispered, with me close enough that I heard something about perimeter cams.

"The security detail is rolling out," Kaori said. "They'll stop our visitors before they get anywhere close."

"And if they don't?"

The most vocal defector was Xin Gomez, one of the three aides who always trotted at Kaori's heels like trained hypoallergenic dogs. I knew that we'd beefed up security since Kaori rolled the Envisioner out of the closet. But this place was still a research lab, not a military base—a fact she'd used to trumpet as a strength because their decisions weren't made by men in uniforms who got stiffies off a little power play.

"We've done the evac drills," Kaori said. "Those who don't want to stay and secure the Theater can take the tunnels to the bunker and wait out an emergency pickup. Reinforcements are on their way. More security drones are already lifting off." She paused, and I could see in her eyes that she was holding back. "But the timing will be tight."

I watched this all from faraway, through a pair of binoculars as I drifted through a frigid sea on a sledge of ice. Shivering, and with hope shrinking away. I had to jam up the courage to look at the tattoo down my thumb to remind myself. YOU ARE HERE.

"And the box? We roll it out through the tunnels?" Xin challenged.

"There are a dozen barriers between the Theater and the front door," Kaori said. "Locked gates. Foot-thick reinforced steel. The safest spot on the continent is behind these walls."

And here, fate scooped up the dice, winking at the challenge with a cooed *oh, honey.*

The white coat by Yusuf broke off and darted to a panel on one of the walls.

"We've got them on satellite," the guy said.

Another one of the screens over the Envisioner shifted to a feed of ants crawling the red desert. He zoomed in on the ants to show that they were actually a fleet of pickups and some squat tank with a roof-mounted gun at the lead. Another wave came into view, through clouds of red dust. Then another.

Civilians with pitchforks my ass. That was an armed militia.

———

Captain Kaori was going down with her ship—she didn't say that exactly, but she was staying in the Theater. Yusuf too. I wasn't going to high-tail it outta there and leave him behind. He knew that and was smart enough not to push.

More than ever, I was sure that the footage of the riot I'd seen in Figueiredo's universe—where he and Tiago chatted in his office before running the halls—was a premonition.

Someone cranked the gravity way, way up in the glass fishbowl of the Compound. Whatever drill sergeant who had dumped the latest hit of adrenaline into my bloodstream had officially hopped into the driver's seat. I was on autopilot, watching my own body move like it was Figueiredo's on screen. Barely in control of myself but somehow keeping my shit together. I only saw Kaori's hands shake once while she unlocked a supply closet by her office before the staff escaped into the tunnels. She reached in and shoved a dozen handguns at whoever would take one. She kept one for herself and stuck it into the waistband of her pants at the small of her back, under her lab coat. Assault rifles had been banned a century ago, though a few black market high-capacity magazine guns were still out there, passed like heirlooms from mouth-breathing anti-government doomsday prepper parents to their kids. As rare as guns were, Kaori wasn't stupid and wouldn't have stranded us here without any defenses.

My feet clunked on the tiles below me, cement-shoed. Jesus. This was really happening.

"Go to the box!" Kaori snapped at me.

She brought me back down to myself. White coats whipped past me as I sprinted back to the Theater and ran my hands spirit-board style over the machine. Begging.

————

I held two scenes in my head, and they wanted to blur together.

```
SCENE A - INT. FIGUEIREDO'S OFFICE - EVENING

Tiago pops into his husband's office to
mention he's going off-campus to grab dinner,
and does Figueiredo want to come? But of
course he's blabbing like always to his
journal and he waves Tiago over, pointing
to the camera like come and say hi. They
catch up a bit about their days until someone
knocks at the door and bursts in with news
that one of the techs is going nuts and
trying to lock the rest of the staff out of
the control room. Soon, the three of them
pound through the hallways on their way to
the Bridge - past the dozen barriers, locked
gates, and foot-thick hepta-carbon walls - to
get to the machine. But the Bridge door won't
close, even with Figueiredo slamming his
badge at the reader and stabbing the buttons
of a control panel. Unless this was a trap
all along. Someone appears in the doorway
but Tiago shoots before the other man has a
chance to even lift his gun.

SCENE B - ENVISIONER INITIATIVE THEATER -
EARLY MORNING

Me, Yusuf, and Kaori hover by the Envisioner
in the dead silence. Kaori snarls into her
```

radio, with no answer from the other end.
A blurry black mass approaches the clear
glass door of the Theater. When they're
close enough, I can see that a goggled man
in black is anchoring Xin to his chest with
an arm around her throat. He levels a gun
at the three of us, separated by the glass
door until Xin weakly raises her hand to open
the door with her badge. Already her face is
turning purple as her other hand claws at the
arm around her neck.

No hostage demands or bargains. The man
doesn't speak before he raises his gun and
shoots Yusuf in the chest before Kaori can
fire a round. I collapse to the ground over
Yusuf, screaming and jamming my hands over
his wound, blood already seeping through
the cracks between my fingers. Shouting and
begging. *No no no no.* And *jesus there's so, so
much blood.* Kaori misses and shoots the wall,
but it's enough to rattle the guy into shoving
Xin at us. Kaori recovers, whipping her arms
to the side, and she shoots him in the side
of the neck. He crumples to the ground.

Everything arced in bolts of lightning across my brain. In the
machine gun rattle of my heart and the bullet wound that I could
swear was leaking blood out of my chest, exactly where Yusuf
got shot in the vision. The scenes were like the projection of my
doc on the wall that I'd shown him. Except I couldn't figure out
which was the trick of the light and which was the wall.

Do you know how long it takes for a grenade to blow after you've pulled the pin?

I don't know, either. But years back, the crowd in the gay bar in Ukraine where I'd been filming spilled out into the street once the police rammed down the door. I'd watched a flash-bang grenade hit the glass-strewn pavement and time had stopped for an instant when the steel canister had bounced by my foot. I didn't have time to think, I just wound up and kicked the thing back and watched the line of police with their riot shields and flak armor scatter.

I don't know how long I was cemented in front of the Envisioner with my eyes closed, only that when I opened them, the last of the other white coats were gone. Only me, Yusuf, and Kaori, now. The game pieces falling into place.

Yusuf's wide eyes beamed like a lighthouse at my side. He looked so brittle that I could snap him at the waist.

"What do you see?" Kaori snapped, which seemed to yank him back to Earth.

"They're—they're inside," Yusuf muttered, blinking down at the tablet she'd handed them. "I'm picking them up on security footage in the main artery."

"Vasquez," Kaori snapped into her belt radio. "Where are you? Did you make it to the bunker?" Her narrowed eyes hit mine. "Did you get anything from the box?"

"Not yet."

A weird calm frosted over me, like the second that the grenade had rolled to me and I knew what to do. I turned back to the Envisioner, hands planted on the facets, and sucked in a breath. We still had time.

The door to the Theater hissed open.

Hands on the Envisioner, me and the machine were one circuit, with electricity sparking between us. I didn't ask the machine. I told it. *Save Yusuf.* The command was a knife jamming through the machine's faceted armor into whatever unknown *thing* waited in the center. I could almost hear the box groan under the stress—beams and armor flexing and grinding—like I warped it into doing something it was never supposed to.

What's *supposed*, Yusuf would ask, shrugging off fates and plans. For a second the whole world free-fell under my feet. That instant of liftoff in the plane that brought me here, vaulting into the sky for the first time with Yusuf at my side.

Snap.

The gunshot was a thick cable splitting, the soundwaves warped like I was diving underwater. Everything slowed into a disaster-movie crawl that saw every brick of a building smashed to dirt, every windowpane disintegrated into fairy dust. By the time the waves of the gunshot rolled past, my head was clear again. I was back in the Theater, my hands still crammed against the machine, until my legs gave out and I hit the floor.

When I opened my eyes, they were level with the unblinking blue eyes of the man who'd barged in here. A thin trickle of blood leaked from a hole in his forehead, where Yusuf—from the look of his arms still outstretched and holding the gun—had shot him between the eyes, and he'd crumpled to the floor.

Xin tittered away from the body and screamed.

19
OBSERVATION EFFECT

The AC had gone on the fritz one weekend early in our days here and my *Quantum Mechanics for Dumbasses* tutoring. The room had smelled of us—of sweat, and spit, and musk. Yusuf had hopped off the bed with its sweat-slicked sheets and scooped up a stray T-shirt to wipe the pearly beads from the hair that trailed down his stomach. The lamp on his bedside table had turned the room into a kids' shadow puppet theater, projecting a huge version of him onto the ceiling.

"You're telling me that if we leave this room and shut the door and there's no one looking at this…" I'd glanced around. "This *lamp,* that it stops being a lamp?"

Alright, I may have been purposely trying to work him up.

"You know I'm not saying that," he'd said. "A lamp is not a quantum event."

"Then refresh my memory, doc."

"Particles are clouds of probabilities that—"

"The wave function," I'd offered. "See, I've been taking notes."

"Right. Do you want me to finish?"

"Yeah."

"Observation is… is a violent action that collapses the wave function in the instant of—"

"People observing is what makes the particles actually real."

"No, no. Think of it as measurement instead of observation. Or something knocking into something else. Nothing about magic, nothing about consciousness making reality."

I'd listened to him talk for a while about the outcomes of this experiment or that one, proving his point and doodling on the windows like he'd loved to. What had stuck with me the most, though, was observation as violence. Collapsing wave-functions and squashing possibilities. *I'm just here observing,* I'd said more than once with my camera in hand at some place where people hadn't wanted me to be.

There are things I observed that didn't make sense, the day of the attack, after the security staff hauled away the body of the black-clad intruder with his new forehead bullet hole and mopped the blood off the floor. After the news that the security drones and reinforcements had robbed the armada of their weapons and kicked them out far into the desert. I didn't ask about the casualties. Panic bled into a slow drip of hours with Yusuf in his bedroom, kissing the knuckles of his steady hands, asking him again and again, are you okay? He said he was fine—if not surprised by how *fine* he felt—and I told him I'd have done the same. Why feel guilty about shooting someone who had a gun pointed at your head?

The *hows* and *whys* niggled me. How did Yusuf get the gun? How did Yusuf, a Ph.D. not a sniper, shoot the guy clean in the forehead without harming Xin? Why did things turn out different than what the Envisioner seemed to tell me would happen, and what did it have to do with whatever *connection*, whatever spark I'd felt when I'd pushed at the machine with my mind? All this building up into static that kept me awake late into the night, eyes pinned to the ceiling.

Kaori, again. *But at the same time, here we are.*

After Yusuf fell asleep, I slid out of bed and looked down at him. The bow of his parted lips. The hairs over his crossed forearms. The two lines between his knit eyebrows, like he was pouting even in sleep. I moved like a ghost, careful not to wake him, as I shrugged into my clothes and wandered back to the Compound.

No Kaori by the Envisioner. No other staff around—she must've given them the day off after the whole fleeing for your life thing. There was already talk of adding dozens more armed security posts in a wide perimeter or moving to a new location altogether. Until then, I traced the invisible thread to the glass door of Kaori's office, finding her sitting at her desk with a cup of tea. Just like old times.

"Can't sleep?" I asked, plopping onto the stiff-backed chair across from her desk after she waved me in.

"Not after today. You?"

"My brain won't shut off."

"How's Yusuf?"

"He's fine. Sleeping like the dead. *Ouch.* I didn't mean to—jesus, given what happened…"

"What happened is he saved us."

"I know. I had no idea he was such a crack shot. Good thing you tossed him your gun."

Her brown eyes, ringed in gold, narrowed slightly. "What do you mean my gun?"

"You had the gun when I turned to the Envisioner. And when I looked back, he did."

"Hayes, I never had a gun. I was watching the security footage on my tablet and trying to remotely lock doors to trap the intruders the whole time we were in the Theater."

My throat ached from whatever brick I'd swallowed. The rough weight of it sank deeper into my gut.

"Do you have the footage from the attack?"

"I'll pull it up."

I scooted around the desk next to her and she pulled up the Theater security footage with me, her, and Yusuf clustered by the Envisioner before the attack. Everything about that moment was still burned into my brain—my hands on the machine, Yusuf shifting on his feet by me—since I'd been replaying it all night in my head. What didn't make sense was how, on the screen, Yusuf held the gun and not Kaori. After a minute of tense stillness, something flashed across the screen.

"What was that?" I asked.

"Must be some dust across the camera."

Dust, my ass. Except that exact moment was probably when I pushed at the machine—or whatever it was that I did—with my mind.

In the footage, the intruder barged in with Xin as his shield. Then Yusuf raised his arm in one fluid motion and the barrel of the gun in his hand sparked to life. But his sudden sharp-shooting didn't make sense. I asked Kaori to show me the hallway footage from earlier that night, when she'd opened the surprise artillery closet and handed out the guns, toting one herself. In the footage she played for me, the Kaori of the past handed a gun to Yusuf and took a tablet from him instead.

My heartbeat soared at the sides of my neck. I flashed back to opening my eyes after I'd crumpled to the floor of the Theater. The vacant blue stare of the dead man on the gleaming white tiles.

"You okay?" she asked. "You look green."

"Yeah."

"I can play it again?"

"No, I'm good."

"We had a riot here, just like in Figueiredo's universe. History does tend to repeat itself."

"I guess."

Only when I was out of the Compound and onto the painted green concrete outside did I let my brain form the thoughts of what I'd known, somehow, since the Envisioner crackled under my hands. The machine showed me that Yusuf would die in the attack, but I changed it. With all the threads, with all the possibilities of what would happen the instant that the man in black with the gun burst through the Theater door, I flung us over into another possibility. I hadn't *just* changed the future events by making a gun appear in Yusuf's hand. I'd somehow changed the recent past so that what I'd wanted to happen—what I'd willed the Envisioner to *make* happen—would be what happened all along.

My head was crammed with hypotheticals and parallel threads and fucked tenses. Of course all that was batshit crazy. As crazy as an alternate version of myself creating a magic machine and sending it on over from another universe.

Proof. I needed proof.

Honestly, the weirdest part of what had happened was when I turned around on the green concrete before even stepping foot into my house to head back to the empty Footage Farm and watch the video of the riot in Figueiredo's universe. Kaori's little *history repeats itself* ditty wasn't some off-hand comment. She didn't do off-hand. She was telling me, *check Figueiredo's footage, you dolt.*

She's so brilliant it's scary, looking back now.

I get how people like Yusuf and the others are brilliant on, like, a theoretical or experimental level—their brains can spin calculations or imagine universes with ten dimensions folded in on each other. To Kaori, this entire world is her lab and all of us are just variables she can tinker with in her experiments. She sees our weaknesses and histories—*I can play on his vanity issues here or her mommy issues there*—and knows how to mold us. How to use her scalpel to splice in the right scenes in the film reel.

I followed her thread to the farm, where I played the footage from Figueiredo's riot. I'd seen it a million times before. Except this time, the man in black pulled a gun and shot Tiago dead.

I've got some ideas. But since I'm not a scientist with any experimental evidence to back me up—though Yusuf cracked himself up with "Which means now you should publish a paper on the topic and try to get it cited"—you have to bear with me.

What if the footage we'd seen of Figueiredo's universe were not recordings of the past, like we figured. Maybe they were future predictions or simulations from the Envisioner. Or maybe the past isn't as solid as we think.

What if certain events between our universes are linked? Entangled—I might want to borrow and completely oversimplify a fancy physics topic while Yusuf looks on patiently and decides whether he should correct me or just let me run with this until I get too confused or bored. What if it was never set in stone who would die during the parallel attacks on our parallel Compounds? Just that Yusuf or Tiago had to, for whatever reason. For balance, even with Figueiredo and me flipping off the multiverse and pushing our thumbs on the scales every now and then. When I saved Yusuf,

I unintentionally dropped the guillotine on Tiago, but the net outcome between the two of them was the same.

Like our universes were each one side of the same coin. *Heads or tails, whose love is going to die?*

I'm going to fast-forward a few days of self-doubt and creeping out of bed to look at my hands and stare at myself in the mirror of the dim bathroom. Wondering what I was becoming while cold anxiety sweat dripped from my armpits. We're short on time.

Kaori found out that the militia had kidnapped and tortured a junior staff member on weekend leave until he'd coughed up the location of the Compound, and then the militarized mouthbreathers had used the evacuation tunnels to barge through the gates. All off-Compound leave was canceled. Goodbye, margarita club.

She, of course, knew the militia was coming and left the back gate open for them. Knocking all the pieces into place so I would connect with the Envisioner and she could test if her experiment worked, but I'm getting ahead of myself. Please see previous notes re: Kaori pulling all the strings.

I waited two days to tell Yusuf. I couldn't avoid him because it would've been too selfish after he literally killed a man to save us. But I knew I wasn't myself around him until we were sitting on his bed by the open window, and I was running my thumbs along his palms.

"Hayes," he began slowly, and with the way he knit his brows together I could tell he was trying hard not to offend me. "We both saw the footage from Figueiredo's riot and saw that his husband died. That's what's always happened."

"No, it's not. I *remember* when I showed you before that he lived. Remember? You joked and said something about how you were glad he wasn't dead."

"I get that you're confused but..." Yusuf trailed. "You're saying that you changed our future and that altered Figueiredo's past? How does that... work?"

The film that I saw from the other world was already becoming hazy, like my brain wanted me to forget what had really happened. Threads and storylines crossing and tangling up.

"I'm saying I know it sounds absolutely batshit crazy, but it's the machine. We know Figueiredo could connect to it. We saw him sending fleets of machines to tons of different universes." I tried to keep my words slow and even. "What if, just like he does, I connected to whatever powers the thing? And used it to... *do* something?"

Yusuf waited a long time before answering, drawing his shoulders up and down with his steady breaths. I could see the battle behind his eyes. All the evidence suggested that I'd had an aneurysm, but something made him want to believe me.

"I've heard you say things about M-Theory or whatever," I said. "Get theoretical with me. Please. *Anything.* What could've happened?"

Okay, so, hypothesis. Tossing it over to Yusuf.

Suppose that the Envisioner could understand the state of every bit of matter in the universe—impossible but remember we're supposing—and use that to accurately predict—can't say *predict* but more like map out—the only possible events of every action, down to electrons bouncing off each other. Suppose that the only way it's possible to change a mapped event is to actually subsume—

that means, like, absorb, Hayes—another universe where the event happened the way you wanted it.

This is assuming that every possible history of every universe exists simultaneously, and new ones don't branch off for every infinite outcome of every possible quantum event. I mean, maybe the Envisioner somehow violates the laws of thermodynamics and the law of conservation of mass as we know them because the system is no longer closed—that is, the Envisioner blasts open the barriers between universes and maybe lets matter and energy flow between—sorry, sorry, I'm just thinking out loud.

Yeah. What?

Okay. If universes are different threads, maybe when you pushed at the Envisioner, or—what'd you call it? When the Envisioner *blinked,* you made this universe absorb another one where the only outcome of the riot was that Kaori handed me the gun, I shot the intruder, and I lived.

Yeah, but how is that different from us using intel from the Envisioner to stop that attack in Cape Town?

Because we followed the laws of physics to stop the bus bombing. We put troops on the ground. We didn't just make the attack disappear. If you pushed the Envisioner and said, "Make me fly," maybe this universe becomes another one where people have wings on their backs, or maybe a precise gravitational wave hits the Earth localized around you and you float for a second. I don't know. The key is, how does this work without violating laws of physics?

That was a lot of *maybes* for Yusuf.

He scooted off his bed and paced the room while he talked. I couldn't think of anything else to say. No words, no stupid jokes. Arms folded behind my head on his pillows, I just let his words calm me down while the goofy half-smile slipped up my lips. After our trip to the observatory, he'd told me he thought he loved me. While I watched him pace, head-down, from the window to the other side of the bed and back again, over and over, throwing out everything he'd ever learned and rewriting laws of nature just to work out a way to believe me—that's when I knew he really did.

20
THE FOOL

After the theories, I let Yusuf get some sleep while I wandered to the Footage Farm before sunrise. Hoping to find some sense with the mapped-out marker-board timelines of Figueiredo's life. I was alone in the grayscale room for a few minutes before the lights cracked to life and I jumped in my chair to see Kaori at the door.

"Have a minute?" she said.

"Yeah. What's up?"

She was still wearing her same wrinkled white button-down shirt and black slacks from the day before. She walked from the doorway and handed me a paper that had been folded down the middle, its sides slightly crinkled from what must've been the heat from her hands.

"Does this mean anything to you?" she asked.

Back to her asking questions that she already knew the answer to, like the first time we met.

I looked down on the paper to read *Superflu, age 43.*

"Not really. Do I have to guess?"

She crossed her arms, the light of my screen casting shadows on her face.

"Did you... *do* something to the Envisioner, Hayes, during the attack?"

She handed me an anvil and nudged me off a cliff with the way my stomach dropped.

"How about you cut the questions and just tell me what happened."

I trotted at her side on the way to her office like one of her trained white coats while she filled me in. She'd been working on some Envisioner calibrations, asking it all the usual questions, and when she asked the machine how she'd die, again—and that still completely weirded me out—she said the answer had changed. Goodbye, embolism at age 68. According to the box she now had a year to live, give or take a few months.

Not just her, either. Close to three billion around the world, thanks to the ease of international travel and open borders and the potency of some virus that won't want to die even in the face of all the drugs that governments will throw at it.

Wildfires raged deep in my guts, burning me from the inside out.

"I think I connected to the machine and told it to change the future it predicted," I said.

"What do you mean *connected to*?"

"Like—*talked* to it. Maybe like Figueiredo would," I told her. "It said that Yusuf was going to die in the attack. And then I told it to save him."

"Well, can you tell it to send a plague that wipes out a quarter of humanity somewhere else?"

"I can try."

Kaori scattered the few researchers in the Theater with a curt *leave,* and when we were alone again, she pointed to the Envisioner.

I didn't need to be told. I pressed my hands against the facets by one of the screens and closed my eyes, reaching out with my mind. I tried to empty my head and find some after-yoga stillness, but that's like telling yourself not to think about oranges and now all you can picture is a giant orange rolling down a rocky incline at you. I didn't feel any of the threads nearby, vibrating like possibilities, only the cool facets of the box.

"It's not like I'm flicking a light switch," I said. "Before it was life-or-death."

Her annoyed sigh into her two-way radio rustled like the air-conditioning vents above. "Would somebody please get Dr. Hassan here?"

I'd like to think a lot of our time together was genuine because Kaori liked that I didn't give a shit about her genius and was more into her detached sense of humor and the way she'd honk like a like a goose with laughter when her mask slipped off. I know the same receptors in her brain that calculated the world in a trillion undulating points of data also blunted her emotions, but I really do remember seeing her smile at me and Yusuf during some margarita club night when she could tell she didn't get some in-joke or look shared between us. She seemed happy for us, really.

Which is why it was even more of a surprise that she pulled a gun.

She said something to me about just needing to pop out for a second, and when she came back it was with Yusuf and two of her lapdogs, the four of them catching up like just another normal morning-shift debrief. Meanwhile I was still toeing the ground with my hands on the Envisioner, feeling for the invisible threads that didn't want to vibrate for me. Yusuf nodded a business-casual good morning to me like an hour ago our naked bodies weren't all wrapped up on his bed.

"Yusuf, would you mind helping Hayes with something?" Kaori asked, as casual as if she wanted the two of us to move a planter in her office.

"Sure."

Then, like a Renaissance painting, I stood by the faceted spider of the Envisioner with Yusuf at my side, and Kaori across from us with her backup, when she reached to the small of her back, pulled out a gun, and leveled it at Yusuf's head.

"What the *fuck*, Kaori?" I snapped.

Yusuf just kind of tipped his head like a dog saying, *huh?*

"Would somebody like to tell me what's going on here?" he asked with more calm than I've ever felt in my life.

"Sorry, Yusuf," she said, over the murmurs of her staff behind her. "I know this is abrupt. I'm just trying to inspire Hayes to do me a solid here and avoid an apocalypse."

"Hayes?" Yusuf asked.

"Nutshell: I changed the future with the Envisioner or something, and now a plague is wiping out a few billion people in a year."

"Huh," he breathed.

"Hayes said he only felt inspired enough when there was a gun pointed at you yesterday," she said, almost bored, now, "so here we are."

"I'd really like if you pointed that away from me, Kaori," Yusuf said.

"Don't worry, there is no way she's actually going to shoot you," I said, camouflaging the panic with fake cool.

"I would prefer not to," she said, "but you are absolutely wrong in assuming that I won't kill one man to save billions."

"I thought we were friends," I said.

"If we were, then you'd understand why I have to do this."

I faced away from them, back to the machine, and squeezed my eyes shut. Trying to drown out the *fuck fuck oh jesus fuck* voice that wouldn't shut up. Willing for a spark, for *anything*, but the thing only felt dead under my palms.

"I can't," I said, turning back to them. "Yesterday I could *feel* the machine, like it was alive. Now it... it's just a machine."

Hands still outstretched, Kaori shifted the gun just a few inches to the right and squeezed the trigger, shooting one of the big screens that ringed the Theater. The noise slammed me back into myself, away from the whitewater rapids of panic.

Yusuf stood absolutely still—which made me love him more—not even flinching.

"The next one is in his shoulder," she said. "You have three seconds."

"Fuck off," I said.

"I'll consider that later, when this is done. That's two seconds left."

I had to try. I slammed my hands on the machine, pressed my forehead against it, and gritted my teeth. *Come on you motherfucker, light up.* I pushed at it, slammed with my whole mind and heart because I really did know that when Kaori said blowing Yusuf away to save billions would mean nothing to her, she meant it.

I told him that I needed his vision, she told me of bringing him here. *I told him I needed his help to change the world.* Traitor.

And just for an instant, I could feel the threads of probabilities, of other universes, stretching out in all directions, with the Envisioners that Figueiredo dropped in—the hundreds of them—connecting each thread like a knot. One glowing spider web that spread out forever and forever. *One second.* The box felt like a part of myself, another body part I never knew I had. I slammed at the strings with my thoughts again. *Keep Yusuf safe. Send the virus away.* I heard the crack of the gunshot, just like before. Except—no—I didn't hear it so much as I *felt* it, like one of the strings the box was connected to had snapped under the pressure of my hands.

Plane turbulence bowled over me. I sagged against the side of the machine. Yusuf moved in a blur to my side and propped me up. Kaori must've felt something in the room, too, some ear-popping shift in the atmosphere, with the way her lips parted and she lowered her gun.

"It's done," I wheezed.

Yusuf's breath was warm in my ear.

"Good," she said.

"What, I don't even get a thank you?"

"Let's check for sure before we start celebrating how you fixed a problem that *you* caused."

I found my feet underneath me and stood up on my own. "If you think we're going back to normal after you pointed a gun at us, you're out of your fucking mind."

Kaori sighed. "I understand your—"

"Don't even," Yusuf snapped.

She pressed her lips together, her hands on her hips—her problem-solving face I'd seen a million times—and turned to her staff, ignoring me and Yusuf.

"Would you please show them to an open dorm while I work with the machine?"

The two men, each inches shorter than both me and Yusuf with their thin frames hidden in billowy lab coats, shared a glance. We could throw down if we needed to, I knew. When I'd been arrested after that douche at Genesis's bar had called her a slur and I'd slugged him, the guy had had thirty pounds on me. I still managed to bust his nose. Yusuf could probably snatch both of Kaori's backup over his head at the same time and toss them clear across the room.

But there wasn't a lot of use in fighting, in giving her the chance to call her new security team with their rubber bullets and Tasers to *escort* us to wherever she wanted us to go in the first place.

I was the first to break away from the machine, to the relief of the two guys.

"This isn't over," Yusuf said when he passed Kaori.

She didn't say a word.

At least Kaori kept me and Yusuf together. No one used the word *prisoners* but what else are you gonna call it when you're led to a room and two people are posted by the door to make sure you don't leave?

"I'm really sorry, Dr. Hassan," one of the guys—Fred, I remembered—said after he opened the door to the dorm bedroom in the hotel hallway, and we all waited at the threshold like vampires before they're invited in. I guess Fred didn't mind so much about locking me up, just Yusuf.

"It's fine," Yusuf mumbled.

"I'd really like you to rethink your definition of fine," I deadpanned.

"We'll round up some water and snacks and bring them to you while you... wait," the other guy said. "And again. Uh. Sorry."

Fred shut the door behind us. Inside the little pod hotel room, I flashed back to my first day here, fumbling around with Yusuf as my only tether. I tossed myself onto the bed with a bounce, while he stood and frowned.

"What the hell is going on?" he asked.

"Kaori said the Envisioner told her that some virus is coming that's going to wipe out a quarter of humanity. She used me to change the outcome. Like what I did with you and the riot."

"I knew she'd try to use you like some lab rat," he rumbled, low. "She's the one who was all about extracting usable information from the machine predictions and now she's forgetting all of that and using you to—to snap your fingers and change things, never mind how fundamentally fucking impossible that is. Any of this. All of us are just tools to her. I knew it, even after the years with her. She fooled me. Even still, it… it…"

I could read the words in his lost eyes. *Even still, it hurts.*

"Hey, it's okay. Come back to me."

"We should've left right after the attack. I should've dragged you out of here when you told me what you did."

"I dig the hero thing, but we both know you weren't going to drag me anywhere."

"We were stupid. This was our fault."

"Don't talk like that," I said, scooting up on the bed. "We'll figure this out. Somehow."

I measured time in the steady tick of his feet as he paced the room and the finger puppets I threw on the wall in the light cast by the desk lamp. Hours could've passed by the time the first knock rattled the door.

"*Finally,*" I groaned, hauling myself off the bed and opening the door.

No bottles of water or food. Fred and the other guy escorted us back to the Theater for round two of Kaori's universal hostage negotiation.

Apparently, I'd nixed the superflu after all, but there were more dice rolls, more questions of the Envisioner, according to Kaori, who by then had left the gun-pointing to the two black-body-armor clad women from her new security detail. Now we apparently were weeks away from a nuclear war that would irradiate all of Eastern Eurasia for tens of thousands of years. I connected to the machine, after a little inspiration from one of the security guards who dragged Yusuf from my side and socked him in the stomach. Then back to our room again while we waited.

A continent-cleaving earthquake. A shudder deep in the Indian Ocean that sends tsunamis all over the world, knocking out coastal cities and drowning island nations. Each of these disasters might as well have been my fault with the way that I held two thoughts in my head, each time I touched the machine. *Stop whatever's coming. But keep Yusuf safe.*

You've heard of the butterfly effect, right? The idea of consequences—how a butterfly flapping its wings can set events in motion that'll cause a hurricane in another hemisphere. This is more like the pterodactyl effect. I summoned a huge dinosaur out of nowhere, and now it's flying around a city with its huge fucking wings and crashing into bridges and toppling skyscrapers.

On our fourth visit to the Theater, I was so drained that my hands were limp against the Envisioner's facets until one of the guards lurched forward and jammed a Taser into Yusuf's shoulder. He slumped against me, heaving breaths, his head lolling to the side as I held him up.

"I know what you're doing," Kaori said, her blank face calm even with me screaming and swearing at her, even with her staff mumbling to each other like *maybe we should say something.* "Stop being so goddamned selfish. Tell him or I will. At least let him be the one to make the choice."

Yusuf couldn't have heard her, with the way he leaned into me, sucking in air and blinking away the sparks in his eyes. The unknown metal of the machine sizzled under my palms when I connected to it again, each time easier than before. Like a muscle I was learning to flex. Each time, the wispy threads that I could almost touch felt more solid.

"I have no idea what you mean," I said.

I shoved away from the machine, flung Yusuf's arm over my neck and half-carried him back to the room.

Alright, I may have had some idea of what she meant.

Yusuf slumped down on the bed and I followed him, giving in to the doubt for a few minutes, the thoughts that followed me since I'd watched the footage of Tiago's death and when Kaori had told me about the plague. Each knock on the door of this tiny room brought with it a new apocalypse that cemented my doubt. All of this was my fault. By saving Yusuf, somehow, I'd messed up what was *supposed* to happen. I'd jammed my thumb in the big multiverse loom, knotting-up and snapping threads, the shockwaves reaching out farther than I could ever imagine. Figueiredo obviously didn't care about any other reality except for his own, with the way he mailed Envisioners off, to hell with the consequences.

Maybe we were more alike than I wanted to admit.

Kaori's words just confirmed everything. *Tell him or I will. At least let him be the one to make the choice.* All this was happening because I wouldn't let him go. So why didn't she just kill him and spare us this torture?

Unless she didn't know everything and wasn't as smart as she thought. Either way, no chance that I was just going to let him die.

Each time she dragged us into the Theater she was giving me another chance to learn how to connect to the faceted box. The nonverbal commands flowing out of my head, down my arms, and into the machine, like with a scratch between the ears I could get it to do whatever I wanted. *Sit, stay. Heel.* How to connect our Envisioner to another universe where Figueiredo had also shoved an Envisioner, with the machines linked and calling out to each other. Everything was connected—Yusuf was right.

The other universes were strings I could feel each time I touched the Envisioner. Each with a certain tension, like they'd give off different notes if I plucked them, with different colors that I could practically taste in some sensory mashup. And whatever fabric the universes were made of—whatever barrier separated them felt flimsy, almost like I could punch through if I tried hard enough. All these things I was beginning to feel even though I'd probably never really be able to understand.

"We can't keep doing this," Yusuf said.

I could barely hear the tired puff of his voice even though he was inches from me on the narrow bed. As much as I needed the practice, I hated putting him at the wrong end of the barrel of a gun each time we were in the Theater. And it would stop soon enough. I threaded his fingers with mine.

"I know. I've got a plan to get us out of here."

"How do you figure we'll get past security and haul it to the garage and break into a car and..." He trailed, jolting up on one elbow. "Wait. Wait. You're joking," he said, his giddy voice saying *please tell me you're not joking* at the same time.

I mean, of course he'd figure things out before I even had to tell him. I couldn't say much else, anyway, because I was pretty sure the room was bugged and Kaori was listening in.

"You want to go exploring?"

"Oh, fuck yes."

So we waited for the next knock.

21
BREAKTHROUGH

I've got a theory about how we're even in this mess.

Sure, it's based on one of the marker-board *The Alternate World* plotlines from one of my Footage Farm coworkers, but let's call it *collaboration* instead of *plagiarism*.

In all the footage from Figueiredo's universe that we'd seen, there seemed to be a giant patch of time missing. Unless it didn't exist.

We called his early journals—the ones of him blabbing into his camera in his basement lab—the Basement Records. Creative, I know. In the videos, Figueiredo was gray and full-faced. He looked both older and younger, minus the lines by his eyes, and with the rounder face of someone who'd physically given up around middle age. We had hundreds of hours of him scribbling equations and explaining them to the camera, and welding panels of gray metal to other panels of gray metal in a showering, glowing rain all over his basement lab. Then he tested little gray machines that had a habit of sparking fires, sending him running around with a fire extinguisher and whooping like a goofball scientist on a kids' show. *Hey kids, sometimes when you shatter the barriers between realities, you can make a mess! Remember to get your parents' permission first.*

Then Tiago showed up in the Basement Records and started helping Figueiredo, who then completed what must've been his prototype Envisioner. They flicked on the machine and ran some tests that me and the others didn't understand, and they must've worked with how much Tiago and Figueiredo celebrated. All leading up to a kiss, bumbling in front of the machine and suddenly shy, after cresting some mountain between them that they'd been slogging up for weeks.

The next footage we'd been able to place in chronological order must've been years after he completed the prototype, based on context clues from the setting and how Figueiredo looked. From a cramped research lab in a university basement to a wide facility that looked like the hangar of a space station. Light from the walls of machinery and screens flooded his face, with cables snaking to the Envisioner, and the databanks where worker-bee researchers droned with tablets and video cameras.

Then another patch of missing time, suddenly they're in a bigger facility with even more staff, all of them in sage-green lab coats. Figueiredo looked leaner, hungry-eyed, and harder. Like he'd turned his welding torch onto his own skin—sparks flying— to become some version of himself that could complete his work.

Sometimes you might see a light flash across the footage, but it could've just been your eyes.

But what if there aren't actually any patches of time missing and Figueiredo blinked his kingdom into existence overnight? The lab. His staff and his power over them. The hard angles of his face in place of the doughy doubt.

Maybe Projectionist Kaori, on her break outside smoking and flicking butts onto the cracked pavement behind her booth at Hayes's Disaster Drive-In, knows all this. How Figueiredo discovered an energy source that powers the machine by collapsing probability clouds down into whatever outcome he wants. How he can change his world by warping probabilities with his hands on the Envisioner, his eyes closed as if in prayer.

I can drive myself crazy wondering about this and whatever horrors Figueiredo sent our way if my coin-flip idea about the relationship between our universes is right. He gave his world all the glory—miracles of science and medicine—and left ours with the shit side of the stick. Plagues instead of progress. My mom dying instead of his. The return of high-waisted pants.

But I guess it's just a theory.

In the tableau of the Theater the night that Kaori held us hostage—I could almost float above the scene and see it as a diorama with little figurines from a kid's fifth-grade history project, like *Hayes First Breaks the Universe*—the FantiSee screens above us were set to a starry sky. Me at the Envisioner with Yusuf at my side, less than an arm's length away. Kaori ten feet across from us, her bored *why are we here again* look on her face and her arms crossed, her three-person security team in body armor with guns pointed at both me and Yusuf, just for kicks.

About an hour before, Fred had knocked on the door of our dorm/prison cell and left us a tray with a couple of slices of lukewarm cafeteria pizza and bottles of water, and my stomach still churned from the taste of soggy cheese. Of course, it was probably mostly nerves.

I ran my hands along the facets of the Envisioner like I was trying to concentrate. Really, I was nervous and killing time.

Sure, I'd seen Figueiredo sending things to other universes and I knew they'd arrived intact. I mean, I was touching proof of that now. In the footage, Figueiredo's hands sometimes crossed the gateways he created, and his skin didn't bubble, or burn, or anything. What I was about to do was possible and *technically* safe. But I gave Yusuf shit about that *technically* word before. *Technically* means *I'll accidentally gate us to the bottom of an ocean.*

This or watch Yusuf die here, then throw myself at the security guards until they snuff me out too.

I closed my eyes and felt for a thread that seemed so close it almost crossed this universe at this exact moment. I tested the string with my mind and its tension felt familiar, somehow—add this to the growing list of shit I can't explain. I knew I had to open a gateway to someplace similar, with breathable air, with gravity that wouldn't rip us to confetti when we stepped through. The thread *felt* right as I tried to steady my breathing, wrestling myself down from a panic attack.

I thought of my mom. I know that sounds weird. Genesis pushed me to go to a couple group therapy sessions after my mom had died, the sight of her gray and frail, and the oxygen tube snaking from her nostrils following me when I closed my eyes. "Don't remember them as they died. Remember them as they lived," the counselor had said between sobs and sniffles from us griefbags. We'd been in my mom's home—the house where I grew up in South Boston—and the home hospice nurse came to get me from the kitchen where I'd been making coffee. *It's time.* I'd waited by my mom's bedside for hours and talked to her, trying hard not to be a mess but mostly failing. My mom had looked at me as her last breaths rattled through her and told me, "It's okay, *querido.*" Even when she was dying, she was more concerned about me, the one who'd been beyond terrible to her when I was a kid and had spent years and years trying to be better.

I knew she'd fought as hard as she could and that *it's okay* had been for her, too. Sometimes you have to give in and let whatever's going to happen just happen. And maybe there's some peace in surrender.

I tried to borrow a little bit of her strength whenever I was making myself sick over something stupid. Or wallowing about how life was sprinting past me all because I wasn't who I'd thought I'd be by now.

I opened my eyes, trying to float through a still pond of memories of my mom, turned my head away from the Envisioner, and grabbed Yusuf's shoulder.

What I love the most is that I was actually able to surprise Kaori. Maybe she thought I'd eventually fall in line after she paraded a million disasters in front of me, or that I wasn't stupid enough to do what I did. Or she thought my little filmmaker brain couldn't possibly understand how the whole network of Envisioners was connected, or she didn't realize how much of the machine and Figueiredo's work I'd be able to understand just by communing with the device.

I guess what I'm saying is that even the C-squad can ace a science quiz once in a while. It's all probability.

I could feel the barrier between this universe and the one I'd found vibrating like the rainbow-swirled skin of a giant bubble. I pushed through with my mind and, with the *sploosh* of a stone tossed into a pond, a shimmery *thing* appeared under my palm across the surface of the Envisioner—a small circle with glowing gold edges that rippled and expanded until it was just big enough for us to crawl through. Just like what had happened in the video I'd seen of Figueiredo sending off the machines.

For a second, I thought, *oh.* Like an almost blasé, *this looks surprisingly normal.* In a time-warping slow instant of realization, it looked like the picture in my eyes of this reality suddenly had a three-foot wide window into Somewhere Else—a room not that different from this one—sliced into it. Which I guess is what pretty much had happened.

Kaori's mouth dropped open into a silent *no*.

I yanked Yusuf and we both tumbled backwards through the window before the gunshots cracked the air.

In the movie version of this story, Yusuf and I will tumble through a wide, black expanse that's filled with glowing spider webs. Like stained glass windows, the scenes of all our possible futures together fill in the spaces between the glowing threads. The special effects team will really blow a chunk of the film's budget. Scenes of us fighting in the rain and getting married under a flowered canopy on a beach. Scenes of us crossing each other on the street, never even looking up, and leaving each other's lives as strangers. In one image, spun from light, we watch the sunset on a park bench, our faces creased from decades of laughter, our wizened hands interlaced.

But at the same time, here we are.

When really, we just fell like we tripped backwards out of an open window—just an instant of weightlessness, and then we landed on our backs on the floor. Well, me on my back. Yusuf landed on my chest with all his weight on me. Most of it on my balls. The glowing circle of the gateway zipped closed as soon as we popped through.

Yusuf rolled off me and I tried to wheeze in air against the sparks flying across my eyes. Except for the crash landing, I felt fine. Overhead, what looked like a greenhouse roof of giant panes of glass and copper girders crowned whatever building we'd landed in. He leaned over on his thighs and peeked down at me, his brown eyes goofy and dancing.

"You okay?"

"Yeah," I grunted, still on my back. Letting myself feel, for a second, the sugar-rush of giddiness because I'd actually saved us. Hopefully.

"It worked," he said. "We're here. Wherever here is, exactly. I think we're in… in… an airport? I had this theory that we'd annihilate ourselves once we touched ground here. Like, antiparticles colliding. But so far so good."

"Yeah. And I'm very glad you didn't share that idea with me beforehand."

I'd seen the doubt in his eyes every now and then about the machine, like even after all he'd seen some part of him thought that all this junk about alternate universes was a hoax. That you could theorize about different realities all you wanted, but if you couldn't get to them or otherwise prove that they were there, the theories didn't mean a ton.

"Where exactly did you send us?" he asked, squinting as he drank in the world around him.

"I'm not really sure. Just through the Envisioner to the closest universe that I could feel."

I rolled over and hauled myself to my feet. We stood in a wide indoor courtyard by this universe's Envisioner, its same hulking spidery shape casting a shadow across the industrial carpet floor of beige and burnt orange triangles. A low pool made of some clear material with jets of water spurting in timed helix patterns gurgled a ways off, in the center of the courtyard, past clusters of brown couches and waiting room chairs. Little rooms aglow with gold light ringed the courtyard. Overhead, deep copper-hued catwalks crisscrossed the air that opened multiple stories up to the greenhouse roof. Recessed lighting in the beams cast a haze of gold onto the glass, like the starry night sky beyond was drizzled with honey.

We were alone except for what must've been a family with bags and rolling suitcases who waited by the courtyard fountain. The only sound was the gurgle of water and the dull thuds as the little girl in the family bounced a ball against the floor. Until a shrieking alarm split my eardrums and I jumped out of my skin. The shrill whirring was so loud that it rattled my teeth. Yusuf's hands flew up to block his ears. An oddly soothing voice cut through the alarm. *Lockdown procedure has been initiated.*

Yusuf and I froze, since the alarm was clearly about us, if the three security guards in dark green uniforms who were sprinting our way were any clue.

"So far so good, huh?" I said.

"At least we're not dead."

"Yet."

I fought just about every instinct to run while the security guards stopped about five feet away, holding up fat black batons. Almost funny to think that I'd just stopped Yusuf from being killed only to have us get gunned down here.

"Why aren't you in the living quarters?" one of the guards said in English. "I'm going to need to see your citizen cards."

"Hold up," another said before we had a chance to sputter some bullshit. "It's…"

"No," the third guard said, her mouth falling agape.

"We're unarmed," I said. "We're just here looking for safety."

I looked to Yusuf, broadcasting *help me out here* with my eyes.

The guard closest to us unclipped a fist-sized radio from her belt. "Cut the alarms," she said into her hand, eyeing us. "You're gonna wanna see this."

———

The three security guards called in a troupe of hazmat suits who ushered me and Yusuf with cattle prod-looking things into a glass and plastic room, where other hazmat suits ignored all our questions about what was going on. I had to mostly drag Yusuf because he shut down. It was like he was in power save mode—completely dead in the face and unresponsive except for his wheezing breath when I called his name. I pressed my hands to either side of his face, whispering to him, "We're okay. We're okay."

If him mentally ghosting on me when things got intense was an indicator of things to come, I'd have to worry about keeping us both safe.

The room stank of bleach. A doctor, I figured, in another hazmat suit swabbed our arms and drew our blood—Yusuf willingly, while three of the hazmats had to come back and hold me down until I bruised because I have to make everything hard. The doctor fiddled with our vials of blood, slid them into a centrifuge, and only when the thing stopped spinning and our vials were the blue of window cleaner did she pull her mask off and sigh.

"All clear," she said into her wrist. "Dial back the lockdown."

"Where are we?" I asked her.

Turns out, we were in Oxford, England. Just not our Oxford. The three security guards with their tube gun things led us past the Envisioner in the beige and orange airport gate area and left us in a wide, book-crammed room that Yusuf said looked like his office in his Oxford. But at the same time, very much *not* his office.

He squinted at a framed picture on the wall of him in a graduation cap and gown standing with his parents. The three of them smiled, with his teeth poking through his too-tight lips because I'm sure he'd been thinking *I'm supposed to smile in pictures.*

"I've got that hanging in my office, too," he said slowly. "But the buildings behind us are all wrong." He circled the ornate wooden desk that looked like a church altar. "I just can't believe we're really in another universe."

"It feels so... *real*, right?" I asked. "I mean. I know it is. But you know what I mean."

The door opened behind us and I turned towards it, bumping into Yusuf who knocked a framed picture over on the desk.

Speaking of real, seeing two Yusufs at the same time felt very much *not*.

Yusuf—*my* Yusuf—froze by the edge of the desk, eyeing the stiff-backed man who walked in and shut the office door behind him. Their faces were riffs on the same idea. The other man was thinner, with deep lines carved into his broad forehead, hard eyes, and close-cropped hair. The face of a principal who wanted both of us to know how disappointed he was, and how he wanted us to think hard about our futures. He clasped his hands in front of his wide-lapelled, white-collared shirt and fat brown tie.

I stood so close to this familiar stranger that his frown gave me frostbite. Beside me, Yusuf swore under his breath.

"You tested negative for the virus," the other Yusuf said. "Which is wonderful news, seeing as how you barged in here. We'll get to that, by the way. But first—*when* are you from, exactly?"

"I'm sorry," Yusuf said. Even their voices sounded different, Yusuf's a softer, gold-toned tune from a brass instrument instead of a tired sandpaper scrape of his other self. "Are you saying you think we're time travelers?"

The other Yusuf pressed his lips together. He did not like being corrected.

"What else would you be? I assumed it was only a matter of time before a future version of myself was able to prove my theories."

"Time travel exists here?" I asked. "Screw this, Yusuf. Let's see some dinosaurs."

For the first time since darkening his office, the other Yusuf squinted at me like I was standing in front of a glaring light. I know I default to humor when I'm uncomfortable, which I've been told more than once is annoying, so I figured his glare at me was because of that. Or he recognized me as Figueiredo—he must've seen the video footage that came as a bonus pack along with his universe's Envisioner.

"That's a joke?" he asked Yusuf, who just shrugged, instead of looking at me.

"We're from another universe." Yusuf frowned. "As improbable as that sounds, we—"

"And how did you get here?" his double cut in.

"I hailed us a cab," I said.

His flinty eyes cut past me to the picture frame Yusuf had knocked over on the desk. He charged past us, snatched the frame, and flipped it over to inspect the glass with squinting eyes. His steady hands hovered over the picture, one thumb whispering over the face of one of the two men in matching tan suits in front of a waterfall. The face that—when I stole a glance before he gently placed the picture back on his desk, facing away from me—looked just like mine.

22
HOMECOMING

It turns out I'm dead in this universe. Bummer. I'll get to that later.

This Dr. Yusuf Hassan—who let us call him *Hassan* so he and my Yusuf wouldn't turn around every time I said their name—was born in Al-Maghrib in Northern Africa to Christian parents, who then fled religious persecution and raised him in France. He made his way as a teenager to what had once been called the United Kingdom, though by the time he enrolled at Oxford, the monarchy had been abolished, and England was now the anchor state of the United Commonwealth. He studied physics with a special focus on comparative universe sub-subatomic particle mechanics, plus he puttered around with quantum time entanglement theory in his spare time. I think I got most of that right. I tried to work my charm on Hassan but he wasn't having it. I checked out about halfway through the conversation because it was like Yusuf and I were interviewing him for a job and Hassan took us on a guided tour of his credentials, stopping just short of whipping out his diplomas.

In his universe, the Farsight—what they called the Envisioner—had been discovered in 1995 when construction workers unearthed it while digging out an extension of London's Jubilee Line underground transit system. Which meant—and here I could see Yusuf's eyes practically roll up in the back of his head in ecstasy—that based on when we'd dropped in, this Earth had enjoyed about a century-and-a-half's worth of progress thanks to the Farsight and its predictions. Plus, they'd been able to translate much of Figueiredo's language once they figured out that it was related to a distant bastard step-cousin of a branch of medieval Portuguese still spoken by a tiny pocket of people in an interior patch of Brasil. Being here was like spying on how the Envisioner would change our own universe.

Turns out Figueiredo didn't gift-wrap his devices and send them off for other Earths to benefit from his technology. He did it because a network of other devices communicating to each other through the barriers of universes—averaging laws of physics and probabilities and a million other variables—boosted the accuracy of his main machine back in his world. Hassan theorized, too, that the locations and possibly even *times* where Figueiredo dropped the machines were variables in some grand experiment. Sometimes, the machines were purposely inaccessible—tossed into deep space or at the bottom of the ocean—just there to suck in ambient data. Other times, it was like Figueiredo had wanted people to find the Envisioners, like the ways in which other civilizations used the machines was a goldmine of data about the inner workings of our little monkey brains, and he could always drop in, borrow, and improve on the technology they'd created. I mean, so long as the worlds didn't blow themselves up right after they discovered the tool.

I'd never understood how Figueiredo could afford to send off these crazy complex machines until Hassan told me how my other self basically had access to every resource in the multiverse and could just build a million more if he wanted. We were all part of his experiment, feeding data to his giant machine that he called the All-Eye, which sounded a little too much like a global surveillance system in a dystopia to me.

So much for Figueiredo, the multiverse's benefactor. He was a selfish asshole and a world discovering an Envisioner was like finding a single flea on a dog except the dog was the size of a galaxy. No matter. The societies of this Earth were able to use the device and decode some of Figueiredo's work and use it to perfect their world. A flotilla of solar panels in the Atlantic and rings of photon-sucking satellites fueled every nation with unlimited, clean energy. Towering elevators dotted the Earth to lug cargo to space stations that were like floating cities, with starliners whisking passengers to colonies on Mars.

The general public knew about the endless threads of other universes because scientists and researchers had been able to tap into the Farsight's network and take a peek at the footage other devices were recording in other worlds. They didn't think they'd ever be able to communicate with other universes, never mind travel there. Scientists had hoped to crack teleportation and faster-than-light travel, based on whatever technology Figueiredo had used to send the devices across the multiverse—probably the same that had allowed me and Yusuf to travel there—but couldn't figure out how. Large swathes of how the machine worked were still a mystery, especially what power source it ran on. The only major disaster associated with the Farsight was when a research team came up with the bright idea to strike its surface with an ion laser to see how it refracted and get an idea of what was beyond the casing. Which blew up the entire facility, killing over three hundred people. They learned pretty quickly that trying to take a peek under the hood of the machine only ended in disaster.

Hassan told us all of this while he led us on a tour of his facility on the way to the refugee dormitory, where we could stay. We were sort of refugees, after all. He hadn't pressed us on how we got there yet because he was still dick-waving the accomplishments of this world, like they were hardwood floors he'd installed in his home with his bare hands. A human life expectancy of two hundred, thanks to organ regrowth and cell-replacement therapy. Half-living mobile cities of organic glass, with buildings that could skitter out of the path of a natural disaster like a millipede running across the floor. Hunger and poverty and disease were all just about the way of the dinosaur, which they'd managed to resurrect along with some other megafauna with some gene-editing borrowed from *Jurassic Park*—which, fun fact, never existed here—just because they could.

Yusuf *hmm*'ed and asked a lot of questions. I knew that decades of studying particle physics and probabilities had made him feel a sort of detachment from one particular reality—freed him, he'd say—but I was still surprised by how chill he seemed while meeting one of his other selves. Mostly the brain-fog and exhaustion after everything that had happened over the past two hours was trying to knock me onto my ass. Given how empty the hallways were of staff, it must've been late in the evening here. The people we did see gave the three of us—twins, though one looked like he'd been in a warzone, and the other was a guy who looked like their boss's dead husband—weird looks and a wide berth.

This place had been more important, once, Hassan told us as we followed him over the beige and orange carpets, through the hallways of empty offices and wide windows that overlooked a meadow. By the time he'd taken over as Director General of the Predictive Intelligence Bureau three years ago, the organization had been past its prime. The world had wrung most of the progress it could out of the Farsight—the actual machine was on the main floor in a spot of honor by a memorial fountain for the Taceovirus victims—and was plateauing on autopilot. Networked computers around the world dialed into the Farsight for near-constant access to its predictive tech, making the initial machine a relic. The facility was mostly used for boring administrative stuff, with the Farsight occasionally fired up to compare probability discrepancies between computers for governmental business, which meant a lot of time for Yusuf to continue his research on nested universes.

Until the plague hit.

We rounded a corner to a wide carpeted area that was once probably a few conference rooms split with folding walls, now filled with six long barrack-style rows of thin cots separated by a few flimsy screens. Close to a hundred people crammed in the space—families with two kids to a bed and their parents on a nest of blankets and clothes on the floor. Single women trying to carve a slice of privacy out of the crowd by rigging up a tent of sheets around their bed. Couples sitting on the floor and eating what must've been freeze-dried provisions out of pouches, with everything they owned spilling out of backpacks next to them. What hit me first was the sound of the place—a low din of a crowded mag-train station with coughing, kids screaming, and low radios playing jangly upbeat tunes that seemed out of place.

Refugees, Hassan told us, of the Taceovirus that wiped out a third of the world's population, with no treatment still in sight. New pockets were still popping up all over disparate parts of the world. There was some evidence to suggest the virus was manmade to silence political dissidents in the wake of the Second American Civil War—the virus literally attacked the vocal cords before killing nearly all of the infected—but no definite proof just yet. And it kept mutating.

The Farsight had solved all of humanity's problems except for humanity, which still had a knack for wanting to kill itself.

The United Commonwealth had closed its borders to the rest of the world and the only way for the non-infected to find asylum in the safe haven of the island was to head to Dover on the coast and quarantine for weeks before they boarded a mag-train to one of the temporary housing facilities like this one.

"How long can we stay here?" I asked. The funk of stale clothing and reheated food for the first time made me realize that me and Yusuf had absolutely no plan about how we were going to live.

"This is only supposed to be a temporary shelter before the refugees can find a permanent home, but some have been here for months," Hassan said.

"There are a few empty beds over there, Hayes," Yusuf said. I could tell he was trying to sound upbeat, but exhaustion was starting to creep into his voice too. "We can—"

"Wait," Hassan said. He clenched his jaw and shook his head slightly, like he immediately regretted his interruption. "Come on. You can stay at my place. For a few days—until you can figure out what you're doing. He'd kill me if I let you stay here."

Turns out the *he* who would've killed Hassan for being a bad host on behalf of his entire universe is me. Or, the other me. Or—the other *other* me, if the first *other* is Figueiredo. I'll have to include a flow chart in all of this or something.

Outside, the curving concrete and glass Predictive Intelligence Bureau building was the bow of a ship against a sea of stars. The three of us loaded into a golf cart thing that whizzed along a solar-panel track through a small meadow after Hassan told it to drive home. The ride to the staff townhouse neighborhood was less than three minutes, which we easily could've walked, but I guess the Farsight in this universe bred laziness. Hassan's house looked like a weathered English cottage squished at the sides and stuck to three other townhouses. He pressed his thumb to a keypad by the doorbell and the door slid open.

He left us in the living room while he dug up some extra blankets in the bathroom closet to make up the couch for us. I watched a small space appear between Yusuf's lips while he circled the room with its beige walls and crowded shelves of books and knickknacks, studying it like the open-air gallery we saw in Beatty. He pressed his hands on the spines of books and from a shelf picked up a tile circle with Arabic calligraphy. Ceramic pots filled with ferns and scrolling vines lined the floors and windowsills.

"Half these things I have in my flat back at home," Yusuf said. "The other half I've never seen before. It's like I'm in two places at once."

Crowning a tiny electric fireplace was the same picture from Hassan's desk, with him and the other me in matching tan suits and holding bouquets of ferns and purple flowers with fringed petals like fairy wings. Me and Yusuf both studied the picture, standing close enough that our fingers brushed at our sides. By then, I could read his face like a spin of the Envisioner and knew what he was thinking maybe more than he did. *What are we gonna do?*

"Our wedding day."

When I looked up, Hassan was lingering by the narrow entryway to the small kitchen, a stack of woven blankets and pillows in his hands.

I know you can't really say if someone is happier than you based on a picture because of course they're gonna be smiling. It's a picture. But my alternate self—floppy hair gelled down in a bowl cut, laughing brown eyes, clean-shaven and tattoo-less from what I could see of his brown legs poking out from the shorts of his suit—really did look happier than I ever have. Hassan looked alive, too, instead of this husk of a man who yanked the cushions off the couch and pulled out a folding bed.

"I dig his shorts," I said. Yusuf shot me a mortified look.

"Rui died in the plague a year after that."

Oh, shit. Which explained why Hassan hated looking at me. Some morbid part of me wanted to know what his funeral was like. Who came, who threw themselves on the casket, sobbing? I clammed up, mostly for Yusuf's sake.

Rui. My mom had bought this tiny hypoallergenic Chihuahua after I moved out and named it Rui, telling me she really wanted to name me that, but my dad thought it was too weird. She must've won out in this universe.

"It's not much, but…" he trailed, looking down at the couch.

"Thanks," Yusuf said. "I'm sure this is strange for you. It is for *me.* We'll be out of here soon. I promise."

We talked for a while over a murky bottle of wine. Rui was a nurse, he said. He'd worked graveyard shifts in an emergency room for years, even when he could've cashed in on the weird fact that he looked like the mythical Dr. Hayes Figueiredo that every school kid read about. Like, *exactly* like him—some walking marvel so that he'd bleached his hair and wore green contact lenses for years in hopes that people would stop gawking at him in the streets. He'd even moved from his small hometown in Madeira, where he'd lived with his mom after his American dad had walked, over to London, just for the anonymity of a big city.

They'd met while Hassan had been vacationing in London, years before the virus hit. What had drawn Hassan to Rui, at first, was just how much he'd looked like Figueiredo. And Hassan had spent months tracking Rui's family lineage and comparing it to what the world knew of Figueiredo's. When Rui had wanted no part of that research, Hassan had begged him with *how can you be so selfish and don't you see that you could be proof of something huge and wonderful?* Hassan had published his findings in a journal anyway, supporting his thesis that this universe was a younger sibling of the one where Figueiredo had created the Farsight. Maybe new universes were popping up all over the multiverse all the time. It had taken a while for Rui to forgive and trust him after that because *fuck theoretical physics,* Hassan had betrayed him and written about his life when all he wanted to do was be a nobody like everyone else.

It had helped that Hassan's paper had gone absolutely nowhere. Like, even physicists hadn't read it, never mind the average person who enjoyed a life of semi-retirement by age twenty-five since basically every industry was automated.

Rui had wanted to make sure that Hassan loved him, and that he wasn't just looking for some Figueiredo knock-off. They'd patched things up—Hassan had sprung for some MDMA intimacy therapy, and they'd cried for hours in a therapist's office with Hassan explaining he'd only wanted the world to see how incredible Rui was—and they'd moved to Oxford for Hassan to take over the Predictive Intelligence Bureau. They'd enjoyed a few quiet years before the pandemic hit. In the early days before the quarantine when the sick had flooded the hospital, healthcare workers had died in record numbers. Rui's mom lost her battle with the virus. Even still, he wouldn't stay home. He'd needed to help.

"The disease shreds the vocal cords," Hassan said, his mouth hammering his words with flat anger. "He couldn't even speak by the time he'd died. We couldn't say goodbye."

He drained his glass and abruptly pushed off the couch, leaving me and Yusuf alone. *Jesus.* The horror movie of this alternate version of myself replayed in the empty theater of my head. And I thought the idea of seeing Yusuf shot in front of me was bad enough. I reached for his hand and squeezed.

"I'm sorry," Yusuf whispered. "I know I didn't do anything to you. I know I have a tough time talking about my feelings. But, holy shit, I would never. Never."

"I know. I'm sorry too. For everything. Or nothing. Just— thanks for being here with me."

In the kitchen we heard Hassan fill a glass of water and glug it down. He was being more generous than I probably would be if I met a guy who was wearing my dead husband's face and another one who was wearing mine. At the same time, if he could hurt Rui by turning him into a research paper subject, I didn't want to find out what he'd have no problem doing to us.

When Hassan came back, he apologized, saying he didn't get to talk about what had happened much. Enough of the past for the night, what about me and Yusuf? Hassan did grow up in a world completely shaped by evidence of multiple universes, which seemed to explain how unimpressed he was about meeting us. He even had a book filled with hypothesized histories of Figueiredo's world on the coffee table by us, the touch-screen pages complete with video stills from footage historians pulled off the Farsight.

Around here was when I spaced out. I dimly heard Yusuf talking about how I seemed to be able to interact with the Envisioner like Figueiredo had. He mentioned Kaori as the head of our Predictive Intelligence Bureau-like organization, and how she probably wanted to slice me up and figure out how I connected to the machine, leading us to jailbreak out of our universe. He stumbled over Kaori's name like the word was hot on his tongue. Give me a break for not jumping in here with *actually she wanted me to kill you or use my freaky gift to change the past and revert our universe back to the one where you died in the attack, which is apparently what should've happened.* All in one day, I'd saved us from dying, had ripped a hole through universes, and had heard the story of how my alternate, saintly self had died while trying to save others, when I would've barricaded myself in a grocery store and waited out a plague while stuffing my face with potato chips. I let the two of them talk physics while I, outnumbered, leaned back on the couch under a blanket and watched the shadow the lamp cast on the wall blur in my eyes. They swapped theories about how it might be the same year on Earth in both our universes, but maybe the nature of the multiverse made room for spontaneous Big Bangs or finite universes tucked within a greater, infinite space. And all the Envisioners or Farsights or whatever you wanted to call them—it was like they sang to each other. They were all networked together across the multiverse, with a little part of each one lighting up once someone in one universe asks it a question.

I saw strings of Christmas lights stretching out into the blackness in my half-sleep haze. Until, later, Yusuf slid under the blanket next to me on the couch. For an instant, I forgot where we were. I only grabbed his hands and held on.

23

KNIFE EDGE

B ut why did opening the portal with the Envisioner work? I've been thinking about it for a while. I haven't met anyone in any of the other universes we've been in who can do it, just me and Figueiredo.

It's hard to separate the *now* and the *then* when everything is all knotted up in my head. I was doing the dishes at Hassan's place the morning after the first night he let us stay there, mostly out of houseguest guilt. With Yusuf still asleep on the couch, I was trying to be as quiet as I could. Of course, since it's me, I picked up a plate and a knife slid off the edge. I stood in front of the dishwasher and in the sliver of a second that the knife fell, I saw both outcomes: it would hit the floor or stab my foot. Either way, I knew I should move but I didn't.

There were other probable futures, sure. The knife would freeze mid-air, defying all laws of physics. Yusuf would teleport out of the pile of blankets on the couch and catch it. Or we'd gotten in a fight and I'd stormed out of the house and wasn't even doing dishes in the first place. But the two most likely outcomes for the knife sliding off the plate were that it would stab my foot or bounce on the floor. If that's the case, Figueiredo is the stab and I'm the bounce. We're the only real outcomes.

That thought isn't great to hold in my head when I remember all the selfish things he's done, like sending Envisioners off to other universes without caring about the consequences. And then I think of all that *I've* done, warping futures and crash-landing into other universes and dragging Yusuf along without even telling him what we were really running from. Maybe me and Figueiredo are exaggerations of each other. Or inversions. But still the same, if that makes sense. Whatever makes us *us* is the same.

I thought of him as my shadow. It sucks to think that maybe I'm his too.

"I'm excited to show you around," Yusuf said, his mouth full of toothpaste foam in Hassan's bathroom the next morning. "The covered market and the Radcliff Camera. The University and my favorite restaurants. And, yes-yes—the library. I spent so much time in a nook on the third floor that I wrote my name on the underside of the windowsill. I wonder if it's still there?"

I was trying hard not to let my doubt drown Yusuf's excitement at playing tour guide for me. Trying to stay where my feet were and returning his giddy smiles in the bathroom mirror, looking for some of that sugar-rush from yesterday. Blunt questions rattled around my head. How long would Hassan let us mooch? How could we find our own place to live if we couldn't prove we were from this country, never mind this world? I'd never been one to think things through, and I couldn't put this all on Yusuf. Especially now, with him whistling in the shower, still riding the upswing of a high. I got it. He was one of the first humans to ever step foot in an alternate universe. He found himself in a world with centuries of progress ahead of his own, with whole new fields of science based off the Farsight to explore.

While Yusuf showered, I headed into the kitchen, where Hassan was pouring coffee into a travel mug. He waggled the pot at me and, when I nodded, he poured me a mug.

"I hope I wasn't too unwelcoming last night." He frowned, looking down at his coffee, mirroring what I'd seen Yusuf do a million times. "Rui was always the one with the soft skills, not me."

"It's alright." I sipped the coffee to stall. "We sprang this on you. You're being way more patient than I'd probably be."

"You can stay as long as you need. I'll keep your secret safe." He looked up, one corner of his mouth wavering into something like a smile. "It's what Rui would do."

"I appreciate that." An awkward breath flowed between us. "And Rui—he sounds great."

Hassan nodded and brushed past me. He'd love to stay and show us around, he called from his bedroom, but work wouldn't wait. We'd have everything we'd need right at our fingertips anyway. He'd left us his citizen card on the counter, which we could scan in town because everything—food, transportation, entertainment—was free for Commonwealth citizens. And we could research whatever else we needed on his Portacle. He popped back out and handed me a tiny, voice-activated, palm-sized tablet, practically glowing. Everyone on the planet carried a Portacle, which was connected to a treasure trove of information pulled from the Envisioner, plus real-time satellite data and the global communications network. It even came with personal assistant AI. You see, he said urgently, in this world all the information ever discovered by humanity was free for everyone.

"It's like a *portable oracle*," he said.

"Yeah, I got that. So, it's a cellphone."

Hassan pressed his lips together. "It's more than that. It's—it's… I knew I should've spoken to Yusuf about this and not you."

Whatever. Hassan left for work. I tapped around the Portacle, unimpressed. I remembered my teacher in high school had told us about how, way before CalTech's Tabula Rasa AI could blank-slate someone's online presence at the tail end of the Cloud Cold Wars, within twenty years of the internet's widespread usage the technology had become completely boring and normalized. Even with phones offering access to all human knowledge, people mostly used the internet to look at pictures of puppies while on the can. Hassan's world wasn't hugely different, where humanity had mass-produced miniature versions of the Farsight and people asked them whether they should have frozen yogurt or chocolate cake for dessert. I guess humans have a way of repeating themselves, no matter the universe.

"Who needs help choosing between chocolate cake and frozen yogurt, anyway?" Yusuf chimed in, frowning at one of ten identical black button-downs in Hassan's closet. He'd given us the go-ahead to borrow some clothes. "Chocolate is subjectively better."

"Amen."

Yusuf pulled on a pair of jeans and a light gray sweater. I found some clothes at the back of the closet that must've been Rui's—ripped up jeans, a T-shirt, and a baggy red flannel. He was into grunge, which I was very much living for. Maybe he wasn't totally a boring saint. I tugged a baseball cap low over my forehead in case anyone would peg me as Figueiredo's double, like Rui. The hat and the flannel made me feel very rough trade. I tossed the clothes we'd stress-sweated and slept in into the oversized microwave-looking clothes sanitizer in the hallway closet.

We trekked out of the gated townhouse neighborhood and towards the train station the Portacle said was nearby. I kept expecting to see flying cars. Even with everything we'd fixed over the past fifty years, this place still made ours look like a shithole. The manicured lawn of the community gave way to a sidewalk with a moving track that threaded its way into what looked like a shopping center made of stone and glass. With this weird, glowing new world waiting for us.

I'm gonna hit pause here in my monologue because I promised Yusuf before he left that I'd think about time.

The sun is high overhead above this pink beach. I slather some more sunblock on my face and arms and plod over the sand back to our camp area for the umbrella I made by tying fern fronds to a long branch. It's still a work in progress seeing as how it doesn't stand upright. Our real umbrella, the rainbow beach one we lifted a few universes back, washed out to sea two days ago thanks to yours truly. Yusuf said I didn't anchor it into the sand right and I lost my shit about how *jesus christ there's more than one way to do things.* He clammed up after that. I'm really not proud of my reaction and I know he wasn't trying to nag but we'd been bickering a lot by then. That night a gust of wind launched the umbrella out of the sand and into the surf. I chased it, naked, into the water, and floundered while the tide swept it out to sea.

Yusuf had the unbelievable grace not to say "I told you so" when I heaved back to our air mattress, shivering with exhaustion and clumped with seaweed. I try stabbing the frond umbrella into the sand, now, and end up stomping it to dried fern bits when it tips over. I really don't deserve him. Or *didn't,* I guess, since he's gone.

I recorded a lot of Yusuf's tutoring sessions with Scarlett back on the Compound. We'd be lying in his bed and I'd say, "Tell me about electrons." Or, "Tell me about gravitational lenses again," when I just wanted to hear him talk. The way his voice cranks up when he's so lit up by whatever he's explaining and excited that I want to hear it. The way he'll stop and laugh, sometimes, saying how I was looking at him made him feel special. I wish I could drop into our home universe and find the camera from my room just so I can replay those days and watch us fall in love all over again.

I recorded some bits with Junior here. Me and Yusuf on a Ferris wheel with cotton-candy pink lights reflecting in his eyes, both of us lost in Neo Cairo's neon maze of streets—him pointing at a street sign and laughing because *damnit, weren't we just here?*— in a world where Ramses II had discovered the Envisioner. His tomb in the Valley of the Kings and Queens featured paintings of a strange giant spider that looked like it was made of the night sky. Wide-eyed nutjobs on TV said it was proof of ancient technology, lost to time, that the Egyptians used to build the pyramids, while scholars rolled their eyes and said the paintings were of a primordial creation god.

I'll try to remember some things Yusuf told me without footage to back me up.

For a while he wasn't convinced that the Envisioner worked in the way Kaori said it did, or that it was even evidence of an alternate universe. The machine was a souped-up modeling device at best. Probably some big hoax. He changed his tune pretty quickly once he was sitting in the living room of his alternate self, having a glass of wine and talking shop.

I asked Yusuf how he thought time worked, especially with this whole multiverse thing kicking around. How it messed with my head that some parts of Figueiredo's world seemed so far ahead of ours—obviously the Envisioner and whatever powered it—and some seemed behind us. The greenish, domed screens on the machine and elsewhere in Figueiredo's lab, the glowing buttons and dials where we had touchscreens.

Yusuf had a rare afternoon off, back before he was co-running the Compound with Kaori. I'd flopped onto his bed and was half-asleep as he traced squiggles on my lower back over my T-shirt.

"I think the better question is what kind of multiverse exists," he said.

We could live in an eternally inflating multiverse where universes shimmer to life because of random fluctuations. Like an infinite ocean, with each universe a bubble that pops up for a comparatively short speck of time. Or in one infinitely large universe with islands of matter—each basically a separate universe—separated by huge distances we could never dream of crossing. Or a multiverse that's constantly branching with new universes for every possible outcome of every possible event down to the quantum level, with each universe a slightly different film?

I appreciated his dumbed-down similes. More so, the way my skin was singing under his fingertip.

"See, now it just sounds like you're making this stuff up as you go along," I said.

He traced another little bubble over the cotton on my back for a new universe that had just popped up.

"Who knows if in another universe you're the one explaining this to me," he'd said.

"I bet."

Figueiredo had tossed the Envisioners into universes that had been in different stages of their life cycles. He'd sent some to universes that could support life, others to Earths crawling with people, others where the forces of nature squashed the machines as soon as they appeared. I pictured the machines dropping out of the skies over cities. Ancient crocodiles swimming around an Envisioner in a murky, primordial ocean.

But then again, we live in a model-dependent reality, which is that our brains use sensory observations to create a model of our environment. Thinking about concepts of infinite time and space could be one big, non-helpful headache, Yusuf had told me. The branches are all tangled up, the scenes of us spliced together into a movie trailer supercut.

In the infinite bathtub of the multiverse there are a million universes where me and Yusuf haven't met yet. I wish them better luck than we've had.

Now, a ways down the pink sand, waves brush against the shore. I know I'm doing this all wrong.

I wish Yusuf was here so I could say, "Hey, look at me trying to wrap my head around what you taught me and apply it to a theory of my own that is probably both wildly inaccurate and over-simplified."

I know this isn't the way that Yusuf wanted me to think about time when he probably meant, like, to think about how insignificant he—or anyone—is in the big picture. Which is why I have to let him go.

24
CRYSTAL OXFORD

The shimmering crystalline snake thing that slid towards us on glowing tracks might have been called a train by some people, but I was not one of them. Doors on its side whispered open like a monster bug inhaling and Yusuf and I jostled our way into the crowded belly. Next stop Oxford Center, a soothing overhead voice informed us, before terminating at London Paddington five minutes later.

Yusuf didn't even have a chance to finish explaining what propulsion technology this world had to shrink the travel time of fifty-something miles to five minutes before the city of Oxford shimmered into view.

Oxford was a fantasy of stone and crystal, of ancient-looking buildings flecked with moss among blocky clear towers, lit a pale blue from the inside. The city center looked more like a cracked-open geode you'd see at a natural history museum and less like something people would build, never mind live in.

"It's… so different," Yusuf murmured in awe.

I pressed close to him in the crowd of the train. Back in the Compound, he talked about bouncing from country to country with his family, thanks to his dad's job as a Peacekeeper for the

UN. I know if any place on Earth felt like home it was Oxford, which changed the course of his life—where he studied, and worked, and met Kaori. This city, this whole world, wasn't his real home. He'd never get back there because of me.

The train slid to a stop and the crowd gushed past us onto the platform of crystal-flecked concrete. And the city beyond—a chessboard of stone and crystal pieces waiting for a giant hand from the sky to make the next move.

"Come on," I said, laughing. "Show me everything."

He turned back to me, one corner of his mouth curved upwards, and grabbed my hand. I was projecting my fear and my doubt onto him, with the half-wild way he smiled, like we were back at the Compound again in the early days, and he was at my doorstep with some thin excuse. I hoped. We jumped onto the platform and the train doors closed behind us.

The University of Oxford wasn't much different than his, Yusuf said. Call it a stubborn English resistance to change that spanned universes. He walked me through rolling green botanic gardens and along the River Cherwell, through St. Mary's Chapel with its curved wooden beams like the bow of a ship, beneath a ceiling the deep blue of a night sky with painted stars. Ornate building exteriors with scrollwork and sculptures of ancient white guys or cloven-hoofed forest spirits guarding the doors. Radcliff Camera, where I was expecting, you know, a video recording device but instead Yusuf waved his arm like an interior designer at a low stone circular building surrounded by a moat of grass.

He ambled over the grass, free from his breakneck pace and stiff shoulders of the Compound. I was laughing and *oh wow*ing a lot, mostly at the sight of this giddy new Yusuf. Here was where scientists discovered the structure of DNA and famous authors I was supposed to know about researched their books, he told me. *White scientists and white famous authors.* Sometimes, he still couldn't believe he'd studied and worked at Oxford, with the country flip-flopping every few years about whether immigrants and ethnic minorities were a part of the *rich tapestry of the United Commonwealth* or if they should *go back where they came from because they certainly don't belong here, excuse you very much.* Even if *where you came from* was a place whose history was, you know, irrevocably fucked by imperialist intervention of the former British Empire. Couldn't make an empire without breaking a few eggs and all that. Back in our world, some of the adjunct professors had found little barbs to fling his way because he had a permanent faculty spot over them. Because how *wonderful* it was that *someone like him*—brown, gay, very much not interested in the words falling out of their mouths—could find a place here over, you know, *typical* Commonwealth citizens?

If I were Yusuf, I would've sipped my tea and asked, "How many papers have you published this term, asshole? Oh, zero?" But he was way more patient than I was and he didn't need anyone's approval.

In this universe, a broom closet took the place of his office, though he couldn't see much else of a difference between the university we walked through and the one he knew so well.

The rest of the city was alien, filled with breathing buildings of glass.

We wandered the chessboard of streets like tourists, our faces glued to the Portacle in Yusuf's hands, while grids of flying cars whizzed around the city's towers in a dizzying geometry. The glass was actually an organic self-healing crystal that both purified the air and slowly grew—the buildings and the whole city expanding inch by inch, day by day, into pre-programmed configurations to house more citizens and refugees. The crystal spires tinged with light blue and violet glowed softly against the gray drizzle.

The University of Oxford was still a tower of learning, but the rest of the city—the world, really—was a playground for art and entertainment. Except for the Taceovirus, the Farsight had solved all the world's problems like poverty, climate change, and hunger. With the United Commonwealth's closed borders, the citizens could pretend the virus ravaging the rest of the world was just a bad dream until scientists cracked the cure. Especially when everyone could distract their brains with massive art installations and immersive holo-films or join one of the roving theatrical troupes that made every street corner their stage. Everything was automated, no one had to work, and most people just had to entertain themselves until they gently died.

A lot of this we pieced together with Portacle research, and Hassan filled in the details later. Parts of the country were sectioned off into themed districts that you could hop between within minutes, thanks to the grav-trains, like a theme park. The retro-future sci-fi dreamscape of Little Eridanus in the southeast, surrounding Canterbury. London was smack-dab in the Victorian cosplay wet dream called Great Britannica. Up around Edinburgh, actors skulking in the shadows as assassins and private eyes lived a film-noir fantasy called Empire City. Cornwall was a living paradise based on Milton's writings of heaven called Neon Eden. In a world where the Farsight mapped out everything— every future, every decision—the people were obsessed with fantasy and the unknown. They'd perfected the world but still wanted to be anywhere but in it. Which the escapist in me dug very much. Especially since Oxford was the capital of the New

Albion district—a witchy King Arthur kaleidoscope steeped in the occult.

We roamed away from the university and down curving streets where silver, fist-sized drones whizzed by, using beams of light to paint the crystal buildings into moss-spotted medieval castles and black-and-white taverns with shingled roofs. I led the way into a tavern called the Prince of Cups which, according to the sign, featured the serving performances of Gwenhwyfar's Magickal Minstrels.

Inside smelled of firewood, roasting meat, and spilled beer. Drones painted the restaurant around us as a squat, wood-beamed room with a long wooden bar and roaring fireplace, where a bard plucked at a lute over the cackle of laughter and clatter of forks. Eight dancers twirled around each other in the center of the room with quick hops of their stockinged legs or flourishes of their skirts, each holding a domed silver platter. The few dozen guests slung tankards of ale and wiped their beer-slick hands on skirts and aprons. Stepping through the front door into this fantasy had made us a part of the play—probably the drones painting us as background characters—as me and Yusuf now wore dark tights and loose, white pirate shirts under velvet vests.

"Nice gams," I said, eyebrow-arching at his legs.

"I feel like a brown Robin Hood."

We dodged the dancers, sat down, and Gwenhwyfar herself made an appearance at our table, at least according to the wooden nametag that was pinned to her green corset. When we told her it was our first time here, she practically cackled in excitement. She'd spent years researching medieval feasts, she said, and folk dances and courtly love lyric poems, all to create this homage to the lost art of hospitality. With a scan of Hassan's citizen card, we ordered some food and cider. She dipped into an elaborate curtsey that made my knees ache and spun away with a ripple of her skirts. I mean, I'd been a waiter to pay my bills, but if she ran the restaurant as a performance piece, more power to her.

I say "restaurant" with some sarcasm because food in this world is absolutely revolting, and this is coming from a non-food snob who's survived for weeks on canned tuna and microwaveable rice because I'm broke. The great minds of this Earth had long ago solved the world hunger crisis by creating machines to 3D-print cubes of algae-based synthetic protein and fiber mixes. Food is a necessity, not culture—it's like flavoring air—plus we were in England anyway, which is not exactly celebrated as a land of gourmands.

Cuisine here—and I say this with a mouthful of salt—uses spices and neuro-stimulating chemicals to fool your brain into thinking you're chomping on paella or curry and not semi-firm mushcubes.

The booze, though. Holy Merlin. A pull of the cider chucked a cherry bomb of bliss that fizzled as soon as the liquid left my tongue. I know I can spin excuses about how I use weed to expand my mind for work or to help me sleep, and that I can drink a little, but alcohol isn't really my jam because it makes me too sick. If I lived here and could order a frosty pint of chemically induced euphoria at every bar on every street corner, I don't know whether I'd have enough self-control not to drown.

One of the drones that buzzed behind Yusuf faltered, flickering to reveal a hint of gray concrete wall before another drone swooped in to pick up the slack.

"So do we stay here?" I asked, brain singing from my latest pull of cider.

"Yeah," Yusuf said through a mouthful of mush that was

supposed to be roasted mutton, according to Gwenhwyfar. "I think there's a joust later."

"No, I mean *here* here. Like, this Earth."

"We're safe. And look at this place. It's incredible. I'll see if Hassan will let me help with his research, and you can—"

"Become a traveling bard."

"Sure. You've got the pipes for it."

"And you're fine with that?"

"Fine with us not going back home and Kaori dissecting you like some lab rat? Very fine."

I kept a glug of cider on my tongue to give me something to do with my mouth as I tried to figure out what to say next. Because I'd maybe *let* him think that we fled from Kaori so she wouldn't treat me as some test subject, instead of really leaving so she wouldn't kill him to avoid some apocalypse.

```
SCENE: FIGUEIREDO'S OFFICE - MORNING

          FIGUEIREDO (sitting at his desk,
          wearing NAREK'S therapist glasses)
     See, a lie of omission is worse
     because you make the other person
     complicit in the deceit.
```

He's right. I know in some not-insignificant way, I'm guilty of shattering Yusuf's idea of his hero, which I didn't let myself think about until then. Letting him think that she didn't care about him at all, when really all she's guilty of is not valuing his life over the entire human race. Like I do.

The cider fireworks fizzled out too soon, its bubbles souring my stomach. That, or the guilt. Yusuf didn't lie, I tried to tell myself.

Couldn't lie, really, since he even said his brain didn't work like that. But I wasn't sure if he was letting himself think through the idea of staying here.

At least he was right about the joust.

The drones zipped and transformed the tavern into a medieval hall with stained glass windows and mosaics of gem-studded chalices, with archways over torch-lit hallways that stretched out into forever. The crowd around us huzzah-ed as a knight in black armor and one in white—because fuck subtlety—rode in on horses and pummeled each other with wooden lances. The white knight knocked the black knight off his horse and the two slammed at each other with swords until the black knight dispatched his foe with a blade through the chest. Then Gwenhwyfar was at my side, pulling me up whispering about *just follow his cues* and *most of all have fun!*

I looked at Yusuf, who just shrugged.

The drones flew around me so close that I felt them as a swarm of bees, fairy-godmothering me into a knight with rune-carved armor and a long, shimmering sword. When a sword appears in your hand, even if it's made of light, and a guy in black armor is charging at you, you know what to do. I swung the sword baseball-bat style into his shoulder.

We parried for a while—moving and grunting—and in my head I was saving the realm or something. I probably looked like an asshole, but I didn't care. Because I should stop worrying about everything and just, you know, *live.* Tomorrow we could go to Little Eridanus and I'd be an astronaut surfing on the edge of a black hole or whatever else I wanted to be. Everything was opening to us, now. I stole a glance at Yusuf, who was clapping in that way that he had to look around first to get a hint about what he should be doing.

I reared back and slashed at the black knight one last time, sending him staggering and clanging to the ground in an over-acted death scene. With how the cheers of the crowd lit me up, I was pretty sure I could slay a goddamned dragon if one busted through the walls.

Still sealed inside my suit of armor, I clanged over to our table and knelt in front of Yusuf, saying something about how I fought for the honor of my king. I was so high off my victory that I didn't really know what I was yammering about. Gwenhwyfar swooped back in—she really was on her toes with the improv—and tugged Yusuf to his feet. She practically had to drag him, now in a long, furred robe with a crown made of captured rays of the sun, to sit at the throne that appeared in the center of the room.

"All hail King Yusuf the Glorious!" she called out with a bell voice.

The crowd repeated her words as one voice, again and again, echoing down the hallways spun of light. Yusuf's face twitched as he tried to smile, wincing slightly with each chorus of his name. Oh, god. He was mortified. *Mortified.* I was such an asshole. I pushed him too far, just like I always did.

25
MUSHCUBES

Figueiredo's shadow voice followed me as I led the way out of the Prince of Cups and onto the train with Yusuf. The voice whispered like my alternate self was leaning to my ear, just someone in the crowd pressed against me. *Do you really think you can live here? You're running because you know the only way to save your world is for him to die like he should have, and you're not letting him make the decision for himself.*

The train rolled to a stop, and we stumbled onto the glass-flecked sidewalk and then over the damp grass to Hassan's neighborhood. Still, the voice followed me.

He had a purpose. He has none here but to love you. You think he'll like trudging to the Prince of Cups every night and playing knights and wizards? He'll get bored and hate you. You will drive each other crazy.

I brushed past Hassan in his kitchen, where he was sprinkling lemon-yellow powder over a big bowl of fresh, steaming mushcubes. His hand with the spice shaker froze mid-air when he saw me, a gap appearing between his lips. I was too in my head to think about how I was being an asshole to him, barging into his house wearing his dead husband's clothes. In the bathroom, I filled the sink with cold water and dunked my face under.

And you—you'll ruin it because you ruin everything. Because you're not actually happy when everything's fine. You're never yourself unless you're at the end of your rope and hanging on by your fingernails.

I opened my eyes, tugged the chain of the sink plug, and watched the water spin down the drain.

Hassan had baked. I didn't have the heart to tell him to stick to science.

His smiling eyes watched me spoon a bite of the spongey thing that was supposed to be strawberry shortcake into my mouth. The metallic taste of chemical sweeteners lanced my tongue. And was it possible he'd added sawdust to the batter? A sliver of whipped-cream-coated strawberry flopped onto my plate.

"Sounds silly, but we'd used to splurge on real eggs and butter, sometimes," he'd told me, slicing a strawberry the size of my fist he'd gotten that afternoon at a farmers' market that was run by an agricultural theater troupe. "Then Rui would whip up a cake and we'd polish the whole thing off in one day."

Hassan hadn't made it for me, I knew. He was fussing over the man whose face I was wearing, whose clothes I was in. Whose eyes glared at me from the walls in this house, this mausoleum for their love.

"So good," I told him through a mouthful of cake that was turning into cement on my tongue. "So, *so* good."

Grinning, he pushed off from the stool at his breakfast counter and started gathering the dishes of our mushcube masala. Yusuf hopped up to help while I choked down the rest of the strawberry shortcake as a favor to Rui. When the dishwasher softly gurgled from the kitchen, we moved to the living room, where Hassan yanked books off the shelf to show Yusuf something they'd been chatting about. They flapped their hands at pages, and each other, and out to the world—smiling and chattering and solving equations already—because if Figueiredo and me were each other's shadow, Yusuf and Hassan were brothers. Twins.

Before I'd handed Hassan his Portacle back, I'd asked it *what do we do?* No luck. *Invalid query.* Hassan had told me that the things have limited predictive power since they're a dumbed-down user-friendly version of the Farsight. I don't know what I expected the thing to say, anyway.

"You have to come to the center with me tomorrow," Hassan said to Yusuf over a world atlas. There were no refugees coming in for a while, so things at work were a little lax. "I'm already thinking about all the research you can help me with." He looked up quickly and had the politeness to add *both of you* even though we both knew I could contribute squat.

He'd dropped his citizen card that I returned to him in a bowl by the front door, which also held his work badge. I wonder, now, if he made a show of doing it—*look, Hayes, where I'm dropping this. I see you. Smile at the birdie!*—but I know that's unfair. That shifts the blame from what I was already planning onto him and away from me, which I'm really good at.

"Quantum time entanglement theory you called it?" Yusuf asked.

"Time travel," Hassan said.

And with those words, I disappeared for the night in Yusuf's eyes.

Look, I didn't blame him. We hadn't talked about the King Yusuf thing and he was probably still embarrassed and annoyed with me. He and Hassan traded theories as I tried to add a *hmm* and *oh, wow* here and there for as long as I followed things. Something about how Hassan hadn't been able to prove his theories about time travel, even with the Farsight. The key could be to exit a universe and then *choose* at what point in space-time you hop back in, like Figueiredo had likely been able to do when sending his machines. Time travel was a problem of scale and observation.

"I get it," Yusuf said. "Like a GPS. You have to be *above* the thing you're exploring to really get an accurate point-of-view."

This was Yusuf's sweet attempt to loop me in again with an explain-to-the-audience movie dialogue simile when he saw my blank face.

"Oh wow," I added, uselessly.

If I was Yusuf, I would've grilled Hassan about every life choice he'd ever made to figure out how our lives had panned out differently. But I'm more interested in my personal history than the *collective responsibility that comes with the Envisioner* and *blah*.

They talked time while I grabbed our now-clean clothes from Hassan's clothing sanitizer, shrugged out of Rui's ripped jeans, T-shirt, and flannel, and tried to pull myself back together.

The ceiling of Hassan's living room was the white of untouched snow. I waited until Yusuf was asleep next to me on the couch, when I whispered his name and he didn't answer. Sneaking out when I was a kid both gave my mom mild heart attacks and taught me how to move like a whisper, dodging creaky floorboards and hopping in and out of shadows. I left the ground-floor window in Hassan's bathroom open a crack so I could climb back in when I was done exploring without having to fiddle with the thumbprint-coded lock of his front door.

Out the front door, over the front porch and down the steps with Hassan's work security badge in my pocket, wearing his gray lab coat that I borrowed from the hook by the door. Over the dew-drenched grass towards the Predictive Intelligence Bureau building in the distance, lit up on the hill like the beating heart of a synth. Quick and quiet over the grass and through a side door with Hassan's badge.

The Farsight was easy to find in the main courtyard of the building, which glowed like the crystal spire-filled center of the city. Already the sight of the faceted spider sent a gurgle through my guts. I steeled myself, pressed my hands to the cool edges of the machine, and crammed my eyes shut, hoping that I could feel the other Envisioners out there.

"What should I do?" I asked that machine.

The domed screen of the machine winked to life, with numbers scrawling across the display. *Reply hazy. Try again.* I knew the *should* was a sticking point. The machine wasn't some friend I could dial up for advice. I needed to ask concrete questions to get real answers. I had to start making my own decisions instead of looking for help from everyone else, never mind a machine. But we'd already *communed* or whatever, so I figured we were bonding.

"Does Yusuf really have to die for the plague or asteroid or whatever to go away in our universe?"

Yes.

"Why?"

Invalid query.

"So whatever disaster happens is my fault?"

I could almost feel the machine hesitate under my hands. *Invalid query. Yes and no. Entanglement through many threads.*

It sounds dumb for me to even say, but I swear it felt like I was talking with the thing. Like, it was trying to understand what to say back, some translation that maybe I would understand.

"Did saving him kill Figueiredo's husband?"

Yes and no. Entanglement through many threads.

"Why?"

Adjacent realities seek a zero sum.

"Hey!" someone called from the catwalks above.

I tipped my head up from the machine to where a security guard called from the balcony of the second floor.

"Good evening!" I chirped back, waving. I banked on cheery confidence and Hassan's coat to help me look like I belonged there.

The guard started towards the stairs at the end of the catwalk and I broke off from the machine to hoof it through the courtyard—*no big deal, just passing through*—down a hallway and out a side door. Over the carpet of the grass again, my head a tangle of threads and *adjacent realities.*

Before my feet hit his porch, I saw Hassan in the shadows, teetering slowly on a rocking chair by the front door. Like my mom catching me sneaking in. *Are you high? Look at me.*

"Did you find whatever you need?" he asked.

"I'm not sure yet."

His rocking chain creaked in the night air that was threaded with chirps from swooping bats above. It was too dark to see his eyes.

"You know, you're nothing like him."

"I'd like to think that's why he likes me."

"I mean Rui."

Sure, how am I going to compete with a dead saint? As much as I wanted to say this—as much as I probably would have before I met Yusuf and he'd sanded down my mean edges that would want to hurt Hassan for being a jerk when he clearly was hurting—I kept my mouth shut.

"Do you want me to say sorry?"

"No. Just an observation."

I left Hassan outside with his observations and crept onto the couch beside Yusuf. A line ran across his forehead above the thick arches of his eyebrows, frowning even in sleep. The three-day stubble painted a dark shadow along his face. If he heard anything, he pretended to be asleep. *Are you awake?* I wanted to whisper. *Invalid query.*

The box told me that he had to die to save our world, but fuck that. We'd stay here, forever. I would keep this secret even if it rotted me from the inside out because I would launch a million asteroids into a million worlds just to keep him safe.

Here's some math for you, courtesy of Hassan.

Let's say there are a hundred Envisioners bobbing around the multiverse. There are likely many times that, but he didn't want to overwhelm my tiny mind with too many big numbers. Thirty of those hundred are free-floating through space. Another thirty are on an Earth but otherwise undiscovered or inaccessible—lodged in an underwater crater, buried miles under glacial ice, floating like a crouton in the French onion soup of the interior of a volcano. Ten landed in universes that are uninhabited for one reason or another—wonky physics or still too early in their histories to support life. Thirty to go. Let's say another ten were discovered but the cultures who found them ended up accidentally obliterating their planets. Now that's twenty Envisioners actively in use throughout the multiverse. And each time someone uses one, it pings the whole network—most importantly the Mother of All All-Eyes sitting in Figueiredo's office.

How long, really, would it take Figueiredo with all his brainpower and resources and technology to poke around twenty

Earths and sniff us out? Not that long, apparently. And much less time if he asked for help.

We whizzed over the lawn in Hassan's little electric golf cart the next morning, the three of us like coworkers carpooling to the Predictive Intelligence Bureau. I was wearing one of Rui's short-sleeved white collared shirts with huge black polka dots over my T-shirt and shorts. I know "borrowing" Rui's clothes again was a touch mean, but hey, Hassan was a dick to me last night and I'd chirped something at him that morning about wanting to dress business-casual for the job. Yusuf didn't seem to sense the whiff of tension between me and his alternate self.

In Hassan's office, the two of them hovered by his computer, which projected 3D models of particles and equations into the air, while I breezed to a corner bookshelf like I was banished to the kids' table with a box of crayons. I plucked out a landscape photography book and was just settling down into a cushioned chair when a whirring shriek hit so hard it could've shattered the windows of Hassan's office.

The noise yanked us into an action flick from my nightmares. Hassan shouted into a comms device while security staff ran past the office window, down the hallway. Here came the other shoe dropping, I knew, because no way were we really going to be safe. Maybe there was a quarantine breach and me and Yusuf would die here, looking into each other's eyes and unable to speak because a sickness shredded our throats. He pushed away from Hassan's desk and ran to my side.

Then just as quickly as the siren sounded, a quiet rolled over us.

Hassan hovered by his computer. I'm assuming he pulled up security footage with the way a projection of the Envisioner in the lobby hovered in the air. Then, a wide oval appeared like someone took a razor and sliced a gateway right through the machine.

This probably sounds familiar to you.

Two people stepped out of the gateway, and it zipped shut behind them. One man, one woman. I knew both of their faces well.

Hassan stopped the footage and zoomed in on the man's face, not that me and Yusuf really needed to get any closer to see who he and his companion were.

"Rui?" he asked.

At Figueiredo's side, Kaori lifted her hands up in the air while the security team sprinted towards them. Her palms may have been out, but it would be a mistake to think she was surrendering.

They wanted to see me alone. Should I have felt flattered?

Yusuf took off his glasses and pinched the bridge of his nose while we power-walked with Hassan and two security guards down the hallway, and over one of the catwalks that stretched across the courtyard. Rui's polka dot shirt stuck to my armpits with all my stress-sweating. Each of my footfalls on the catwalk rattled in my hollow chest. As much as my heartbeat was already cranking up, abso-fucking-lutely was I jumping at the chance to meet Figueiredo. Me at the window of that gay bar in Ukraine, again. Watching the blinking lights of the police cars speeding down the street towards us. The rational voice in my head that kept telling me that I should put down my camera and run was drowned out by the other voice. So loud that everybody else must've heard it. *Come on, I fucking dare you to come here and mess with me.*

"Should we start charging tolls?" Hassan asked the air. "Who else did you invite to crash on over here? And you're just going to let Hayes walk into an obvious trap?"

Before I could even open my mouth, Yusuf snapped, "I don't control him. He can make his own decisions." Over the burnt orange carpet, we plodded across a scaffolding of shadows cast from the skylights above. Then, after a few swears in Arabic, he murmured just loud enough for me to hear, "Be safe. You know we can't trust them."

Hallways, rooms. We changed hands from one security detail to another like a suspicious package before they led me to a large room that was split in half by a glass wall. From the doorway I could see Kaori sitting on a single metal chair on the other side of the glass—a straight-backed metal hornet—while Figueiredo paced the wall behind her, seething at me.

I'd stared at the hard angles of his face for hours and hours, never thinking I'd ever meet him. Never wanting to, with the way his voice rattled in my head, looking for the gaps in my armor. His undercut hair that swooped down into his eyes that he'd absently brush away while yammering to the camera. He wore his usual gold-rimmed glasses and dusty green lab coat even away from his lab, screaming for all of us that he really was the great scientist. I swept my eyes over him with a detached fascination like I was studying a film still. Even though he wouldn't look at me, I could feel the heat of his rage, like his footsteps left a trail of lava.

Kaori—in a black turtleneck and pants, asymmetrical bob framing her face with uneven parentheses—just waited. Her legs crossed, her interlaced hands resting on one knee. I slid into the chair across from the glass wall.

"Hi, Hayes," she said. "You left without even saying goodbye."

Through the glass, her voice carried a hollow buzz. As a kid, I'd gone camping, once. I'd been invited by one of my friends from school—more likely pushed by his parents to invite the poor city kid—to get out into nature for a weekend. In the woods, one of us had stepped on a hornets' nest and the whole swarm swirled out of the ground and attacked us, the air buzzing with wings.

"Goodbye," I said. "Now, how about you leave?"

I kept my eyes on her and away from Figueiredo, with the looking-through-someone-else's-glasses queasiness he was kicking up in my stomach.

She shrugged. "As soon as you come back with us."

"I don't think so. I have a joust tonight."

She tipped her head. "I'm intrigued. Sounds like you've been having fun. While I've been trying to avert a world-ending cataclysm."

"Sorry, I would've asked about you. I guess I'm still annoyed about the whole threatening to kill Yusuf thing."

"I get it. And you look well. Unburdened by the deaths of billions."

"And you look like a low-rent assassin."

Back at margarita club, that would've killed. She didn't even blink.

"Thanks. Sorry it took so long to find you."

"Yeah. It looks like you couldn't do it on your own."

I bobbed my chin at Figueiredo, who was still leaving scorch marks on the floor behind her. For just a second, a dark flash hit her eyes until her cool mask of gold slid back into place.

"A temporary colleague. Seeing as how Yusuf abandoned his post."

"How'd you get here?"

"How'd *you* get here?"

Figueiredo lunged forward, pounding on the divider and screaming something I couldn't understand, his spit flecking the glass. I didn't need a translator to tell me that the way he pointed and screamed roughly meant *this is your fault*. I only jerked a little, even as my pulse sprinted so hard that I could feel it in my eyes.

Kaori snapped something at him in his language and he pushed away from the glass and punched the back wall. So—*what the actual fuck*—she'd learned his language in the past two days Yusuf and I had been gone, or she'd known it all along.

In the woods, during the hornet attack, we'd flailed at the bugs all around us and barreled through the trees, swatting branches and tripping over roots. When I'd looked down, hornets had been stuck to my shorts. "Hornets bite so they can get a better grip to sting you a bunch of times," my friend's dad had told me when he'd cleaned our wounds.

"Who *are* you?" I asked her.

"I am the one person—the *one person*—who is thinking clearly."

"He killed my husband, Nakamori," Figueiredo snapped in a thick accent. "He will fix this. He—he does not deserve all that I built... this existence. This face. This *genome*."

"I didn't kill anyone. Please fuck all the way off."

"Gentlemen, let's stop with the dick-swinging." Kaori cast barbed glares at us. "Alright. Here's how we fix things. Hayes, you and Yusuf are returning with us—"

"The hell we are."

"—to our home universe where you'll connect with the machine and set the paths right. We're too far away, here, for the ripples to hit and everyone has to be in their original vector in the multiverse because—"

"Adjacent realities seek a zero-sum," I said. "I got it."

Kaori's smile stung. "You've been studying?"

"I'm a quick learner."

"Clearly not. Look where we are."

"Why am I even here, Kaori? I'm digging the cat-and-mouse thing we have going on, but you know I'm not going to let Yusuf die. Not to mention I don't even understand how I can change the *past* with the Envisioner."

"All of timespace exists simultaneously and linearity is a human model-dependent construct, you *bckxxfkljakkxxb*." Which is to say that I didn't understand what Figueiredo said at the end, until Kaori cut him off.

"Should we bring in Yusuf and see what he thinks?" she asked. "You are here alone out of respect to him and the years we worked together, and absolutely nothing to do with you. I assume you haven't told him that because he's alive billions of people will die as the scales that keep the multiverse in balance try to reset themselves." Her sting, again and again. "I'd prefer to spare him that pain."

The ground quivered beneath me, tectonic. I tried to steady myself by locking my eyes on my calloused hands in my lap.

"I get it," she said, gentler. "I care for Yusuf too. I know I haven't… haven't treated him in the best way. But this is the kindest thing I can do for him. Come back with us and connect to the machine. Separate the threads and set them right. He won't even know. He won't be scared. And then he'll just be—gone… like he should've been. You're messing with things that you know nothing about. You have to change the past to fix the future."

"Did you spin the box and ask it what I was going to say?"

She sighed. Her eyes fell to the floor and she shook her head, all the sarcasm and exasperation leaking out of her voice. "I didn't have to. Just remember that I tried to do this kindly."

Figueiredo reached into his waistband behind his back—whatever he had hidden there shrouded by his lab coat—pulled out a chrome ray-gun thing that looked like a kid's toy and pulled the trigger, unleashing a blast of pink light.

26
ENTANGLEMENT

If I could just hit slo-mo here for a sec as the shatterproof glass between my intact body and Figueiredo's rage is not living up to its name very well—big chunks flying apart and spiraling in fractals of jagged death in the air—I think that explaining some things would really help.

Why didn't the security team check them for weapons, you ask?

Here's what me and Yusuf pieced together from a history book that he'd flipped through earlier in Hassan's house, along with some guesswork.

Guns in this world were just not a Thing. A mass-shooting in America in the early 1990s led to a nationwide ban on assault rifles that soon spread to most of the industrialized world. When the Farsight was discovered here a couple years later, the free exchange of scientific advances led to a United Nations wet dream of global cooperation. Science and diplomacy would save them all, and there was a big show of ceremonially disbanding armies and dumping weapons into plague pits that workers filled over with cement while politicians shook hands nearby.

The age of human violence was over. For a century and a half—at least until the biological warfare of the Second American Civil

War—the world was a big family around a campfire, strumming the guitar and singing and advancing human rights and all that. Guns, kids learned in school, were like siege warfare or the Crusades: a cruel and barbaric part of the past that humanity was really embarrassed about. Besides, no one needed guns. Advances in synthesized food meant no one hunted with rifles anymore, not even for sport. All of this Figueiredo must've known, because he has a giant machine that's connected to a million universes, including this one.

Besides all that, even though the Predictive Intelligence Bureau housed refugees, there was little security since the displaced people weren't going to rise up against the one nation that would take them in. The security guards there weren't exactly top brass, and I walked into the room thinking the two people who likely wanted me dead had at least been patted down.

We were also all thinking about Kaori and Figueiredo as just two people—geniuses, sure, but still contained and way outnumbered—and not the forces of nature that they really are.

Got it? Back to just before the snowstorm of glass that's still spinning out in slo-mo.

Figueiredo whipped his arm from behind his back with the muscled grace of a gymnast on the rings. Kaori shifted just ever-so-slightly to her right, her hair swaying, out of the path of a pink blast of light from his gun. My mouth fell open into a drawn out *oh, fuuuuuuuuuuuu—*

Cue the glass speeding up into real time and me trying to dive out of the way.

What I'm saying is: yeah, I really wish they'd checked Kaori and Figueiredo for weapons, too.

———

I cracked my head on the ground. The pain was so bright that I swore I'd been struck by lightning.

A rain of glass shards from the obliterated wall tinkled around me while I flopped over, gasping for breath. My eyes hit the scorch mark on the wall behind where I'd just stood. Figueiredo draped his lab coat over the shards on the ledge of the former glass wall and then vaulted over. Next thing I knew, his blurry-edged body was above me, and then he lifted his gun to blast out the door that led to the hallway.

Shouting, somewhere. Conking my head on the floor had fucked with any sense of time. Locusts with glass-shard wings swarmed me as I tried to crawl over to the hallway away from Figueiredo, slicing up my forearms on the way. Dizzy shadows burst into the room, only for him to launch them against the walls. He must've been 'roided up or wearing some sort of superhero exoskeleton with the way he brushed off Yusuf and the security guards like biting flies.

I knew Figueiredo wasn't going to kill me because he needed me. Right? That didn't stop him from reaching down, hauling me up by the collar of Rui's polka dot shirt, and slamming his fist into my face.

Fireworks. Shards of glass dazzled my eyes. It felt like the front part of my skull caved in under his fist.

"You didn't have to do that," came Kaori's bored voice.

He ignored her, dragging me as I thrashed against his inhuman grip and snarled out animal noises. With a sigh, she climbed over the wall and her booted feet crunched over the shattered glass. In the hallway, something knocked into us from behind and I careened onto the floor again, rag-doll limp, with Figueiredo toppling over me. His gun clunked on the carpeted floor.

The blood in my eyes smeared my view of Yusuf, Hassan, and the two security guards from before. Yusuf snapped forward, grabbed Figueiredo, and shoved him at one of the walls of the narrow hallway.

In my mild, I-probably-have-a-concussion delirium, I remember thinking, *my boyfriend kicking ass for me is surprisingly hot.*

Another guard flicked his hand to extend a collapsible baton and used it to pin Kaori to a wall. The thing must've been electrified with the way she jolted and clenched her teeth. Yusuf slammed Figueiredo into the wall again, hard enough that his head knocked back against it. The other guard lanced Figueiredo in the side with an electrified baton.

Through the kaleidoscope of brain-spins and blood in my eyes, I barely kept track of anything. Screaming over alarms. Kaori yelled at Yusuf to *ask him why you're here.* A squad of five security guards with their batons rounded a corner and joined the drunken bar brawl in the hallway. Yusuf helped pin Figueiredo against the wall but was also somehow at my side and lugging me up by my armpits.

"Let's go," he snapped.

"Oxford Center," I heaved. "We can get out of here and the drones can…" I winced my next breath and spat blood. "…can camouflage us."

"No. I can keep you safe here."

I just kind of smiled, all gooey and delirious, letting him half-drag, half-carry me out of the fray. Hallways. Catwalks. My spinning eyes up at the greenhouse ceiling of this place. A meat-locker of an elevator that, for some reason, pitched us underground. I don't remember much else before I blacked out.

Against the screens of my closed eyes, I could see the hazy form of a demon, its forked tongue flicking out to taste my fear. The thing dug its talon-tipped feet into my chest, keeping me from sitting up.

I opened my eyes to salt-white lights that blasted from a steel ceiling. My head lolled, my eyes trying to make sense of the surroundings. Bare gray walls. Bare gray floors. Steel tables. Black anacondas of thick wires that slithered from the ceiling into a hunk of rock on steel legs that glowed like the spires of Oxford. Hassan was a shadow in front of the machine, checking wire connections and spinning dials. I looked around for Yusuf until I realized, gut sinking, that it must've been Hassan who'd dragged me from the brawl in the hallway, not Yusuf. Give me a break. I'd had blood in my eyes and an earthquake in my brain.

I was also now tied to a reclining surgical chair with what looked like duct tape and extension cords.

"Where are we?" I burbled. "And why the *fuck* am I tied down?"

"Relax," he called. "You're secured so you don't fall over and crack your head open. You probably have a concussion or twelve. The cerebral anti-inflammatory meds that I gave you need some time to work. I also cleaned the glass out of your wounds. You're welcome."

At my side a bloody wad of gauze clouded a rolling triage table. A sharp metallic funk that reminded me of Hassan's maybe-toxic strawberry shortcake filled my mouth. The duct tape bit into my arms when I tested its strength.

"Don't move too much," he said, floating closer to me. "The ready-graft is adhering to your skin. Your face is busted up pretty badly."

"Where's Yusuf?"

"Not sure. He must be helping security with the doctor and your friend." Hassan looked up, frowning. "Dr. Figueiredo seems... *angrier* than I pictured. I suppose you really shouldn't meet your heroes."

"Okay," I huffed. "I appreciate you patching me up, but I have to get Yusuf and we have to catch an Envisioner ride out of here. A whole universe couldn't hold Figueiredo and Kaori, never mind whatever room you guys are gonna lock them in."

"You can't leave," he said, tipping his head a little, like *obviously*. His widow's peak of cropped hair pointed to the furrow between his eyebrows. "Not at least until you help me get Rui back."

"Wait. What? He's—he's *dead,* Hassan. What do you want me to do?"

He flicked his hand at the mess of wires and the hunk of rock behind him. "I've made some improvements to the Farsight. You'd be amazed at what you can do when you're stuck in a museum in a quarantined nation. Living off grief and boredom."

The machine behind him pulsed with light from deep inside its crystal form. If the Envisioner was a spider, this was some type of enormous frozen jellyfish, luring with delicate, icy lights before it stung.

"Don't tell me you made a time machine," I said.

He shrugged. He and Kaori really did have that detached boredom for everyone around them down pat. "Not really. It's more a *navigation* device. Once you connect us to another universe and we step through, we will use it to find a specific point in this universe's greater landscape of simultaneous space-time before Rui got sick. We gate to that point, retrieve Rui, and then we bring him back here to the present where he belongs, with me. At which point, you're free to leave."

"Sounds so easy," I said. "I bet you have every possible universe-ending paradox all worked out."

"Time is one continuous, entangled moment," he said, waving me off. "The multiverse is resilient. You being here is proof."

I flexed against the duct tape again, to keep from screaming. Still no budge. Just the dizzy spins of my head thanks to Figueiredo's fists and the claustrophobia of my arms clamped down at my sides.

"How will that even work?"

"I've run the necessary simulations. There are still some things, though, I haven't figured out. About you and Dr. Figueiredo. How does your connection to the machine work, exactly?" he asked, poking at the blood-spotted bandages on the table beside me. "Blood? It can't be just genetic. Rui never could access the machine's restricted functions. And his hair, and dust from his skin, was all over our house. His pillows. I can still smell him there. I grew a patch of his skin and grafted it to my palm, but I still couldn't interface."

Jesus. He stank of sweat and grief as he stared down at one hand. With the bare floors and walls of whatever basement lab we were in, with Hassan's distant eyes—we could've been in Figueiredo's first lab from his early footage. History couldn't stop repeating itself. Just me and Yusuf jogging the track outside the Compound, never really going anywhere.

And I was probably going to die here, my body divided up into little slides all over this doomsday basement lab.

"Do you think Rui would want you fucking up timelines and universes for him?"

"I suspect, once he realizes he's still alive he'll forgive me. You'll have to ask him yourself."

You're nothing like him, he'd spat at me the night before. This close to me, Hassan's eyes were the same as Yusuf's when he'd roll off the bed and draw on the window as he'd explained some physics concept. Smiling at first, until he forgot I was there and he lost himself in his own mind.

The door at the other side of the room flew off its hinges and clattered to the floor.

Yusuf, the *real* Yusuf, plowed through the still-smoking doorway. He didn't have to ask anything—me duct-taped to a chair, Hassan nearby, fresh off his master plan monologue—he just planted his feet and fired.

The kickback from Figueiredo's gun jerked his arms, futzing his aim, and the pink fizzle of light grazed one of Hassan's shoulders. Where was my sniper that had saved us on the Compound? Hassan still careened backwards, though, writhing on the floor and clutching his shoulder. The air stank of burnt barbeque. Yusuf dashed the space between us in an instant.

"You okay?" he asked, his hands fumbling at the duct tape that tied me to the chair. One of his glasses lenses was cracked, some light-cloaked drone painting him as a pirate with a spider-web eyepatch.

"Yeah. Thanks. Scalpel. Over there."

He sliced me free and helped me up. Hassan hadn't been kidding with the whole *concussion* thing, with the way I swayed against Yusuf.

"Where's Figueiredo and Kaori?" I asked.

"Rotting in a cell by now, I hope. Another squad of guards rolled in with tranquilizer guns. I ran after you guys but couldn't find my way through the lower tunnels for a while." He glanced back at Hassan. "Did I really do that? Is he dead?"

"You shot me in the goddamned *shoulder*," Hassan snarled, still bent over.

I'd seen enough movies where the villain—is that what he was, now?—skulked to their feet and pulled out a hidden gun, so, no thanks. I kicked him in the stomach twice, toppling him onto the floor.

And then we ran. Through the halls. Dead ends. The alarm split the air again, which maybe meant that Hassan was coming after us or Kaori and Figueiredo broke free from whatever cell the rent-a-guards had shoved them in.

Up maintenance stairways in blind panic until, finally, we found the lobby and ran at the Envisioner. Me with my arms outstretched like I was rushing a quarterback, and Yusuf with one hand on my shoulder. My hands connected with the machine and for a few agonizing seconds nothing happened as I tried to clear my head and feel for the threads of the other universes. The wispy spider web of light. I pushed at the first thread I felt with my mind and the gateway opened. No time for thinking or hesitating. We jumped through.

27
THUNDERSNOW

This was not supposed to be a thriller.

Especially with how all my films are people sitting around and talking about their feelings, I didn't expect my life to have explosions, and face-punching, and evil geniuses who look like my boyfriend monologuing at me while I'm tied to a chair.

The idea of a life eating dinner in front of the TV every night makes me want to chew on salted glass, but all this is dialed-up too much, even for me.

Anyway. I'm taking a break from storyboarding this all out for you since my throat has turned to sandpaper. I kick on over to our campsite, fish another banana-coconut out of our stash, and slam it on a rock to suck out the juice.

Maybe I was too hard on Kaori that last bit, talking about her like a spy flick henchwoman. It's easy for me to paint her—and even Figueiredo—as faceless stock villains and we're just running for our lives like innocent heroes with moving backstories. When I'm thinking of myself and Yusuf and she's thinking of the billions of lives I may or may not be responsible for eventually killing. When I walked into that glass-walled room with her and Figueiredo and before she even opened her mouth and I just saw her eyes, I knew she was right. But I also knew she was wrong at the same time—because she *had* to be. Because I wanted her to be, like how you can hold two thoughts in your head that should cancel each other out. God doesn't exist but then also there's a god who's personally interested in my specific needs and mainly uses his magic to help beautiful, rich people win awards.

I should say that I thought of Kaori a lot when I tried not to love Yusuf. When I tried to say goodbye. Here on our pink oasis world before I told him the truth and he still wanted to be around me, I'd walk off and commune with the Envisioner, alone, for hours. I wanted some of her cool distance, some of her cracks painted over with gold. I peeked through the glowing web that connected devices across the multiverse. I dropped in and out of the footage each device had recorded like I was shuffling through TV shows. I could *feel* traces of us in other threads. In that universe we never met. In that other one we broke up and destroyed each other's lives. In a million others we never even existed because we are small and not that important, even though what I'm doing here maybe radiates out and puts countless other universes in jeopardy.

Each time I made up my mind to surrender, whatever goodbye I'd planned evaporated when I walked back and found Yusuf cross-legged in the sand with a book on his lap. His halo of messy curls. His eyes—glinting behind the replacement glasses he'd lifted from another universe—were somehow surprised to see me each time. *Oh, hi.*

So, there. I'm sweeping my leaf blower behind the rows of seats in the movie theater and showing you all the trampled popcorn and candy bar wrappers. Kaori was right all along, I knew it, and I'm a selfish piece of garbage. But don't tell me I didn't try.

We jumped through the gateway in the Envisioner, landed in knee-deep snow, and I topped over onto my chest, my face cracking through the frozen crust of white. The gateway zipped closed behind us. I pulled back and traces of blood from the scratches on my arms gashed the snow with red.

The cold felt good against my scalding skin and throbbing face, with the tight patch under my eye of what Hassan called a ready-graft—which must've meant it was healing the wounds from Figueiredo's fists. The refreshing feeling lasted all of two more seconds until the bare skin exposed by my shorts and Rui's short-sleeved shirt registered the *holy shit*-level of cold. Of course the closest universe that I could feel when I'd touched the Envisioner was home to a frozen Earth, because why would things ever be easy?

We'd landed in some type of featureless storage bay with concrete walls and a huge rolling garage door open behind us, which let snow tumble in on frigid winds. The Envisioner, laced-over with frost, was a hunk of coal against the thick carpet of white. Everything was too quiet, muted by the cold. Just the sound of my heavy breathing and Yusuf's footsteps as he crunched through the snow.

I hauled myself up and he brushed crusted chunks of snow off Rui's shirt. My T-shirt was underneath and I was looking forward to tossing my blood-spotted souvenir from Hassan's house, but I needed all the warmth I could get.

"You okay?" he asked.

"Yeah. Sorry I couldn't find us a beach planet."

"It's fine. I burn easily."

The snow burned my bare shins. *I thought we could spare him the pain,* Kaori said, her steeped-tea eyes the softest I'd ever seen them. I don't think so. I'll take the pain if I have to, not him.

"Sorry Hassan turned out to be a psycho. I assume he wanted to slice you up and see how you connect to the Envisioner?"

"Something like that."

"What was that *thing* in the lab?"

"Time machine to get Rui back. I think I was supposed to be the battery?"

"No. No way." He paused, shivering. "If we're being honest, I'm curious to see if that would've worked."

"If we're being honest, you probably shouldn't've told me that."

He grimaced.

I circled back to the Envisioner and tried to find us another Earth to land on. But when I touched its surface, all my shaking hands felt was the frozen, hard shell. I was too cold, with my head still on spin-cycle from Figueiredo's fists, to be able to reach out and find the threads. The threads that I could see were spun of clouds. Fluffy and slipping through my fingers when I tried to hold on. Whatever anti-concussion meds Hassan had pumped me with were taking their sweet fucking time.

We crunched through the snow to the open bay door and stepped out. Under the pale blue sky, a featureless plain stretched all around us, white like the cotton balls my mom glued to constructed paper during craft time with me when I was a kid. Yusuf shivered in his long pants and T-shirt, framed against the whiteness like a painting in a gallery. The wind whirled small cyclones of flakes from the top of the packed snow. Down the plain—two miles away? Ten?—I could just make out a smudge of brown that maybe was a building, but could've been a pile of dirty snow. I grunted against another arctic gale and pressed my arms in close.

"There might be people down there," I said, pointing at the distant shapes.

When he said nothing, I turned to find him staring off into the pale sky, where I noticed for the first time that the hazy giant marble of the Earth looked down over us.

"Jesus," I breathed. "No way. We're... we're not."

"We're on the moon."

We explored the facility for a while, mostly to look for things to keep us warm. Yusuf had the smarts to bring Figueiredo's gun with him into this universe, which he kept tucked into his waistband since it was pretty clear this place was deserted. I just needed a little time to focus, I said, and I could try the Envisioner again and get us out of here in no time. The whole building wasn't much bigger than the Theater in the Compound back home, with just a few glass hallways, a kitchenette littered with empty potato chip bags and microwaveable meal packets, and the wide room with the open bay door and the Envisioner.

No staff, either. One by one, we opened doors to little cubby rooms to find the unmistakable shapes of bodies under blankets. They'd either frozen to death or starved. Or maybe both.

We found some matches in a first aid kit in the kitchenette and made a small fire of stray paper by the open bay door. Gray wisps curled up to the sky. *A gift to you, oh ancestors.* Still, almost too cold to even move. Yusuf shivered and blew air over his hands. The vision in my right eye was fading into a shrinking spotlight. Soon enough I'd have a killer migraine.

I waited long enough to be polite and then went back to the staff bedrooms. I tried not to look down when I pulled two blankets off bodies on the beds. Still, I couldn't get the Envisioner to open up under my now-numb hands. I draped a blanket around Yusuf's hunched shoulders by the fire and he had the sense not to ask where I'd gotten it from. The light outside was flat gray and darkening, telling of the coming night and the deeper cold it would bring.

Shadows from the fire played over his face, with the flames reflecting in his eyes. Some ancient instinct wanted to tell me that we'd be safe if we just stayed by the fire, away from whatever animals wanted to stalk us in the dark.

But we both knew what needed to happen. No other choice. We had to walk.

I couldn't take clothes off a corpse. I just couldn't. The thought of breaking the legs of a body frozen in the fetal position just to get some pants off made me want to bury myself in the snow and surrender to the cold. I found a roll of duct tape in the kitchenette first-aid kit and made pants by taping another blanket around my shorts and bare legs.

More blankets around us, with pillowcases around our faces—trapping our breath—and then out into the expanse of white.

I had no idea how to tell time as we walked with the wind whipping our blanket capes behind us. Maybe ten minutes passed, maybe an hour—convulsing with shivers and trying not to chip my teeth with their rattling—when I realized we were going to die here. The thought came on like a chill, at first, then a burn. Then a numbness that crept up from my legs and around my whole body. A storm dumped swan-feather snowflakes around us. Someone would find our frozen, intertwined bodies months or years from now. I'd survived an overdose and had woken up connected to tubes and with cracked ribs from puking so much. Me and Yusuf had jumped from universe to universe, dodging bullets and ray-gun blasts, and possibly homicidal versions of ourselves, and now we were going to fall into the snow and hold each other while the clouded-over Earth looked down at us, like, *big fucking deal.*

We stopped a few times so I could blow hot breath across Yusuf's reddening hands and rub the life back into them. The chill was starting to seep in through my eyes and numb my brain, leaving me too cold to even panic. Settling down and just taking a nap wouldn't be bad, my body wanted to tell me. It wouldn't hurt for much longer.

"We're almost there," he chattered. "We gotta keep going."

My sweet, brilliant idiot lying to me. The dome down the plain seemed anchored at the exact same distance, no matter how far we walked towards it. I thought about turning around and trying the Envisioner again but with my numb hands, I knew it wouldn't work.

The voice in my head started when I ducked against an arctic gale. *You can't run forever. You need a plan.* One foot, then the next crunching through the snow. *You have to kill them. Or at least him, so Kaori can't follow you.* The voice in my head was Figueiredo's, or maybe it was mine. They sounded the same, now—the Storyteller voice gone hoarse after a night of yelling on the dancefloor and sucking on cigarettes. The end of the word *you* stretched out into a long moan of *ooooo.* Then it folded into a blaring *mmmmm* that seemed to grow louder and louder as I kept my face down against the cold.

"Hayes, someone's coming."

My neck creaked towards the gray blur streaking towards us. When it got closer, I saw that it was someone with insect-like goggles and a thick, fur-lined coat plowing over the snow on an all-terrain vehicle. We froze in our tracks. The person rolled to a stop a few feet away and pulled up their goggles to get a good look.

"We saw the fire," the person said, some guy best I could tell by the stubble on his face. "How'd you get all the way out here with no gear?"

"Please," I chattered. "We're freezing. Can you get us outta here?"

"Yeah." He hopped off the ATV and I saw for the first time that he was dragging some improvised cargo sled that looked like it was made from a door and some canvas and ropes behind his beat-up three-wheeler. "It's five klicks to the hotel. Hang on. I'll get us there as fast as I can."

Me and Yusuf clambered onto the sled and laid down. The guy tucked blankets all around us with surprising tenderness before he jumped back onto his ATV and darted over the snow.

Yusuf squeezed his eyes shut. But we were together. His breath was on my face and I was whispering into his ear over and over again, against the drone of the ATV engine. *We're safe. We actually did it.*

Speeding across the snow on the improvised sled felt like we were falling sideways the whole time. The three-wheeler engine growled a minor chord, a long, drawn-out *ohhhh*. Owe. *You owe it to him.*

I held on to as much warmth as I could, shivering under the blankets until the Hotel Selene drifted into view.

Our goggled, ATV-riding savior's name was Riz. He puttered his ATV to a stop in the valet semi-circle in front of the hotel by a fleet of a dozen or so others, along with golf carts and things that looked like souped-up camera dollies. Me and Yusuf shifted up in the sled to eye our surroundings. Nearby, frozen plumes of water burst out of a marble fountain and hovered in the air. The domed, terra-cotta colored hotel rose three stories out of the white blanket of the snow, the huge sign with Hotel Selene in looping script dim against the darkening sky. A woman in a toga lounged on the final *e* in Selene, the letter stylized as a crescent moon. Beyond the tall glass doors of the hotel, a lobby of marble and rich silk glowed with warmth, all of this under the half-Earth that lingered overhead.

None of this looked like it belonged here.

The pillowcase wrapped around Yusuf's face slipped off in the wind. I pulled mine off too, letting the cold air sear my lungs.

"Joel?" Riz asked, looking to Yusuf. "Are you back already? And where's Niall and Jerome?" Then he looked at me, and I swear I could see the exclamation point bouncing off his head as recognition shifted into *huh?*

I sighed. Here goes. Soon, I'd meet the version of myself in this universe who was an axe murderer or anti-vaxxer guru fraud or something. "Take me to the other me and we'll explain everything."

I almost cried in the hotel foyer, letting the slightly musty air thaw my bones. Riz led us deeper into the lobby with its alcoves with statues of gods and goddesses holding bows and bunches of grapes, their togas draped over long kaftans. Past circular sofas of gold velvet and murals of gold sea monsters and mountain hunts. An empty check-in desk decorated with a mandala bordered in a Greek key design and gold phoenixes frozen in flight. Rich silk curtains—dusty with disuse—paired with white linen. The place must've been beyond beautiful once, before the cobwebs and the tattered edges of the sofas, before the smell of stale bodies. Like Santorini by way of the Silk Road.

Yusuf's hand brushed mine as we trailed Riz, our blanket capes dragging on the floor behind us.

The room that Riz led us into had probably been a restaurant bar and dining room, once, like in one of the boutique hotels in Boston where I'd film a wedding reception that saw guests slinging back thirty-dollar martinis. Our feet sank into the thick red carpet while overhead crystal chandeliers hovered like enlarged snowflakes. A wall of windows looked out onto the snow-covered plain, with all the tables and chairs pushed against the other walls to make a broad clearing in the center of the room for what could've passed as the ruins of a huge pillow fort.

Maybe thirty guys lounged on mattresses and pillows on the floor—arms lazily draped around each other—or piles of sofa cushions and blankets. I couldn't guess the theme of whatever costume bash had them lazing off a communal hangover. Some wore open silk jackets with Mandarin collars, which looked like uniforms from the hotel. Others in ripped military uniforms and T-shirts, scraps of suit jackets and what looked like animal furs. The air smelled of warm bodies and spilled booze. Glass shelves behind the bar nearby reached up to the ceiling, each bottle backlit and looking like a glowing cell under a microscope. If outside was the apocalypse, here was the after-party.

And lazing on a pile of mattresses at one end of the mass of bodies was a man with my face. Framed by the wall of windows behind them. He laughed at something one of the guys below him said, his wide smile showing his teeth.

Funny story. In this universe, my alternate self was a filmmaker turned Hollywood auteur director turned career-building mega-production company owner. Mostly, though, he seemed like a skeezebag.

I'm skipping past some of the *oh my god how is this possible* talk after Riz introduced us to my alternate self. His name was Logan, which my mom had told me my dad had wanted to name me, only for her to veto it because it sounded like they were naming me after Logan Airport in Boston. I'm also pretty sure that Logan was so bombed that Riz could've introduced him to a cartoon character, and he would've said, *yeah, sounds about right.*

Logan warmed up real quick when he realized that we might be his ticket off this frozen wasteland. More on that later, too.

Just how did he and thirty or so other men get here? Here's my best guess based on what he and Riz told me that night, then whatever else I could snoop by hanging out with some of the guys and reading between the lines.

They were all supposed to be stars.

Logan's last superhero noir had netted the studio a few billion worldwide—never mind the toys, and licensing, and video games—so they'd basically given him a blank check for his next flick. I couldn't believe how lucky he was. I couldn't even imagine the kind of films I'd make if I had that freedom. Logan decided his follow-up would be an arty military space action-drama called *The Jungles of Andromeda.* But there were no more jungles in America and shooting in front of green screens was so unbearably *over.* Logan had a better idea: this would be the first film to shoot entirely on the moon.

The People's Republic of Měnggǔ had offered to foot the production and host the entire crew in their new luxury hotel. They'd been trying to market a huge section of Luna One—their domed, terraformed habitat on the moon—as the newest over-the-top luxe travel destination and wanted the buzz of having a blockbuster filmed there. The studio had hesitated, at first, about following up Logan's massive flick with a comparatively quiet film starring four leads and a bunch of background actors journeying on America's first space battleshuttle to find a new homeland for their dying planet.

"That's exactly the genius!" Logan had screamed in meetings. Think of the hype, the built-in marketing plan about the movie filming off-world. Never mind all the labor laws they could skirt in the legal gray area of another country's satellite territory. Plus, he'd *deserved* a three-month shoot that would basically be a tropical vacation with a bunch of hot men.

He'd been really good at convincing people of things.

His casting techniques had never been a secret. His pool parties, his auditions in hotel suites or club VIP lounges. How he'd always been surrounded by a seemingly endless roster of beautiful men with sculpted shoulders and muscles striping the sides of their ribs like fish gills. *Muses*, he'd be quick to say about the men who'd *inspired his art about the beauty and ugliness in all of us and blah*—who he'd plucked from gym locker rooms or on the beach. Models/actors/personal trainers/servers had flocked to him at parties and had introduced each other to him because he'd basically made Joel Hassan, casting him out of some no-name off-Amsterdam play in New York City and look at him now. Multiple franchises under his belt, along with his billboards hocking cologne and watches, plus he'd followed Logan from flick to flick as his uncredited creative partner.

Besides, Logan had still been handsome then. Before the gristle of exile on Luna One, before the scars across his nose and the pink splotch over the right side of his face after he'd tried to fix one of the weather habitat systems but just ended up whacking it with a wrench and getting a face full of steam. He'd been fit and tan, even if his face had been pulled too tight to hide the wrinkles of two decades in the California sun. He'd made the boys laugh and made their lives comfortable while they hung around him, and when they'd wanted to leave he'd wished them luck, and made a few calls to get them their next gig.

I mean, I've banged sketchier guys after a sidewalk sale outside of a WeHo club at 3 am, a lot of the men he'd cast had decided, *so I might as well get on my knees and think of my name in lights.*

Riz told me all of this as I tried to keep my face still, imagining just when in Logan's life he became a monster. Maybe because he'd gotten all he'd ever wanted. All *I'd* ever wanted—though I'd give it up to keep from becoming a gross shark like him.

The green jewel of Ménggǔ's twenty-mile-diameter lunar habitat had been visible from the Earth. At the center of the circle had been a wide complex of research labs and dorms with a few other satellite stations dotted around. With all the nation had learned about terraforming and weather architecture, they'd hoped to build a second dome that would test the large-scale stability of their findings before they irreversibly changed the Earth. They'd dreamed of drought-resistant forests that would grow in months and suck carbon from the air, with tree roots boring deep into the soil to purify the irradiated ground water. Decades of unchecked climate change had fried the Earth—withering jungles, shriveling the Nile, carving a new desert from Vienna to Warsaw across Ménggǔ's Eastern Province. They'd planted a prototype jungle on the edge of Luna One and had watched it flourish into a green paradise. Untouched groves of pineapples and hibiscus shrubs, with neon blooms the size of dinner plates. Waterfalls spilling into crystal pools fringed with birds of paradise. The perfect place to build a hotel, right by the supply spaceport, to woo investors with the unlimited future of Luna Two.

Logan had gotten the green light and they'd have free run of the place for the whole production. First, though, he'd had the bright idea to travel to Luna One with the cast for two weeks ahead of the shoot so they all could *bond* as a creative unit.

Joel had been cast as the commander of America's first Space Armada and his soulful brown eyes could carry a lot of the movie's weight. With betrayal and mutiny at the heart of the story, the cast had to live together to develop a real chemistry—a collective heartbeat, Logan had swooned. When Joel's second-in-command stabbed him in the back, he wanted the audience to feel the blade.

Week one had been a paradise of lobster kebabs and ketamine. Of caviar and cocaine, and boys breaking off into groups to scatter into the palms surrounding Hotel Selene's infinity pool. Week two, Logan had taken a couple of cameras and led the cast into the jungle for four days of camping, and rehearsals, and shoots to test the mood of the script, completely incognito without even a satellite phone for the studio to harass them. They'd pitched tents or slept in the open air under the hab dome with its fake sunsets to mimic Earth. They'd cried, and talked about their dead childhood pets around campfires, and frolicked through more chemistry screen tests in glades of palm trees.

By the time they'd gotten back to the Hotel Selene, the staff had already peaced-out in one of the shuttles that had been parked outside of the dome. Best that the crew could tell by scanning the hotel security footage, the asteroid had hit Earth while they'd been doing their trust falls. Everyone else in the research stations of Luna One had already evacuated. Radio silence from Earth, too, which hung in a dim crescent in the sky.

That was nearly a year ago. In the weeks of silence that had followed, the snow had started falling, and an Earth warped with dark clouds looked down on them. Some part of the hab's weather system had malfunctioned. The pineapples and the hibiscus had withered. The infinity pool had frozen into a block of ice looking for a giant martini to cool. Goodbye tropical paradise. They'd abandoned the other floors of the hotel and had moved into the restaurant to conserve energy and wait for the rescue that wasn't coming.

Logan had led them all here. He'd trapped them but also had saved them, in a way. The blame was murky—nothing as easy as it had been those days in the jungle—though they tried to wrestle some of that joy back. They were pack animals, now, and Logan would look out for all of them. They still had cases of beluga caviar and slabs of wagyu beef in the freezers of the kitchen. All they had to do now was drink and eat and fuck until they starved to death in the best five-star hotel this side of oblivion.

"You should see the footage from those four days, though," Logan told me, outside on the deck by the iced-over pool. A single palm frond tried to struggle up from the snow. We had the same buzzed hair, the same slightly stooped shoulders. Honestly, we were way more alike than I was cool with—he was the gritty, sleazier reboot of me. He offered me a drag on his cigarette—oregano, he said, since they'd ran out of tobacco and weed a while back—but I waved him off. "Fucking beautiful stuff."

He flicked the cigarette and the red spark died against the snow.

28
PACKED

We needed a plan but first I had to get Yusuf out of here.

Dinner was beef sliders that Logan cooked to order on a small griddle at the bar and served with ice-cold martinis. No one seemed especially interested in the details of how or why we were there. Happy hour had started around eleven that morning. I mean, I'd almost passed out after learning about the Envisioner, and here we were, two for two in the blasé reaction department.

The food line was a mish-mash of worn silk pajamas and military costumes under hotel bath kimonos. Me and Yusuf grabbed some grub and stuck to the fringes, away from the other guys who sat in a circle on the floor. After he was done playing chef, Logan floated to the circle to hold court, wearing a wolf fur, complete with a head, which was out of place even with all the other costumes. The only light came from floor lamps scattered among the mattresses and blankets.

Yusuf's social batteries were running low, his brown eyes locked on the stray melting chunk of ice in his barely touched drink. Even after making the rounds, we still hadn't met Joel. I could see Yusuf, fresh from pulling me off Hassan's operating table, drafting theories in his head. Probably worrying over what kind of human wrecking ball Joel was, and what that meant about himself.

"You need anything?" I whispered to him.

"Hmm?" He furrowed his brow, looking up. "No. Just…"

"Yeah. I get it. This is all a lot."

"Right." He frowned at his martini glass. "And I don't know that I can stomach an enhanced evaluatory—a drink right now. I'll be right back."

After I watched his slightly stooped shoulders as he walked back to the bar, I turned to Riz, our official tour guide.

"Where's Joel?" I asked him.

"He took a couple of the guys and left," Riz said, flicking his eyes at Logan and lowering his voice. "Every few months he'll say something about being sick of Logan's shit and he'll up and leave. But there's nowhere else to go to. They said they were gonna move to one of the research stations or something." He wiped the beef grease off his chin and licked his thumb. "He always comes back."

Logan, propped up on a pile of mattresses, his arm around a guy in a military uniform with another dressed as a bellhop dozing on his leg, didn't seem to mind that Joel wasn't around. The light of the nearest floor lamp cast their shadow as one unified blob on the ceiling.

I didn't have to poke with the Storyteller voice too much for Riz to start dishing. A year of exile with the same group of guys must've made him hungry to talk to someone else.

Joel had known what he was getting into when he started hanging out with Logan. *Dating* was too casual a description since they'd lived together in L.A. since he'd been cast in the film. They'd never been exclusive, though if Logan could form an emotional bond—the jury was still out on that—it was with Joel.

And Logan had been charming, and hilarious, with his passion for work beaming onto those around him like a spotlight.

Being trapped here had just dumped gasoline on all of Logan's selfish habits, whether he knew it or not. Or cared. The wolf pack had quickly found themselves divided into a pecking order based on whoever Logan—or both Logan and Joel, at first—had been sleeping with at the time. And they'd all wanted him to want them but couldn't place just why.

I mean, I got the draw of the wolf pack in theory. I knew how the lines between friends and lovers blurred. When you could be both at the same time but maybe also neither, and you tried to do it all with kindness though that didn't always work out.

It's condescending, but I couldn't help but feel that this level of entanglement could never be Yusuf's jam because navigating his own feelings and explaining them to me was hard enough.

"What's with the wolf coat?" I asked Riz, bobbing my chin to Logan.

In the beat of silence, low laughter floated over to us. Dinner was about done and a few of the guys were making rounds collecting dishes. Riz pulled from his drink. His breath smelled like the ATV exhaust.

"The first few weeks alone, after the disaster, were rough. The snowstorms lasted for days. We didn't know how long our supplies would last. We rustled up some ATVs and solar carts and started exploring the whole hab looking for other people or a way to get back to Earth. A couple of days in, we… we found this zoo."

I looked down at my clean plate and really didn't want Riz to keep going.

"Research station, I guess, with animals in these glass cell things. Anyway. They were stuck there. Rabbits, a bear, giraffe.

The wolf had eaten its cellmate. They were all starving. We were gonna set them free in the hab but they'd have no food out there and honestly, that seemed cruel."

"You didn't…" I trailed, my stomach spinning.

"*I* couldn't. None of us could kill them. Logan had to. He did it fast. As kind as he could, I guess." Riz tried to laugh, and I know he meant to break the tension with a joke if that's what this was, but it came out weird. "Giraffe is way sweeter than you'd think."

Looking back, I'm not saying that I'd crawl into the wolf pack while the Grim Reaper smoked a butt off stage right and waited for his cue, but I get it.

Let's say I'd never met Yusuf and got mixed up in all of this by myself, with Kaori and Figueiredo chasing me across universes, into one purgatory after another. Sooner than running forever, I'd probably find some cozy place to land, swallow a bellyful of pills, and settle down for a long nap.

Yusuf made me want to fight.

I told him that the night before he left me on the beach, when I was still trying to convince him to stay. The words were mostly a compliment, but I'd be lying if I said that there wasn't a niggle of annoyance there. A hidden weapon. A razorblade in the birthday cake. *How dare you. You made this hard for me because I would've just given up. You made me want to fight.*

Me and Yusuf left the wolf pack after dinner for a private room, our arms piled with pillows and blankets because the guys said that the rooms away from the restaurant got chilly at night. I finally shrugged out of Rui's bloodied shirt—officially mine, now—and the rest of my clothes, and watched the mess of the last day spin down the drain of the shower. Yusuf hopped in after I was toweling off. The mirror fogged as I tried to scrub the blood from my shirt at the sink.

"I never thought I'd miss frozen pizza dinners at the Compound," he said, his voice echoing in the marble-walled shower.

"I hear that."

He smelled of fancy bar soap and mouthwash when we slid under the covers of the huge bed in this hotel room that neither of us could ever afford, like some weird honeymoon we didn't want. The wolf pack had pulled the floor-to-ceiling curtains off, probably to use as blankets. Two mahogany armchairs were tufted in red fabric, with gold fringe hanging off the seat. I could see the Earth hanging in the starry sky through the window. I missed the cheap Gold Rush Hotel in Beatty, now that the gold rush was long over.

We were safe for the first time since escaping Hassan's universe, giving me the chance to unpack everything and try to cobble together an exit plan. The funhouse-mirror-horror-show of seeing Figueiredo in the flesh, with the shockwaves of anger that blasted off him. How weird it was to see him and Kaori together. Her working with him was a betrayal, but I knew she wouldn't see it that way and she'd only offer some cool dismissal. *Those are the feelings you are bringing to this, but they are coming only from you.* Then how she told me she was dragging me and Yusuf back to our home universe so I could set things right. *We're too far away, here, for the ripples to hit and everyone has to be in their original vector in the multiverse.* A big part of me wondered why with all Figueiredo could do—dropping into whatever universe he wanted, maybe changing his own world by willing it—he couldn't just grab ahold of his All-Eye and kill Yusuf to revive Tiago.

If we all had to be in our original universes for whatever changes we wished on each other to actually take hold, that meant that me and Yusuf could never go home again.

Something colder than our trek through the snow crept into me. Yusuf rustled the sheets, the sound as faint as the falling snow outside. Neither of us could find sleep. I could tell he was wrestling with something, but I couldn't always be the one to tease it out, as much as I wanted to. I couldn't push. I needed him to let me in, when he was ready. I ran a thumb over one of his eyebrows.

"We can't run forever," he said.

"I know." I inched closer, his breath sweeping over my bare skin. "We have to stop them."

"Yeah."

Don't say it. Don't say it. He closed his eyes. *Don't say we have to kill them because that's not the kind of thing that you can just drop before bed.* The chilly dread frosted over me, even through the piles of down blankets.

After a while, he turned away from me. He was so still that he must've gotten some sleep. I stayed awake most of the night and watched the edges of the giant dome that separated us from space bloom with the pink of a fake sunrise.

Bitterness cut through the fog in my brain. The cappuccino that Logan made for me the next morning at the bar, while Riz led the wolf pack through a yoga session in the middle of the ring of mattresses, helped me melt the doubt that had frozen in my chest last night.

Step one in my plan—I wouldn't exactly call it a master plan because I could hear Genesis's tinkling laugh like, *oh, honey*—was to get allies. Even with Yusuf in my corner, Kaori and Figueiredo had the brains and god knew what other tricks. If we couldn't outsmart them, maybe we could outman them.

Logan wiped down the bar top with a rag. I still wasn't sure what to make of him. He was layered—even if most of those layers were gross—but he was trying to make their lives here as comfortable as he possibly could.

"I'm trying to keep them busy and active," he said, nodding to the group, wavering in their tree pose. "Yoga. Scavenger hunts around the hotel. Cooking lessons. It keeps the cabin fever at bay for a while."

"Good idea."

Yusuf was burning miles on the treadmill in the basement fitness center after saying he needed to clear his head. He'd scrounged up a pair of shorts and a T-shirt from one of the guys. If we had any hope of getting out of here alive, we needed his brain. Besides, as much of a help as he was dealing with mad scientist Hassan, navigating imploding gay relationship dynamics was more my wheelhouse. I was happy to do the recon work.

I tried not to stare at Logan while he steamed milk for more cappuccinos for the guys. Seeing Figueiredo and Rui had prepared me for a kind of curious distance from other versions of myself. I had to stop thinking they were all different versions of *me*. Me with a different haircut. Me with a mustache in a palette-swapped crowd of other me's. Because however this universe existed—if each one was created at the same time or if they split apart at different points—we were different people.

For the first time, I was thankful for my all-but-ignored docs that I'd blown my money on, for the watch parties that Genesis had hosted at a popup club where I'd bought cheap beer for everyone. I watched Logan's pulled-tight face and his eyes that drank in the sights of the lean bodies of the men who he probably thought, on some level, belonged to him. Success, and ego-stroking, and money had warped Logan into this person who felt he was owed something.

"I need you to get us out of here," he said. "Even with rationing, we've got three, maybe four months, tops, before our food stores start to run out."

Riz's voice floated over to us. *Now we move to corpse pose. We're going to stay here a while. Just breathe.*

"Do the others know anything?"

"Joel. And Riz has some inklings."

"We've got people tailing us who want us dead," I said after pulling on my cappuccino. "Help me with them and I'll drop you off in whatever Goldilocks universe you want."

"You've got a deal."

He clinked my mug with his champagne flute of vivid orange mimosa.

Kaori and Figueiredo had taken two days to find me and Yusuf in the last universe. Less than that, really, because maybe they never would've found us if I hadn't snuck out of the house and used the Farsight alone at the Predictive Intelligence Bureau. I'd only ever used my mojo on the Envisioner to emergency eject out of one universe and into the nearest one. And that had already almost killed us once. I needed time to practice with the machine and see if I could hone whatever connected me to it. Practice, meaning touching the machine and connecting to it over and over again—basically lighting up the whole Envisioner network and flicking on a big HERE WE ARE for Figueiredo to see.

When I was halfway through my cappuccino, Yusuf joined me and Logan at the bar, smelling of salt with a storm-cloud of sweat down the front of his borrowed T-shirt.

"How did you guys get here from Earth?" he asked. We hadn't found him a new pair of glasses yet. One of the lenses was still a spider web of cracks from the tussle back in Hassan's world.

Every time Yusuf spoke, Logan's eyes lingered on him. A heavy weight of a stare that if I'd been at the business end of it at a bar back home I'd tell the guy, *ease up, man. I'm not a fucking cheeseburger.* Logan sputtered through something about a spaceport nearby, where the ship from Earth had dropped them off. Then a shuttle van had whisked them from the port and rolled into a freight airlock in the basement that separated the dome from the barren lunar surface. I could see the pieces falling into place in Yusuf's head.

"Sorry," Logan said, blinking away some cobwebs in his eyes at the sight of Yusuf. "It's just so weird. You look exactly like him."

"Yeah." Yusuf cleared his throat.

"Sorry you guys are in a fight," I fumbled. "Or, something."

Logan waved me off. "He'll be back soon. Especially now you guys are here. He'll definitely want to meet you."

"You told him we're here?" I asked.

"Yeah. He took one of the two-way radios with him. Sometimes he picks up and listens. Sometimes he doesn't."

"What'd you say?"

"I said two guys who look just like us dropped in through a machine in the middle of nowhere and that it means we're getting outta here." Behind us, the wolf pack wrapped up their yoga session and flooded the bar. Logan flitted away from us to play host, pouring mimosas into flutes. "I said, 'Baby, come home.'"

I watched the muscles working at the sides of Yusuf's jaw.

One week, moths invaded the Compound. They'd fluttered in the cones of light cast by the spotlights in the Theater. We'd all found their little brown, withered bodies in the cabinets of the kitchenette and in our rooms. They'd driven Kaori absolutely bonkers. How the hell did the things get into her supposedly airtight facility?

I'd caught a couple of moths, held my breath as I'd stuck them to cotton swabs dabbed with petroleum jelly, and zoomed my camera in real close. I'd been dicking around, unsure of what I was going to do with the footage. Yusuf had been sitting on my bed, flicking over some Envisioner readouts of the day on his tablet. Scarlett was hooked up to my laptop on my desk, with the footage of the moths projected on one wall. The things had struggled against the goo—twitching their spindly legs and antennas, their trapped wings leaving brown dust on my hands.

"That's cruel," Yusuf had said.

I barely looked up from my footage. "What? They're moths."

"You'll mind when you're the moth."

It hadn't really been a fight, but close enough.

Through the hallway after we left the wolf pack for some quiet, I could already see the argument swirling behind his eyes. The patch of sweat down his borrowed T-shirt mimicked the abstract birds on the foil wallpaper surrounding us.

"We can't take them with us," he said, once we were inside our room.

"We won't. But we can help them find someplace safe to land."

"I'm not saying I don't feel bad." He crammed his fists beneath his crossed arms. "It's just too many variables. We barely know what we're doing as is. And we have no idea about the consequences of matter from one universe hanging around in another, never mind what we're already—"

"You'll mind when you're the moth," I cut him off.

His sigh was a white flag. He looked down then back up again, his annoyed smile like *you got me, you asshole*. He pushed off the wall and walked into the bathroom, where he peeled off his sweaty clothes and stepped into the shower. I watched the droplets on the glass shower door warp his naked body.

"I'll handle the human variables," I said to the spray of water. "You just keep working a plan, doc."

The shower and the bathroom vent drowned out his answer. I plopped on the bed—already making a mess of the neat plain of the duvet that he'd carefully smoothed out with his hands that morning—because I could hear Figueiredo's low whisper.

```
SCENE: A CUSHY HOTEL ROOM, WHERE FIGUEIREDO
SITS IN A CHAIR FACING THE BED WITH A SNIFTER
OF BRANDY IN THE LAMPLIGHT, AS IF HE'S PAID TO
WATCH HAYES AND YUSUF GO AT IT - NIGHT


                    FIGUEIREDO
          Interesting that you believe saving
          thirty men will make up for killing
          billions. Please.
```

Figueiredo's whisper stretched out into the low mechanical whir of solar engines and tires outside. I looked through the wall of windows, out over the white canvas of snow, where six guys from the pack whipped by on ATVs and a flatbed truck to drag the Envisioner back here.

29

COSTUME CHANGE

D id I mention the guns?

Logan had been filming a military flick, and along with the cast, the first shuttle from Earth had dumped a bunch of supplies on Luna One. Sewing machines for the costumers—which the pack had used to Frankenstein together some winter gear—lighting equipment, more food, and a crate loaded with enough guns to arm a militia. Sure, most of the ammo was blanks for filming, but the studio's insurance company wouldn't let the production film off-world without a security detail. Four of the wolf pack were hired guns packing actual heat. Plus, Yusuf still had Chekhov's ray-gun lifted from Figueiredo in our hotel room, stashed in one of the nightstand drawers.

The four security guards and two others had ridden off to drag the Envisioner back here from the abandoned building that me and Yusuf had bombed into. It didn't take a whole lot of convincing, Logan told me, since the box was their only shot off this ice cube. They'd hauled the Envisioner down a freight elevator and into the underbelly of the Hotel Selene.

Logan led me, Yusuf, and Riz past the tapestries of the lobby and into gray tunnels to the freight airlock. Down a dim hallway that was lit with red overhead safety lights, a tunnel from purgatory into hell. The hallway ended at a thick set of metal double doors to the left of a huge window that looked into the steel box of the airlock, where the Envisioner waited for me. The door set in the airlock's far wall was ringed in more red lights and led out to the suffocating surface of the moon. A few gauges, switches, and a row of spacesuits were the only colors in the gray cave of my workroom.

"That's the thing?" Logan asked.

"That's it," I said.

"So it… predicts? It'll tell you what I'm gonna say next?"

"Something like that."

"Then what the hell does that say about free will?"

"Yusuf, you wanna take that?"

"Not really."

Logan scratched absently at one front tooth. "Remind me," he said to Riz, "to turn this into a screenplay when we're outta here."

Yusuf warmed up a bit to all of us being here in the bowels of the hotel, seeing as how it was mostly his plan. I'd have two armed guards in the airlock at my back the whole time, with two more beyond the doors that led back into the hotel. Four guards were ready to shoot at Kaori and Figueiredo or whoever else dropped unannounced through the machine and all I had to do was run through one door and we could vent the airlock out to space.

All our plans and preparations, even a fire drill when we rehearsed how long it would take the doors to the hotel hallway to open and the guards to rush in as my backup.

Maybe you're getting annoyed with me and wondering why, now that I had free access to an Envisioner, I wasn't just connecting to it and changing the future into whatever I wanted. I could trap Kaori and Figueiredo here, or have them explode in confetti, or melt the snow and let the wolf pack frolic in their tropical paradise again, or something.

The simple answer is that I didn't know what would happen.

Saving Yusuf and altering the world back home was an accident. Kaori wanted to pin all this blame on me for the asteroid that was headed to Earth or whatever else, but I had no idea what I was doing. Once I knew that unnaturally changing the events of the future could throw the whole world and maybe the universe out of whack, I couldn't do it. Even if it would benefit me. I had a choice. What would happen to everyone was now my responsibility.

Besides, changing things would make me the monster that she's convinced I am.

The training montage of me working with the Envisioner is pretty boring. Just two days of me and the machine in the airlock, with two bodyguards at my back and two more beyond the airlock doors that led to the hotel tunnels. Bowing my head and running my hands along the machine, trying to quiet my mind and feel the threads of the different universes. While at the same time, tense with the very real possibility that at any moment, Kaori and Figueiredo could pop out of the machine that I was close enough to brush my eyelashes against. Feeling for hours and hours like I was in a car skidding over the ice and not knowing if I'd crash.

Hours trickled through my hands on the machine's facets, like when I was in a flow state in the middle of editing a doc. I'd never had uninterrupted hours with the Envisioner like this, even back in the Compound. I made sure to open portals to other universes and pop back into this one again quickly, thinking if I could light up a bunch of Envisioners throughout the network, I could hide my tracks.

I may have been still recovering from getting my head knocked around with the way, for the first time, it felt like the machine had a personality. Something a little fierce or impatient, like a dog I had to soothe and gain its trust. I sucked in deep breaths to douse the fire in my gut because just about anyone I know would tell you that I've never been patient.

Somewhere in the middle of the give and take with the Envisioner I could feel beyond it—*through* it—to the network of other machines in other universes. How each universe was like a thread with a different tension that, if plucked, would ring out with a different note, and the music would ripple over my ribs. The threads that felt the closest to this universe—Hassan's world, my own, even an unfamiliar thread that was probably Figueiredo's— felt like they'd ring out in similar notes.

The machine had told me something before about how *adjacent realities seek a zero sum.* I never really understood why keeping Yusuf alive meant dooming a whole world. Him and Tiago seemed like a fair trade for each other. A life for a life and all that. Yusuf was everything to me, but what was he in this whole equation? I clenched my jaw and tried to shape this into a question to ask the Envisioner, and before I could even open my mouth, I saw the flashes behind my eyes. I don't know if they were just my brain cranking out its own theories, or if the machine was trying to get me to understand that Yusuf was part of some chain reaction. That even if he wasn't saving lives directly—billions of them— something he does will impact humanity. Down the line someone will use his research to get us off Earth before another disaster and we'll spread to other planets. City spires and traffic jams and fast food on Mars.

Or maybe it was Tiago. Another flash, another premonition through a cracked kaleidoscope. Maybe when Tiago lived like he was supposed to in his world, something he did to the All-Eye backfired. Figueiredo never thought big enough, did he? And hadn't the All-Eye been Tiago's idea anyway, and were they really using it to its full potential? Tiago cranked the machine past its red zone for an experiment and the fail safes fizzled, with the whole network of machines across the Afro-Asiatic Union and India shuddering apart. The machines controlling the power plants and the rail lines. The mini modules in every home busting like baby atom bombs. With Tiago gone, all those people wouldn't turn to ash in one giant explosion that was like the sun leaning in for a big kiss.

I don't know which vision was real, or right. What I did know was that the machine was trying to tell me that the debt of all those lives had to come from somewhere.

That didn't matter when I needed to take Yusuf far, far away from here. To find some safe place where Figueiredo couldn't even drop in. I could almost feel the thread of some distant safe harbor for an instant before it slipped out of my hands. Some gold note like sunlight on my face and warm, pink sand under my bare feet, before it vanished away again.

Figueiredo was a sour note, a clangy minor chord through all this that made me stop, chug some water, and let the guys watching my back take a break. I'd seen footage of him opening gateways into other universes as easily as twisting a doorknob and dropping Envisioners in. He could open doorways to anywhere he wanted instead of just connecting to another Envisioner that was already there, which—as far as I could tell by flying by the seat of my pants—was what I could do. When I met him and Kaori in the interrogation room in Hassan's universe, they seemingly had no idea how I was able to even jump from my universe in the first place. I could do what other versions of me couldn't, even if I wasn't as strong as Figueiredo.

Yet.

He wasn't better than me, as much as he sneered that I didn't deserve this link to the machine. He fucked with entire universes just to get whatever he wanted and yet *I* was the selfish one? He would chase me across the multiverse until he trapped me and made me kill Yusuf. And everything came so easily to him—his brains, his staff falling all over themselves for him, his ease at messing with hundreds and hundreds of universes, and all I was asking for was to stay alive with the man I loved.

"Uh, Hayes?" one of the security guards asked.

I opened my eyes and the two guards near me winced through gritted teeth. A low scraping sound that must've been coming from the machine frizzed the hair at the back of my neck, with a pinching overtone that whined higher and higher. The facet under my hands almost quaked, like the tar pit of envy or anger or whatever it was that I felt towards Figueiredo could overload the machine's systems and it would blow—vaporizing this hotel and everyone in it—if I would just let it. The minor chord in me, amplified through the machine, called to whatever trapped power was inside. Whispering, *let me out.* I could almost see Figueiredo's eyes, hear his voice that, for the first time, sounded scared. *This is not what the machine is for.* And his little whine sounded so, so *good* because what the fuck did he know, after all, when both me and the machine really wanted to see how it would play out if I just held on a little longer?

"Sorry," I mumbled, stepping back from black box.

I tried, for a while, to feel for the threads again for someplace I could bring us all. The quiet in my head was gone.

I skipped dinner and happy hour in the hotel restaurant, where Logan had decided tonight was the superhero disco, and the wolf pack was tying curtain capes around their shoulders and doodling sigils on their bare chests with stray markers. Like some summer camp craft game, only with more vodka, with their laughter rising over the driving electronic thrum of music from the ceiling speakers.

I know Yusuf wouldn't have cared if I cut a mask out of a pillowcase, stayed with the boys, and stumbled back to our room to him before the sun came up. My throbbing head had other plans for me. I found him asleep in our room, propped up in bed in the lamplight, bare-chested, with his superhero secret-identity black glasses and a hotel magazine limp in his lap. I shucked out of my clothes in the dark. I switched off the lamp and crept into bed beside him, tossing an arm over his chest and burying my face into the curve of his neck.

"Hey," he murmured. "All done with work for the day?"

"Yeah. I think I got us a way outta here. Found us a tropical paradise with indoor plumbing and pool parties to drop right into."

"Uh huh."

The starred sky where the Earth watched over us streamed light through the wall of windows. I could just make out Yusuf's heartbeat at his collarbone, above the dark patch of hair at his chest. *Thump-thump. Thump-thump.* The steady metronome of him. His breath was the rolling tide of the ocean on the shore.

We slept for a while—behind my eyes was the dreamless black of space between stars—our door barricading us against the music from the party. The low bass thrummed like the heartbeat of some huge, underwater animal. Louder. Then, louder again, the shockwaves of liquid sound flowing through me until—*jesus*—I bolted up in bed at the pounding on the door. Yusuf rustled up by me and winced against the invasion of light from the window. More slamming and screams at the door, with something that sounded like breaking glass on the floors above us, but that couldn't be right.

I whipped out of bed while he fumbled in the slice of light for his glasses and clothes. I ripped open the door to find Logan in the dim hallway, half of the pink burn wound on the side of his face covered with a drawn-on hero mask of pen ink. He shoved his two-way radio at me.

"Joel's back and he brought some company," he said.

I turned behind me to Yusuf, who was silhouetted by the wall of windows. Outside, a beam of light swept over hulking shapes, for an instant lighting up the shadowed faces of a crowd gathered on the snow.

30
THE TOWER

Before I even pressed the button on Logan's two-way radio and said a gruff *hello,* I knew who would be on the other end.

"You have thirty seconds to get outside." Kaori's voiced cracked through the quiet room. "This warning is not for you. It is for the people inside the hotel. Unlike you, I do have some regard for other lives."

I already felt like a crumpled candy bar wrapper after my Envisioner session, exhausted from an adrenaline hangover. The sound of her voice sent a cold jab of steel through my heart. Yusuf flapped his hands at me, mouthing something. I ran to the wall of windows by his side, ready to snap at him to get away from there, when I saw what he meant. Outside, the small army—including a mini-tank thing with a searchlight pointed at the hotel—was positioned behind the frozen pool, beyond the deck right outside of the restaurant. They didn't know me and Yusuf were holed up in our separate room away from the pack.

"How the fuck are they out *there* if they came through the Envisioner? Did they blast through the airlock doors?" I asked.

"Not that I heard," Logan said.

"There must be a second Envisioner on this base," Yusuf said. He turned to Logan. "Did you know that?"

"I didn't know there was one here, never mind two," he said. "Jesus fuck, I barely know where I am right now."

"Twenty seconds," Kaori crackled over the radio again. "I'm not kidding."

"Let the others get out of here, then," I snapped at her.

"Whether they leave here safely is up to you."

"But they have *nothing* to do with this."

"They are insurance. No more bullshit. Figueiredo has his finger on the trigger of the roof cannon on this little muscle car that he brought over. He wants to pull it."

"And how the fuck will blowing us up help if you need me to fix what I did to our universes?"

"If you're dead and can't interfere with the Envisioner anymore, that is a sacrifice you are forcing on us. You and Yusuf need to get out here. Now."

Yusuf looked at me with his steady brown eyes and a thread of understanding passed between us. Logan was here to shove us out into the snow to save his pack. I couldn't fault him for doing exactly what I would have done in his position. We'd have to take him down and run to the Envisioner if we were going to leave here alive.

Under the sloppy ink of his drawn-on mask, Logan's eyes were flat steel.

"Take the boys to that thing downstairs and get them out of here," he said. "I'll buy you some time. Me and Joel should catch up."

Yusuf grabbed the radio out of my hand before I had time to sputter something.

"We're coming," he growled to Kaori.

Maybe I should think about the strands of the multiverse as loops instead of threads, since the same things keep happening over and over again. Collisions seem to knock us off course until we swing back around to see histories repeating. That militia storming the Compound, this army storming the hotel, me and Yusuf barreling down hallways that might as well be the same. A lazy palette swap by the Art Department since they were crunched for time.

I grabbed Figueiredo's gun.

I had to take charge since Yusuf was numb, again, for the first minutes of panic—sprinting to the hotel restaurant and yelling at the wolf pack to follow us. Someone flicked the lights on after last call at their superhero disco with the dazed way they looked around, all *oh, you're who I've been necking for the past hour.* Only Logan followed a straight path—oddly calm through the swirl of curtain capes as everyone careened around him—to the glass sliding door that led to the pool deck. The last I saw of him was the back of his body as he stepped out into the frigid night.

The pack scrambled through the hotel lobby behind us, sobered up by the panic, with Yusuf back in his body and leading us in a full-out sprint. My lungs ached for air as I ran, my feet matching the machine-gun pace of my heart. In the corner of my eye, blurred shapes darted just beyond the revolving glass door of the hotel entrance. Of course Kaori and Figueiredo were smart enough to have teams at all of the entrances, and somewhere behind me, glass exploded and booted feet slammed on the marble. Another squad poured down a stairway from the other floors. The first rattle of bullets hit so hard I thought I was bleeding. Just the screams and the boots and one of the invaders in their faceplates screaming, "Get the fuck down!"

Caped wolves crumpled to the ground around us, tackled by men in body armor. I fired a few shots from Figueiredo's gun into the fray. A smoke grenade fizzed past us when we ducked into a stairwell to get to the lower tunnels. One of Kaori and Figueiredo's marines pounced at us from around a corner and I spun away, only to knock into a wall and lose my grip on Figueiredo's gun. The thing clattered to the floor, kicked by guys in the pack. No matter. Still, me and Yusuf ran.

A stitch in my side—the loop of the outdoor track at the Compound when we had just met—and somehow, *somehow* we slammed to a stop at the first door of the airlock with the Envisioner just beyond and a dozen of the wolf pack with us. The invaders on our heels twenty feet back.

No time to wait for anyone else. Yusuf slammed one of the buttons on the control panel by the door and it creaked—achingly slow—open. We crammed through before the door even widened all the way and soon he was whipping around—slamming buttons and sputtering *how do we lock it, how do we keep them out,* as the door rolled closed. The armored guys were already at the door and screaming *we've got them!*

"Okay," Yusuf heaved. "This is an airlock. The only way to keep the inner door to the hotel locked is to open the outer door. Just a crack." He jerked his thumb to the thick bay door that led out to the moon and our suffocating, oxygen-less death. "Just a tiny crack. But Hayes, you need to move. You need to be fast."

My hands were numb. "Okay," I said. Then again, to try to convince myself. "Okay."

The surge of my heart in my ears cranked the sound on everything else way down. The muffled, distant noise of the wolf pack shouting as the armored men outside fired bullets into the shatterproof glass window. Yusuf tapped around at a few panels and the outer door snuck open—such a tiny space that I couldn't even see it—but the angry red lights that ringed the bay door flicked on. A sign above the inner door flashed to life. *Airlock engaged.*

As tiny as it was, the gap in the bay door was sucking the room of breathable air, I knew. My hands flew to the machine and I begged it, *get us out of here.*

The gateway glimmered open beneath my hands, offering a glimpse of a white room—always white, always gleaming with metal and windows, and pressed lab coats—of some other research facility in some other universe. I widened the gate for the guys to bolt through until it was just me and Yusuf in the airlock, my skin already cold from the venting air, with lava flowing under the surface. The machine wanted me to keep holding on. To crank the frequency of the sound that was rattling both between my ribs and deep beneath the gunmetal casing way up—to test the limits of the machine's power. Letting us jump to safety through the open gateway just before the whole thing smashed apart, taking Kaori and Figueiredo, the whole hotel, and probably half the moon along with it.

"We need to go!" Yusuf yelled over the spray of bullets on glass.

Maybe I was looking for it, but some softness in his eyes, in the middle of all this, seemed to give me permission to do what I had to.

"Yeah," I said. "We'll come back for the other guys."

He knew to lie. "Yeah."

In that second, I knew, *you monster, Hayes. He's doing all this because he thinks he's saving you from them.* I pushed at the machine with my mind—almost the same way as the very first time that started this whole mess—now with more control instead of blind panic. Gently, coaxing the Envisioner that shivered beneath my hands like a raging horse to dial back down from a supernova to something that the airlock doors could hold. This had to happen. I didn't want to light the fuse—my body vibrating like a plucked string—but they were forcing my hand.

Blow.

I grabbed Yusuf and we jumped through the Envisioner's glowing, circular gateway. It zipped closed behind us just as a panel from one of the airlock walls sliced through and clanged into the opposite wall of the hospital we'd landed in, if the white room surrounded by glass cubicles with prone patients hooked up to monitors was any hint. I barely looked up at the stunned, painted faces of the wolf pack and the staff in purple robes and surgical masks who screamed at us in a language I didn't recognize. Then, whooping alarms, and guards with clear face shields and batons, and I didn't have time for this again—to learn the rules of a new place and stick around for a few days and hope that maybe, *maybe* we were safe this time. What was left of the wolf pack was safe here, and the best thing I could do for everyone was get as far from them as possible.

I whipped back to the Envisioner with Yusuf's hand tight in mine, my other hand on the machine's facets. I opened another gateway and we jumped through to a grassy field. Through another to a bombed-out military outpost. Another, on stage at a university auditorium where we crashed the speech of a suited speaker at a podium two feet away. Faster and faster—in wild panic and barely able to suck in air until the weird calm of exhaustion weighed me. I had nothing else in the tank. Tearing through universes, farther and farther away from the train wreck of Hotel Selene and our old lives. A dozen or so gate jumps later, I could barely hear Yusuf at my side, begging, *Hayes, you gotta stop,* over the zipping of gateways that I slammed open and closed. One last one.

I reached out for that thread I could barely feel when I'd practiced with the Envisioner in the airlock, the one that had promised warm sun and pink sands. Kaori and Figueiredo must be ashes on the moon, I knew. We were safe and this all had to be over. I grabbed the thread, held on tight, and gated us through.

And that's how we ended up here on our pink sand safe harbor, the final thread in the multiverse before everything dissolves into meaninglessness.

I'd like to tell you that the other guys in the wolf pack who we left behind made it. The guys who came to the moon to be on the big screen, even if only for a few minutes in the background, so that some little part of them could live on even when they were gone. I didn't know them. I hadn't even talked to all of them, but I knew that they didn't deserve what happened. Even if you want to blame Logan for trapping them there, or them for being stupid enough to follow him. Or greed, or lust. Or me, or anyone else.

I'd like to tell you that they made it, so let's say they did. The airlock doors held back the blast and the armed men trying to shoot out the window told Kaori and Figueiredo that the Envisioner must've overloaded. There was no way that me and Yusuf survived the blast—it was a miracle even that *they* did—so at least that part of their mission was successful. They could all head home and pat themselves on the backs. Kiss their kids goodnight and all that.

Weeks later, I asked the Envisioner left what had happened to Logan. The machine hesitated—by then I could read its moods, like it was my dog when it was stubborn or snippy. *Just a boy and his predictive machine lounging in the sun.* I could mostly get it to show me whatever I wanted. Video simulations on its screen of the past, or the future. Alternate timelines. Which sounds like fun until you spend a day getting drunk in the sun while your boyfriend isn't speaking to you and you ask the machine to take you on a joyride of your past. And the thing is like, *you sure?* Soon enough it plays you footage of happy times, sure, the birthdays, and the documentary release parties, and Genesis dancing on stage as you watch in awe, and the first second your eyes met Yusuf's outside your little cabin in Connecticut.

And then, because you ruined all that and you want to pick at the scabs that have hardened over your heart, you ask it to punish you. So you sit there and torture yourself with every high school embarrassment, or time you got wasted and made a friend cry, or when you were too careless with someone's heart when they were really into you and you dated them because you were bored, and then *jesus,* you're watching your mother cry at your bedside the time you overdosed. And then you're watching her die, again and again, withering away to a cancer months before the cure is found. Through the snot and the tears and the blubbering you see the one person on this Earth— the one who loved you before you knew how to love yourself—die again and again.

Anyway. Logan.

He slid open the glass door as me and Yusuf ran with the wolf pack out of the restaurant. He crunched through the snow, shivering, in his pen eye-mask with his tasseled drape-cape trailing behind him. *What the fuck?* one of the guards whispered to another. The floodlight on the mini-tank swept over him as he walked closer.

"Where's Yusuf?" Figueiredo screamed. "He comes out too or we're going in after him."

Joel, at the front, spotted the ruse first. He could see through the painted mask and whatever costume Logan was wearing for another one of his stupid theme nights to try to make being here less miserable.

"That's not him," Joel said. "It's Logan."

I'd like to think that Kaori and Figueiredo had twisted Joel against Logan. I don't know why. What I know about their relationship sounds pretty shitty, but I'm rooting for any couple that looks like me and Yusuf.

Let's say Kaori and Figueiredo had dropped in through a second Envisioner on the moon. Two are just as probable as one in a universe, I guess, when either option is just shy of zero, unless the scientists on this lunar base had built a second one themselves. Or Figueiredo had a spare lying around. Either way, Kaori and Figueiredo had found Joel and the others he took with him when he'd exiled himself from the wolf pack. Joel told them that two other people had just dropped in there, too, according to Logan, and had made it to the hotel. Best that I can tell, Figueiredo and Kaori had already been on the moon while I'd been working with the Envisioner, thinking I was stalling them by opening dozens of portals. They'd already found me, but Figueiredo wasn't making the same mistake twice and going in hot. He took a few days to haul in his tank and the Navy SEAL team and do a little recon before they stormed the hotel. And maybe Kaori had promised Joel—because Figueiredo would not give a flat fuck—that she'd take him and the rest of the wolf pack off this wasteland if he'd just lead them to me and Yusuf for a peaceful exchange. Because that alternate reality makes what really happened—Joel lifting an arm and shooting Logan square in the chest before he crunched through the snow one footstep closer—less awful. That someone you once loved could put you through such hell that the only relief you'd ever find was shooting him and peacing out of there.

Logan flopped backwards in the snow on his cape and looked up at the Earth as the hotel incinerated behind him.

31
GOLDILOCKS ZONE

'd yammered on and on in my head about how I would do anything to save Yusuf. And Lady Pythia, one hand on the Wheel of Fortune, had clocked me with a wry smile and asked, *Oh yeah? Prove it.*

I killed to save him.

I waded out into the water of our pink sand beach and tried to cool my skin, half expecting steam to sizzle around me. The reflection of my face rippled across the water. The sunlight dazzled my eyes. No turning back now. I'd carry an echo of the Envisioner exploding wherever I went. I'd hear it when I closed my eyes. My first thought in the morning, what would hit me out of nowhere when I crossed streets would be, *people are dead because of you.* Yusuf shivered when I held him on the sand, even with the dry heat of the beach. We were safe now, I said, more for me than for him. His eyes crammed closed, his head replaying all the explosions and the screams. At least that's what I figured, since mine was too.

I thought of Genesis a lot, that first night my thrumming body wouldn't let me sleep. In my delirium of exhaustion, we were getting brunch some Sunday and swapping stories about our Saturday nights. She'd killed herself for what she believed in. One life, and it was her own. I'd blown up an army. I could see her leaning back and playing with the paper napkin on the table, cracking, *You always have to one-up me, don't you?*

I forgave her, hot tears spilling out of my eyes, just as I passed out from pure exhaustion.

I waited until sunrise to ask the Envisioner if the blast had killed Kaori and Figueiredo, because I wasn't sure I could handle the answer. They were alive, the machine told me, but trapped in the rubble of the hotel. I spilled this to Yusuf and we agreed to keep a lookout. He wouldn't let this kill our mood, though. We were safe, and alive and together.

The questions in my head echoed like the fading explosion. Safe, yeah, but for how long? Could we run forever? I followed Yusuf to the shore where he shucked off his clothes and rinsed off in the water, splashing me and laughing when he caught my eye. I couldn't pummel him with my doubt, so I swapped those questions out for others.

Where do you go from here, when everyone who tries to help you winds up dead or tries to kill you or use you?

We tried to think of it as one long vacation.

I gated us from the Envisioner on our beach to another one in some version of New York where the machine was perched on a platform in Central Park, lit up with soft pink light like a war memorial. A security guard yelled at us to get down and we bolted, laughing—two teenagers sneaking out past curfew instead of two men on the run. We walked all night, hand-in-hand, talking about where we'd go and what we'd do now that we were free. What worlds we wanted to see together. No one would ever understand us better than each other, with all the weirdness and trauma we'd lived through. The squat buildings of the city were covered in soot. On the sidewalks, people in long skirts and heavy wool jackets wore long-beaked facemasks against clouds of dust that the aboveground trains belched into the air.

We agreed, wordlessly, to Not Talk about What Happened back at Luna One, besides a quick thank you from Yusuf for doing what I'd had to do. After a couple of days, the guilt of what must've happened to the rest of the wolf pack weighed on me. Mostly, and if I'm being totally honest here, finally being free from Kaori and Figueiredo—temporarily or not—had me closing my eyes with my face tilted towards the clouded-over moon above and breathing deep. Somehow, the life I'd been living had been somebody else's, and now it was actually my own. Right?

Sure, the hours wandering with him were romantic, but we had no money and no place to sleep. We dozed on park benches once the sun rose, my arm around Yusuf and me pinned down by the sweet weight of him, while pigeons plucked at the grass by our feet. I stole us pasties from street vendors and the occasional wad of cash from the tweed jacket of someone on the train platforms. The stern face of Queen Victoria IV glared at me from the red-inked bills. I wasn't proud of dusting off my childhood shoplifting skills, but we had to eat and Yusuf didn't have any better ideas.

We skipped town before long. We crashed in a dorm at the University of Nairobi where researchers were using the machine to break the light-speed barrier. Then the private mansion where the woman who'd found the machine was using it to manipulate the stock market. At the top of a dry hill in the north of Portugal, the Envisioner spat us out at the pre-Roman megalithic sanctuary of Panóias just before dawn. We walked the huge granite stones carved with flat altars and rectangular slits to catch rainwater, with signs pointing out inscriptions to infernal gods, and how the strange machine at the top of the granite hill was likely proof of the existence of some advanced, undiscovered civilization. The groundskeeper chased us away, screaming about how kids always left beer bottles around for him to clean up.

A dizzying trip to Singapore where the Envisioner powered the city that existed half in this world and half as a digital creation, its streets aglow with billions of AI citizens and their shimmering bodies spun of light. With bridges made of crystallized star-glow that rose into a holographic, mirrored version of the city that stretched across the sky. We tried to follow the crowd onto one of these bridges and almost fell off the side of a building and into the spires below us.

Yusuf's wide, bright eyes at each of these new worlds, his laughter at karaoke bars and wonder at networks of teleportation pads, delayed the sinking doubt in me for a while. Because how much of a future do you have if you can't put down roots? If you can't make friends or hold a job?

We spent days between gate jumps on our pink sand beach where we could be alone and let our guards down. Yusuf slept in the sand with his head propped on a balled-up hoodie I lifted from our last jump. Figueiredo followed us even here, on the edge of the multiverse, as the disembodied shadow voice. *You think you're safe, but you'll never be happy.* To shut him up, I séanced with the Envisioner that was half-buried in the pink sand, knowing I could get stronger. I'd already one-upped him by lighting the fuse of the Envisioner at the Hotel Selene, but he could still do things with the box that I couldn't. Footage clattered in my head of him opening gateways to whatever universes he wanted and tossing machines inside, starting this whole mess. As easy as chucking trash out a car window. I didn't sleep that night until I was able to squeeze my eyes shut and find the thread that felt like the familiar tension of home. I could almost see my place in South Boston. I opened my eyes and the glowing circular gateway under my hand was a window into my apartment. The smell of wet wood and old coffee. Eyes stared at me from the walls around my bed, the long-dead men dressed as cops and carpenters, their open shirts over muscled chests, torn from the pages of antique beefcake rags. My old life that I could step back into if I wanted, or take Yusuf there with me, but the gateway would close behind us and we could never leave.

And all of that belonged to someone that I used to be, anyway.

We fell into a pattern, gating into a universe and hanging out a while, sticking to crowded places in case Kaori and Figueiredo had escaped the rubble and tracked us down. I had to stop asking the machine on the hour because it was driving me crazy. Instead, I killed them in my head. I showed Yusuf how I could gate anywhere, regardless of whether the universe had an Envisioner or not. I saw the spark in his eyes—the scientist who wanted to observe, and study, and theorize—that had faded a bit over weeks of travel. Interesting, he said, but maybe not useful right now. Worst case scenario, I'd drop us into a universe and we'd be stuck there forever, with no Envisioner as an emergency exit. Handy or not, the new ability made me want to lean in and see what else I could do.

Dropping by our alternate selves seemed like a recipe for disaster, based on our last jaunts. Still, our lack of money and permanent place to live had us fudging the rules a bit. In one universe we sweet-talked our way into the luxury condo building where that version of Hayes and Yusuf lived. *Whoopsie, forgot our keys again. Would forget my head if it wasn't attached, blah blah.* The doorman buzzed us through and in the condo, we found a spare key fob hanging by the front door of their unit. The first thing we saw when we stepped inside was an instant camera at a small table for odds-and-ends by the door, across from a wall mosaicked with pictures. Years of pictures with the two of them celebrating birthdays, cheesing on beaches, bright pinioned birds resting on their shoulders at zoos. A sliding door to a huge patio offered views of downtown Boston that looked pretty close to my own, with its glass towers, canals, and floodgates holding back the Atlantic.

The other Hayes and Yusuf were on their honeymoon, according to the digital wall calendar in their marble kitchen that was bigger than my entire studio. Best we could tell, they were finance bros, which squashed any guilt-pangs I had about spending their money.

For almost two weeks we slept in their bed and ordered takeout from the lobby restaurant and charged it to their unit. We strolled the city in their clothes. Yusuf swapped his cracked glasses with a pair he'd found by the bathroom sink. I played tour guide and we hoofed it all over the city—sitting in the nosebleeds for a game at Fenway Park, gliding across the water of the Public Lagoon in one of the swan boats, watching the gauzy jellyfish float by the two-story glass seawalls that surrounded the South Boston waterfront and kept Boston Harbor at bay.

I tagged along with Yusuf as he audited a physics class at MIT, saying he was a prospective grad student. He ended up raising his hand so many times and chiming in during the lecture that the professor planted her feet and asked him, *perhaps you'd like to teach this class instead of me?* Yusuf popped up out of his seat and dashed to the front of the class to pluck the marker from the professor's hand and sketch diagrams on the board while he spoke.

I hid my laughter with a throaty, fake cough. I loved him so, so much.

We were happy for a while, probably longer than we had a right to be. It was beautiful and mundane—tossing clothes in the dryer, sorting the recycling, sleeping in and then rolling out of bed to hit a diner down the road—a preview of some future we could have. Maybe no wedding ceremony and honeymoon was in the cards for us, but we were in this for the long haul, whatever we decided our lives would look like. And I wanted all of that with him, with the way he made me want to be more of the person he saw in me. With the way that he shut up the rotating cast of heckling voices in my head, how he canceled the production of their shitty *here's how Hayes is a fuckup now* scenes before they even started.

Sheets soft as cotton candy in their huge bed where I kissed down Yusuf's neck, past the hair across the valley between his chest, following the archipelago of moles down his torso. We opened a bottle of wine. He slipped on a pair of white briefs and stepped out to the small bedroom patio, a floating island of blue tile above the city, just big enough for two chairs and a small table where we could have coffee in the mornings and talk about our days.

"We can do this," Yusuf said, in profile against the twinkling city lights. He sipped his wine, his grip so soft on the glass that it looked like he could drop it at any second. "We can find a universe where we can make this work. Some pre-Digital Age version of Earth where it'll be easier to fake identities. We can get jobs and find a place to live. Or some version of Earth where the you and me there are already dead. Or, or maybe—maybe we talk to the guys here and tell them what happened, and we can share their identities. We can work something out. You and me."

The cool breeze rippled goosebumps over our bare skin. With our weeks and weeks of universe-skipping, winter was just around the corner.

I changed him from the man who could barely unknot the feelings in his own head and explain them to someone else, to this different version, with his soft eyes. I'd never asked him to change for me, and maybe it was more that he was showing himself to me and I just couldn't wait to see more. No one else had talked about wanting a future with me. I almost told him to wait so I could run to the instant camera by the front door and snap a picture of him like this—wrapped in blue shadows from the bedroom, his bed-mussed curls a dented halo, the swoop of one corner of his lips. But I didn't want to interrupt the moment just to document it.

So.

What if we slam the brakes and say *the end* here? Fade to black.

In the writers' room of my pink beach, my co-writers beside me in the sand below where Junior rests on her rock—a coconut, a dried fern frond, and a granola bar wrapper—don't look so convinced. They've been working with me on this film treatment as the sun slowly soft-boils my brains. Ending here is perfect. Hayes and Yusuf are still together and happy, and we even set them up for a potential sequel, a whole goddamned franchise, of their universe-hopping adventures. Coconut is unconvinced with his hairy eyes. *Yes, but did Hayes actually earn that ending?* Fern Frond has been undermining me all day, so she won't be any help. Granola Bar Wrapper just wants to go on his union smoke break.

Fine. I'll keep going.

I joined Yusuf on the bedroom patio, and together, we leaned on the railing. I had to hold my breath, with the constellation of city lights behind him, and try to burn this moment into my head.

The diamond lines of car headlights in the streets, the glowing necklace of white on the Longfellow Bridge over the Charles. Yusuf building us a future with his words—one that I wanted so much but knew would never happen. At least not here and not like this.

32
FLASHBACKS

Yusuf swore he saw Kaori and Figueiredo in a crowd by Downtown Crossing, close to the time we'd have to leave this universe because our alternate selves would be back from their honeymoon. He'd skipped out of the condo that morning like he had the past few days, leaving me to sleep in. He'd come back with coffees or soup dumplings or some other surprise, just like our first days at the Compound when he'd drop by my little temporary house on the green concrete with a few T-shirts or snacks from the cafeteria and some excuse for us to hang out.

He wasn't sure if it was them. He only saw the backs of their heads, but the doubt was enough to smash the fantasy we'd been honeymooning through.

That was the same morning my mother called this Hayes and left a message on the machine. She was alive in this universe and I had to see her before we left. As much as Yusuf begged, *you can't. She'll know something is different and won't understand.* I settled for borrowing our doppelgängers' car and parking outside of the hospital she worked at to watch her leave her nursing shift in her pink scrubs and orthopedic sneakers, turning her jacket collar up against the cool breeze.

All I could do was hold my breath and think, *wait, wait*, because her ghost was shivering through me. I cried, squeezing Yusuf's hand and wheezing in the car, my tears leaking all over my face. I cried at seeing her, and for meeting Yusuf against all the stupid odds and being there with him. I cried for losing Genesis and for her believing in something enough to die for it. For a million other things I couldn't name. Yusuf let me lose my shit for a while as he eyed the other cars in the parking garage, ready to floor the gas if someone came too close. Finally he said, "We have to make another jump."

He was right. We drove back to the place that wasn't our home.

As much as we both wanted to stay there forever, we packed a couple of backpacks from the closet with supplies—a couple of changes of clothes, some sunblock, and canned food. Yusuf snagged a Red Sox hat and tugged the brim low over his eyes. I snapped a picture of him, my tourist, with the instant camera by the door and stuck the picture to the wall with the others. Yusuf loved it, laughing, *how long until you think they'll notice?* We cleaned the place as best we could. I grabbed an air mattress and a couple of sheets from the closet and slung the whole cloth-covered bundle over my shoulder.

Soon, like a couple of travelers, we breezed into South Station where this world's Envisioner waited in the center of a web of glowing pads that teleported people all over the world. I touched the machine and we were gone in a blink. No one would've even known we were there.

We stayed on the beach for a long stretch, and I worked with the Envisioner enough to unlock God Mode on the video game that was my life in the Compound, thanks to a combination of recordings from Kaori's Envisioner and security camera footage from the Theater that she'd uploaded to the machine. Unwittingly gift-wrapping it to the whole Envisioner network where people with admin-level privileges—me and Figueiredo—could access it.

I knew I was missing something, which wasn't so unusual for me.

Yusuf was off for a walk to get supplies, he said, though I suspected he needed a break from me, wandering off in the bright, humid morning. Which I understood. I carved tracks in the sand around the half-buried Envisioner for a while. I'd talk to the thing when I was alone, partly out of boredom and partly out of stress relief after all we'd seen. I ran my hands over the facets like I'd seen Figueiredo do—like I'd done a million times by then—and coddled the machine like it was a tantrum-throwing dog. *Gentle, girl.* The swirling mind of the thing calmed a little at my touch, and at the same time, a sense of flow washed over me like I was hours into a doc-editing session.

I felt the other Envisioners and all their histories spread out across the multiverse, that same way you can walk into a dark room where someone is hiding and just know you're not alone. The spider webs stretched out and out, and I was getting closer to the center.

Show me how we got here, I asked the machine.

I didn't really know what I was looking for or expecting, but the Envisioner did. Its screen blinked to life.

In her office, Kaori pressed her hand against one cold glass wall, smudging the equations she'd scrawled in green marker. She was so close to something that it hurt, and her thoughts swirled around in my own head. Something jabbed at her brain. The good kind of hurt—the hurt of picking a scab, of biting the inside of your cheek.

She'd already combed through most of the footage after copying and dumping a decade's worth onto her private server. The facial recognition algorithm she'd written allowed her to single out footage of just Figueiredo, trimming away everything else, so she'd seen him alone in his facility at night. Both the footage from the Envisioner and his various portable recording devices. The hours and hours and hours—his obsessive narcissism and self-grandeur so clear, even though she couldn't understand all his language yet, though she was learning fast. The years he'd spent recording himself at his desk in his closet-sized university office and his garage lab. How his university had hired that universe's version of Yusuf—either as another professor or as Figueiredo's assistant, she couldn't tell—and then he'd made his breakthrough and built his prototype only a few weeks later.

She didn't know yet what linked Figueiredo to the machine. She didn't need to know, really. That was for her staff to piece together, later. There would be decades to figure it out, and books to write, and she'd pioneer entire fields of physics and quantum resonance imaging to pierce through the shell of the machine to see what's inside, what foreign energy the thing ran on. Right now, Hayes just had to be similar enough to Figueiredo for the link to activate, and then she could guide him. Help them prepare for natural disasters and regulate the climate. Keep them from annihilating themselves with nuclear weapons or genetic warfare. The problem with Figueiredo—well, *one* of them—was that he wanted to be a god.

But she could make Hayes a tool.

They were genetically near-identical, meaning the connection wasn't just a simple gene link. What else made up a person, a consciousness? Memories. Emotions. *Don't say love, don't say love.*

If E was the Envisioner link and F was Figueiredo—her marker squeaked in the footage that I had to blink through the tears to see—and H was Hayes, she could map this out. What did she need to do to H to make him the percentage of F that activates E?

$$(H)^y = \frac{x}{F} = E$$

She didn't have forever for trial and error. *Don't say love, don't say love.* But there was something that would change him so fundamentally—his body chemistry, his hormones, his memories—aligning him closer to that percentage of F, maybe. What happened to Figueiredo before his breakthrough?

He'd met his Yusuf. He'd fallen in love and changed himself—became more ambitious, tried harder. And Yusuf had helped with the research, too. She had to bring them together.

"You're talking to it again?"

Back on the beach where my feet were, I blinked from the Envisioner to see Yusuf with a T-shirt full of dark purple coconut things bundled in his arms, his sunburned forehead wrinkled at the sight of me.

"Just trying to find answers," I said.

"Find anything good?"

The cold look in Kaori's eyes in the footage scraped barbed wire across my chest. I had to tell him what I'd just seen, but I was still slogging through what it meant for both of us. How he bucked against the idea of fate and how stupid and impossible it was because nothing was ever supposed to happen a certain way. So, sure, forget about fate. Would it change how he felt about me if he knew that we only even met because Kaori was messing with us like we were an experiment and she was watching us from beyond the glass?

I couldn't hold it in, not after I'd already been keeping so much from him. He squinted against both the bright afternoon sun and his worry at seeing me crouched in the sand like I was praying to the machine.

"Kaori played us," I said.

"What do you mean?"

I sucked in a breath, wiping the sand off my knees and avoiding his eyes. He dumped the coconuts onto the sand and sat down in front of me.

"She's known everything all along, about the Envisioner, even the right order of Figueiredo's footage. All of this was a game to bring me and you together so she could—I don't know—make us fall in love. Make me similar enough to Figueiredo that the Envisioner would link to me and she could use me to change the world however she wanted."

"Well. Huh."

"It's like none of this was ever real."

"What, this?" He brushed the back of my knuckles, twisting his mouth in a smile. "Don't be stupid."

"Hey, watch it."

"Of course this is real. We're real. Does any of this change how you feel about me?"

"No."

"Did she make you feel anything? Could anyone do that to you? Who cares how we met?"

"Yeah." I wiped at my face.

"That machine doesn't offer any answers. Just more problems."

I knew he was right. He took me by my hand and I helped him lug the coconuts back to our camp where we made dinner by the fire, slamming the coconuts with rocks and watching the liquid inside slosh onto the pink sand below.

———

I got pretty good about covering our tracks. Usually, we leapfrogged through a couple of universes before we headed back to our oasis. I felt the *thrum* of dozens and dozens of threads across my ribs and simultaneously opened gateways to a bunch of other machines to try to throw Figueiredo off the trail.

We slept on our air mattress on the sand and roamed the little island while the sun warmed our skin. Then, we fell back into our pattern. We'd drop into another universe for supplies, or to laze on a real bed, or wash in a real shower, though something was always wrong in each place we ended up. We'd stay a day and I'd get restless and say that we should leave. I could see the arguments building up behind Yusuf's eyes, the things that I knew he wasn't sure how to say, and I was a jerk for not asking. *Are we jumping again because you can feel Figueiredo coming or because you're bored?* I ignored it because opening each new gateway was like a big middle finger to Figueiredo and Kaori. Especially Kaori. Because if they could do whatever the fuck they wanted, why couldn't we?

I was strong enough by then that I could open a small portal to any universe we'd already been in just by recognizing the tension of the threads when I touched the Envisioner, and I didn't need to connect to a second machine. I started using my fancy new portal tricks to pinch us some things from finance bros Yusuf and Hayes's world, which seemed like a safe bet. Supplies, at least at first. I'd stick my hand on a facet of the machine, open a gateway into a supermarket, and grab some things. Never mind that whoever was in the store saw a hand appearing out of thin air and grabbing a blueberry pie off a bakery shelf. I grabbed a jug of milk to wash it all down from another store, and when I leaned out of the portal,

I caught the eye of a mother with her kids who screamed and dropped her carton of eggs on the floor.

"Where'd that come from?" Yusuf asked when I walked back to our camp with the pie and the milk. I just shrugged.

I pinched a video camera to replace my baby, Scarlett, that I'd left at the Compound. And a couple of blankets, lanterns, and logs of quick-start camping firewood. It was so easy. And each time I opened a gateway to nick something, the fireworks started at the back of my brain, the fizzles of euphoria like I was on the dancefloor and the DJ was so plugged into my body that they played the song I didn't even know I'd needed to hear. Everything else just melted away against the bass thudding in my chest. *You can keep going. You've got this.* As much as I wish I could say it was Figueiredo's voice in my head, it was mine. Saying the same things I'd tell myself when I'd been hiding in a bathroom stall for ten minutes so I could delay ordering another drink at a bar. *You'll know when it's too much and you're not there yet.*

Snatching the rings for Yusuf took skill that I'd like to think even Kaori would be impressed with. I opened a gateway into a jewelry shop somewhere, but the kicker was that I opened it *inside* the jewelry case. If I'd been able to do half this shit as a kid, my mom wouldn't have pulled fourteen-hour shifts at the ER and I could've gotten her the best doctors in the world when she got sick. I couldn't change the past—not yet, anyway—and I didn't know what size Yusuf's fingers were, so I just grabbed an entire little velvet tray of men's gold rings and zipped the gateway closed to the screams just beyond it.

I plucked the rings off the tray and tossed the empty thing into the sand. The tide would rise, soon enough, and pull it out to sea. In the moonlight, the rings in my hand glinted like stars.

When I padded through the sand and back to our campsite, Yusuf looked up from the book he was reading by the light of the fire and a nearby lantern. His eyes landed on the backpack full of my latest haul.

"Are those things we need?" he asked.

"All we need is each other." I plopped down onto the air mattress and flashed him a goofy smile, still sizzling from all the gateways I'd opened. I'd be up all night, now. "Everything else is icing on the cake, right?"

"That doesn't answer my question."

"What? I just got some stuff to make this place a little more homey. No big deal."

He pressed his lips into a hard line. "You're being an asshole and that's not you."

His words doused cold water over me. His eyes yanked some plug deep in my gut, sending my insides spinning into a deep drain. I would've snapped at Narek about this, or Genesis. I would've cocked my *how dare you* and *do you know what I've been through* guns. But we both knew that Yusuf was right, because while he loved me he could also slip into his white lab coat and observe what I was really doing. And he must've known that he was the only thing keeping me from leaning into the pull of the machine and whatever it was that I was becoming.

"Huh," I said, just a puff of air. "I'm sorry. And I appreciate you being no-bullshit with me."

He tried to smile. I couldn't sleep that night. I rolled off the air mattress and hid my pocketful of gold rings under a log in the fern forest. Because what the hell was I thinking? What, was I gonna ask him: *Will you take this stolen ring and be my Subject B?*

I thought that Yusuf yanking me back to myself fixed things, until he started going off on his own some mornings, beyond the quick trips to grab us coffee. Just to wander, alone, and I'd wait at home, holding my breath. When he came back it was like he shrank further into himself. Finally, we dropped back to the beach one day, and he walked off without a word. He ignored me as I called out to his back. I couldn't run after him because I didn't want to fight and wanted to give him space. And honestly, this had been coming for weeks.

He shrank to a speck, far down the pink sand. I made a fire at our camp and only started to worry come nightfall. At least the fire would draw him back here.

Hopefully.

He wouldn't meet my eyes when he finally returned. His body was dark against the sky—starred and painted over with a haze of pink like whatever planet we were on was sailing through fog. The muscles at the corners of his jaw worked again and again. I'd shredded a palm leaf into strips and had been braiding and re-braiding it for hours.

He sank into the sand and the cannonball of his weight ricocheted into me. Shadows from the fire played across his face. The iridescent beetle shells of his eyes. When he finally spoke, I could barely hear his flat voice over the waves.

"Hayes, what are you not telling me?"

33
A FRAYED KNOT

His question was a trap, of course. He knew everything.

We'd jumped to an alternate version of Montréal during a festival where people had hung garlands of flowers outside their windows and all along the streetlamps of St. Catherine's Street. Yusuf had left early one morning—I asked the Envisioner to show me what happened and it spun together a video that I only watched for a few minutes before it hurt too much—to walk the flower-bordered streets. When a voice had called out to him from a table outside a little café, he'd turned to find Kaori. Just Kaori, in a gray knit cardigan and her glasses, like they were running into each other on the Oxford campus a million years ago. She'd smiled at him and said he was right on time. He'd thought it was an alternate version of her that belonged in this world until her lopsided smile gave her away.

What are you not telling me?

He stared at the useless palm leaf in my hands and couldn't bring his eyes up to mine. Out of everything I've done, the one thing I'd take back is lying to him when he asked me for the truth.

"Nothing," I told him.

"I know you're lying. I ran into Kaori. Our Kaori."

"You know she'd... she'd say *anything* to get us to follow her back to—"

"Please. Just—stop."

His eyes hit mine. Even in the dim light from the stars and moon overhead, the hurt that I could see there knocked into my chest and bowled me over. An Envisioner detonation behind my ribs.

"I need to hear the truth from you."

"You wanna hear that I'm saving you?"

"Don't do that. Don't turn this around into you doing something heroic for me. I left our universe because you made it seem like Kaori was going to use you to change the world into whatever she wanted. Not that she needed you to fix some mistake you made."

"The mistake being keeping you alive."

"At what cost? I don't want to die, but how can I live knowing that because I'm alive *billions* of people will die?"

"But that's not *your* fault. And it's not like I knew what would happen when I told the machine to save you."

"You didn't know what you were doing at first. I understand that. But when Kaori told you how she discovered the new future because of what you did, you made the choice to take us on the run. You didn't let me choose. You hid this from me. Like... like I'm a child you have to protect. Like you didn't trust me."

"Because I *knew* what you'd say."

I sounded angrier than I was proud of. In the silence, the waves lapped at the shore behind him.

At the café in Montréal, he'd sank into the chair at the table across from Kaori. They sat for a minute in silence until a server dropped off a cappuccino for him, which she'd ordered before he'd walked by. She'd probably asked the Envisioner what he'd want to drink, of course.

"You deserve to know what's really happening," she'd said. "Even if Hayes won't tell you."

She'd said it had been Figueiredo's idea—his *mistake*—to chase us. She was trying to appease Figueiredo so he'd let her access the All-Eye, which was her fault for putting her own wants over the safety of the world. She'd known all along that all she'd needed to do was lay it out to Yusuf. Stick to the math. *All of this is the universe trying to right the equation.*

"I'm sorry." Something pulled at my throat. I dropped the palm frond and reached for Yusuf. His hands were rough—callouses dotting his palms—and I flipped them over and traced the lines there with my fingertips. When he looked up, I squeezed his hands.

"It's not that I didn't trust you," I said. "I just knew what you would say. That *this* would happen. That you would come and tell me that you being alive is not worth billions of people being dead."

"I'm not worth—"

"Because you're not selfish like I am. But I *need* you. And… and… you're the one who told me that every history is equally possible or equally valid or whatever. Just *choose* the one where you stay alive and we can be together."

I was losing him. My reasons unraveled in his hands that blurred in my eyes.

"I'm *asking* you to choose," I begged.

We sat on the sand for a while as the fire burned nearby and the waves lapped higher on the shore. The air smelled of salt and smoke. And regret. He crawled to my side and we leaned against the mattress together, watching the logs burn down to embers.

"I wish I didn't know."

I could barely hear him over the crackling of logs and the breeze. I almost thought I won him over, honestly. Maybe I was wishing too hard or I didn't know him as well as I thought.

We sat in the dark, just watching the tide roll out. We slept a little. I watched the sunrise and Yusuf crawled over to the mattress. Then the next morning he told me *I can't do this anymore,* wincing against the sunlight. I knew he was trying to look at me and see the person he fell in love with, who I still am, but the weight of all the lives hanging in the balance dragged him down.

"We're not white-flagging," I said. "I'm not bringing you back to the Compound. Him and Kaori will kill you."

"What, you're going to keep me here?"

"You know I won't do that."

His sigh was the sea breeze through the ferns.

"I know. I don't—I… Then take me back to Beatty."

"Alright."

We're tied together. What hurts is that I could see in his eyes that he knew this too, the way I grabbed his hand and we walked over to the Envisioner with our steps in synch. I opened a gateway to the universe where we met. A while ago, I'd be discreet about where we portalled into a universe, but the jig was up, so screw it. Right on the sidewalk it was.

Yusuf stepped through the glowing circle that separated the pink sand from the concrete. My hand lingered on the Envisioner, keeping the gateway open.

"I'll figure this out," I told him through the window between worlds. "I know I will."

He smiled just a little. I could tell he wanted to believe me, but I guess I wouldn't believe me either.

"You know where I'll be," he said. "I'm only waiting a few days."

Then, smaller, in a way that broke my heart into a million fucking pieces—because with all the freewheeling and cowboying through universes and kisses in impossible landscapes, he'd never *really* sounded scared. Until now. "Please don't make me go to them alone."

I closed the gateway, stepped away from the machine, and the distance from him pulled me inside out.

So there. You're all caught up. Yusuf bailed on me this morning and I've spent all day flapping my gums at a blinking red light on the camera. Now, let's roll credits and hit the floodlights over at Hayes's Disaster Drive-In to let people know it's time to clear out. I'll watch them blink against the glare and start packing up— folding their lawn chairs and shoving coolers of beer back into their trunks. And then they'll drive away, leaving me here alone.

My ass is sore from sitting on this rock across from Junior, my camera, for hours and hours. I stand up on stiff legs, kill the recording, and wander over to our campsite stash.

The sun hovers low on the horizon of the beach, like one of those days in August back home where I'd swear the summer would never end. I chug from one of our canteens to soothe my throat, dry from hours of talking. I tried to be honest for the camera but I'm sorry if I ever made myself out to be something other than a selfish person who lied to the only man who's ever really loved him.

Yusuf's gone but still I feel him here, since we're all bound up and tangled together. His hairs on the pillows of our air mattress. His history books in the fern forest library. He left his stolen Red Sox hat on the mattress. I wonder if the happy, rich, and married versions of ourselves noticed the picture I took of Yusuf and I stuck to their wall. If that and the nagging feeling that the place isn't exactly like they left it are driving them crazy.

Maybe it's mean, but honestly, I find that hilarious.

Give me a break. I'm tired and at the end of my rope, just hanging by a knot I tried to tie.

Dinner is a couple of protein bars that I fish out of our hole-in-the-sand refrigerator. I shrug out of my clothes and dip into the warm water of the ocean. I'm killing time, I know, wiggling my toes in the sand and watching the skin of my fingers wrinkle. Watching the light through the water ripple and warp the tattoos on my bare skin. The Wheel of Fortune on my foot buried in the sand, the wolf on my thigh, the lines of poetry that I'd written, thinking I was so deep, banding my arms.

Voiceover: A sad man alone, by himself in his sad, empty world.

The voiceover flubs the line. Take two: *A sad man alone and weaving the beginning of a plan.*

My feet brush against something slick and hard beneath the sand, what must be a shell. When I nudge the thing with my foot, I feel a ridged opening. I squat to fish it from the water and find that it's a green glass bottle, the label worn off long ago. I huzz it as hard as I can and watch it flop once against the top of the water. So much for being here on this world alone.

I've been practicing, feeling the energy of the machine and testing its limits. Opening portals and seeing how long I can keep them open—one, then two at the same time, then three. I don't have any weapons for what I know I have to do, so I might as well try to become one.

Even before Yusuf left, I'd wander off and hang with the Envisioner, giving us both some alone time. He'd catch up on sleep or some reading, and I'd pace the quarter mile out to the machine that he didn't want to be near, especially after the explosion on Luna One. We dropped into plenty of research stations and private labs during our jumps, though no one we spoke to could really give us a good answer about how the Envisioner works. Or what else it can do besides predict, like be used as an improvised explosive device under the right—or wrong—hands, for example.

Right now, Yusuf's probably drifting off to sleep in a hotel room alone in Beatty while I'm planted in the sand in front of the Envisioner, the stars leaking light down onto me. He'd never admit it—and maybe he doesn't quite understand it himself—but I think he's a little scared of me now. Strike that from the script. Let me edit. More scared about what I'll do for him.

Kaori couldn't predict what I'd do either, even with her big brain and big machine, before me and Yusuf bailed from under her thumb.

I can see all the threads, all the Envisioners Figueiredo tossed out into the multiverse, so clearly now that it's just me and my girl here. I can reach out an invisible hand and pluck them, against the tick-tock metronome of my heartbeat, to spin a disco tune pulled from one of Genesis's shows. Thrumming the threads lights a sparkler of bliss on my tongue like the cider at the Prince of Cups tavern back in Hassan's Oxford. Maybe my head's fried from sunstroke. Maybe I'm finally getting what Yusuf felt before I met him—how a billion possible histories means that any moment or outcome isn't so special. That's the problem with infinities, I guess. Nothing matters more than anything else.

Except that I feel like the one pulling the strings.

I know when you look up at the night sky, you're supposed to feel all small and overcome with wonder at the universe and *blah*. I feel that, too. But when I look up, I always feel—for that first instant—like the center of fucking everything.

The strings in my head only seem to snag when I think of Kaori. *I thought we were friends,* I said to her that first time she pointed a gun at Yusuf in the Theater to *inspire* me to connect with the machine and change the future. *If we were, then you'd understand why I have to do this.* Then her trying to bargain with me in Hassan's lab.

Sure, keep blaming her, Figueiredo's shadow voice scrapes through my head. The strings vibrate—taut—like with just a little nudge they might just snap. I can almost see the researchers with their white coats in their white rooms, swarming around a dozen Envisioners, all *we're seeing some unusual energy spikes.* Like I could just let the fire in my gut light the fuse on all the machines throughout the whole network and then sit back and watch the fireworks. Like the footage I saw of Figueiredo pacing his gray hangar full of Envisioners and opening gateways to drop the machines across the multiverse is so hokey, now. *You think you're hot shit, but you can't even touch what I can do.*

Some part of the machine under my hands quivers like a dog skittering towards me for comfort at the sound of fireworks exploding outside. She flicks her ears back and flashes me with her big, melty eyes. A whine, pushing her wet nose into my hands. *Easy, girl. Easy.*

It's time to go.

The air mattress finally deflated during the night. I roll off the packed sand with one hell of an adrenaline hangover thanks to the Envisioner. The pink sand and the turquoise water are the same watercolor still-life of a perfect beach morning. Goodbye to my sorta paradise, to me and Yusuf skinny dipping and wandering the tropical fern forest naked. Joking about sunburns on our bare asses. Kissing coconut water from each other's lips.

I ask the Envisioner about what I should do and what the future will be, but she plants her feet and won't budge. Instead, she spins me equations, and star charts, and a recipe for the rice pudding my mom used to make, just because. Like, *you're on your own.*

Fair enough. I'll decide things from here on out.

Back at our campsite I pull on my paint-splotched khaki shorts and Rui's polka dot shirt, the fabric sandpapering against a sunburn on my shoulders. I lid my dome with Yusuf's Red Sox hat, already knowing that when I see him I'm going to make a crack about *just popping by to drop off something you left behind.* And if—even after this nightmare—a hint of a smile touches his eyes, I'll know we can make this work.

I snag Junior and a roll of duct tape from the supply stash, then wiggle my feet into a pair of Yuppie Hayes's running shoes. One last look around our campsite, feeling Yusuf so close he could be standing behind me, before I turn and hoof it towards the Envisioner.

I lift Junior, flip her viewing screen so I can see my face as I talk, and cheese for the camera.

"I guess this is all a warning," I say, white waves rolling behind my back, this after-credits scene that sums up the whole film. "If you ever find one of these fucking machines on a mountaintop, or on an asteroid, or whatever—just do yourself a favor and leave it there."

Cut.

I stick Junior to the side of the Envisioner with long strips of duct tape and then jump through.

34
THE HANGED MAN

I know that things seem like they're building, here. That in the movie version of this, I'd amass an army of other Hayeses and together we'd storm Figueiredo's universe. There'd be this big adrenaline-boner of a fight sequence where my army and his security team pick each other off one by one, until it's just me and him left, running around a hangar filled with tarp-covered previous models of the Envisioner. And then we both strap ourselves into mecha-like battle exoskeletons and try to punch each other's dicks off.

But I don't have an army behind me. Basically everyone I thought I was friends with in the multiverse is either dead or wants to kill me. Logan. Hassan. Kaori. I don't have time to win different versions of myself over to my cause, and Yusuf was always the more likeable one, anyway. And seeing as how I dropped the camera, I have to stop running my mouth and actually do something.

I'm not telling Yusuf—not yet, anyway—that I'm going to try to jam a red-hot poker right into Figueiredo's All-Eye and destroy the whole Envisioner network. I've tried to do it from the beach here but the All-Eye is too strong and I can't get it to heel from this far away. I'll just have to work my mojo in person.

I gate from the beach and into Yuppie Yusuf and Hayes's universe, appearing in the glass-and-chrome skyscraper of South Station. I wriggle through shoulders and elbows of people teleporting to their morning commutes and out into the street, where the city smells of rain and wet autumn leaves.

If I was telling Genesis all this like I was bellyaching about some guy backstage at one of her shows, she'd practically scream at me, *hey asshole, didn't you learn anything about keeping secrets? Don't you get that the worst shit you've done in all of this is keeping Yusuf in the dark?*

This is the last time. I swear. I *swear.* Because I know Yusuf will just say I'm going to get myself killed. He's probably right.

And sure, I don't want to die. Not out of self-preservation. I mean, I care as much now about my own personal safety as I did when I dry-swallowed a few extra pills from the plastic baggie I scored from one of my friends—which sent me on a direct flight to overdose land—knowing that someday I'd figure out whatever's beyond that black wall when I close my eyes. (Just kidding, it's probably nothing.) But if I could toss myself into a volcano to keep Yusuf safe, I would. Genesis had taught me, after all, to fight with my life for what I believed in and loved. And how to finally take the stage, for real. So, I have to stay alive to fix this, even if he never wants to see me again. And if I die before I right things, he'll be left to watch the world burn, feeling with all of his gut that it's his fault and knowing he can't live with himself.

My heartbeat cranks way up because I know that with Yusuf gone absolutely nothing matters anymore. I don't matter. He's the only thing keeping me tied to whoever I was before this, the only thing keeping me from *really* giving in and plugging into the machine like I know I can. Which I thought was keeping me strong and grounded, but right this second, I'm not so sure.

Because Figueiredo is a monster and look at all he can do, with forces of nature bending with a flick of his hand. I can be the monster to save Yusuf, because maybe I'll never get to look in his eyes again. And the only way out of this is deeper in.

I can do what I need to, and he never has to know.

First, I need supplies.

A shop on the street-level of Yuppie Hayes and Yusuf's place sold these at-home cloaking devices. We wandered in one day when we were crashing in that universe, and I listened while the salesperson yammered about the features of the flat, little disks. How you could toss one on a side table and it would paint holograms all over your room, letting you swap out your wall colors or the look of your furniture without having to buy new pieces. The world had dumbed down this military tech enough that you could turn dishes in the sink and piles of laundry invisible before company comes over, instead of running around and cleaning in a mad dash.

I ignore the salespeople asking if I need help and shoplift the disk, barely even needing to try. This cloak of invisibility isn't a suit of battle armor or some other tech from another universe that Figueiredo has probably already stolen and improved, but it's all I have. Besides, I'm the weapon, now. My skin singes and my molars feel like they could crack under the cranking of my jaw muscles.

Back on my pink beach, I swear the Envisioner knows what's up. I run my hands over her facets, hushing her with my head. She knows what I want her to do and she doesn't want to budge. I can see Kaori and Figueiredo in the Compound back home in flashes, like a night after a bender that I'm trying to remember. They're looking for us, taking turns asking questions and spinning the dials, with Figueiredo laying his hands on the machine like

I am now. He waves here and there in the Theater, talking of *you really should create a wider berth here in case of large brane-incision kickback* and *perhaps I'll allow you provisional access to the All-Eye if things here go smoothly.* Kaori nods, taking notes on her tablet, cowed for him like I've never seen her for anyone else.

Tell them I'm dead, I nudge the machine.

She plants her feet, stubborn, not wanting to lie. Instead of yanking on the machine's leash, I rub her behind the ears until her tongue lolls out. *But it's not a lie, right? What did Figueiredo say about all of space-time unfolding simultaneously? I'm dead already, somewhen. Just fudge the timeline a bit.*

I feel her hesitating until she rolls over, flashing me her spotted belly for a rub. A spark flicks out into the Envisioner network and I can see Kaori's eyes flitting to the screen in the machine on the Compound.

"They're separated…" she trails. "Yusuf's nearby—some hotel in Beatty. And Hayes… I think he's dead?"

Figueiredo's eyes flash with steel. "Bring Yusuf here."

Well, fuck.

The machine is a little trickster, flashing her teeth, her tongue lolling out. *You can save Yusuf or yourself, but never both. Now, why don't we play a little game?* Mystic Lady Pythia in her glass booth by the restaurant shrugs, bored. *Your lucky number is green.*

When you're already dead to the only people you care about, you start giving zero shits about yourself.

I've got no idea what they'll do to Yusuf. The machine wouldn't cough up what Kaori and Figueiredo are planning. I have to be fast. As far as Figueiredo and Kaori know, their plans are already fucked anyway, with me dead and unable to set the threads right once everyone is in their universe of origin. But when you're insane with grief you'll try anything.

Like invading a research compound in a foreign universe on your own, for example.

I can see that kid in Cape Town taking the backpack bomb from the man in his doorway, and my hands quake just like his. I'm alone here on the beach, with the fern trees in the distance crushing in. Weighing into me and watching. Every breath is a struggle against the boulders on my chest.

I try to feel for Figueiredo's world, reaching out with my mind to trace the knotted threads and thorny vines that lead to the All-Eye at the center of this whole network. I feel a heaviness—a resistance—when I try to latch onto the thread that ends at Figueiredo's machine, like the thing does not want me gating through. I can almost see his version of the Theater, crowded with his sage-coated techs, where the machine lurks like a giant black mass on an X-ray, its black tendrils creeping out to infect the world around it. I pop over to one of the tendrils and follow it until it splits into dozens of others, all leading to what seems like a room in the same compound with Envisioners waiting in the dark. All spinning calculations and feeding them to the main machine, all of them connected with cables like veins flowing to the pulsing heart of the All-Eye.

I flick on the camouflage disk in my pocket and the little thing works its magic, bouncing light beams away from me and dropping an invisibility cloak over my shoulders. Ready as I'll ever be, I guess. I cast one last look at this beach that became mine and Yusuf's home, in so many ways, before I gate through.

At first, I think that my eyes are still crammed shut since the long room I've landed in is so black. The darkness crushes me, seeping into my mouth and stealing my breath. I almost scream and chicken out, slamming into blunt shapes and tripping over snakes on the floor. After a minute of stumbling around, my eyes adjust to the dim red overhead lights and the candy-colored pulses from the dozens and dozens of Envisioners in this airplane-hangar-sized cargo bay. Each one signals to the others in a bioluminescent language I can't make sense of. I dropped through an Envisioner about halfway between the sliding double doors that probably lead to the rest of Figueiredo's facility and the far wall that's studded with red safety lights. No one else is in here with me, as far as I can tell. I move like a shadow anyway, over the Envisioner cables that line the floor like snakes waiting to strike. Nights dodging creaky floorboards to sneak out when I was a kid, creeping out of Hassan's house and leaving Yusuf in bed—the memories all blur together.

The door doesn't budge when I approach it. I slam my hands against it, not that I think I'll do anything, but needing the pain. Needing something to pull my mind away from my ragged heartbeat. I press my head against the cold metal door and try to just breathe. *Try.* Shaky shoulders with each pull of air.

On the side of the door, around eye-level, waits a little screen that blinks when I look at it, before flashing green. The door's lock clicks. I open the door and cold air blasts across my burning skin. Me and Figueiredo are the same, right down to the eyes. I freeze in the open doorway, waiting and glancing down the bright white hallways with their glass walls. I can almost feel the tree roots of the cables from the room of Envisioners snaking under the floor and leading to the All-Eye. I don't have time to search the place, and I could use a distraction and a chance to get as many people as I can away from the All-Eye, anyway.

Back in the cargo bay, I lean down to where the Envisioner cables twine together before slithering into a duct in the floor. I run my hands over the cables and pick one that seems to link to the farthest machine, by the back wall. I don't need a building-leveling blow like on Luna One, just enough to cause a distraction.

I nudge the cable with my mind—throwing the dice, touching the lit match to the fuse—and then I sprint as fast as I can down one of the empty white hallways. The explosion, like two icebergs smashing together, is so loud it vibrates my skull, rumbling the ground and the walls around me, almost knocking me over. The noise dumps another gallon of gasoline onto the runaway blaze of my heartbeat. A second of silence after the explosion, and then come the whooping alarms and the green-coats running down the halls. I'm still invisible, as far as I can tell, as I cram my hands against my ears. Tripping over my own feet while I wriggle away from the green-coats that stream down a hallway in the flickering lights. I can hear Yusuf in my head, trying to show me through the maze of the Compound on my first day there, then his words trying to calm himself down. *Earth. The Solar System. The Milky Way.*

Up ahead I spot an enormous glass fish tank of a room surrounded by what looks like a jungle of dew-tipped trees and hanging moss. Figueiredo must've upgraded to a new facility since the dim, gray one I saw in his footage. In the center of the room, a faceted black crag that's huge enough to hold up the sky rises through the floor and bursts through a hole in the ceiling. I hug the wall and run through the door against the stream of green-coats, knocking into one who doesn't seem to notice with all the panic. Of the few people still in the room, scrambling between control panels, no one sees me. No Figueiredo either. He must still be with Kaori on my world.

I stop, in full view of the hulking, irregular mass of the All-Eye with its hundreds of screens like unblinking eyes. As big as a small house with manic additions added over the years. Its blunt facets the red-black of dried scabs, dull even under the lights from the ceiling and windows. The thing rests on dozens of bent metal columns that look so much like muscled human legs that I have to tear my eyes away as my stomach spins. The All-Eye, and the dozens of thick black cables that leach from it, ruptures through the ceiling and more of it must hulk through the floors above. Probably connected to thousands more machines in the rest of the facility.

So here we are again, rewinding back to the beginning with me walking over a tightrope to the Envisioner, the first time I spotted it. Dizzy and reeling from the height and trying not to look down. Shrouded in glass walls, the whooping of the alarm is the caw of a night bird.

The lights flicker again before snapping off. With a crack I can feel in my bones, red overhead safety lights switch on and cast the room in red shadows. The heavy air is a sour metal tang in the back of my throat. Ignoring my screaming pulse at the sides of my neck, I reach out to one of the facets of the machine. My hands snap back against the fire that ignites in my brain. Because I can feel a million threads at once—a million universes all interconnected by the whole poisoned web of these machines, with Figueiredo's hands everywhere, pulling the strings. Each a slice of razor wire into my scalding skin. Already so tight that if I pushed just a little, I could short out the whole network and smash every one of the Envisioners to bits. And probably myself to dust, too, which at least would drown out the screaming in my head.

I don't know how I'm going to get out of here when all of this is done, if blowing the network doesn't rip me down to atoms first. But that doesn't matter once I touch the machine again, gritting my teeth against the fire, and can see Yusuf. I can see him finding me in the woods the first day we met and slipping into his white lab coat—his black glasses resting on his nose, the shadow of stubble on his cheeks—in a room that looks like this if you squint hard enough. I can see him in a hotel lobby in Beatty finishing up his breakfast of powdered eggs and bad coffee when one of the electric cars from the Compound rounds the cul-de-sac outside. Kaori steps out, shielding her eyes against the glare of the morning sun, and rests one elbow on the car roof. *Just here for the carpool.*

Yusuf sees her, nods, and knows it's time.

I can see the hospital that we jumped into after fleeing the Hotel Selene, and a million other places and worlds like it that use the machine to power cities, and satellite arrays that capture solar energy, and god knows what else. I can see the machine stuck in the side of the asteroid in our universe that started this all. And maybe I shouldn't punish everyone else for the shit that Figueiredo and I can't get right.

No more time to think, though. I close my eyes, already feeling the match ignite, when a pulse rips through me like someone is yanking at the All-Eye like it's a leashed dog with a shock collar.

Figueiredo storms out of the glowing gateway in the side of the All-Eye, already screaming at his staff who scatter out of the room. I freeze, hands still stuck to the machine, an invisible ghost in this haunted house. Just the two of us, now. Of course. This is always how it had to end, right? All of the dice throws leading us here, all the shell games. He tears his blue blazer off his white collared shirt and hurls it to the ground, stomping on it as he screams at the walls.

And then he stops. His back rigid, he turns in a slow circle, one finger resting on his chin. His eyes hit me, which I *know* can't be true since I'm still camouflaged by the light-bending device. The safety lights make the whole room look like an aquarium with blood in the water.

My trapped breath sears my lungs.

I just really wish he'd apply himself more, a teacher sighed at my mom a million years ago.

Figueiredo's other hand reaches into his pants pocket and pulls out something that looks like a slim black pen. He clicks one end and I hear the faintest whisper above my surging heartbeat as the thin veil of the invisibility cloak slides off my shoulders.

Lips that look like my own twist up into something that could be a smile. I preferred the yelling.

"Ah," he says with the low voice I heard in my head this whole time. "You're here."

As much as Kaori wants to blame me, he's the reason why we're all in this dumpster fire. More than all the other versions of myself I've met, being in this same space as him feels like if we get too close, we'd smash each other apart. Anti-matter and matter obliterating on contact.

"I thought I would drop in," I say with a shrug.

The shrug and the snark help so much. The character, the armor that I slip into to keep me from vibrating right out of my body.

"You know, I'm actually surprised," he smarms. "Which I find *very* interesting."

He buries both hands in the pockets of his pressed khakis, walking closer until he's a few arms' lengths away. I drop my hands from the All-Eye and turn to him, keeping my face still.

"Oh, good."

"How'd you get the machine to send us a false reading?"

Another shrug. Focusing on him instead of the All-Eye monster behind me helps slow my manic heartbeat. "Your pet has a new favorite dad."

"Mm." Two steps closer to me, slow and unafraid over glowing-hot coals. "Now, you have a word for this, yes?" He flicks one finger between us.

"Invasion," I offer.

He shakes his head. "Surrender."

I can't tell if he's playing the role of the patient diplomat bogged down by the seriousness of this negotiation or whatever. Heavy accent or no, I'm sure it took him all of a week to become fluent in English. His thin gold glasses that reflect the light, his patient half-smile—everything about him bugs me with how it's scripted. Some smug, smashed kaleidoscope version of myself that seems like the worst things that Narek accused me of brought to life. He's got to have a weapon on him somewhere, but if he really wanted me dead, I'd be a pile of ash already.

"You know that's not why I'm here," I tell him.

I can see Figueiredo's hard angles in the lines of the All-Eye and the rest of his machines, his chin and cheeks in their facets. We're both standing with our hands resting high on our hips with our heads tipped to the side. I step back and cross my arms across my chest.

"While we're sharing." I bob my head to the side, towards the machine. "How does it work?"

His tired sigh is what bugs me the most. How sinking down to my level to even *talk* is beyond exhausting.

"Beyond the hull is an initial singularity shrouded in a time-dilation field. Every time you ask the machine a question, it dials the singularity forward and observes the conditions of that universe iteration. Compared with the data from the Farsight network, the machine then provides the most likely outcome to the query before compressing the simulation down again."

"Oh."

"It's fine. From what I know of you, I don't expect you to understand. I could speak to you about matter resonance memory, and cross-brane entanglement, and meta-universal inflection points but your world's grasp of nature is…" He trails, already bored of my existence. "Nascent at best. Except Dr. Nakamori. She has perspective."

"So you're saying it's a universe machine."

He pauses. "I suppose you could call it that, with the most absolute basic understand of… Never mind."

"And how do we *connect* to it?"

Even facing off like this I can feel his gross need to celebrate himself and his achievements, like his endless video journals monologued to audiences only he could see.

"Each device carries with it an internal sample of my blood. Neural-linked admin-level functions like brane incision and selective branch collapse—what you did by choosing a specific future outcome and imposing it onto your universe iteration—are coded to my genome. And I studied branch collapses for years— *years*—before even attempting. And only to further my research and progress, even when my staff became insipid."

I almost shiver, picturing him slicing open his veins again and again to feed this gunmetal spider, when he wasn't creating and destroying universes every time he dialed the machine. This fucking monster. Maybe there's another version of *us* in there. Or we're stuck in someone else's machine as they lean in and ask a question, sending us all on our useless track loops, over and over again.

"Then how do you explain me? Other versions of… *us*… who I've met don't have the link."

"I suppose it is statistically significant that you can do what you can."

Oh, fuck him so hard. That's probably the biggest compliment he's ever given to anyone.

"We're the same."

"You're mistaken if you think that every possible event that produced every possible one of your ancestors played out the same in each universe. You may think those others that you met are *you*, but they are products of different variables. Different ancestors here and there, different environmental factors—different minerals in the soil that grew their food, even—which all impacted their genetics. We're all approximations of each other."

"But if any two of us *are* the same, it's us."

"You are fractionally more similar to me than the others, at best. I am curious to study a blood sample, if you're offering. Perhaps we share the most common genome out of all the iterations due to similar large-scale histories."

"Intellectualize it all you want. I don't like it either."

He shrugs. "What is this *like?* You're attaching human observational importance to the result of residing in adjacent universes that exist as different expressions and often opposing outcomes of the same variables. Two sides of a coin flip. A dice roll."

"Two bullets aimed at two different husbands. Tiago must love this kind of pillow talk."

He can't hide the flare behind his eyes, though just like Kaori and her mask, it's gone in a second. I internally toss myself a high-five for finding his wound between his plates of armor. I'll just keep jamming with the knife. *How's that for brane incision?*

"Go ahead and think I'm a monster," he says. "Your thoughts leak out of you because you're too soft to keep them in. Tiago surviving the riot in my universe was my *rightful* outcome. You loaded the dice."

"You can spout shit about probability and variables and fuck all. Rightful my ass. Your problem is that you think you're special, deep down. That you deserve whatever you want. That you can *do* whatever you want."

"You've altered reality so deeply that your actions have rippled out, pulled an asteroid off its predicted course, and *hurled* it towards your planet to try to balance the scales again. Please tell me how I'm the one acting irresponsibly. You only even *met* Yusuf because of the Farsight. You are indebted to me. I'm pulling rank."

"Rank? Oh my god. Meanwhile, you've fucked with I don't even know how many universes just for your own research."

"I swear, Hayes. I swear." He walks so close that I see the red webbing his eyes as he stabs the air with one finger. "I'm sending you back to your world. Dr. Nakamori will aim a gun between your eyes, and you will separate the branes and set our universes right. Then you can go back to your miserable life—alone, because that is how you always will be. Do this or I will implode my world just to watch yours burn."

You know just what to say, Narek would observe. I guess he's right. My skin blasts heat and sears the floor under my shoes. I've been coming at this all wrong, with nerves and fear and whining. When I should just take a cue from Figueiredo and give into the anger. Now that we're at the end of this tangled line, it's so clear— so bright it's like winter air freezing my nose—that he doesn't know anything. Even with his millions of machines and this giant eye hulking behind me. He doesn't know that I am more *him* than he is.

"I'm embarrassed that I thought you were this better version of me when I first saw your footage," I say. "I could practically *hear* you following me around and making fun of me like a shadow. I guess I was that stupid."

Figueiredo throws his hands, his face smeared into a bitter grin. "Look at you—this weak, self-important man who makes little movies instead of doing something useful. Who can't make a goddamn decision and always needs help. Dressing like a child. Poisoning your brain and body and marking up your skin like a criminal. I'm the real thing. You're the bad copy."

"You know, I'm surprised you even want Tiago back," I start, some part of me surprised how I can shape my voice almost like his, the stab of a dull knife. "I might be an idiot, but even *I* could see how you hated him as much as you loved him. How you envied him so much it tore you up inside. How you never could've built your first machine without him because he was the one who found the energy source. The spark. The secret when you were too blind and stupid and high off your own brain to see it. And it killed you, didn't it? Tiago's mind? Because you never *really* wanted an equal. You wanted someone around you, just close enough to work the spotlight and take none of the credit."

I'm so close to the All-Eye that I can almost feel it quaking. Like it's scared of me.

"You don't know anything," he spits.

"As much as you think you're at the center of all this, he made you. And you're *nothing* without him, and that absolutely terrifies you and—"

He rears back and swings a fist. Once it slams into my jaw, I reach for the All-Eye and open a gate in an instant, sending us both tumbling through.

We topple onto each other, thudding to the pink sand of me and Yusuf's beach. Figueiredo's head knocks into mine but I'm so radioactive with adrenaline that I don't feel a thing. Only my fist against his cheek. Once, twice. Like I should've punched the TV screen back in the Compound the first time I saw his face and heard his voice. Again and again. His nose sprays blood on both of us. I hurl him off me—both of us heaving and snarling like animals—anchor him by the collar and shove a fist full of sand in his eyes and mouth.

The second he claws at his face, screaming, is all I need.

I pounce up and touch the Envisioner, opening a gateway beneath both me and the machine, sending us both freefalling and leaving him stranded there, finally. Swiping at his blood-smeared eyes and alone.

35

THE UNIVERSE MACHINE

First me and then the machine drop onto a rolling meadow of red grass. I land right on my ass with a jolt up my tailbone. I plop backwards to the ground, spent, and look up at the perfect blue sky for a while, sucking in breaths and trying to slow the manic heartbeat at my neck. The red grass is soft under me, the breeze over my bare arms smells of warm dirt and pollen.

Stranding Figueiredo away from his machine and anyone else is worse than killing him, I figure. But I know what I have to do next is worse.

I stay in the meadow just long enough to swallow a few mouthfuls of cold water from a nearby stream and wash his blood off me, my hands still shaking from the memory of my fists pummeling his face. In the reflection of the water, my face is warped and wavering. I'm almost done with all of this. Just a few more portals to wrap everything into a neat knot and maybe I can ignore the damage I'm probably doing to the multiverse, too. Another mouthful of cold water slides down my throat, frosting my insides.

I'd planned on dropping into the Theater back home and just wormholing the Envisioner there a million universes away, cutting us all free from this poisoned web. And sure, that would save Yusuf, but then he'd have a front-row seat as the world burned around him, and he'd just blame himself. And me. And grow to hate us both, probably. I can't do that to him. I never asked for this connection to the machine, and I didn't know what I was doing when I nudged it that first time to save him, but I can't let myself off the hook either.

Besides, the All-Eye already showed me a hint of what I need to do. I can feel the weight of the giant machine like it's a black hole I've been circling my whole life. Like the night I overdosed was me remembering, somehow, that I'd be here in this exact spot giving into this riptide that I've been running from for years.

I really don't want to be the one pulling the strings. Then there's Kaori with her wry smile offering, *but at the same time, here we are.*

I wrack my brain for a while, cramming my fingers into the red grass and the dirt, begging for some other way. *Nothing will work,* the machine tells me, and I can practically see her big melty eyes because she's sorry and knows this isn't the answer that I want to hear. *Nothing will work and you know why.* Adjacent realities seek a zero sum. Too many lives here on the scales, on our little dust-specks of planets drifting through space. Genesis on stage her last night, knowing that her cause was bigger than just her one life, and knowing what she needed to do.

I can't go back to Yusuf for help because I know, as much as he'd be relieved to see me alive, deep down, he'd sooner off himself if that meant saving the world. And I can't let him do that.

So give me some distance, right now, when I'm digging in the grass and cramming red dirt under my fingernails. When I'm pounding my fists into the ground and screaming. Give me some of Kaori's observations, for fuck's sake, her marker-board equations where she has everything sketched out with zero emotion. Or give me her steady hand holding up a gun to Yusuf's head because she knew he had to die or billions would. And she was more than ready to pull the trigger.

I know all the parts of the equation. All the excuses and the wars I wage with myself, raking my nails along my thighs and ripping at the grass. I can't destroy a world to save him. I don't know how I can take on that weight. Worse than that, though— what's unbearable, what would end me—would be watching him die. A coin flip: him or a world. Except I'm the magician and it's a fake coin, anyway, and I control what side it'll land on. I'd say there's no other way, but that's a lie.

With that, I make up my mind.

"You ready, girl?" I call back to the machine, so, so tired.

She doesn't answer, of course. Hands on the facets, I reach out with my mind and don't feel the same resistance that I did when I tried to gate in through the All-Eye before. Because the king is toppled and the machine at the center of this web has been waiting for this moment the whole time, so it unlocks the door and I gate through.

Inside the empty glass fish tank of Figueiredo's Theater, someone cut the alarms. Shapes seem to move in the trees just beyond one of the glass walls, but it's probably just my fried brain seeing snakes slithering in the branches. Thick and black like the cables that stick out from the All-Eye. This thing with its red-black scabs of facets like the wounded body of a giant beast.

I touch the machine and the only threads, the only universes that feel close now, are filled with different versions of me and Yusuf. The versions of us in their high-rise in Boston that overlooks the twinkling city, coming home tanned and exhausted from their honeymoon and spotting the picture of Yusuf that I stuck on their wall, and wondering just how that got there. They must've taken it but can't remember exactly when. Time doesn't mean much. Hassan is marrying his Rui and burying him at the same time. In decades to come, when the researchers who fled Luna One before the asteroid slammed into the Earth return to their base to salvage the technology there, they'll find a frozen, bombed-out hotel and a withered body with a curtain cape in the snow. And all the different versions of us that still haven't met, but will. The stupid, blind luck that had me and Yusuf even alive on our Earth at the same time lights me up, and then I can feel all of the threads glowing like the sparklers Genesis waved at her last show.

I know that the All-Eye is trying to show me that all of this is a loop. That the universes were already entangled and Figueiredo knotted them even tighter together when he started breaking through the barriers and tossing his machines inside—each a snag, a snarl. That time flows differently through all the universes and *past* and *future* don't mean a whole lot. *Adjacent realities seek a zero sum.* And I already screwed with things once when I saved Yusuf in place of Tiago at the start of this mess. A life for a life. A world for a world. I could just portal the asteroid away, out of the path of our Earth, which would still leave us with a debt and I would just be stalling. Like every time I pushed at the machine back before we went on the run, and each change was a dice roll leading to a new world-ending disaster.

There's one last loop to close in another adjacent reality—as close to *mine* as mine is to Figueiredo's—something that must happen to balance the scales and then we can be free. I know where to pay the debt of the lives impacted by Tiago and Yusuf's work, and how to balance this whole mess of an equation. And maybe this one is easier because I've already seen its aftermath and I can tell myself that I'm just playing a part.

All of this has already happened, with time folded in on itself like the rumpled sheets of our air mattress on our beach. When this whole journey has been about rocks in the sky. And fate and probability, and the tiny instant when both of those seem like the same thing. And blind luck—the Envisioner that Kaori's team found on the Endovelicus asteroid and then dragged to Earth. And the rock that obliterated Logan and Joel's Earth without warning, while the wolf pack lounged in the tropical forest under the fake sky of a dome on the moon. How it never really made sense that their world had the technology to build a habitat on the moon but couldn't spot an asteroid on a direct course to Earth until it was too late. Unless it appeared literally out of nowhere.

Honestly, maybe Figueiredo dropped my Envisioner—and it is *mine*, now, all of them heeling for me like I tell them to—way out on that asteroid because he wanted the data from my universe but wanted me nowhere near the machine. Either to spare me from it or because he knew I'd turn out to be so much like him, with our realities brushing together, that I'd drop-kick him off his throne and take his crown.

The universes flap against each other like the sheets on the clothesline my mom strung across her small deck. She escaped a drowned island to watch the water lap at the sidewalks around her home where she was raising her son, alone, and he skipped curfew again last night. She looks up at the cloud-wisped sky, and, *Jesus Cristo*, what was she going to do with him?

I'm quaking inside. Someone must've cranked open an airlock door because all the air is gone. I can't breathe. I know if I do this—and I have to, there's no other way—I have to leave this all here, in this reality. I can't bring the weight with me because I know, day by day, it'll crush me until there's nothing left. No other choice, though. No turning back.

Still, I suck in a breath and hold it until my lungs burn. My heartbeat in my ears is a countdown clock. *Tick tick boom.* Stretching out the final moments before I really become a monster for as long as I can. I cram my eyes closed and reach out with the whole web of machines to see a little rock floating in my universe, which feels so close by. I open a gateway there, wider than I ever have—each machine in the whole network strumming like a plucked string—wider until a shimmering window of light opens, offering a glimpse of a little blue and white planet that doesn't look like much. The rock sails through the glowing gateway and I snap it closed, leaving just the blackness between the stars behind.

"Show me," I say in one ragged heave.

One of the huge All-Eye screens above me flicks to life.

Because the only thing worse than watching is not watching. When you decide to take billions of lives just to save the one that you love, the least you can do is watch and not be a goddamned coward. You owe it to all of them. You owe it to the man who you're doing this for, who never asked you to do this in the first place, and who you can never tell. You owe it to yourself because you've been a burden to everyone around you—to everyone who ever loved you—and now you have to take on this weight. So you watch.

And here, I'm already zooming out. I'm saying *you* when I mean *I,* casting myself as a character and treating all this like a script. Maybe to give myself some distance from what I'm doing, maybe because there's probably another me that's watching this play out, on another Envisioner screen in another universe. So what would you do?

I step back to get a better view of Logan and Joel's Earth—so blue and green, swirled over with clouds like piped cake frosting—

across the screen. I force myself to live here in this moment. Shoulders heavy and already shaking, my eyes burning while they're stuck to the screen because I'm afraid that if I blink I'll miss the impact.

I can barely see the streak of light that sails against the blackness of space and slams into America over the Great Plains. Petals of fire from the blast rocket into the air and I can hear screams in my head, and the shattering bones of the Earth echo across my ribs. I shake and sway and lean onto my thighs to barf a puddle of yellow sick onto the gray floor. I must've begged the All-Eye to stop somewhere between my sobs and ragged breaths because when I lean back up on my weak legs, the screen is blank.

The yellow puddle of puke on the floor expands until it hits the soles of my dirty shoes.

I take all the screams and the impossible weight and the images of fire raining down from the sky and pour it like glowing toxic waste into a metal drum and push it deep, deep down. I wipe my mouth on the bottom of my dirt-caked and blood-splattered shirt. I wrap myself up in film reels and doc still printouts that stick to me like armor. In my head, I see the film treatment character sketch of who I'm supposed to be—*Hayes Figueiredo, early 30s, damaged but trying to laugh through it and definitely not someone who just scorched an entire planet to dust*—until it feels almost familiar. I'll spend the rest of my life pretending to be the person I used to be, and maybe after a while I'll start believing it.

36
BRANE TRUST

The wide, white-walled room of the Theater back in my universe is just how I remember it when I gate through. The FantiSee screens above offer a clear afternoon sky and a fake sun with no warmth. Seabirds swoop across the blue, cawing and dive-bombing for fish. My mom used to say that the noises they made sounded like they were asking, *"Quem é? Quem é?" Who is it?* She'd flap her arms, running on the beach with me as a kid, and laugh an answer into the sky for us. *É Maria e Hayeszinho!*

The Theater is empty except for Kaori, who must know it's me before she even turns from the machine.

"You look good for someone who's supposed to be dead," she says.

She levels me with her tea-colored eyes, squinting at how I look like I crawled to the Compound over broken glass. And *jesus*, how did we get here, light-years away from knocking back margaritas? I can feel Yusuf nearby, somewhere, in the maze of white halls. Tethered to me by a tight string, even when we're apart. The three of us are game pieces stuck to a board and neither me nor Kaori want to make the first move.

What would the Before Hayes say, now? *Can I get a line, please?*

"Thanks," I say, flatly. Snark—yes, that's him. I bolt on a crooked smile that jabs pain through my split lip. "Where's Yusuf?"

"Here." She tips her head, her calculating face when she's scanning an Envisioner readout.

Already, I know she can see I'm a different person than the one who dropped in here a year ago, so obsessed with his dumb little problems that seemed so huge.

"He thinks you're dead," she says, so low I can barely hear. "You made him soft. I could see when I picked him up from the hotel, and the way he shook when I told him about you, how different he is. I know you think that's a compliment. But…" She sighs. "I suppose you're here to Hotel-Selene me? Blow the whole Compound and everyone here just to take me out?"

"No. You're not that important."

She actually laughs, sending the uneven lengths of her hair swaying. When the sound dies down, there's only the low hum of the ventilation between us. She narrows her eyes just a little.

"I take it you removed Figueiredo from the equation?"

"Something like that."

"Fuck that guy, right? You know, he gave me such shit about what a good *start* I was running here, but if I wanted to understand the true nature of reality, I could be his research monkey." She pauses again. "But no, that's not it. Something's different." Her eyes dance just a little. "You didn't. You did? Did you?"

I shrug. Overhead on the FantiSee screens, seabirds flap their wings through their perfect sky, laughing again. *Quem é? Quem é?*

"Now you get it," she continues. "Adjacent realities seek a zero sum. You sent the asteroid into another Earth?"

"I made a calculated decision."

"I didn't think you had that objectivity in you. I'm surprised and… I don't know. Proud?"

"I'm not nondescript anymore, I guess."

"Well, don't get ahead of yourself."

She asked the machine about me even before I got here the very first time. I can see her gritting her teeth at the microphone and spinning the dials again and again. Trying to force some order and predictability on me when all I do is floor it around the corner into a giant puddle of entropy, splashing it everywhere. I can see her spinning webs in her head of all the things she can do with the machine now that we're all safe. But she won't admit that she doesn't understand love and that she doesn't know what I will do for it. Or if I am as dumb as she and Figueiredo think. Too late to wonder, anyhow.

I feel something inside the machine quake as soon as I touch it, a dog flapping its ears down at me and wagging its tail now that I'm home again. Kaori is rooted to the floor, unmoving. She doesn't even try to stop me. I push with my mind and open the gateway beneath the Envisioner. Off in the distance, muffled by the wind that whips up from the portal, Kaori screams something. I almost lose my balance and teeter through the gap in the floor just beyond my toes. The machine bombs-away through the portal, which zips closed again in just an instant, unknotting us from this whole mess. I can almost see the Envisioner dropping through the air a million universes away, running free from all our meddling. Leaving me free from the temptation to undo anything or change anything else ever again.

The doors across from me *whoosh* open and I search Yusuf's face, his crinkle-cornered eyes, his eyebrows that furrow and carve deep lines in his forehead. *What?* I watch the thoughts collide into him. One corner of his lips swoops up in a question mark, his eyebrows knit together, and his beetle-shell eyes—the ones I've seen smiling at me on a leaky air mattress on our beach paradise and cringing as I bowed to him in Oxford and called him *My Lord* and flashing to mine in panic just before I detonated the Envisioner on Luna One. *How?*

Our whole journey was worth it. And if you want the truth— even though I know it makes me a monster—watching the asteroid slam into an Earth that wasn't mine was worth it just to see the relief flood his eyes.

Leaning back on the hood of one of the Compound's electric cars, the sky above us is an ocean of stars. I bundle the thin blanket a little tighter around us in the night air that's cool, even here in the desert.

We're quiet, now, an easy silence settling over us after the tears in the Theater and running to each other and holding each other up so we wouldn't crumble. With me whispering *I'm sorry* into his ear over and over again, until his arms knotted around my waist, the tight bands of iron that gushed the air from my lungs. We walked the track a lot in silence that afternoon, me not wanting to push, until he was ready to ask what he needed to.

I peeled off my sweat-plastered clothes in his bathroom and didn't recognize the bruised face and body in the mirror. Under the spray of the scalding shower, I watched the dirt and dried blood wash off me and mar the white tile. Trying to fool myself that the water was washing away some of the weight strapped to me.

Afterwards, I told him what happened. Or, the version that me and Kaori are sticking to in whatever weird truce we've drawn between us. I might've taken away the Envisioner from her, but I'm giving her what she really wants in exchange for her silence. For this relative reality that we built between us. The story of how I used the All-Eye's positioning system—the same thing that allowed Figueiredo to pinpoint where in thousands of universes to drop his machines—to open a gateway and send the asteroid sailing harmlessly off into a distant corner of the solar system. Instead of the truth of how I burned Logan and Joel's Earth to ash to save ours.

I'm not proud of the lies but I know they'll get easier, now that I left Hayes the Monster in the other universe, and I'm already breathing into the right beats that Before Hayes knew to hit.

I know Yusuf told me a million years ago that secrets are poison. I'm more than willing to let this poison flow through my blood for the rest of my life so long as that means being able to sit and look at the stars with him even for one more night.

"I thought you were dead," Yusuf says after a while.

"I'm sorry. I had to throw Figueiredo and Kaori off the trail. I didn't know they'd track you down and she'd tell you."

"But how could you do that to me? I thought I'd never see you again."

His glinting eyes flick to mine and I bury my face into the side of his neck.

"I was kind of making stuff up as I went along. I had to take out Figueiredo and then jump back into his Compound as fast as I could while the place was still in chaos."

"Still—"

"At the *start* of this, Yusuf, when I saw you die in whatever future the box wanted to show me. I knew I would've... would've..."

"Done anything to get me back."

"Yeah."

"Me too. But..."

"So we're even. We both died for each other and came back. Kinda."

He waits, working the muscles at the sides of his jaw.

"What did you do to Figueiredo?"

"I stranded him on our beach without an Envisioner."

A tiny spark lights up his eyes. "I would've done worse. And Kaori? How'd she not kill you for taking away her toy?"

Here, I hesitate—pulling away from him and wincing.

"I told her I'd cut a doc and give her the hero edit."

"Wait, what?"

"What's the neatest ending? I used my freaky connection to the machine and end up in a lab somewhere with people trying to copy it, or genius Dr. Nakamori blasted the asteroid out of the sky and saved us all? Honestly, it's the safest bet for us, too."

"Hmm. And you're fine with the lie?"

"Some lies are fine, I guess. Sometimes. If no one gets hurt. Let her have the spotlight if she wants it."

I look up again at the sky. One of the points of light that I thought was a star moves, so it must be a plane. *When you wish upon a jetliner.*

"And you?" I dare to ask. "You don't mind the lie?"

"As long as me and you can just leave all of this. But no more— no more making decisions for the entire universe anymore, Hayes," he says out of the corner of his mouth. "You're not Figueiredo. You're better than that."

I don't let the lance of guilt show in my face. "Alright."

He's quiet again for a long time, so long that I think he fell asleep, though his eyes are still drinking in the stars when I look back at him. I spot the hope there—like that night a few weeks ago when he was on the balcony overlooking a weirdly unfamiliar Boston and dreaming up our future—and know that whatever happens, I can't let him down ever again. I'll spend our whole lives making up for whatever pain I caused him.

"Where should we go, now that all this is over?" he asks.

"I'd say some new city, but I think the both of us have done enough exploring for a while."

"Familiar might be nice."

"You could teach again."

"I'd love that. And you need to finish Genesis's doc."

"I can do that anywhere. Like Oxford. You think they'll take you back?"

"In this specific scenario? Why not?"

"So we move to Oxford, the real one, and you can show me around."

He makes a small noise that might be a *hmm* in agreement, his eyes lost up at the sky again.

"We'll open a bar and call it the Prince of Cups." I squeeze his hand that's beneath the blanket. "Huh?"

He blows air out of his nose as a laugh, rolling his eyes at me. "I'm not wearing tights again."

A breeze blows past us, smelling of the dry, red earth. The hood of the car isn't super comfortable, but here, we're both safe. And when we done with stargazing, we'll head back to our little temporary house for one of the last nights ever, and we'll fall asleep in each other's arms.

37

AFTER CREDITS

D r. Kaori Nakamori looks up through the visor of her spacesuit's helmet and into the velvet blackness of space, overcome with wonder even though time is running out. In just a matter of hours, this asteroid she's standing on will pummel the Earth, wiping out all of human history in the blink of an eye. And the visions—no, *premonitions* due to her uncanny mental bond with the machine— that have plagued her for years, ever since she and her team spotted the machine wedged in between two craggy outcroppings of the asteroid, will finally come true. The rain of fire over Paris and the streets of Barcelona. *We'll miss you, Mona Lisa. Goodbye, Gaudi.* The scorched bones of the planet where Machu Picchu once stood. She draws a breath—steady even with all the weight on her—and waits just a second longer. A single tear rolls down her cheek. For an instant, the teardrop reflects the starlight.

Mostly, she wishes her parents were alive to see who she's become.

I know I'm supposed to be watching the climax of the movie, but it's way more fun watching Yusuf instead. We're tucked in the corner at the back of the theater because I didn't want to bug other people in the audience with what I knew would be Yusuf's ongoing monologue of corrections on the glaring inaccuracies of the movie. *Because really*, he argued before the opening title card even faded away, *it may be science fiction, but the science should be first. It's right there in the name.*

"That asteroid has basically zero gravitational pull," he sighs, squeezing the bridge of his nose. "How is she walking on it? She and the machine would just fly off it and float into space."

"Shh." I squeeze his thigh with a hand that's sticky with fake butter from the tub of popcorn that I just housed. "You're gonna miss the best part."

I've already seen this twice.

The first time, I had a tough time looking at the screen when it showed the Earth puttering around and waiting to get knocked out of the sky by the asteroid. I tried thinking about Before Hayes, but he didn't help much, and Hayes the Heartless Torcher of Worlds is dead by the All-Eye where I left him. I guess I'm still trying to figure out who this Rebooted Hayes is, the one who tries his best and isn't following a script anymore, even if it took me a while to get here. And somehow, on the mornings that are hard to get out of bed, Yusuf pops his head into the bedroom to say something like *hey, I have to leave but there's a pot of coffee on*. And I remember who I am and how I got here. And how I'd do it all again if I needed to.

Dr. Nakamori knows she's on this asteroid to make a sacrifice. With all the wonders the Oracle Box promised—new advances in clean energy and medicine, a whole multiverse to explore—she knows what she has to do. Even with everyone doubting her, just as they have her whole life.

"I'm setting the Box to blow," she huffs.

"Doc, don't be stupid! We need it!" her second-in-command, Amir, squawks over the comm-link in her helmet. He's a composite character, a mash-up of Yusuf and a bunch of other researchers. At least they got the hair right, Yusuf said when he first eyed the actor.

"Think of what the Oracle Box has *already* given us," Amir begs her. "We can't just throw it away."

"All that'll mean *nothing* if the planet is a pile of rubble, Amir. For *once*, I need you to trust me," she shouts, already the plan building behind her steely eyes.

"Oh, what the hell," Yusuf moans, so softly that I can barely hear.

Alright, so basically there's not a single scene in this movie that's anything like the documentary footage that I cut together and released to the news three years ago, right after Yusuf and I left the Compound. *That* footage saw Kaori opening a portal directly to the asteroid, overloading the Envisioner, and tossing it through to blow the rock to a million pieces. I even added footage of the Compound staff cheering her name in the Theater after they'd stopped that bus bomb in Cape Town. *Dr. Nakamori, you just saved humanity!* But I get the need to make the script a little sexier for wide release.

I heard Kaori got a story consultant credit, though how she could find the time away from running the Near-Earth Defense Program on China's lunar base to prevent another potentially world-ending event is beyond me. And all that after the speeches and the books and the sit-down interviews about her work because of the *shared duty for humanity* and *cooperation and empathy that spans universes* and *blah*. I heard rumors on the doc boards that Kaori cloned the Envisioner tech and is going to reboot her own program to surpass even Figueiredo's work. Teleportation. Gravity control. Information recovery from a singularity. An Einstein-Rosen bridge linking a point just outside Earth orbit to Mars, where we can become a multi-planet species so the next time a rogue rock in space tries to snuff us out, we won't be a lone, easy target.

Who knows the truth. She must be happy now that she's in the spotlight, which means she'll keep my secret safe. Not that she has any interest in destroying our lives, because we just don't mean that much to her.

Anyway. I'm not in the movie. Thank god.

So, Dr. Nakamori decides to crank the power way up past the red line on the Oracle Box and open a portal. The silver gateway back to Oracle Command shimmers into existence ten feet away, but can she make it, in the precious seconds before the machine vaporizes her? No time to hesitate—and even if she dies, she knows that she's saved all of humanity, and that's really all she can ask for. She's beyond exhausted, but still, she sprints with her whole heart and dives through the portal to safety, just as the asteroid explodes to dust behind her.

A gray drizzle pelts us on the sidewalk outside the theater, with the ring lights from the marquee glowing through the fog. The theater is way bigger than the little indie house in town where I just showed a rough cut of *Project Genesis* to a handful of people—some of them my students there for extra credit—ahead of its official premiere at Genesis's old vaudeville theater in Boston next week. That's okay. I'm not really a blockbuster guy, anyway. I plan on checking out a few story leads while I'm back there, dragging Yusuf along to show him around. I might be tempted to ask Genesis's cards if those leads will turn into any real stories, but I buried them in the desert as we were leaving the Compound. My goodbye to her to stop worrying about the future, now that I remember how she helped me become a better person. To dedicate myself again to the positive changes I could make, in my own ways, and try to let go of the rest.

"It was fun," I offer Yusuf, nudging him. My breath comes out in a cloud that already floats away.

"It was." He links an arm with mine, hitting me with his eyes that seem quick to laugh, lately. "Different enough from reality to be entertaining."

We slurp down a couple of bowls of ramen at the Covered Market and wander a while, in no rush since Yusuf's on winter break from teaching, before heading back home. I don't think I've ever been happier than in our small, drafty flat with Yusuf—both of us learning together which light switches do what and which floorboards creak. After I shake off the drizzle from outside, I break out the bedsheet and Scarlett. I had to replace her screen but she's still in decent shape. I queue up my favorite thing I've ever filmed, that quick bit of me and him at the observatory back in the Commonwealth. Which Yusuf must've known I'd want to see— after the explosions, and the special effects, and the beautiful lies of the movie—because he rustles around in his office for a few minutes before popping out with his small telescope and opens the doors to the tiny balcony off our living room. He points the telescope up at the sky.

We can't see that many stars here most nights. But the clouds are supposed to clear later, and besides, we have the time.

ACKNOWLEDGEMENTS

Hi, you made it this far! Thank you. I really hope you enjoyed this book. I hope you saw a part of yourself in it. Especially if you're the type of person who, at some point in their life, was described by someone else as something like, "you're too much of…" or "you're not enough of…" I hope you don't listen to those voices, and you stop and remind yourself that you're pretty great.

A number of pretty great/generally wonderful people helped me get this story into the world.

Eternal, multiverse spanning thanks go to my agent, Naomi Davis of BookEnds Literary Agency. For the exact reasons that (many) people said no to me and this book, Naomi not only said yes, but also, "let's go bigger, weirder, and more queer!" And they provided lots of bursts of positivity, advice, and motivation along the way.

Thanks to my editor, George Sandison at Titan Books, for going on this ride. For his many key reads and insights that helped me write some of my very favorite parts of the book, and for his humor and patience. Thanks to Elora Hartway for her thoughtful and thorough edits, along with Michael Beale, Andy Hawes, Paul Simpson, Adrian McLaughlin.

Special appreciation to Julia Lloyd for creating the beautiful cover. Thanks to the publicity team for all of their hard work: Katharine Carroll, Kabriya Coghlan, and Sarah Mather. And to everyone in general at Titan for taking a chance on not one book, but invested in my career.

Big shout-out to wonderful writer, editor, artist, and human Cory Skerry. For seeing my short stories in the slush-pile years ago and campaigning for them, for the invaluable and detailed advice on stories and earlier versions of this book (not to mention life/career stuff). You should stop and read his short story "Antumbra" right now. Thanks for becoming a friend. Thanks, too, to writer and editor Spencer Ellsworth for editorial advice, and the I-Park Foundation for two life-changing fellowships.

My parents, Manuela and Victor, are my heroes. They both moved to America from Portugal in their teens and learned English, then devoted their careers to educating under-served communities in Fall River, Massachusetts. Between working multiple jobs, they instilled in me and my sisters a deep love of travel and an appreciation of our heritage. Among a million other things, thanks Dad for the stories you made up while taking us on walks around the neighborhood; thanks Mom for the sci-fi TV nights where you took us to other worlds.

Thank you to my sisters, Sophia and Cassandra. Two amazing women, mothers, and writers of beautiful stories (I can't wait for you to hold their books in your hands, too). Sophia for introducing me to a ton of art and culture picked up by her always curious mind. Cassandra for her unflappable kindness and humor, and for not only being the best twin, but a friend. And to my whole family for the love.

To my friends, thanks for the gifts of your friendship and support. For the laughter, and trips, and costumes, particularly the last couple of years when the world turned upside down. I'm so lucky to call you friends.

To Ruby for the love and the long walks.

Thanks to Eamonn, for everything, always.

ABOUT THE AUTHOR

Nathan Tavares is a writer and editor living in Boston, Massachusetts. *A Fractured Infinity* is his debut novel, and his short fiction has appeared in *PANK* and elsewhere. He is also a journalist—placing a special focus on boosting the work of historically underrepresented communities—with pieces appearing in *GQ, OUT, Boston* magazine and other publications.

For more fantastic fiction, author events,
exclusive excerpts, competitions, limited editions and more

VISIT OUR WEBSITE
titanbooks.com

LIKE US ON FACEBOOK
facebook.com/titanbooks

FOLLOW US ON TWITTER AND INSTAGRAM
@TitanBooks

EMAIL US
readerfeedback@titanemail.com